José Leon Machado was born in Braga, in the Minho region in northern Portugal, in 1965. He served in the Portuguese Army between 1988 and 1989, having been posted to the Azores Islands as a communications specialist. Returning to Braga, he graduated in Humanities from the Portuguese Catholic University, received an MA in Portuguese Language and Literature from the University of Minho, and a PhD in Linguistics from the University of Trás-os-Montes e Alto Douro in Vila Real, where he is Professor of Semiotics and Portuguese Language and Culture. A prolific scholar and literary critic, he has also written many short stories and ten novels. His first work to appear in English translation, *Darkening Stars. A Novel of the Great War* is about a young law student who was drafted to serve as a platoon commander in the Portuguese Expeditionary Corps sent to Flanders in 1917. What happened to him and the men under his command, the small and great miseries of their life in the trenches, their links with what they left behind and what they lost, and the incomprehension they met upon returning home, are some of the main lines of this moving and historically accurate portrait of one of the most turbulent periods of Portuguese history. It is also a story of love and of a young man's inner struggles and personal growth, his determined search for peace and happiness, along a path strewn with destruction and trampled dreams.

Milton M. Azevedo (PhD, Cornell University) is Professor of Spanish and Portuguese at the University of California, Berkeley, where he teaches courses on linguistics, stylistics, and translation issues. He has translated books from English and French into Portuguese and written books and articles on Spanish and Portuguese linguistics as well as articles on literary translation.

Karen C. Sherwood Sotelino (PhD, University of California at Santa Cruz) has translated novels, short stories, and technical texts from Portuguese into English. She has also taught translation at Associação Alumni (São Paulo, Brazil) and Portuguese language and translation at Stanford University, where she is currently Visiting Scholar in the Department of Iberian and Latin American Cultures.

José Leon Machado

DARKENING STARS

A NOVEL OF THE GREAT WAR

**Translated from the Portuguese with Notes
by
Milton M. Azevedo
and
Karen C. Sherwood Sotelino**

Edições Vercial

Title of the Portuguese original: *Memória das Estrelas sem Brilho*
Copyright of the Portuguese original: José Leon Machado, 2008-2012
Title of the English translation: *Darkening Stars – A Novel of the Great War*
Copyright of the English translation: Milton M. Azevedo and Karen C.
Sherwood Sotelino, 2012
Cover illustration: Paul Driver

Ed. Vercial, Braga (Portugal), 2012
Internet: http://alfarrabio.di.uminho.pt/vercial/evercial

ISBN: 978-989-700-088-1

Legal Deposit: 340445/12

Printed by Publidisa

For José Saramago

While the sun, or the light, or the moon, or the stars, be not darkened, nor the clouds return after the rain.

Ecclesiastes, 12:2

In battle the Captain loves the knight who, having fled, returns and attacks the enemy strongly, better than one who never turned his back nor ever performed an honorable action.

St. Gregory

Life should be a simple gesture of withdrawal, like a secondary actor who leaves the stage without saying the last word, which did not belong to him, but just left, no longer needed.

José Saramago

CONTENTS

DARKENING STARS

A Novel of the Great War

I

I am staying home with the maid while Aninhas and my mother are spending a few days in Póvoa de Varzim with Aunt Generosa, who is sick and needs some help. Afonso, my eldest son, is in his first year of engineering at Coimbra. Pedro is at the seminary in Braga, studying for the priesthood. And my youngest, Inês, is at a boarding school for young women in Famalicão.[1]

My first night alone was uncomfortable. I had more war nightmares. That was why, at dinner, on a sudden and inexplicable impulse – because I do not, nor have ever had any expectation of dallying with the servants – I asked Guiomar to sleep with me.

"Good Lord, sir!" she exclaimed, rather offended, as she set the soup tureen on the table. "I'm a good girl."

"I know you are, Guiomar. That's why I'm asking you."

"I don't get it, sir. You're teasing me, or trying to make me look silly."

"If you'll sleep with me, I promise not to touch you."

"And you think you'll manage that, sir? Wouldn't that be like playing with fire? And besides, why do you want me to sleep with you, sir?"

"I'm not used to sleeping alone, and I get horrible nightmares all night long. Having someone's company makes me sleep well. I swear by our Lord Jesus I won't lay a hand on you."

"Holy Mary Mother of God! And what if Dona Ana finds out?[2]

"Only if you tell her."

"Even if I don't, she might easily find a strand of hair in the sheets, or notice my smell, and then she'll fire me."

"Well, you can always wash the sheets."

"I don't trust that, sir. In these situations women are worse than dogs."

"You mean they're perceptive."

"Yes, sir."

"Listen here, Guiomar: what if I promise you a new skirt and blouse?"

"Promises, promises, everyone knows they're as fickle as the wind. Besides, it's not just Dona Ana finding out. I'm afraid you'll take advantage of me, sir. You see, sir, no man has ever laid a hand on me, and I plan on keeping it like that all the way to the altar, if I ever meet someone who wants me."

"Of course you'll meet someone. A girl like you deserves the best in this world, and in the next too. Come over here, sit down next to me and join me for some soup."

"Oh no, sir! My place is in the kitchen. I'm going to check the stew on the burner."

Guiomar dashed out of the dining room. It took her a while to bring me the tureen of stew. She set it down on the table, cleared away the soup plate and stood there, waiting. I helped myself to a chicken thigh, some collard greens, and half a potato. In fact, I was not very hungry.

While I dined, I watched her out of the corner of my eye. She was nearly twenty five and somewhat clumsy, the result of her upbringing and the rustic atmosphere of her childhood. Her skin was very fair and she had big, blue eyes. Her brown hair fell in two long braids. She was solidly built, with wide hips and a generous bosom. Because she was such a good cook, Aninhas had hired her when she was still in her teens.

I ate some of my chicken thigh, a leaf of collard greens, and the potato. After drinking a glass of wine I stood up from my chair.

"Won't you have no more, sir?" she asked.

"No, Guiomar. I'm not really hungry."

"But you barely ate..."

"I'm feeling a little under the weather. I'm going to my study to do some reading."

"Shall I bring along some tea in a little while, sir?"

"Yes, please do."

I sat down in one of the armchairs in the study, next to the warm fire where the Boche bronze insignia with an eagle and the motto, *Mit Gott für Koenig und Vaterland* – a war trophy I had brought from Flanders – hung over the mantelpiece. I took up Raul Brandão's novel, *Húmus*, and resumed my reading.[3] An hour later Guiomar came in with the tea tray. I set my book aside and asked her to sit down in the armchair opposite me. Out of respect for Aninhas, who usually sat there, she refused. She poured my tea with three teaspoons of sugar and handed it to me. That was usually Aninhas's role, but since she was away, Guiomar felt it was her duty to take her place.

"You know, sir, I was thinking about what you asked me," she said, somewhat embarrassedly, wringing her hands in her apron.

"And...?" I said, taking a sip of my tea.

"If you promise that you won't take advantage of me, sir, I'll let you sleep in my bed. It's small, and the room's a bit cold. But if we settle in, we'll fit, and it ain't so cold with an extra blanket."

"Guiomar, you're a good girl. I promise I won't lay a hand on you. You've already earned your new skirt and blouse."

"All right then, if you'll excuse me, sir, I'll make up the room."

"Well, don't go overboard. Just tuck yourself in and I'll be along shortly."

"Don't forget to turn off the lights and put out the fire, sir. The last thing we need is some kind of disaster."

As she walked toward the door I studied her figure from behind. She was really not a seductive woman, but still, I was not indifferent to her rustic looks.

I took up the book once again and read, "Only insignificance allows us to carry on with life. Without it, the screaming lunatic inside us would have taken over the world. Boundless strength is concentrated in insignificance." It was a depressing book. I made another valiant effort to finish the last paragraph of the chapter, "We are all here, waiting for death!" I closed the book and sat for a while, staring at the Boche insignia.

When I knocked on Guiomar's door in the attic, she asked me to come in, but without turning on the light. I stripped down to my skivvies in the dark, dropped my clothes on the floor, and climbed into bed. Although it was not big, it accommodated the two of us perfectly. The room was indeed cold.

"Get cozy," she said, tucking the blankets around us.

Then we both were silent. I managed to fall asleep, but in the middle of the night I had a nightmare. I dreamed that thousands of Boche soldiers were coming at me. Someone next to me was firing a Lewis machine gun. The bullets were like water and the enemy troops did not fall, but kept on coming, getting closer and closer. We ran out of ammunition and one of them charged with his bayonet pointing at me and stuck it into my arm. I hollered out in pain and Guiomar held me by the shoulders anxiously, "What happened, sir? Are you all right?"

When I heard her voice, just like in similar situations with Aninhas, the Boche soldiers turned into mist and the nightmare was over.

"It's nothing, Guiomar," I said, still half asleep and rubbing my injured arm. "It was just a dream."

"About the war, right?"

"Yes."

"My godfather, he was in the war too, and he used to have bad dreams. Go back to sleep, don't be afraid, I'm right here next to you."

We went back to sleep and I did not have the nightmare again.

In the morning I woke up with Guiomar facing me. There was enough light coming through the slits of the small oval window for me to see. I admired her as she slept, her fresh face, her eyes still shut, and a faint smile on her lips. I touched her forehead and hair. She sighed softly, opening her eyes. Then she grimaced briefly at finding me next to her, and quickly recovered her sense of reality. In a soft, lazy voice, she said, "Good morning, sir. Did you sleep well?"

"Yes, Guiomar, I did. Thank you for the company."

I got up, gathered my clothes from the floor, and left the room.

On the following days, we kept sleeping together, without ever mentioning it as we went on with our daily lives. At nighttime, she would go to her room and I would meet her there a little later. We fell asleep side by side and would invariably wake up in each other's arms. I had no more nightmares.

Several days later, when I was checking the white wine barrels in the cellar with Delmiro, one of my day laborers, I asked him nonchalantly, "So, when are you going to get married, young man? It's high time."

"Well, sir, to get married, a man's got to have someone to get married to."

"And can't you see your way clear to winning over one of the local girls?"

"There ain't too many available, sir. And those there is, they want a man with a situation, or with a little something of his own. And as you well know, sir, I ain't got neither."

"Well, Guiomar's a good girl, and she wouldn't say no," I said, testing him.

"Guiomar?" he said, surprised.

"Yes, Guiomar."

"But she's my parents' goddaughter. She's like kin."

"What's wrong with that?"

"What's wrong, sir? Well, godchildren ain't supposed to marry their godparents' children."

"That's news to me."

"Well, sir, you just ask Father Ruas. He says it's written in the books."

17

"You mean in Canon Law."

"That's right. The Church forbids that kind of marriage 'cause it's assestuous."

"You mean it's incestuous."

"Something like that. Anyways, it's like we was brother and sister. Before God, that is."

"I see. But Civil Law, which carries more weight than Canon Law, does allow that kind of marriage, you know. Therefore, there's no legal impediment. The priest's got to marry you, whether he likes it or not."

"That may well be, sir. You ought to know, 'cause you've read the Law, and I can barely read. But what really matters is if she likes me."

"And who told you she doesn't? She's got her eyes glued on you when you walk by."

"Is that so?"

"Like I'm telling you. The other day, when I sent you on an errand and it got dark before you came back, she was worried to death."

Delmiro kept silent while he inserted a tap into the barrel.

"So she likes me?" he said finally, as if to himself.

"When you have a chance, talk to her and ask her to be your girl. I'm sure she'll agree."

"Do you really think so, sir?"

"I certainly do. But listen to me," I added, somewhat tongue-in-cheek, "no hanky-panky around here, do you hear? Let's keep things decent. And as soon as she agrees to be your sweetheart, you'll talk to the priest and marry her."

He laughed and promised he would not touch a strand of her hair until the priest had blessed them. To help start him out in married life so he would have the means to support his wife and their children, I promised to put him in charge of my best estate. He was ecstatic at the news and swore that, by Christmas, he would drum up enough courage to talk to Guiomar.

"And why not now?" I challenged him.

18

"You know, sir, I got to feel my way first. To go about it slowly, like I don't mean nothing. Otherwise the bird'll fly away. And at Christmas I can always give her a gift. That's how you catch women, with gifts. They all go crazy about a hat or a handkerchief."

"I see you know a lot about women."

"Not that I got much experience, sir. But you know, sir, I've learned a lot from my sisters. Having two sisters at home can come in very handy at times."

"Let it be by Christmas, then. Let's hope you won't let the bird fly the coop. Mind you, another hunter might come by."

"Don't you worry, sir. That bird won't fly away. May I go blind if I let that happen."

And he sealed his promise by kissing his thumb crossed against his index finger.

Two days later the mailman delivered a telegram from Aninhas, asking me to fetch her in Póvoa do Varzim. Her aunt was better.

"Tomorrow I'm going to pick up Dona Ana," I told Guiomar at dinner time.

"Yes, sir," she said, a little disappointed at the news.

"Please get some flowers for the house, will you? There must be chrysanthemums in the garden. They're in season."

"Chrysanthemums, sir?"

"Yes, why not?

"They're dead folks' flowers. They go on tombstones."

"But it seems to me that right now we have no other flowers. And I'd like the house to be cheerful to receive Dona Ana."

"I'll see what I can do."

"And as to our deal, Guiomar, let's keep it confidential."

"Confi what, sir?"

"Mum's the word, girl. We haven't done anything wrong. But even so, Dona Ana wouldn't like to know you've been sharing your bed with me."

"Don't you worry about that, sir."

I took three twenty escudo[4] bills from my wallet and handed them to her.

"This is for your new skirt and blouse. If anyone asks you where you got the money, just say you saved it."

"But that's too much, sir."

"You can always buy a hat and some shoes."

"Even so, there'll be some to spare."

"Well then, keep it for your trousseau."

Guiomar held the bills in silence for a few moments.

"For my trousseau?"

"That's right, for your trousseau. Every girl ought have a trousseau, right? Wouldn't it be a shame if a young man asked a girl to marry him and it turned out she'd forgotten to get bed sheets for their new home?"

She seemed happy with the idea. She pocketed the bills and, after some hesitation, said, "Forgive my asking, sir, but tonight you'll also..."

"Oh yes, Guiomar, if you don't mind, I'll be coming to your room."

"Oh, I don't mind, sir. I don't mind at all."

And she went to the kitchen, wobbling like a turkey, to fetch the grilled steak for me.

When, two hours later, I said good night to Raul Brandão and went up to the attic, I found Guiomar's room softly lit by the full moon rays seeping through the cracks in the oval window. I lay down next to her and, unlike the previous nights, she turned to me and covered my face with kisses. While she kissed me, I felt her tears. I tried to calm her down with kind words and caresses. But the young woman was beside herself with excitement and my self-control began to waver. She grabbed one of my hands and guided it to one of her breasts. When I resisted, she asked, "Don't you like me, sir?"

I told her I did, but that I wasn't there to take advantage of her. And I started to get up to leave.

"Don't go away, sir, stay with me. It's our last night. Make me happy. I know I'll never meet nobody that'll like me. It's just a dream. I'm too ugly for any man to like me."

"You are a pretty girl. You'll certainly meet a good man who'll make you happy."

She sat on top of me, let down her hair, and, in spite of the cold, took off her nightgown. I kissed her large breasts and lingered on her nipples, while caressing her back, shoulders, and neck. Meanwhile, she rubbed her sex on my loins forcefully, as if possessed by a sneaky devil. I slid my hand under her thighs and felt her, wet and throbbing. Guiomar sighed and wept, I do not know whether from pleasure or sadness, though surely not out of pain, as I had not yet penetrated her. I asked her gently to lie on her back, and let my mouth and hands go all over her body. I licked her pubis, nibbled her clitoris, taking in her scent and moistness. As I did this, I felt her hands caressing my hair. She had stopped weeping and I heard her sighs, broken by cries, "Oh my God! Jesus! I'm in heaven!"

I knew that moment could be dangerous. The young woman was excited and, if I got carried away, I might get her pregnant. I entered her slowly, controlling my natural impulse. Her excitement made penetration easy. If she was a virgin, I did not notice the difference. Nor did I notice any blood to indicate she was. Might she have lied about it? Perhaps. But the fact that there was no blood, as a physician friend had once explained to me, did not mean anything. Some women do not bleed. I was not thinking about it at the time. I played my role as best I could and, after the young woman had cried three or four times, I pulled out without ejaculating and lay down on my back. I was afraid to impregnate her and mess up her life. And mine, to be sure. We lay like that for a while, looking at the ceiling, catching our breath. Then she turned to me, with a smile of happiness, pressed her nipples on my chest, and whispered, "If this wasn't a sin, I'd swear I was in heaven."

"This is no sin, Guiomar."

"But Father Ruas, at church, says it is."

"Priests do it with their maids whenever they get a chance."

21

"That's true. The priest at Esmoriz[5] has three children. Everybody knows it."

"See?"

"Oh, sir, I never thought it could be so good. I've always heard the older women say it hurts and only the men have a good time."

"When people like each other it's good for both of them."

"But you don't seem very happy, sir."

"I didn't want to make you pregnant, Guiomar. That's why I pulled out before I felt the way you did."

"So you didn't feel anything, sir?"

"Seeing you feel it was enough for me."

She did not seem convinced and asked what she could do to console me. I told her it was not worth worrying about. I felt fine. She started kissing me, and insisted she did not want me to be disappointed. I said if she felt like it, she could caress my penis and kiss it, if that did not bother her. She must have remembered I had felt no qualms about sucking her juice and smelling her, and she went at it eagerly, and in a little while I burst into a swell of fire and pleasure.

I got up early, climbed onto the Ford and drove to Póvoa de Varzim to fetch Aninhas. During the trip I promised myself that my bedroom trysts with Guiomar were over. It was bad for the young woman's future and it would be worse for my relationship with my wife and children, if word got out. Besides, with a little push, we would soon have a wedding.

I did not think marital unfaithfulness, categorically condemned by contemporary morality, is any more important than a boy's prank. Love is to be given and to be received. Everything else is sheer prejudice. Furthermore, I did not love my wife any less because of that episode. I may be accused of machismo for saying it, but deep inside, I would not like to find out she was also promiscuous, and that instead of visiting her sick aunt, she had been spending a few days with some dandy.

II

There are four kinds of men: guileless, like Rato and the soldiers I commanded in Flanders; ordinary, like Captain Rebelo and the other two second lieutenants in my company; demagogues, like the politicians who sent us to war to fight for their interests in the name of the fatherland; and enlightened. I consider myself an enlightened man, with a sense of responsibility, even though, like anyone else, I am given to passions which, in the course of my life, have often left me in awkward situations. I have tried to do good; not hypocritical Christian good works, in hopes of some reward after death, but acting selflessly and cutting no deals with some almighty god.

The war ended twenty years ago today. For me, it is still not over. Actually, for the last twenty years, in my mind I have been crawling through the mud of the trenches, taking cover from bullets and shells, hearing the heavy guns booming and the machine guns rattling. Sometimes I wake up drenched in sweat, clutching Aninhas.

I have a recurring dream that leaves me with a taste of blood in my mouth. I blow my whistle and lead my platoon over the top, aiming my pistol at no man's land. We slosh forward in the mud and through the shell holes, after the guns on our side have gone silent. The Boche machine guns and rifles start singing. Bullets crack overhead and beside me. We all hit the dirt and nobody knows if the man next to him is dead or alive. The wounded moan, the only ones that show any sign of life. There is a pause in the sound of the enemy weapons. The Boche are conserving their ammunition. Since I am the platoon commander, I force myself to stand up and blow my whistle, signaling a new charge and pointing toward a crater-like hole. About half of my men stand up and move forward. The weapons start singing again. That is when, racing ahead, I feel lead piercing my chest, tearing up my heart, coming out my back, as if a lance had run through me. I fall down slowly, my hands on my chest, my eyes wide open in the darkness, feeling excruciating pain and the life oozing out of me with my blood.

It is an odd dream, all the more so because I never took part in any attack or raid against enemy lines. I can only explain it by the dread everyone felt that some day we might get orders for a raid. But that would have been unusual, because the Portuguese Expeditionary Corps in Flanders was primarily charged with holding its positions, rather than attacking or raiding the enemy's. Still, the commander of our division, keen on impressing the English, would sometimes order a raid. The purpose was almost always the same: to capture prisoners and check out the enemy trenches. It was a rare occasion when we had no wounded or dead brought back on stretchers. And we wondered what for. The soldiers captured were privates or low-ranking, noncommissioned officers who knew little or nothing about offensives and counter-offensives. Like us, they just followed orders. And the enemy lines were not much different from ours: muddy holes protected against bombardments by sand bags, forming a tangled maze dotted with machine gun posts and pools of stinking water.

Maybe the only difference was that the signs in our trenches were in English, which most of us could not understand anyway, while their signs were in German. I once suggested to the Captain of our company that he might recommend to the Major of our battalion to tell the Colonel of our brigade to mention to the General of our division to suggest to the General commanding the Portuguese Expeditionary Corps that, in meeting with the English generals, they might decide to have the signs displayed all over our trenches translated into Portuguese. Captain Rebelo gave me an amused look and said he had already thought of that but had put it on the back-burner when he realized that, by the time the proposal reached proper channels, the war would likely be over. I said he was too optimistic about the end of the war. He laughed, "Come on, Vasques, don't you get it? I know this war's going to last. The big brass are having fun playing with their little colored flags, tin soldiers, and painted cardboard trenches. When the war's over they won't even notice."

The Captain was very encouraging. Fortunately he only talked like that to the officers, or to some of the more reliable sergeants. In front of the troops, his talk was always cheerful, "Hang in there, boys, this war will soon be over. A couple more weeks and the Boche will surrender, and then we'll get our marching orders to go home."

And the soldiers believed him, or pretended to, and then they would put more effort into cleaning and maintaining their equipment and the trenches.

I do not like to talk about the war. At home everyone knows that and the subject is rarely brought up. Sometimes an unsuspecting guest, having heard I went to war and got wounded in one arm, asks a question. I get into a bad mood and clam up. Some have found that offensive. But you simply cannot discuss the war with someone who did not go through it. No matter in how much detail you tell about the horror we went through, they never fully understand it. Some look at you in disbelief, as if such atrocities were not possible. They think we exaggerate just to show off our courage. They think we went to war as if on vacation, for a government-paid holiday in France. We can only share the horror with someone who was also there and saw the dying men's bloody wounds and heard their shouts, someone who buried his head in the mud to dodge the shells and saw human body parts scattered on the ground with rats crawling all over them. No matter how much I wish to forget, it is the stench of the trenches that fills my nose when I take a walk in the country after the rain. In a tree felled by the wind I see that soldier with his leg severed by a shell fragment. The moment I heard his shouts I ran toward him. His comrades were around him, one of them holding the leg like a useless object. I came up to the soldier and he grabbed my tunic and cried, "Sir! Tell me I won't die, sir!"

And I, maybe more scared than he was, kept on saying he wouldn't die, that it was just a scratch. He died like that, clutching my uniform, as if a lightning bolt had struck him. The others had to help unclench his fingers from my tunic. I saw seven of my men die, two shot by snipers while smoking a cigarette, three killed by shell fragments, another shot dead when a comrade accidentally pulled the trigger, and one frozen to death while on guard duty on a trench parapet.

The soldier I watched dying while clutching my uniform was from a nearby village. When I came back I called on his wife to offer my sympathy, even though the War Ministry had already sent her an official letter of condolence. The family was poor and the soldier had left three children behind. The woman came to the door of their hut. She was dressed in black and did not ask me in. I started giving her my condolences. She cut me off me brusquely and told me to go away, yelling insults at me, "Thief! You stole my husband from me!" I left in a hurry, before she could throw a pan at me. I did not visit the relatives of the other dead soldiers.

In the trenches, habit eventually made me indifferent to everything – the smell of excrement, rotten flesh, gas, burned gunpowder, mud, dampness, cold, the constant booming of the heavy guns. Our strategists used to explain such indifference as the result of our military instruction before going to the trenches, and of the war experience itself. When I came back, everything and anything – the smell of manure, a shot fired by a dove hunter, a firecracker on a holiday – would annoy me and suddenly drag me back to that scene of horror.

You just cannot talk about war with someone who has never been there. In the last twenty years, I have kept my memories to myself. Every year the veteran officers and sergeants of my old battalion hold a luncheon. Once they even organized an excursion to Flanders to revisit the place where, for about two years, they watched their youth drift away and their friends and acquaintances die. I did not go on the excursion, and I went to only one luncheon, at Captain Rebelo's insistence. I hear that every year fewer veterans show up at these reunions, because so many of them have died from lung diseases caused by mustard gas, tuberculosis, and wounds that have sapped their health.

Since my return, my contact with the war has been through memoirs published by one veteran or another, which I collect. I have a few dozen, of variable value either as literature or as documentation. Some are more jingoistic and praise the courage, bravery and valor of the Portuguese soldiers. Others are more critical, either of the performance of the Portuguese Expeditionary Corps in Flanders, or of our politicians' decision to drag the country into the war. A few books, written by junior officers, limit themselves to describing daily life in the trenches. These I have read with interest, feeling that somewhere out there, someone has been suffering as much as I have. Finally I lost interest in those books and stored them away in the attic, not so much out of fear of being tempted to leaf through them again, but so that no guest would come across them in the library and bring up the subject.

It may sound contradictory for me to say that I find it painful to talk or hear about the war when I am in the middle of recalling it. Actually, I have read somewhere that writing about what torments you is a way of exorcising it and rendering it harmless. Except for some doggerel written when I was a student, I make no claim to being a writer. While in the Army I wrote service reports, and since then I have been writing legal briefs. It would just not do to become a writer now that my hair has turned gray. You have to make room for the youth. And insofar as I have learned from the few magazines and journals that come my way, there is no dearth of people keen on turning the world upside down with literature. As for me, I will content myself with filling out a few folios that I will probably burn after the exorcism has been completed.

Sometimes I think that our war effort was pointless, that the millions dead on both sides between 1914 and 1918 can never be justified. That the loss of innocence and energy of the young who got back was a total waste. The world, in fact, has not become any better. Many thought the Great War would be the war to end all wars and afterwards the world would live in peace forever, because the horror of it all was so enormous that no nation would ever have the courage to start another conflict. A hopeless illusion. Right now the world is preparing for a new war, which will likely be far more terrible than the last. Germany has rearmed and Hitler is waiting for the slightest pretext to start a war. One of his strongest motives will be the Germans' need to get even for the humiliation suffered when they were forced to sign the Armistice. I fear for my eldest son. I could not stand to see him leave for the trenches – and this time, probably for the wrong side. But which side is right and which is wrong? Salazar is as much an ally of the English as a sympathizer of Hitler and his nationalistic, patriotic, and totalitarian politics. I hope our Prime Minister will have the common sense our republican politicians lacked and not make the mistake of selling our young men to a foreign power in exchange for political support for his regime.

I have promised Aninhas not to mention our Prime Minister. She is afraid the political police might search our house and find something compromising in writing. Three years ago some political big shots of the New State[6] paid me a courtesy call to ask for my support. I booted them out and now it is quite likely the police have a file on me. But I could not care less about that. In the previous regime they had a file on me for being anti-republican, and this time around I am undoubtedly listed as a sympathizer, or maybe a militant of the Communist Party. Politics, which has ruined this country, leaves me cold. At least this kind of politicking, which tolerates neither competing opinions, nor competing tastes. We are under a regime in which everyone has to dance to the same tune and enjoy picaresque *fados* and folksy songs about the so-called Fátima apparitions.[7]

I have just paused, wondering whether I should delete this last musical reference. Not out of superstition or religious fears, which I do not have, but out of respect for Rato's beliefs. Rato was my orderly in Flanders. After the war he went back to France and I did not see him again until two days ago, when he showed up here, hat in hand and gray-haired. He is older than I and must be about fifty now. I never figured out why he was drafted, since he was married, had four children, and was then nearly thirty years old. In 1916, anxious to round up cannon fodder for the French trenches, the War Ministry did not bother to select the draftees carefully. The basic norm was that nobody was exempted, except – but this was not in writing – members of the Democratic Party, which was in power at the time, and their relatives, nephews, godsons, and friends.

As I was saying, Rato showed up at the house two days ago and asked to talk to me. My daughter Inês, who answered the doorbell, thinking he was a bit of a simpleton, told him to wait by the main stairway, then came to tell me.

"There's a man wanting to talk to you, Dad."

It was early on a Sunday afternoon and I was reading in my study.

"Who is he?"

"I don't know him. He says his name's Joaquim."

"There are lots of men named Joaquim. Who the heck can he be? Didn't you tell him we don't need any more day workers?"

"I did. But he assured me that's not why he's here."

"What does he want then?"

"He insists on talking to you."

"What's he like?"

"Middle-aged, maybe a little older than you."

"There are many men like that."

"He looks a bit simple, although he's not poorly dressed. He's even wearing a suit and tie."

29

"Could he be a policeman?" I asked, alarmed.

"I don't think so. I told him to wait outside. Shall I tell him you're not in?"

"No, it's all right. I'll come and find out what he wants. If he's come here to talk to me, it means he has something important to tell me."

"Anyway, be careful."

I put down the book, walked down the hall to the front door and saw Rato, his hands stuck in his pockets, leaning against one of the granite vases at the foot of the stairway. Other than his gray hair and a paunch, he had not changed much. His mustache, combed and waxed at the tips, was just the same.

"Rato?... I asked."

"Lieutenant... sir?"

I walked down the stairs with open arms and slapped him on his back. He seemed surprised with the reception. My slapping must have hurt him, for he grimaced in pain. Only later did I find out he had lung trouble.

I invited him to my study and had him sit down in one of the armchairs. He took out a pouch of shag and paper, rolled himself a cigarette, lit it, and asked if I wanted one. I declined, saying I had quit smoking. I had had enough smoking in the trenches. He inhaled and coughed hard, which worried me.

I introduced him to Inês, my youngest daughter, who was home from school for the weekend. She smiled and he nodded in response. Then I asked her to have Guiomar bring us something to drink. Rato said we shouldn't bother, he'd just dropped in to say hello and wouldn't stay long. I told him that visitors – and particularly such a special visitor – deserved to be well received by the master of the house.

Minutes later Guiomar walked in wiping her hands on her apron, looked at Rato in disbelief, and cried, "Godfather?..."

"This is Guiomar, your goddaughter," I said.

He got to his feet, bewildered. Recovering from her

surprise, she came up to him, and said, "Your blessing, God-father."

Rato gave her his hand, which she kissed, saying, "It's been such a long time since I last seen you! We was all thinking something might've happened to you."

"Well, here I am, finally. And you've grown up," he remarked, looking her over. "You've become a very pretty girl, no doubt about that."

"Fine, you'll have plenty of time to catch up on some other occasion," I said. "I suggest you invite Guiomar to your house. After all, as her godfather, you still owe her an Easter gift for every single one of the last twenty years."

We all laughed in agreement. Guiomar asked what she should bring to honor the guest. A bottle of champagne, I told her, the special kind, with a foreign label. She protested she couldn't tell them apart. It would be best if I went to the cellar and picked out what I wanted.

"Didn't your mother send you to school?" I asked.

"Yes, sir, she did, but I've only learned up to the letter P. The others I didn't have no time to learn 'cause I had to come and work here."

"All right, then. You'd better see to your duties. We'll manage for ourselves."

"I'll bring you some codfish fritters later."

I took Rato down to the cellar. We did not open the champagne. I offered him a white wine from last year's harvest. We spent the rest of the afternoon down there, with our memories of laughter and horror, drinking wine and eating Guiomar's codfish fritters. With Rato I could talk about the war.

III

I was in Coimbra when I received a telegram from my father saying I had been drafted and must return home as soon as possible. For whatever reason, I remembered that Maria, one of our maids, had suggested I make a promise to Our Lady of Delivery, the patron saint of her village, to free me from military service. I am sure she believed I was called up for not having followed her advice.

A number of fellow law students had also received their marching orders in the mail. Before leaving, some of us got together at Joaquina Cardosa's tavern to drink and gripe about our bad luck. Comparing notes, we found out that most of us had a police file. Some because they were brawlers, others because they belonged to political parties that opposed the government, still others because they were monarchists. As I have already mentioned, I too had a police file. As soon as I arrived in Coimbra, because I was friends with a group of students with monarchist views, the police wasted no time in classifying me in that political faction. Actually, I had no sympathy for the republicans on account of their incompetent mishandling of the government, nor did I have any for the monarchists, who were backward and stupid. I hung around with them simply because I had known them since we were teenagers at school together in Braga. Our get-togethers in Coimbra were more about brandy and broads than about political conspiracies.

In 1916, after the government impounded the German ships anchored off the Tagus harbor, that Germany declared war on Portugal. The government of the so-called Sacred Union immediately decreed general mobilization and Afonso Costa [8] and his gang were eager to dispatch Portuguese cannon fodder to Flanders. The English, who initially had looked down on the offer, were finally sweet-talked into accepting it by Afonso Costa's fantastic promises, which he would never be able to fulfill.

When I got home I found my parents rather worried about my future. My father tried pulling strings but got nowhere because of his monarchist background. He was close to sixty and I think I never once saw him smile again.

Later in life he had married a much younger cousin, my mother. Even though it was a marriage of convenience, they knew each other well and had always liked each other. He was fond of telling how my mother had a nun's soul and was convinced, at age thirty, that she would remain a spinster. He saw her during a family funeral and proposed. She thought her cousin was joking, but he was in earnest. They got married and my father brought her to his estate, named Quinta⁹ de São Francisco. I was born shortly afterwards and my mother, as he used to say, became the happiest woman in the world.

I once asked him why it had taken him so long to get married. He owned up to me that while living in Lisbon he was several times close to tying the knot, but had always dodged it. Lisbon women were nearly all flighty.

"I was warned about that danger by Carlos da Maia and João da Ega, who knew their way around Lisbon women."

"You got to know those two?" I asked.

"Did I get to know them?"

He told me how he and those two, and a few other fellows from the Civil Service or the Diplomatic Corps, used to get together in orgies and drinking bouts that nearly always ended in the beds of Lisbon's shameless women.

"Did you go to brothels?" I asked, rather indignantly.

"Come on, son, how naive can you be? That way you'll never get ahead as a lawyer. Do you really think men in our position would go whoring in the Alfama?¹⁰ There was no need for that. There were young and fresh married ladies with traveling husbands, with whom you could have a good conversation. And there were Spanish women. Carlos da Maia, for instance, was crazy about them. But they were really prostitutes. I mean, they went to bed for money. However, they were clean prostitutes a man could afford to be intimate with without endangering his health. When there were no married ladies handy, we hired a bunch of Spanish women. I didn't much care for them. They chattered too much, even while a man was trying to get the job done. No, I much preferred married ladies. More discrete, and eager to do things right, if you know what I mean."

And he summed it up, "Therefore, my son, if some day you move to Lisbon, enjoy life but make no commitments. When you decide it's time to start a family, get married to a girl from here. Our girls are more serious and you'll be certain that her children are your own."

My father had once been elected a deputy for the Progressive Party. He often said the time spent in Lisbon had been the period in his life when he had felt most useless. The capital city had ruined his best intentions and purposes. He gave up politics a little before the end of the century, came back to the North, got married, and devoted himself to nobler causes, such as skinning clients in his legal practice in Braga and managing his estate.

"There's no way to fix this nation of scoundrels, idiots, and crooks," he often commented while taking a break from reading *A Monarquia*, sitting in an armchair by the fireplace or in a canvas chair in the shady garden of our house. *A Monarquia* was a newspaper linked to Portuguese Integralism, whose director, the Count of Monsaraz, had been one of my father's pals in those Lisbon revelries.[11] Being of a monarchic persuasion, my father subscribed to it because he thought it was the most unbiased at the time. The other papers, he said, were either Catholic, and thus unreliable, or republican, no more than mouthpieces for a regime for which he had no sympathy. I recall him saying that in 1919 *A Monarquia* was out of circulation for about seven months, on account of a series of typographers' strikes, a class ideologically controlled by the republicans.

Back home from Flanders I found my father rather gaunt and downcast. He gave me a long hug, as if trying to absorb all the fright and suffering I had gone through in the war. Fear of losing his only son had made him agonize for two years. My mother was crying at his side, and when he let me go, she covered me with kisses and tears. She wanted to know everything, and since I would not oblige, she was annoyed and kept on insisting, until one day my father told her gruffly to leave me alone. I did not feel like talking about it. During the first weeks, I sleepwalked around our estate in a daze, gazing at the trees and feeling the sun, trying to readjust to the world where I had been born and grown up. I found it odd not to hear the big guns rumbling in the background. I could hear the sparrows, the wind through the trees, and the squeaking of ox cart wheels on the road. My parents worried about me and wanted to take me to a doctor. My mother suspected I was like that on account of Libaninhas's marriage. Not wanting to wait until my return, she had married someone else.

A doctor friend told them there was no cure for my condition. Only time can cure melancholy. It was then that my father had the idea of giving me an automobile, a 1913 four-seater Minerva made in Belgium. He had bought it for a good price from the heirs of a man who had returned rich from Brazil. Red and with two big golden front lights, it was one of the best automobiles at the time. It incorporated technology that only years later would be available on other makes. However, it was slow and heavy, used a lot of gasoline, and was uncomfortable, particularly when it was rainy or cold. The dealers in Braga advised me to get rid of it when I bought the Ford about three years ago, but I paid no attention to them. It is still sitting in the garage next to my father's old buggy. My son Afonso tinkers with it in his spare time, trying to make it run.

I used to take off in the Minerva early in the morning, stop by Rato's house and take him along if he had not yet left for work. I would hardly say a word, paying attention to the road's curves and potholes. Rato enlivened our trips talking about the war. But I am not going to write about that now. I have yet to tell how I was drafted and found myself dressed up like a soldier, shouldering a rifle and marching to the sound of drums and trumpets.

Given the shortage of Army officers, the government had opened a Reserve Officers School in Oporto. I was sent there and in a few months I was commissioned a second lieutenant and posted to one of the Braga regiments. Normally, it took four or five years to train a career second lieutenant at the Military Academy. However, since there were so few of them, they had been promoted right away to higher ranks, and we reserve officers with only three months' training would have to do their job. I was in charge of training a thirty-recruit platoon to go to Flanders. I was assisted by a veteran sergeant named Rosado, who had seen service in Mozambique. Even so, if anything went wrong I was the one responsible. Of those thirty men uprooted from their villages in Minho, only three could read and only one of these could write. Few of them knew the name of the President of Portugal, and most thought that King Manuel II, deposed in 1910, still reigned. They did not have the slightest idea where France was, and they wanted to go back as soon as possible to their villages, their families, and their corn fields. They did not want, as General Gomes da Costa[12] later wrote, "to intervene in a war whose causes they did not know." The draftees were not the only ones who felt that way. It was a generalized feeling in the Army. Only a few officers, out of patriotic stupidity, career interests, or simply affiliation with one of the republican parties, tried to encourage the troops.

One of these was the Colonel commanding our regiment. Maybe he did it because he knew he was not going to be sent to France. Every morning at parade, he blathered in his shrill voice about duty, the defense of the Fatherland, valor, sacrifice, and the certainty of victory. He painted the Germans as enemies of humanity, rabid dogs that had invaded France, forcing us

36

to leave behind our loved ones and native soil to go abroad and show them that the Portuguese would sacrifice their own blood in the name of liberty. Some of us smiled but made no comment, just in case there was a snitch nearby – and there usually was. Later on, I found out that the Colonel's speeches did not necessarily reflect his feelings. The War Minister, that other criminal, General Norton de Matos, a real bear in uniform, had ordered all regimental commanders to indoctrinate the troops, in an effort to build up morale and make them understand that their sacrifices would not be in vain. I suspect the order had been inspired by Minister Afonso Costa. He and João Chagas,[13] that scoundrel posing as a philosopher, had led Germany to declare war on Portugal, thus paving the way for the Portuguese expedition to the muddy fields of Flanders.

During the last few years I have reached the conclusion that Afonso Costa and his henchmen were behind every political crime committed in the name of the Republic. If he did not pull the trigger, he certainly ordered the assassination of King Carlos I and Prince Luís Filipe in 1908. He was responsible for nearly all public disturbances after 1910, in which hundreds of people died. He was responsible for Portugal's entry in the war, and his hands are covered with the blood of the two thousand soldiers buried in Flanders, another five thousand wounded, many of whom died shortly afterwards, and twenty thousand more victims of a variety of diseases contracted in the trenches. And I am convinced he was behind the assassination, in 1918, of President Sidónio Pais,[14] who was the hope of a ruined and rudderless nation. Afonso Costa died in Paris last year, exiled and abandoned by those who had supported him. If an avenging God exists, may Costa be tormented in Hell more harshly than any other sinner.

Afonso Costa also shares the responsibility for the dictatorship under which we live. With their political squabbles and their petty vested interests, the republicans have thrown this country into disarray. And as a result of General Gomes da Costa's attempt to restore order in 1926, we now have a dictator. I have to recognize that our beloved Father of the Nation has imposed order and straightened out finances. Nevertheless, when I look around, I see the same misery. In the days of democratically elected republican governments, we were at least able to denounce it – even though it did not do any good – whereas nowadays we have to keep quiet, if we do not want – as Aninhas fears – to be thrown in jail.

Since I am not a political animal and politics to me is no more than a distant rumble, I find my indignant prose rather odd. Let me get back to the recruitment and training of the thirty men that were entrusted to me.

With Sergeant Rosado's assistance, I tried to turn that bunch of peasants into soldiers who, at the sound of an order or a bugle, would obey as if they were a single body. They learned to march, salute, stand at attention, present arms, recognize insignias of rank, wear the appropriate uniform for each occasion, and jump to attention, yelling, "Yes, sergeant!" or "Yes, sir!" Weapons training was more problematic. They practiced with nineteenth century rifles, clumsy and heavy, many of them muzzle loaders and hardly any in working condition. Even if they worked, there was no ammunition for target practice. So we would just run around the Montélios woods outside Braga, coached by Sergeant Rosado, aiming at the enemy and simulating shooting by shouting, "Bang! Bang!"

In early October 1916, it was with a twinge of pride that I watched the ceremony in which the men in my platoon swore allegiance to the flag. We were ready to leave for the Tancos training field[15] to take part in the joint exercises of the Training Division commanded by the doddering General Tamagnini, who would command the Portuguese Expeditionary Corps. Up to that point the recruits had been getting along fine. Compared to toiling in the fields, their work in the Army was not hard at all. Though far from scrumptious, chow was abundant and a few even put on weight. They each had a bed with sheets and a blanket, clothing, medical assistance, and even a small allowance. Every now and then, they could go out to drink in some tavern in town, or spend their money on a whore. Many of them, particularly the unmarried, were even convinced that military life was not that bad after all.

I found out, with disgust, that military life stirs up the most aberrant in man. I saw those plain, naive recruits become ruffians, drunkards, homosexuals, or addicted to prostitutes.

At the Tancos training field, however, the recruits' good impression of military life vanished fast. In the vast treeless prairie where the training grounds stretched, thirty thousand men chewed dust and mud. The gigantic camp consisted of tents that sheltered us neither from the dust nor from the first autumn rains. We went back to Braga by mid-November, worn out by the poor conditions and the exhausting training. After watching the final exercises, some of the top brass realized that if we went to war at that point we would all get killed, not for being an easy target, but from bumping into one another. Our military tactics dated from the mid-nineteenth century and our weapons had seen service during the French invasion in 1808. However, Minister Norton de Matos, after watching the field maneuvers from a distance, proclaimed them a success and announced that our soldiers were fully prepared to defend the Fatherland.

However, in the absence of marching orders, apparently because there was no transportation – the English hesitated to provide the ships needed to ferry the Portuguese troops to France – our Colonel was ordered to furlough his men until further notice. Everyone packed up and went home on leave. It would be a vacation before departure. I, too, went home and found my parents worried. Unless there was a drastic change in plans – always a possibility under the Republic – my going to war was a foregone conclusion. The soldiers did not know that and we were under orders not to say anything. If pressed, we were supposed to say we believed the war would end soon and then our departure would no longer be necessary.

Some of my mother's relatives came to spend Christmas Eve with us and, in spite of the children and their games and carefree happiness, the tension of departure was in the air. My parents feared something might happen to me in Flanders.

The day before Christmas Eve I mounted my horse Ruddy and rode to visit my fiancée, Libaninha. Even though we had seen each other only a few times since I had been drafted, we wrote each other regularly, exchanging kisses between the lines, with words of love and longing as conventions allowed. In those days you could not tell a woman everything openly, particularly if there was the danger of someone else reading our letters. The norms of seduction and common sense kept us in check.

I rode to Quinta de Santa Madalena, where my fiancée lived with her parents, Mr. Arnaldo Fontoura e Azevedo, who had made his fortune in Brazil, and his Brazilian wife, Dona Eleutéria. With the money made in the meat business in São Paulo, he had bought the estate with the house, which he had restored according to colonial taste.

I rang the bell and a maid led me into the living room. I greeted Libaninha with a kiss on her hand and she tilted her head, calling attention to the maid in charge of chaperoning us. Libaninha offered me a wicker chair, sat in an armchair upholstered in red velvet, and we began to exchange pleasantries about the weather, so as not to shock the maid with the things we really wanted to say and do. I had once suggested we could speak French so the maid would not understand us, but Libaninha rejected the idea, as her mother might not like it.

"When will you be leaving?" she asked.

"I'll go back to barracks in a few days. There are things to be organized, I don't know exactly what. All the more so now that the soldiers are on leave."

"And do you know anything about leaving for France?"

"No, I don't. And even if I did, it would be confidential."

She laughed, "You don't think I might pass that information to the enemy, do you?"

"Of course not, Libaninha. But those are the regulations. We're not supposed to reveal anything to civilians."

"Not even to your fiancée?"

"Not to your fiancée, nor to your parents, nor to your wife."

She became serious and said, "If you really leave for France, we'll have to put off our wedding."

"That's right."

"May God make the war end, so you won't have to go."

She grabbed my hands and held them, causing the maid to cough lightly.

"Libaninha, when this is all over, and it'll be over some day, you'll have me here, if you still want me to be your husband."

"How can you think I wouldn't? You're a silly man."

And she pressed my hands more firmly, which made the maid cough again.

I told her what was tormenting me, "Something might happen to me in France. Just imagine if I'm seriously wounded, or crippled..."

"Oh my dear Luís!"

She knelt down before me and covered my hands with kisses and tears. The maid coughed louder and said, "Please, Missy, behave yourself, or I'll call your mother."

We were upset when we said goodbye. Libaninha had tears rolling down her tanned cheeks.

Since it was still early, I decided to stop by Rato's house. He was one of the best soldiers in my platoon. Too bad he was illiterate, or I would have recommended him for the corporals' course. Even so, I appointed him my orderly. He took care of my uniforms, made my coffee and tea, and ran my errands in the barracks and outside.

41

His wife answered the door, surrounded by several children. I counted three and had the impression she was carrying
a fourth. She told me her husband had gone to clear a well and
would only be back at night. I asked her to tell him to come
by the estate, as I had something to give him. And to make
sure he would, I explained it was a little something for their
Christmas Eve dinner. The poor woman thanked me profusely
and promised he would come over the next day.

IV

A new year began, three months went by, and the war was still not over. The conflict, which according to politicians and military strategists should have been settled in a little over two months, had been dragging on by then for nearly three years. By the end of January 1917, the first Portuguese battalions departed for France. A few officers had left in December, some for England, others for France, for specialized training in trench warfare. Since I was in the infantry and did not require much specialization, I was not called up. In April, my regiment was ordered to prepare the Expeditionary Battalion for departure. The soldiers were called up one by one. After all those months of military inactivity, they arrived at the barracks totally lacking in motivation. Some could no longer march in step and had forgotten many military regulations. To prevent desertions, home leaves ceased to be granted. Those wishing to say goodbye to their family would be able to do so at the railway station before departing.

I managed to secure a day's leave to go home to say goodbye to my parents. Rato found out and begged me to go by his house and tell his wife. That way she could come to the station with their children to see him off. I promised him I would and so I did. It was convenient, since he lived near Quinta de Santa Madalena, where I would go anyway to say goodbye to Libaninha, and it was not far from where I lived.

That was the last day I spent with my parents before departure. I arrived mid-morning by public transportation, a horse-drawn eight-seat coach. Buses were not common – in fact, I think they did not yet exist in Portugal. The first time I saw one was in France.

My father was waiting for me at the coach stop with the family buggy. In 1917, Portugal was still technologically in the nineteenth century, and mentally in the seventeenth or maybe even further back. I had many doubts about our performance in the war and shared them with my father during the drive home. As he brought the horses to a stop before the stairway he said, "Despite all the evil and terrible things this war stands for, maybe it will bring the light of development to our country, so darkened by ignorance, the misery of the poor, and the corruption of the powerful. Even if it does no more than that, son, it'll have been worthwhile."

My father was trying to encourage me, to make me believe the war had some acceptable purpose. It was not the patriotic, meaningless speeches and proclamations we heard from generals and politicians, as when senile General Tamagnini justified our going to war with the notion that Portuguese honor had been offended by the enemy. Well, everyone knows it was the Portuguese Government that offended Germany by impounding some German merchant ships anchored at the mouth of the Tagus River, thus triggering a declaration of war. If we really had to fight, we should do so in Africa, where our colonies and their people were being attacked by German forces. That is where the Fatherland should be defended, and not in Flanders, as proclaimed by the government and by the top brass who represented it in the barracks. Before our departure, while handing me my newly shined boots, Rato once asked me how it was possible for us to go and defend our land in someone else's land.

"What if our land was really attacked? By the Spaniards, for example? How could we defend it if we are far away, in France, which I don't even know where it is?"

I refrained from telling him my true opinion, which would surely stir up his skepticism. I just said maybe the government knew the Spaniards would never attack us. He did not seem much convinced, but did not insist. He commented that the younger soldiers wanted to know why they had to go to France to fight on someone else's land. They asked him, and he didn't know what to tell them.

"The problem, sir, is that they just don't get what they hear from our Colonel, from our Major, and from our Captain. They just don't get why they got to leave their land, their family, their fields, their jobs, to go and defend what ain't theirs. There's even a rumor that the English are paying Minister Afonso Costa a pound for each soldier he sends to France. Do you think that's true, sir?"

As the oldest soldier in our platoon, Rato was a kind of father figure for the others. Some of them, though married and with children, sometimes acted childishly and griped about their bad luck in having been drafted, while back in their village single men without family responsibilities had been let off for being related to a local boss or someone with influence. Rato, with his down-to-earth wisdom, so shrewd, clever, and tactful, cheered them up. To avoid conflicts and jealousy, I never showed my admiration and preference for him in front of the others. But they knew I respected him and so they found it natural that I should have picked him to be my orderly. They saw Rato as the bridge between the command and the troops, and they knew they could count on him as a mediator. And without their realizing it, I yielded to his requests and petitions, without ever going against regulations.

Our people have the bad habit of relying on someone to pull strings for them. Since they are certain they will never get what they want by legal means, they resort to someone with influence. They do this all the time, even when they do not need to. This is simply because they do not believe in justice, laws, or regulations. They think such things are for the rich and powerful. The poor depend on favors to survive. Someone once wrote that in Portugal pulling strings is a public institution. And in the Army, more than anywhere else, those words hold true.

A soldier would get a tear in his pants and, instead of handing in a requisition slip for a new pair at the uniform section, he would ask Rato to put in a word with me, so I would then put in a word with whomever was in charge of the uniform section. At first I resisted this approach, but since I could not change it, and to avoid being considered inflexible, I started playing along in that comedy.

Rato's true name, as I said before, is Joaquim, Joaquim Domingues, that is, but he preferred to go by Rato. Privates were usually called by the name of the village they came from. Rato was the only exception. Officers and sergeants were entitled to be called by their last name. But we all knew every one of them had been given a nickname. After the war, at my insistence, Rato finally told me my nickname: the Wretch. That's what the men in my platoon called me behind my back: the Wretch. That was not too bad a nickname, considering the Company Sergeant Major was known as Shitface, and the Captain as Hotpiss.

I once asked Rato where his nickname came from. When he was a kid, he said, he was so small and agile that he could get through any wall, fence, or hedge to steal fruit, just like a rat, and so the kids called him Rato. The nickname stuck, and he did not mind it.

Memory, when prodded, can be like an overflowing river. The muddy water spreads unevenly over fields and woods, and it may or may not go as far as the houses. Memory floods these folios in hasty scrawls and it takes me a while to realize how far the flow of words has reached.

Let us go back to the point where my father and I got off the buggy and climbed the stairway. My mother was waiting at the door. I embraced her and we went in to have lunch. That would be our last meal together. I had to go back to Braga by the end of the afternoon. We sat at table practically in silence. After lunch my father opened a bottle of port that must have been more than fifty years old and proposed a toast, "To your return, alive and in good health, as soon as possible," he exclaimed, lifting his glass.

We clinked our three glasses together in unison.

Then I went to my room and filled a suitcase with clothing, mostly socks and underwear, and a few books. I recall having picked out a pocket edition of *The Lusiads*[16] and a couple of books of poems. It was a way of remembering Coimbra.

I considered changing my uniform to show up at Libaninhas's more comfortably dressed. I looked at myself in the mirror: the cap on my head, the uniform made of coarse, blue-gray fabric, the black boots that Rato had spit-polished to a high gloss, the wrap puttees, and the leather belt with the empty holster – regulations forbade carrying the pistol on leave. I decided to go as I was. After all, I was a soldier, and maybe she would like to see me dressed like one. They say women are crazy about men in uniform. This would be a good chance to find out. But the real reason to go in uniform was more practical: when I came back, I would not have time to change, which took too long, particularly to wrap the puttees around my legs.

Old Felício, our caretaker, brought me Ruddy, who seemed happy to see me. I patted his neck and mounted. With the horse trotting along I made good time. The surrounding fields were covered with green, yellow, and purple. I felt a sudden urge to run among the flowers and cavort with Libaninha.

I dismounted, tied the horse to a ring on the wall, pulled the doorbell wire, and waited for someone to answer. A maid I did not know appeared at the top of the stairway, went back inside and after a while asked me to come up. I was greeted by Dona Eleutéria, Libaninhas's mother, who was surprised to see me in uniform.

"The maid said a policeman was here to see Libânia, and I was so startled I almost pricked my finger. But it was you after all, Master Luís," she said in her Brazilian accent, more affected than sweet.

She looked me over from head to toe and said, "The uniform becomes you, Master Luís. You look more like a man."

"You're too kind, Ma'am," I said.

Libaninha came to the living room a little later. She had surely been making herself attractive for the policeman, and impressed me as being dressed more for a ball than for saying goodbye to her fiancée on the verge of going to war. As I kissed the hand she offered me, I told her she was very elegant and it would be a charming memory to take to France with me. The mother probably did not like my flattering remark and cut us off, asking her if she was not going to offer me something to drink – a glass of wine, or some liqueur, or a cup of tea. Libaninha was confused and I said I did not want anything, thank you very much.

"You look very smart in uniform, Luís," she said. I sat down in my usual chair, she in another, while her mother, sitting in the armchair, resumed her embroidering. We were immersed in a bewildered silence. Libaninha looked at me out of the corner of her eye and then stared at her hands, wringing them nervously. Usually, when I came from Coimbra, which did not happen every week, that was how our Sunday afternoon courtship transpired: her mother embroidering, or else a maid keeping watch, and we facing each other, exchanging occasional comments between long silences. Sometimes I felt like taking her to run in the fields. That even happened occasionally, especially when the weather was good and we managed to dodge our chaperone.

"When are you leaving?" she asked.

"In two days."

"Two days? Why didn't you write me?"

"I did. The letter must be on its way. I mailed it yesterday. Actually, we were told about the departure date yesterday. I didn't even expect to be able to come home to say goodbye to my parents and you. But the Colonel finally granted me a leave."

Libaninha stood up and started walking around the living room, repeating, "You're leaving! Oh my God, what'll become of me!"

Her mother stopped embroidering a white rose on the edge of the fabric and exclaimed, "Stop that, young lady, or I can't concentrate. I've already missed a stitch." She turned to me, "But why didn't you warn us earlier, Master Luís? We'd have made arrangements to offer you a better reception. My husband'll be annoyed when he finds out. He'd want to say goodbye to you and give you some advice. After all, God willing, he's going to be your father-in-law. Too bad he's gone to Vila Verde on some wine business and will only be back late tonight."

I felt a bit confused at the two women's reaction. My explanations were not enough and they seemed to be blaming me. I stood up and said, in the most natural tone I could muster, "Well, ladies, if you'll excuse me, I'll be on my way. I still have to make a few stops before leaving. I'm sorry about this situation. Please believe me, I didn't mean to create it. Now if you'll allow me..."

Seeing my reaction, Libaninha burst into tears. I went to the door, took my cap from the hat rack and, as I was putting it on, she came over and held me, saying she loved me and could not stand my absence. Her mother jumped to her feet, dropped her embroidery, and started yelling, "Libânia, behave yourself! Get away from your fiancé at once! A nice young lady doesn't behave like that!"

But Libaninha would not let me go. She embraced me even harder, soaking my face with her tears.

"Libânia!" her mother insisted. "Let go of your fiancé at once, or I'll tell your father and he'll show you a thing or two!"

I pushed her back just a little and kissed her forehead. She kissed me on the mouth, and then her mother hit the ceiling. She yelled at me to get out, screaming hers was a respectable home, and sent Libaninha off to her room. I touched the visor of my cap in a salute – a gentleman to the end – and left. During the ride back it dawned on me that, without meaning it, Libaninha and I had broken off our engagement. And I was not wrong. Of the many letters I sent her from France, one of which asked her to offer Dona Eleutéria my sincere apologies for the incident, there was only one reply. It was brief:

The Honorable Second Lieutenant Luís Vasques:
I write to request that you cease to write me, since my parents neither appreciate nor allow the continuation of our engagement.
Yours sincerely,
Libânia Maria Perrini Fontoura e Azevedo

I could hear Libaninhas's mother's voice behind her curvy handwriting. Well, I had flaunted convention, or allowed it to be flaunted, and in the Portuguese society of that time – Catholic, moralistic, and hypocritical – that was unforgivable. Losing my fiancée was a very hard blow.

As I rode through the gate of our estate I realized I had not stopped by Rato's. I pulled the reins and turned around. Two kids who were playing by the door of his house got scared when they saw me.

"It's a policeman!" one of them yelled. "Scram!"

They vanished and I just stayed on the horse, waiting to see if one of them was brave enough to come out. Finally, one of them took a peek from behind a corner of the house.

"Come here, my boy," I said. "Go and call Dona Vicência."

"Yessir!"

He ran inside and in a little while Rato's wife appeared. She was a portly woman and, judging by her belly, long gone with child. When she saw a man in uniform she was scared, fearing bad news. I greeted her, "Good afternoon, Dona Vicência."

She shielded her eyes from the sun with her hand and, recognizing me, said, "But it's Master Luís!"

"Your husband asked me to call on you."

"Something wrong?"

"No, everything's all right. No need to worry."

"Do come in, Master Luís. You know, this is just a poor family's home, please forgive the mess. But I'm sure there's a stool for you to sit a while."

I dismounted, tied the reins to a sturdy grapevine clinging to the wall, took off my cap, and walked in. It was not exactly a house, rather a shack with a tile roof and no ceiling, so the wind came in and quite likely the northerly rain as well. There was only one room, which slept five people and also served as kitchen, living room, dining room, coop for a dozen hens, and den for half a dozen rabbits. The latrine was probably in the backyard, among the vegetables.

A smallish blonde girl was peeling potatoes.

"This is my Evangelina. Come on, girl, say hello to Master Luís!"

"Good afternoon, Master Luís," she said, blushing intensely.

I sat on a small stool by the unlit fireplace and Dona Vicência dropped herself into a chair that had seen better days. The two children, bursting with curiosity, sat down on the dirt floor nearby.

"Delmiro!" she called, "Go get the bottle of brandy that's under the big bed and fetch a clean bowl, so we can offer Master Luís a drink."

I did not have the heart to refuse. The bottle was nearly empty. Still, the boy managed to fill up the bowl and hand it to me very carefully, making sure the brandy would not spill. I took it and started sipping. The brandy tasted good after my disastrous visit to Libaninha and I felt my anger subside.

"That's my man's bottle. I don't drink. It may be bad for the baby," the woman said, patting her belly. "He likes to have a swig at night before falling asleep. Straight from the bottle. He couldn't finish it 'cause they called him to go to barracks."

I felt momentarily queasy when I realized I was drinking brandy with Rato's slobber. I hid my revulsion and drank the bowl dry, reassuring myself that alcohol kills germs. Later on, in the trenches, I would get used to drinking rum with the slobber of a hundred and fifty soldiers.

"And how are things, Dona Vicência?" I asked.

She told me that since Rato had been called up, they'd started having money problems. There just wasn't enough to feed the family. He'd been able to put in a couple of months' work after coming back from Tancos, but now that he'd been recalled she didn't know how she was going to pay rent and feed the children. Until the baby was born she couldn't work like she used to. Farmers didn't like to hire pregnant women. They ate too much and didn't work enough. And she couldn't count much on her relatives, since her brothers and brothers-in-law were just as poor.

"I hope to God my man won't go to war and they'll let him come home."

I felt uncomfortable, just as though I had to tell someone about a relative's death. Finally I told her that, unfortunately, we would leave in two days. Dona Vicência looked at the children, shed a tear, and asked why her husband had not come to say goodbye. I explained that, to prevent desertions, soldiers were not allowed to leave the barracks. If she wished, she could tell him goodbye at the railway station. She said she could not leave the children alone and, in her state, it would be very uncomfortable to go to Braga on those poor roads.

I had to acknowledge she was right. Rato could not demand such a sacrifice from his wife. If I had known, I would have petitioned the Colonel to let Rato come along with me. After all, he was my orderly, and that might be an excuse. But there was nothing I could do now.

I set the empty bowl on the stool and took my wallet from the inside pocket of my tunic. I took out all the money I had and gave it to her. I do not remember how much it was, but it was probably enough for the family to get by without much trouble for two or three months. She tried to refuse it but I lied, saying it was her husband's savings, which he had asked me to keep and give to her in case he went to war. She believed me, or at least seemed to, and almost embraced me. I told her to send their eldest, Delmiro, to the estate the next day, as my father needed someone to take care of our pigeon roost. If he wished, he could stay on as a servant and go to school. Dona Vicência was very happy with the news and saw me to the door.

I untied the reins from the grapevine and mounted Ruddy. It was a thick, old grapevine, through which years and years of sap had run to provide wine for two or three generations. I saluted Dona Vicência and turned the horse toward home. I still heard her say, "May the Lord protect you."

The children ran after the horse a ways but gave up when I put him into a trot since it was getting late.

I said goodbye to my parents for the time being – they promised to be at the railway station to see me off – and went back to Braga. But first I told my father Rato's eldest son was supposed to come by the next day, and asked him to take care of him and give him some work. My father was surprised and I explained that I owed Rato, who was my orderly and would leave for France with me. He smiled.

"Well then, a blood pact! One for all and all for one!"

"Not quite," I said. "The truth is that as long as he is around, I'm sure I won't get a bayonet stuck in my back. He's quick and a good shot."

"Let's hope he's also quick enough to avoid getting shot himself."

It was a very pleasant afternoon. The apple trees were covered with pink blossoms, the potato fields were magnificent, and the trellised vines already showed small grape bunches among the leaves yet to be cleared away. That April was on the dry side, good for the grapes and for the wine. By harvest time there would be only old men, women, and children left. Those who had not been drafted and belonged to the Democratic Party had office jobs and would not soil their hands with manual labor.

That was the last time I would see the village until I came back from the war. Or maybe the last time, if I did not come back. But I was not worried, not at that point, anyway. The colors of the landscape and the smell of the fields made me feel, at least until I reached the barracks, at peace with myself and with the land.

Since I did not get back on time to dine at the mess, I went to eat some liver steaks in a tavern, where I found Captain Rebelo, alias Hotpiss, drinking with the other two second lieutenants from our company, Coutinho and Nogueira, and two others from the second company. They told me the next day we would march in full kit as far as the Sanctuary of Bom Jesus do Monte.[17]

"The men petitioned the Colonel," the Captain said with a mocking smile. "They want to ask Christ to protect them in the war."

"Let's hope no one will run away," said one of the second company officers, lifting a bowl of red wine to his mustache.

Actually, no one deserted. I felt disgusted by the officers' tendency to talk disdainfully about their subordinates. How could they command men they did not trust or treated like idiots? In Flanders, when push came to shove, it was those coarse poor devils, who had been yanked from our country's hills, marshes, and fields, who truly showed valor, devotion, and selflessness. The ones who ran away, who malingered, or got an influential friend to secure them a transfer to the rear, were those who should have set the example.

V

Having been sent home on leave in November, the soldiers started thinking they would no longer have to go to war. It was a big letdown when they got the mobilization order in April. Even so, only three soldiers failed to report to barracks and were considered deserters. They showed up the night before departure and explained they had not received the order. It was never determined whether the post office had failed to deliver it, or if they, having received and ignored it, finally decided to show up, out of fear or shame. But since they got there on time to leave with the battalion, the Colonel decided not to punish them.

In spite of that small incident, our company behaved honorably and exemplarily, irrespective of the opinion most of its members might have held about Portugal's participation in the war.

Twenty years later I can see that if I had been in their shoes, I would have run away. But since I was an officer, I had to set an example. What prevented me from deserting was that I knew I would have had nowhere to hide. For a private, it would be relatively easy to cross the border and find work in Spain. An officer would stick out too much, and besides, he would not subject himself to working in the fields like an ordinary day worker.

Once in France, I asked Rato, "Why didn't you run away?"

"Where to, sir?"

"To Spain."

"To Spain? Among those yacking bums? No way. Besides, if you want me to tell you the truth, sir, we was all excited about going to war, to see a bit of the world and get away from that miserable life. I guess that's why there was so few desertions."

On our last day of preparations, when the march to the

sanctuary of Bom Jesus do Monte was to take place, junior officers were ordered to check every single soldier's uniform and equipment. The Expeditionary Battalion formed up at seven in the morning and we remained on parade until nine, inspecting the contents of the knapsacks and making sure every man had all the items on the list authorized by the General Staff. As it turned out, most men had neither the complete uniform nor the full kit, and so had to be outfitted again. One was missing a pair of boots, another a shirt, still another some pieces of his mess kit or an ammunition pouch. Excuses varied – the missing item had been left at home, or stolen, or simply lost. I found out later that some had sold pieces of their equipment for drinking money. Luckily, none of them was from my platoon. At nine o'clock, after the Major had reported the battalion to the Colonel, we set out for the Sanctuary, all the soldiers with knapsacks on their backs and rifles slung on their shoulders.

We ate lunch at the foot of the stairway, where two kitchen carts issued chow and drink. Two hours were allowed for the more devout soldiers to do the Stations of the Cross and pray for divine protection. Those wishing to go to confession could do so at the church with Father Cruz, the Chaplain who would accompany us to Flanders. Quite a few men, though worn out from the march, did the additional penance of the Stations of the Cross, set up in small niches along the stairway all the way up to the Sanctuary. They were either very pious or, as our Captain said, very much afraid to die. There was much talk about a sergeant who joined the soldiers and, catechism in hand, stopped at each niche to read the appropriate text and lead the prayer reciting the rosary. That sergeant came back from Flanders in one piece. During the April 1918 offensive he was captured by the Germans, who found him in a machine gun nest, out of ammunition and surrounded by the bodies of his crew. When he got back he left the Army and joined a Carmelite convent. He is probably still there.

We got back to barracks shortly after four in the afternoon. It was a lot easier coming down. The men were exhilarated. The weather was good, the march had not been too hard, we had eaten well, and the devout ones had been able to perform their devotions. Both coming and going, we were cheered by the people we ran into along the way.

The night before departure, practically nobody slept. The men were restless. The march had not calmed them down. Some said that, as long as we had to go, we might as well go right away. They would wrap up the war in a jiffy and come back home with a medal on their chests. Even without having seen any Boche, some already hated them.

"I'm gonna learn them fuckers a lesson!" Private Tibães kept saying to his comrades.

"Atten-shun!" Corporal Fontes yelled.

They all stood at attention as I walked in.

"Relax, men," I ordered. "So, what's going on here? Nobody feels like sleeping?"

"This is the last night we'll spend on our land, sir," Private Frossos said, sitting down on one of the bunks and starting to roll a cigarette.

"The last night will be on the train."

"Oh, that one don't count."

"How come?"

"'Cause, sir, it just ain't on our land no more."

A few nodded in agreement. Frossos, having asked permission to speak, explained that our land ended as we crossed the Ave River, or stretching things a bit, when we crossed the Douro River. I disagreed, saying that continental Portugal went as far as Algarve.

"Sure, we all know that, sir," he said. "But, begging your pardon, sir, that's mixing things up. The land we was born in is one thing, and the country's another. We're Minho people. Anything below Minho, or above it, is foreign lands."

Not feeling like arguing about territorial borders, I ordered them to go to bed and try to catch some shut-eye. They might not have another chance to sleep in a bed with sheets anytime soon.

"Ain't no beds in Flanders, sir?" Private Tibães asked.

"Insofar as I know, only at the hospital. And may God protect us from ending up there."

"In that case, where do we sleep?" asked Private Soutelo.

"From what I've been told, we take a nap where and when we get a chance."

They were silent, pondering what I had said. I wished them a good night and, as I walked out, I thought perhaps I had talked too much. What did I know then about Flanders and the war? Only what I read in the papers, duly censored at the source, and what I heard at the officers' mess.

Reveille sounded at seven, and after breakfast every man placed his baggage at the entrance of the barracks, duly tagged with his identification number, the platoon number, the company number, and the battalion number, to be taken by truck to the railway station. At nine the battalion's four companies, each with three platoons and totaling about 960 men, formed up on the square facing the barracks. A little later General Simas Machado reviewed the battalion and greeted each officer individually. I saluted him as prescribed by regulations, he returned my salute and offered me a clammy hand. We exchanged no words, but to me he looked like someone that had been plucked off a desk and decorated with stars in a hurry.

Around ten o'clock we marched in route step to the station to the sound of a military band. Our obsolete rifles had been left at the barracks, since the English had promised to issue us with modern weapons in Flanders.

As we paraded through the streets of Braga our shoulders and caps were showered with flower petals and shredded colored paper thrown from the windows by young women and ladies, as if we were characters in a Corpus Christi procession. Clerks, workers, and a few merchants appeared at the door of the shops to watch the band and the soldiers go by. Passers-by waved their hats. Even though they did not know us, they wished us good luck. A couple of priests out of morning mass blessed us. But our men only had eyes for the young women, who smiled at them. The soldiers looked back, smiled in return and nearly tripped on the comrade in front of them.

It was a sunny day and the flowers in the city gardens filled our eyes and our minds with pleasant memories. We soon reached the station square, overflowing with people. Our families had come to say farewell and it was hard to prevent the soldiers from falling out. The Colonel, who had no experience with crowds, had ordered to have the platoons fall out one by one, to avoid mixing the civilians and the military. But that did not work, and everyone, privates as well as noncoms and officers, broke ranks to exchange final words and embraces with their families. Even the men detailed to guard the train and the baggage walked out of their posts and got together with their folk.

Since it was hard for the families to recognize their young men among so many soldiers dressed exactly alike, we had to look for our loved ones in the crowd. I found my parents easily. My mother stood out in a light blue dress I liked and which she certainly had worn for me. My father stuck out in height among the common folk, with his white, unfashionably long hair flying in the morning breeze. They were in the shade of a blooming horse chestnut. I remember the intense aroma of those flowers as I approached.

"Here we are," I said, "ready for the war."

"You don't look good, son. Did you sleep poorly?" my mother asked, concerned.

"I practically didn't sleep. We spent almost the whole night seeing about last-minute details. I'll have the rest of the day and the whole night to sleep."

"But you don't like to sleep on trains. You always used to complain when you travelled to or from Coimbra."

"That was when I was used to soft beds, Mother. But

since I've joined the Army, I've had plenty of time to get used to sleeping anywhere."

I turned then to my father and said, "Actually, you're the one who doesn't look good, Father."

He looked down at his shoes and said, "Yesterday morning we had a visit from Mr. Arnaldo Fontoura e Azevedo, young Libânia's father. He came over to complain about an affront. He accused you of behaving indecently toward his daughter in Dona Eleutéria's presence, of having besmirched his daughter's honor, and he demands satisfaction. What have you done to the young woman, son?"

"Me? Nothing. I went over to say goodbye and she embraced me, sobbing and kissing me, in front of her mother. Dona Eleutéria didn't like that at all. But what could I have done? Bawl out my fiancée and demand that she behave properly? Even if she were doing something indecent, which wasn't the case, I wouldn't have said anything to her."

"That young woman is really shameless!" my mother cried.

My father laughed. The shadow I had seen in his eyes disappeared.

"And I was thinking," he said, "that you had made her pregnant and were leaving us with a grandchild!"

"Well, you stand warned that if Libaninha has a child while I'm away, I'm not the father."

My mother told us to be quiet. That was no way of talking in front of a lady, especially when there were so many people around.

"A decent woman won't let herself be led into an improper situation," she added.

At that point we heard the bugle sound muster, and my father, drawing the conversation to a close so we could say goodbye, said he had left Mr. Arnaldo Fontoura e Azevedo with the promise of a sound dressing-down for the rascal who had so shamelessly abused his daughter's honor.

60

We all laughed. I embraced my mother, who gave me many more kisses than Libaninha had two days earlier, and I embraced my father. My head reached his neck. He took my cap off, kissed my forehead, and said, "Come back in one piece. You owe me, not one, but a dozen grandchildren."

He took off his signet ring with our family's coat of arms and, grabbing my right hand, put it on my ring finger.

"This is your punishment for misbehaving. Wear it at all times, honor it as your ancestors did, and return it to me without a scratch."

"That's a big responsibility, Father. I don't know if I'm up to it."

"That's what I once said to your grandfather when I left for the Lisbon wars. That ring saved me in a brawl I got into in a fado tavern, when I smashed the teeth of a ruffian who meant to slice my belly open."

"I didn't know you used to get involved in that kind of adventure," I said. "I always thought your time in Lisbon was spent in the company of the nation's aristocracy and important politicians and intellectuals."

"A fado tavern is open to both ministers and ruffians, assuming there's a difference. When you go to Lisbon, if you have a chance, go find one of those taverns. The best ones are in the Alfama district."

"That's enough, Simão!" my mother said. "How can you tell our son to go to a fado tavern?"

My father apologized and winked. My mother then handed me a small package, "This is for you to eat during the trip. If you need anything, let us know. I know Flanders is far away and I can't send you anything that might spoil. But we can always send you a few sausages and a cured cheese."

I put the package under my arm and started wading through the crowd toward the assembly area. The crowd swayed and the soldiers began to fall in. I shoved my way across the square and managed to reach my men. Fortunately, Sergeant

Rosado had already formed up our platoon.

From the crowd came shouts of farewell, applause, and grief, while white handkerchiefs waved. I heard a woman scream, "They're taking my man away and I'll never see him again!" People got less excited when the military band struck up the national anthem, which was listened to at attention. The crowd calmed down. No more cries were heard. The tears on the faces of parents, siblings, children, and wives, were not from happiness or patriotic pride, but rather from fear and despair. My father, far away, his head towering over the crowd, looked straight ahead. He neither smiled nor cried. I glimpsed my mother's handkerchief, wiping, or hiding, her tears.

When the anthem was over, we were ordered to enter the station and get on board. After calling roll on the car assigned to my platoon, I went to the officers' car. The train whistled and departed in a few minutes, filling the station with smoke.

I sat next to Second Lieutenant Nogueira, who commanded the second platoon, and he asked, "Where have you been?"

"Just out there," like everyone else.

"You were one of the few who didn't report to the reviewing stand for the hand-kissing."

"What reviewing stand?"

"Didn't you see a stand next to the station, with the Mayor, General Simas Machado, commander of our division, the Colonel of our regiment, and all those other civilian and military officials that people call stuffed shirts?"

"No, I didn't."

"Well, all those stuffed shirts made a point of shaking hands with every officer in the Expeditionary Corps. You seem to be the only one who missed the honor."

"Did they also give out sweets?" I quipped.

"Sweets and other gifts were given out by other corporations, like the Brotherhood of Our Lord Jesus of the Steps and the Brotherhood of Our Lady of the Tower. Some pious ladies gave the soldiers stainless steel medals of the Sacred Heart of Jesus, ideal for trench use, and holy cards of Our Lady of Candelária. They're both very miraculous and sure to protect you in a tight spot."

He pointed to the medal pinned to the lapel of his tunic and took a crumpled holy card out of his back trouser pocket.

At the station entrance a group of ladies waited with two baskets full of red carnations ready to be inserted in the muzzles of our rifles. They were disappointed to find we were not carrying rifles. Even so they handed out the carnations.

"What about the sweets?" I asked.

"Unfortunately, I didn't get there on time. The soldiers stuffed their pockets with them. There just weren't enough for everyone. As for the saint medals and the holy cards, we'll hear about them. Some soldiers picked up three or four and the latecomers ended up with nothing. You'll see what an active black market there'll be. I'm sure they'll try to push them onto the English when we get to Flanders."

"You may be mistaken about that," I said. "The English, as good Protestants, are iconoclasts."

"Well, they can always sell the saint medals and holy cards to the French."

"If there are any left."

The train ride was slow and uncomfortable. We stopped at a few stations, but since it was a special train, everyone had to stay on board. The families who could not go to Braga showed up at the stations between Braga and Campanhá. The soldiers waved goodbye out of the windows.

Everyone ate what he had brought along or had been given by his family. I unwrapped my provisions and shared them with the officers of our company, Nogueira, Coutinho, and Captain Rebelo. I had codfish cakes, chicken thighs, a sausage, corn bread, and a bottle of white wine. The others shared what they had.

In Campanhá, officers were allowed to get off the train

for ten minutes to drink coffee at the station bar. I paid for mine with a fifty cent coin. My change included a shining four cent piece, surely newly-minted. Back on the train, sitting next to Nogueira, I rolled it through my fingers. It was silvery and the heads side showed the bust of a young woman representing the Republic. The charm and gracefulness of her face was nothing like the other coins of one escudo or fifty cents, where the woman representing the Republic looked too masculine.

Near my window a group of people, probably members of a family, were gathered around an officer. Among them there was a young woman wearing a pink dress and a hat with a green ribbon. She was beautiful. Her face, which I saw in profile, was astonishingly identical to that on the coin. The train whistled, they said goodbye to the officer, and he climbed aboard. The young woman looked at the train windows and our eyes met. She smiled at me, or so I thought. The train left the station and she stayed behind, like a fleeting dream. I put the four cent piece away in the left pocket of my tunic, separated from the other coins, leaned my head on the bench and tried to sleep.

At dawn the train pulled into the Alcântara-Mar station and we started detraining by platoons. The sun had not yet risen and the atmosphere was gloomy. Scattered street lamps lit the way to the anchored ship. Having slept poorly in overcrowded third-class cars, the soldiers looked somber and restless. Most of them had never seen a ship, let alone one of that size.

I recognized General Norton de Matos, the War Minister, standing by the ship, as if making sure his merchandise was delivered. Next to him was an English general and the ship's captain.

When the sun rose the men had already climbed down to the hold to drop their gear and pick out a bunk. Most of them climbed back on deck to see the Tagus and the rows of houses. Other than a Military Police patrol, an occasional sailor, or a family member waving goodbye, the dock was deserted. Leaning on the railing, Nogueira said, "Here we are, going to defend the interests of these ungrateful Lisbon people who forced the Republic upon us, and not one of them has come to applaud us and shoot fireworks."

Nearby, a group of sergeants listened to a captain from another battalion that had come on board with us, "This Tagus River, which saw our glorious caravels depart for India, and watched the Portuguese heroes returning covered with gold and glory, today proudly watches us departing for the exalted mission of defending the Fatherland, which, in a moment of agony, has asked for the blood of our youth!"

"That captain," Nogueira whispered, "is either an ass, or else his father is a deputy for the Democratic Party."

"Or maybe both," I suggested.

A little later I heard someone calling me. It was Rato.

"With your permission, sir?"

"At ease," I commanded when he came near.

"I'd need to have a word with you, sir,"

"Shoot."

"In private, if possible, sir."

I said goodbye to Nogueira and stepped aside with Rato.

"Go ahead."

"It's about the wife. Did you give her my message, sir?"

"Oh yes, I went by your house and talked to her."

"I didn't see nobody at the station."

"You have to understand, Rato, in her state, it would be too hard for her to come and say goodbye to you. Sorry I didn't tell you earlier, it just escaped me. But since you're the interested party, you could have asked me."

"I didn't want to bother you, sir. Besides, I didn't have a chance."

"Never mind. She'll write you."

"She can't write, sir."

Rato looked down at the deck, then at the other bank of the river.

"Don't worry. You'll find a way to exchange news. She and the children were all right."

He was silent.

"Are you all right?"

"Yes, sir. I mean, I feel fine, only my bones are aching after that train trip. We was packed like sardines in that car, we couldn't even stretch our feet. But as for the rest, nothing hurts. It's just something I got here in my chest, seeing the others saying goodbye to their folks when I didn't have nobody. The wife and the children couldn't come, that much I understand. But my brothers, my mother, my in-laws, that's what I can't figure out. After all the favors I've done them. Some of the men was seen off by their neighbors, nearly their whole village, even by the bailiff."

"Those are the world's contradictions," I said. "Never expect applause nor praise, and be content with what life gives you."

I no longer remember if I told him exactly that or if I read it in a poem by Ricardo Reis.[18] If he did not write it, he certainly could have.

"The sea is really big, sir," Rato exclaimed, changing the subject, maybe because he did not understand the quotation.

"This isn't the sea, it's the Tagus River," I explained.

"It's quite wide for a river, sir. The Cávado, which runs by our land, is a lot narrower."

"Here the Tagus is wider because we're close to where it empties into the sea. Have you never seen the sea?"

"Never, sir. It's too far. My father saw it, when he went to Africa to kill blacks."

"Your father was in Africa?"

"Yes, sir. That's where he done his military service. His commander was a certain Mouzinho Something-or-other."

"Mouzinho de Albuquerque."[19]

"That's it. My father used to tell he went by ship. He was at sea many days and nights without seeing land. But there

66

wasn't no submarines then. The only danger was for the ship to be caught in a storm, or to hit a rock. But now they're saying our ship might be sunk by a German submarine. They say it runs underwater like a fish and has got a cannon that can shoot through a ship's hulk and send it down."

"It isn't exactly a cannon, because cannons can't fire underwater. It's a torpedo. It's a risk we might run if we were spotted. But there's no need to worry about that. We're being escorted by three English destroyers. Those anchored over there, see? If a submarine tried to attack us, most likely it would go under."

"But if it's already under, sir..."

"If the destroyers detect a submarine, they'll throw dynamite charges in the water and blow it up. Tell the boys not to worry. This is like an excursion. Damn it, we're going to see France! And at the government's expense!"

"Yes, sir. Well, with your permission, sir, I'll be leaving."

"Wait. I have a question for you. How many medals have you got?"

"Medals, sir?"

"Yes, medals. I mean, those saint medals the ladies were giving out at the station."

"Oh, those. About eight. Since I didn't have nobody to say goodbye to, I took advantage of them. But why do you ask, sir? Ain't you got one? If you wish, I'll give you one of mine for free."

"No, thanks. I already have one," I lied. "You may go now."

"If you need me for anything, just call me, sir."

"I shouldn't be needing you. Besides, privates aren't allowed in the areas reserved for officers. Therefore, you may consider yourself on leave while we're at sea."

"On leave?"

"Yes. You're excused from taking care of my clothes and shining my boots."

"Thank you, sir."

He clicked his heels, saluted, and went to join his comrades. I remained looking at the horizon. It was a grey day, which was not good for the men's spirits. In spite of that, a group of photographers, accompanied by an English general, were walking around the dock, aiming their cameras at the ship and the men, who struck grotesque poses.

Around ten o'clock, the ship weighed anchor and moved away from the dock, only to cast anchor again in the middle of the river. We sat there the whole day, bored with looking at the water and the two banks, where we could hardly distinguish anything. They served us two hot meals and, a little after two in the morning, the ship weighed anchor again, steamed down to the mouth of the river and headed north.

VI

Rato came back to the estate, this time not for a visit, but to work. I asked him how things had gone for him in France. I wondered, because his wife had complained he never sent her any news, nor any money. She had brought up the children alone as best she could, working as a day worker at the nearby estates. When it was time to harvest rye, corn, or grapes, I used to see her working on our lands. When I did, I would then ask my father or Old Felício to double her wages, unbeknownst to the other day workers, to avoid a repeat of that passage in the Gospel – Matthew 20, if I remember well.

When Rato returned home, wearing a suit and tie but penniless, he told his wife he had been robbed. All he had left was a small bag with two shirts, some underwear, his shaving kit, and a comb. In Paris, while waiting for the train, he had to relieve himself, but he couldn't handle his three suitcases filled with his savings, clothes, and gifts. He asked some elderly Frenchmen, who looked like decent folk, to keep an eye on his suitcases. They said, "No problem, go and do what you have to do in peace." He took along his small bag, but when he got back he found neither the elderly Frenchmen nor his other suitcases. Besides his small bag, he had only his train ticket, his passport, some change in his wallet, and his hat. Otherwise he would have had to beg.

I did not believe that story and told him so. He swore to it, but later he was to tell me what had really happened.

After listening to his story, Vicência had received him with open arms. She had forgiven him those years of absence, abandonment and silence, the lack of news and not even a hint that he was all right, and the dire need she suffered to bring up their children.

To help Rato's family's financial situation, I hired him to clear three old wells, clogged with mud, rocks, and weeds, and nearly dry in summer, and to dig a new well near the house for domestic use. Since that job required two helpers to operate the pulley, he brought along Fernando, his middle son. I had his older son, Delmiro, who was already working on the estate, pitch in. Every day in the middle of the afternoon I went by to see how work was progressing and brought them a carafe of white wine with some codfish fritters or codfish cakes. Rato, from the bottom of the well, thanked me profusely, not for himself, since he ate little, but for his sons, who were young and needed sustenance.

He suspended himself on the rope and the two young men used the pulley to hoist him up. He always had a hand-rolled cigarette dangling from his lips, even while doing tasks that required effort, like shoveling mud or dirt into a pail at the bottom of the well. He coughed constantly and I told him he should not smoke while working.

"It's a vice, sir," he replied. "Without a cigarette I can't do nothing. I caught the vice in Flanders. Everybody smoked. Do you remember how we used to get tobacco packs with our daily rations? It would be a waste to throw them out or give them away. And in the trenches it always helped to pass the time and feel warm inside. That's how I started smoking. And now I can't do without it."

"Don't give me that line, Rato," I replied, somewhat annoyed. "I also used to smoke a cigarette every now and then. It was a way to relieve the tension of being in the trench, to feel less lonely, with that little light in front of my nose in those pitch-dark nights. Sometimes it was the only light we had in that hole where we slept, or rather, where we took cover from the shells. But when I got back, I no longer felt any need to even touch a cigarette."

"You was lucky not to catch the vice, sir. That was a very good thing that happened to you..."

A coughing fit prevented him from going on. One of the young men slapped him on the back lightly, trying to relieve him. Rato spat out noisily, red-faced, and then, having calmed down, stuck the butt back in his mouth.

"That was a bronchitis fit, sir. Sorry about that, it's a trench disease, 'cause of that damned dampness."

I felt sorry for him and wondered if it was a good idea to have him working in such a damp and unhealthy place like a well.

"Rato, you should let one of the boys get down the well and clear it, and you could work the pulley."

"That wouldn't do, sir. They don't know the trade. And besides, I ain't got the strength to pull the pulley no more. We'll manage, sir."

Back home, I told Aninhas about my concern for Rato's health. I told her I owed that man my life and that everything I could do for him was a lot less than what he had done for me, without expecting anything in return. She suggested that, if I cared for him so much, I should take him to a doctor. So the next afternoon, when I brought them the wine and fritters, I told him I would be taking him to a doctor to check his lungs. He was surprised and protested, saying he was not sick.

"It's because of that bronchitis," I explained. "I don't like that cough."

He said no, the bronchitis was chronic, or whatever it was called, and there was no cure for it. In France, Constance had made him see a doctor several times, with no results.

"You mean Madame Constance Gavroche. Or were you so intimate with her?"

Rato was silent for a moment, chewing on his cigarette butt, as if regretting having talked too much. But he could not go back.

"Yes, of course. Madame Constance."

"No, Rato, not 'Madame Constance.' You ought to know that's how whores are called in France. Decent ladies are called 'madame' plus their full name, or just their husband's name, for short. She is Madame Constance Gavroche, or just Madame Gavroche."

"Well, I always called her Constance, or Madame Constance, and she never complained. Just imagine if we called my Vicência 'Madame Vicência' or 'Dona Domingues.' Wouldn't that be funny."

"But we should respect the uses and customs of those who aren't like us. In France that's how you address a married lady."

"Then I must have stuck my foot into it many times."

He paused again and added, "Did you know she died, sir?"

"No, I didn't. I'm very sorry to hear that. She was a very good lady."

"She died three days before I came back from France."

"And what happened?"

"Some day I'll tell you, sir. Not today."

"I'll be looking forward for it. But just to make sure you won't die too, tomorrow at nine I want you at the house. I'm going to take you to the doctor. The boys may take the day off or help with something else. There's plenty of work to be done."

He showed up on time. From the top of the stairway, while knotting my tie, I asked if he had had breakfast, which he had. Aninhas brought my jacket, I kissed her and went to get the Ford. Rato helped me open the garage doors, I backed out, he got in and we drove off. The road, once muddy or dusty, depending on the weather, had been paved by the local government, thanks to my father's influence.

Rato sat next to me in silence. He was wearing his suit and tie. I asked how things were coming along with his wife and children.

"Everything's fine, sir. When I was on the train, crossing France and Spain, I wondered if Vicência would forgive me for all them years without no news. I was afraid she might tell me to go back to wherever I'd been until now."

"And what happened?" I asked, pulling over to make way for a hay-loaded ox cart. Hay was mowed early in the morning, before the sun got too hot.

"I got off at the station in Braga and found transportation to come here. I was impressed when, instead of a horse carriage, I got on an *autobus*, or whatever they call it here. I got home by the end of the day. My youngest daughter, Maria de Fátima, was cooking dinner. I walked in and she was scared 'cause she didn't know me. She was born during the war, and when I got back and left again, she was still a baby. She's turned out a pretty gal. She's the only one that ain't gone to work for quality. Vicência's kept her at home to help her and keep her company."

He told me that when the young woman saw a stranger with a few days' stubble walk into the house, she thought he was a robber. She waved a knife at him and started screaming. Rato asked her to calm down, saying he meant no harm. Then, after telling him you shouldn't walk into someone's home without calling or knocking, she asked who he was and what he wanted.

"I'm your father. And you must be Maria de Fátima."

The young woman was so surprised Rato thought she was going to faint and fall down. He helped her to sit, sat down next to her, and they looked at each other for a while. Rato felt his fatherly instinct resurge when he saw his daughter so attractive and grown up. When the young woman recovered from the surprise, she told him her mother had gone to harvest corn for a farmer and should be back soon.

"I asked her about her brothers. She told me that the eldest, Delmiro, was working as a servant on your estate, sir. Fernando was working as a day worker. Evangelina had got married and was living in Matosinhos." [20]

He was silent for a moment and asked if he might smoke. I told him no. He was going to have his lungs examined and it would be better if he did not have any traces of tobacco. He put away his rolling paper resignedly, and I asked, "And when Vicência got home, what happened?"

"She walked in, tired out from work, and saw us sitting by the fireplace."

She recognized him right away but did not seem surprised to see him. She looked at him briefly, went over to the clay water pot in a corner, drank deeply from an aluminum mug, and wiped her mouth on the sleeve of her dirty shirt. Then she went over to the fireplace, grabbed an iron rod and lifted the lid of the cauldron in which the stew was simmering. She asked her daughter if she'd already put in the potatoes.

"Yes, Ma", she answered.

"Then what are you waiting for? Go pick the collard greens for the stew. Then go to the salting trough and fetch a piece of rib roast. Your father's thin and needs sustenance."

After the young woman had left, husband and wife sat face to face, gauging the passage of time. Vicência was thinner. She had a few white strands, her sun-tanned skin was wrinkled, and a few teeth were missing.

"When I met Vicência, sir, she was the prettiest girl in town. She had beautiful brown hair, wavy and long. Her eyes was brown, almost matching her hair. My youngest daughter's got her hair, but I don't know where she got them blue eyes. One of my grandfathers had blue eyes. Maybe that's where she got them."

Vaguely recalling Mendel's laws, I explained that for someone to have blue eyes, there had to be at least two people in the family who also had them, either the parents or the grandparents. And if his daughter had them and her parents didn't, it was because two of her grandparents had had blue eyes. Rato found my explanation complicated and did not care much about it. He just said, "Well, sir, if you say so, it must be so, 'cause you learn them things from your books."

And he went on with his story. The two sons got home a little later and Vicência, helped by her daughter, handed out the bowls of stew. The young men vaguely recognized their father and asked for his blessing. They were of marrying age, but since they were poor, they could not find a bride. They had been called up for military service, but since there was no war they were placed in the reserves.

74

At night a problem came up. There were three beds. The two young men slept in one each, and mother and daughter shared the third. Vicência was not ready to share her bed with her husband. All the more so because he had a lot to explain. The two young men ended up cramped in a bed and Rato slept in the other.

"I hadn't slept with the wife in more than eighteen years, sir. And the truth is, I didn't feel like it. And since I've been back, we've yet to get together. Even though she don't say nothing, and she don't accuse me of nothing, I know she ain't forgiven me for being away all them years without sending no news."

I told him she had good reasons to act that way. After all, he had behaved like a rascal. She had been abandoned by her husband and stuck with four children to bring up. Rato did not contradict me.

We crossed the bridge over the Torto River and he went on, "The next day, Vicência woke up early, sent the boys off to work, and before she left for work she asked me if I had anything that needed washing. I said I didn't. Well, that sure surprised her. Then she asked me about my bags. That's when I told her they was stolen, with all the money I had. She looked at me in that way she has of not letting you know if she's sorry for you or just laughing at you, and she said, 'I don't want no bums here. If you want to eat, you got to work.' I promised her I'd find work. There's got to be someone needing a spring cleared or a well dug. Then she went to work and I hung around the house. I drank a mug of barley tea and ate a piece of bread Maria de Fátima gave me."

His daughter offered to wash the dirty clothes he had on.

"While she washed my clothes and hung them to dry, I went out to the vegetable garden in my long johns and started picking weeds. While I was at it, she got a few pieces of the uniform I'd brought back from Flanders, which the wife kept in the chest with the bed sheets. The pants was yellowed from wearing and washing, but I could still get into them. The shirt was big. I put them on and I've been wearing them for work."

I told him to come by the house and ask my wife to give him some of the clothes I no longer wore. There would surely be some trousers and shirts that he could use, even though I was taller and slightly heavier. Vicência or their daughter could certainly fix them for him.

We arrived in Braga in less than fifteen minutes. The day before I had made an appointment by phone with a lung specialist I knew. I parked and took Rato to the doctor's office. I went in with him to follow the examination and hear the diagnosis. It really was chronic bronchitis. To alleviate his coughing the doctor prescribed a syrup and a strict diet, and forbade him from smoking.

"And what about a little drink, at least, Doctor?"

"Only at meals, and only a glass."

"Could it be a bowl? At home we don't use glasses."

"Just a small bowl."

And so they worked out a compromise. I would have to quit bringing him a jar of white wine. Well, I could still bring him some codfish fritters.

I thanked the doctor, who had been my contemporary at Coimbra, paid his secretary, and took Rato to lunch.

"Do you have a favorite restaurant?" I asked.

"A restaurant, sir? That's for the rich. Twenty years ago there used to be a good tavern not far from here. Let's see if it still exists."

I hesitated but did as he wished, and we went looking for the tavern. It was still in the same place, and we sat at one of the few tables not taken by bricklayers and house painters. I told Rato to order and not worry about the bill. A young woman in a worn-out apron came over and he ordered fried codfish with lots of rice with beans, a mug of red wine for him and one of white for me.

I reminded him of the doctor's recommendations and

he said, "Beginning tomorrow, I'll start drinking a small bowl. This is by way of saying goodbye."

The codfish and the rice with beans were delicious. The wine was nothing special, but in a tavern you cannot ask for the sky. I paid a pittance for our lunch. We left quite full and took a walk around town, reminiscing about some old sins that will be mentioned later.

Rato started following his diet in a more or less intermittent manner, just as he took the medicated syrup and refrained from smoking, and soon I began to see him gain color, put on weight, and cough less. When he finished clearing the wells, I showed him the spot near the house, next to a camellia shrub, where I wanted him to dig a new well. He looked at me in a funny way and asked, "And how do you know this is where the well should be dug, sir?"

"I don't understand your question. If this is where I want..."

"But it can't be done just like that, sir. A well can't be dug just anywhere."

"I know. That's why I want it here, where it won't get in the way."

"Sorry to be so stubborn, sir, but suppose we dig here and then don't find no water?"

"So what? We'll dig deeper."

"That's like playing the lottery, sir."

"You mean we risk not finding water. What do you suggest?"

"We got to find the spot where there's a water vein, sir."

"And how can we do that?"

"Just give me a minute, sir."

He went up to an olive tree and cut a small branch with his clasp knife. He removed the leaves and the secondary branches, grasped the ends, and made an arch. Then he walked around aimlessly, searching for a water vein. I felt like laughing but soon became serious when I saw the branch dipping without Rato even moving his hands.

"This is where we got to dig, sir. The water vein runs between seven and eight meters below."

"But that's not the ideal spot. It's more than ten meters away from the house."

"Begging your pardon, sir, it's the branch that tells if the spot's ideal."

"And if you're wrong?"

"Not the branch, sir. Never."

He came back the next day and, helped by his sons, started digging. Three weeks later, having reached eight meters twenty, he found water. He filled a bottle directly from the vein, came up on the pulley operated by the young men, and put it in my hand.

"Go ahead, sir. Please taste it."

I tasted it. It was water, and very good at that. But just to tease him I said, "So the branch was wrong."

"Wrong?" He looked at me in surprise.

"The water appeared at eight meters twenty and not between seven and eight meters."

"That wasn't the branch's mistake, sir. It was mine. I'm out of practice. I ain't done this kind of work in a long time."

"And how do you know the water is at seven, eight, or nine meters deep?"

"I don't. The branch tells me."

"So, if the branch says it..."

"The branch says it, and it's right. But we don't always get it right."

"And how does the branch tell it?"

"By the pressure it makes, sir."

"So you mean you more or less know at how many meters the water is, by the pressure of the branch on your hands. Is that it?"

78

"That's about it."

I asked him to teach me the technique and we went looking for another place on the estate that might be an ideal spot for digging a well. He got two identical olive branches, one for himself and the other for me. I tried to imitate him, holding the green branch in my hands. It took a while for something to happen. Under a vine, his branch started dipping. I came near, but mine would not budge.

"Hold on to it, sir. Hold on to it."

His branch had already bent down but mine remained straight. Obviously, I was not cut out to be a dowser.

VII

When I recall our voyage from Lisbon to the port of Brest in France, I feel like heaving. Those three days have become so engraved in my stomach that my reaction is nearly instinctive. My father had advised me to go by train. It was safer, more comfortable, and less nauseating. Actually, when the idea that officers might leave for France by train circulated in the barracks, I do not know what fit of devotion made me and the other officers in our battalion reject it and decide to travel by ship with the troops instead. I simply thought it would be shameful for officers to enjoy privileged treatment. I even said as much to the other two second lieutenants, Nogueira and Coutinho. The point is that the Army's actual need to send a few officers to Flanders to prepare for the troops' arrival was being used as an excuse to avoid boarding a ship.

So we agreed to accompany our men on the sea voyage. It would be good for morale and discipline if they saw us on board. Nevertheless, we came to regret it, not only because of the poor conditions on the ship, but also because of something that nearly ended in disaster.

First of all none of us, beginning with the Major commanding our battalion, understood why we had to go down to Lisbon to board a ship when we could have done so in Oporto, saving us a day's travel. The northern battalions were forced to undertake a long and uncomfortable train trip to Lisbon, only to travel up north again. If the ship had stopped in Oporto we would have been spared the discomfort and saved time. But that was not what the top brass, our own and the English, had determined.

As the ship steamed beyond the Tagus River into the ocean, the men started getting seasick. The holds were filled with moaning, vomiting, and stench. The day after we left Lisbon, around two in the morning, as we went past Cape Finisterre on the coast of Galicia, a violent storm broke out. It was an April squall, late and untimely. Huge waves washed the deck and the ship shook so badly that the troops, with little or no experience at sea, feared we would sink. The waves burst noisily on the hull like explosions. Someone sounded the alarm and the men started screaming we had been torpedoed by a German submarine. The troops panicked and climbed out of the hold onto the deck, screaming in the dark, *Mother of God, have mercy on us! Oh my mother, I'm drowning!* The English sailors and the ship's captain were flabbergasted at our soldiers' deplorable behavior. Though weakened by seasickness and fear, the other officers and I waded into the crowd of soldiers trying to calm them down. Having recognized me, the soldiers from my platoon grabbed me, weeping and crying they did not want to drown like cats. I told them everything was under control and the ship would not go under. But they would not believe me, and every time a wave blasted the hull they started screaming again.

The English sailors had to chase off a group of soldiers who had climbed onto a lifeboat and were trying to cast off. A few had knelt down on deck and were praying while rain and sea water ran down their faces. With the help of the sergeants and a few soldiers who kept their cool – some of them, fishermen from Apúlia or Esposende, [21] used to sea storms – we managed to herd the men back to the hold.

When we returned to the officers' cabins, we hardly knew how to hide our embarrassment. That incident did little to enhance the image of the Portuguese soldiers before the English, whose rather low opinion of us had led them to question all along the advisability of sending our troops to France. Now the degenerate landlubber descendants of the sailors who had once crossed the unchartered oceans were reduced to a bunch of frightened hens soiling themselves during a storm.

By dawn the storm had let up. We proceeded to call roll by platoons and found out two men were missing from one of our companies. Someone claimed having seen them falling into the sea during the storm. Their company commander tried to find out if they had ever got on board. Their platoon comrades testified they had been seen on the train to Lisbon, and later on the dock, which meant they must have boarded the ship. They were listed as our first two casualties, even before we had reached the battlefield. After the war, the two men reported to their regiment's barracks in Braga and confessed they had deserted. Questioned by the Commandant, they explained that when they had got to Lisbon they had fallen out a little before boarding time with the excuse of taking a leak and had run away. They were the true heroes of that clownish troop.

During the day there was a medical review. The only ailments onboard were seasickness and the resulting digestive troubles. Considering the chow made by the half-breeds the English hired as cooks, it would have been a miracle if we had not had the runs. Obviously, that could have been prevented with a simple seasickness pill. Millions of francs, pounds, and marks were spent in that war to invent and produce the deadliest devices – cannons, mortars, grenades, machine guns, poison gas, tanks, airplanes, submarines and Lord knows what else – but nobody thought of inventing a simple pill to prevent seasickness. That would have avoided a bad beginning. And a bad beginning always leads to a bad end.

During my three days on board there was hardly a moment when I did not feel seasick. I tried to fill my time with reading. Nobody felt like talking. My fellow officers were in the same situation. Only the battalion commanders got together with the English to fraternize. I do not know how they did it, since the wine available on board was dreadful and, besides water, there was nothing else to drink. Perhaps the ship's captain had a bottle of port or rum in his cabin, but if he did, I doubt he would have shared it with a bunch of dumb Portuguese.

Having reread what I have written, I recognize I am being somewhat unfair to our allies. Regardless of what they might have thought of us, undoubtedly not very complimentary, the

English were always flawless and truly reliable in the trenches. Even though you cannot make friends with an Englishman, since they are too cold and self-centered, you can have a good time with them in wholesome camaraderie, particularly if you have a bottle of port handy.

Relationships among the English have always perplexed me. It was understandable that they hated the Germans and Austrians, whose fault it was we were stuck in the muddy trenches, under fire and among rats, fleas, ticks, and lice. But I was shocked at their hostility toward one another. Each battalion was like a tribe that had more or less latent conflicts with the other battalions in the same division, even when these came from the same town or region. It was not surprising that the English should dislike the Scots, the Welsh, the Australians, the French, and the Indians. I often heard them say that the French were a bunch of sissies who stuck their head in the mud like women whenever they heard a shot. That was an exaggeration. Although there was some rivalry among the Portuguese battalions, on account of more or less tolerable regional idiosyncrasies, it never amounted to more than a few jokes exchanged by soldiers from Algarve, Alentejo, Beira, Minho, or Trás-os-Montes, all of them united against those stuck-up, thieving fado lovers from Lisbon. But there was no comparing those rivalries with the prejudices of the English against one another and outsiders.

On the third day the ship reached the bay of Brest. It must have been lunch time, for I remember we were summoned to the mess to eat a funny-tasting soup and bacon. We remained anchored for two days, without permission to land. The troops, recovering from seasickness and from their fear of being torpedoed, were more energetic and had regained their color. They had managed to get to France in one piece. A few more meters and they would be stepping on solid ground. And that is why they could not figure out why they had to wait on board for two days.

The reasons had to do with logistics. Train transportation to Flanders, as well as lodgings, had to be arranged. Also, the French authorities were concerned that our soldiers, being foreigners and speaking no French, might get mixed up with the locals in Brest and cause trouble. And so we spent two days gazing at land from the deck.

Leaning on the railing, I was watching the ships entering and leaving the port. There was not much new going on and I soon got bored. I remembered the four cent coin, pulled it out of the left pocket of my tunic, rolled it through my fingers, feeling the smoothness of its polished sections and the relief of the face of the young woman representing the Republic. It was a nice coin, and a nice young woman. I wondered who might have posed for it.

"With the sea like a lake and the ship so steady, things ain't too bad. We could even get used to it," I heard someone say next to me.

I turned and saw Rato looking toward the port.

"So that is France, sir?"

"Well, Rato, how are things?" I asked, without answering his question and pocketing the coin.

"Not bad, sir. The crossing was a bit rough, but with God's help, here we are to keep going."

"Did you also get seasick?"

"I sure did, sir. From our battalion, the only ones that didn't was the fellows from Apúlia and Esposende. Everybody else got wiped out. I thought I was going to barf up my guts. And the worst, sir, is when you ain't got nothing left to throw up and keep on retching. I guess war, no matter how bad, can't be no worse than that, sir."

"Nothing is worse than war," I said.

"You say so, sir, but you ain't been to war yet."

"But I've read a lot about it. That's something."

"If you say so, sir."

Whenever Rato said that, it was because he did not agree

84

with me, or thought I was talking nonsense. It was his more or less polite way of letting me know.

"Do you need anything, sir? Since we got on board, I ain't got no chance to do my duty as your orderly."

"Don't you worry about that. You'll be doing it when we get to barracks. For the time being just take care of yourself, and that's plenty."

"You know, sir, the men want to go ashore. They're fed up with this ship. They can't stay in the holds 'cause of the stench of barf and, begging your pardon, of piss and shit. Up here on deck it's cold. The food is bad, and the wine, worse."

"You know the orders. When we go ashore we'll go directly to the train. And I don't know when that'll be."

"And what should we do to kill time?"

"Play cards."

"That's what we been doing, sir. But it's already caused trouble. There's a few suckers that play cards and get cleaned out. Some are flat broke."

"Have you been playing?"

"Every now and then, sir. But I ain't won much."

I suspected he was lying. Rato was not the kind to lose at cards. I reminded him that regulations forbade playing for money.

"We play for beans, sir."

I did not ask where they found the beans. It was not worth it.

"Have you got any medals of the Sacred Heart of Jesus left?"

He made a gesture of dismay.

"Unfortunately, sir, I lost them on the night of the storm. They must've fallen out of my pocket. Or maybe they got stolen. But if you insist, sir, I might manage to get you one. How much would you be willing to give for one?"

I laughed at Rato's cleverness and he realized I was not serious.

"You know, sir? Them medals have got to be real miraculous. Someone's got the idea to say they was blessed by the Pope, and now everybody wants one. Our fellows been selling them to the guys in the other battalions. There's even been some fighting, a couple of black eyes and broken teeth."

I gave him a look of displeasure.

"That incident hasn't been reported."

"Oh no, sir. And it won't be. The men don't rat on each other. Anyone that snitches, gets it."

"What do you mean, gets it?" I asked, already guessing the answer.

"He gets punished, sir. They just beat the shit out of him."

I started thinking that while the big brass worried about the dangers awaiting us in the trenches, the soldiers, who should have been acting like a single body and soul, were smashing out each other's teeth. I was astounded by the illiteracy, ignorance, and savagery of our troops. I thought of blaming the Republic and those who ran it, but they were not solely at fault. They were guilty of betraying their own ideals and doing nothing to free the people from ignorance and misery. They had seized power for their own advantage, while keeping the nation mired in its centuries-old apathy and traditionalism. But they could not be blamed for centuries of physical and moral slavery, the glorification of ignorance abetted by the Inquisition.[22] Those who were responsible were long dead and could no longer be held accountable.

The ship finally moored and the troops went ashore. We were met by some paper-pushers from Headquarters, all spit-and-polish in their shining insignias, and eager to order us about. Our soldiers had to leave behind their knapsacks with all their belongings, to be transported by cart later.

With some effort and much shouting of orders, we managed to form up the battalions along the dock. There was another roll call and the equipment was double checked. We marched toward the railway station. We were on French soil. The townspeople gawked at us with curiosity, wondering where such a filthy crowd might have come from. Due to the lack of basic hygiene conditions on board, many men had an overgrown beard and looked more like convicts than soldiers, although the two were not mutually incompatible.

In spite of our appearance, we managed to arouse some sympathy among the people of Brest. Through the clouds of dust we kicked up while marching through the city, we saw white handkerchiefs waving and children and young women smiling. Rato confessed later that he had never seen so many beautiful women. For us Portuguese, used to our women's dark complexion, those slim, fair, blonde young women looked like a host of angels.

A special train was waiting to transport us to the front, more than eight hundred kilometers from Brest. The troops were assigned to the cars. Next to each one we found stacks of rations for three days: cans of corned beef, meat-and-beans soup, preserved fruit, cheese, and crackers. Inside each car there were two wool blankets for each man. Everyone was delighted with such luxury after having crossed Portugal in a tin train and the ocean on a ship that made us throw up our guts. Nogueira commented that those were the last luxuries due to a man about to be hanged.

Once our battalion had boarded, the train started out, went through Brittany toward Rennes, a little to the south, and then swerved northward. We crossed Normandy as far as Rouen, Picardy as far as Amiens, and finally reached Calais in Flanders. I travelled on a first class car with the other officers of my battalion. I sat with my fellow junior officers, Coutinho and Nogueira, and Captain Rebelo. As we watched the landscape flying past, we exchanged impressions about the war and what awaited us at the front. I realize now that we did not have the slightest idea about trench warfare and the dangers ahead of us. We saw the war in terms of big cavalry and infantry charges, with bayonets pointing at the enemy. That was what we had been taught at officer training courses. And that was what we passed on to the troops.

Coutinho, who had left behind a civil service office where he used to spend his days writing deeds, was the one in our group who took war most seriously. "We're here to fight for an ideal," he said. "For civilization against barbarity. France deserves that we shed our blood for her, because France is the cradle of civilization, the assurance of progress and liberty."

"Oh, come off it, Coutinho," said the Captain, puffing on a foul-smelling cigarette, "I can't figure out your admiration for France and the French. They even invaded us in the days of Bonaparte, that chicken thief! And it wasn't easy to kick them out. They liked Lisbon's pleasant weather so much they wanted to stay on."

"But sir, France is the land of culture and the torch of civilization. And we, being civilized Portuguese, are bound by a moral duty to defend her."

"I don't know that France's the land of culture and the torch of civilization. What I do know is that Portugal has entered this war, not because of any love for France, but because our interests in Africa are at stake. Also, because England has an alliance with us, or we with England, which the English actually couldn't care less about, but which we like to remind them of. And because the government wants to consolidate the republican regime and gain support inside the country and abroad. We know what's happened in our country: the republicans have generated a lot of bad blood because nobody wants to lose their hide for someone else's land. And outside the country, it remains to be seen if Portugal will get anything in exchange for our promenade in Flanders. So spare me your idealism."

Coutinho was stuck. Reducing Portugal's participation in the war to a mere play of interests seemed too petty to him. Where was the ideal? Were we going to war without having a cause to illuminate our soul? Although I kept quiet, I thought our participation was completely dispensable, both for us and for the Allies.

The Captain stubbed his cigarette out and went on, "Coutinho, you should ask your soldiers why they are going to fight. Do you know what they'll tell you? Nothing. They'll tell you nothing, because they don't know. They're going to fight because they're made to fight – by the Republic, by the government, and by us, who command them."

We opened one of the soup cans, enough for four, heated it on a kerosene lamp, and served it in our individual mess kits. The Captain, as the senior officer, tasted it and turned up his nose. "The English really can't cook," he said. "They can't even make soup worth eating." We tasted the soup and confirmed its awful taste.

"They must have added pickles and lamb lard," Nogueira commented. But since there was no alternative menu and we were hungry, we proceeded to eat the soup in moderate spoonfuls.

"Better get used to it, because this is what's waiting for us in the months ahead," said the Captain through his fat-smeared mustache.

"The war is about to end," said Coutinho. "I guess we won't have time to get used to this soup."

"You're an optimist, Coutinho. That's good for you and for the troops. Your optimism even makes me think, for just a few seconds, that our humble contribution will be able to decide the course of the war."

After the soup, which we ate with crackers since there was no bread, each of us attacked a can of corned beef, a brownish paste made with beef and other hard-to-identify animals.

"I'm going to miss that good ham from Chaves,"[23] said Nogueira, rolling his tongue over his teeth and palate.

Meanwhile it got dark. We bundled up in the blankets and, in spite of the cold, managed to sleep in relative comfort until daybreak.

Although the trip took a long time, we could not say it was unpleasant. The landscape was different from anything we knew in Portugal and diverted our attention from the noise of the wheels on the tracks. We wrote letters, to be posted only after we got to our destination, read and talked. The train stopped at some stations to refuel.

In the rear cars, the soldiers entertained themselves playing cards – for beans, as Rato said – singing, telling dirty jokes, and getting into fights that usually ended with a black eye and a few broken teeth. Nothing to worry about.

VIII

When they saw me depressed in the weeks following my return from Flanders, my parents suggested I should get in the automobile and take advantage of summer to relax a little. Getting back alive from the inferno of war was a gift from God and it would do me good to enjoy what a shell fragment or a bullet could have deprived me of. I went alone on my first few trips but soon got bored. The problem was I had no one to talk to. The roads were, and still are, in disrepair and, except for the more picturesque places where I occasionally stopped, those trips became tedious. I once had a flat tire and had a lot of trouble changing it. It would have been much easier if someone had been there with me. It was nightfall when a goat herder, on his way to the corral with his two dozen goats, came by and lent me a hand. Otherwise I might still be there. That is why I decided to invite Rato. It was the end of July, and he was going about the village without a regular job, unused to the sun and the heat, not quite believing he was still alive and back in the land where he had been born. To make a little money he helped farmers, husking corn or spraying insecticide. But he did not care about those jobs. I found him in a tavern, called him aside, and asked him if he would like to come along on my trips. He looked at me warily, stroked his mustache, and said, "I'm at your service, sir. But there's a catch."

"What?"

"What shall I tell the wife? That I'm going on vacation with you?"

"You can tell her I'm hiring you as my valet and that I'm going to pay you well for your services."

"Even so... You know, sir, she'll want to know where we're going and what kind of work I'll be doing."

"A valet is like an orderly, he does a little of everything. You can tell her you'll be washing and cleaning the automobile, seeing about my meals, and taking care of my clothes, as you did in the Army."

"But that was in the Army, sir. Over here that's women's work."

"You sound like you're grasping at straws not to come along. But if you don't want to, I'll understand."

"Why do you want me to come along, sir?"

"Just for the sake of coming along. I don't like to travel alone. Besides, something might happen to me, and I'd like you to be nearby."

He wetted his mustache in his bowl of wine, and smacking his tongue, handed it to me.

"And where will we be going, sir?"

I took a sip and made a face. That tavern's wine managed to be worse than the wine we drank in the trenches.

"Tomorrow morning we'll go to Coimbra," I said, returning the bowl to him. "I'm going to get my papers in order at the university. My father wants me to finish my studies. I have one more year to go."

"If you come by my place as you leave, sir, I'll be waiting for you."

"Make sure to pack what you may need. We'll be away a few days."

And that was how my travels with Rato began.

We arrived in Coimbra by mid-afternoon. The town was practically deserted. Most students had already left. A few were hanging around to try their luck at the final round of exams. Nothing had changed. The war, despite having taken some students, had not changed the habits of that old, gloomy university.

I went with Rato to the Law School Registrar's Office. We leaned on the counter and waited. Five clerks, engrossed in rubber stamping folios they picked up from one pile and stacked onto another, made a point of ignoring us. I cleared my throat to attract their attention. They must have been deaf. The only sound in the room was the cracking of the rubber stamps on the folios, like intermittent sniper fire. Rato, standing by me, whispered, "Wouldn't it be better to call them, sir? Maybe they're absent-minded and ain't noticed we need help."

"Better not," I said. "These fellows are cranky."

"And we're supposed to stand here like dummies waiting for them to notice us?"

"Don't talk so loud! If you annoy them, they'll find a way to send me away and I won't get anything done."

Rato would not accept that and exclaimed loud enough for everyone to hear, "Attention to the Lieutenant!"

One of the clerks, the only one who was not rubber stamping, looked up at us indignantly. The others remained indifferent.

"Now see what you've done!" I growled between my teeth.

"Take it easy, sir. We got to show them desk riders they're here to help us."

We waited for about five minutes, maybe longer, until one of them deigned to help us.

"So, what can I do for you, Doctor?" he asked, approaching the counter in no hurry. In Coimbra, after the freshman year every student was called "Doctor."[24]

I explained what I needed. I wanted to register for the last year and sign up for two exams in September. The man pointed to an official notice tacked on the wall and signed by the Rector. The deadline for registration was July 15. Since it was already past, I would have to file a petition, which would likely be turned down. I explained I had just returned from France, where I was doing my military duty, and was not aware of that regulation.

"I can't be bothered with that," he said. "Regulations are to be obeyed."

I asked for a form, for which I had to pay, and wrote out my petition, underscoring my status as a former serviceman. To justify my absence for over two years, the clerk required a military certificate, to be attached to the petition. I promised to bring it in September, when I came for the exams. Since I wasn't registered, he said, it would be better to talk to the professors. Maybe they'd not mind examining me and entering the grade after I'd registered. One of the professors wasn't in Coimbra. Maybe I'd be able to catch him, the clerk said with a sarcastic smile, sunbathing on the beach in Figueira da Foz.[25] The other should be around. The clerk glanced at the clock and said that the professor should be attending the afternoon mass at the University chapel. If I went there, maybe I'd still catch him at communion.

And so I went, on the double, with Rato trailing behind, to the chapel located next to the Joanina Library.[26] As we arrived the faithful were coming out. I recognized Professor Oliveira Salazar and, out of breath, called him. He stopped and turned his aquiline nose to me.

"What do you want?"

"I'd like to have a word with you, Professor, if possible."

"Certainly," he said courteously, but with no alteration in his austere demeanor. "What is your problem?"

"I have just got back from Flanders and I'd like to take the Political Economy exam in September."

"So, a returning hero!" he exclaimed, ironically. "I assume you were at the front on April 9."

"I was," I said, after a brief hesitation.

When someone asked me about that battle, it was usually to make accusations of cowardice and incompetence against the soldiers who had let the Germans cross the lines they were guarding on that day.

"It was a major battle, from what I've heard," he said, looking down at his shoes. "The responsibility for that disaster does not lie with the men who were there, and who were only trying to do their duty. It lies with whomever sent them there."

He was silent for a few moments and started walking toward the square, hands behind his back. We followed him.

"What did you do in Flanders?" he asked, looking at the clocks on the university tower.

"I was a second lieutenant. I commanded thirty men in the infantry."

"How many died?"

"Four on April 9. This man," I indicated Rato, "is one of the survivors."

The professor looked at Rato and then again down at his black shoes, so highly polished that they shone in the sun. His mind seemed far away. He started walking again and, without turning, asked, "You are Vasques, aren't you?"

"Yes, sir, I am."

"I remember you in class. You always seemed a bright and sensible young man. All of a sudden you stopped coming to class."

"I was drafted and had to drop out."

"I understand. I assume you're here because you intend to finish your course."

"That's right, sir. I'd like to take the exam in September."

"All you have to do is to sign up for it."

"I've tried. Unfortunately, because of regulations, they won't let me sign up until I register again."

"Then why don't you?"

"I thought I'd be able to do just that by coming here. But it's more complicated than that. The registration deadline's past and now it'll depend on a petition to the Rector that I've just filed. But judging from what a clerk at the Registrar's Office told me, I'm afraid it'll be turned down."

The professor took a little black notebook out of the pocket of his black coat and penciled down my name.

"Don't worry. I'll see to it myself."

"I don't know how to thank you, Professor!"

"You have nothing to thank me for. Heroes don't thank poor mortals like me. I'll be looking forward to seeing you at the exam in September. What you have to do now is to grab your course readers and catch up. Maybe there's still time."

We nodded to each other and separated. As I left the square, I looked back. The professor was standing in the middle of the square, looking again at the clocks on the university tower. Nine years after our meeting, he was appointed Minister of Finance.

"So this is Coimbra, sir?" Rato asked, while we drank lemonade at an outdoor cafe on the main square. "I'd always thought it'd be more lively, on account of the students."

"It's quite dead. Without students, Coimbra is worse than Beja."[27]

"I knew a guy from Beja. He was a cyclist in Flanders. Died in the battle."

The battle. We were silent and gazed at the empty square. We had lost hundreds of comrades, killed or imprisoned, and we could not understand which hidden force had prevented us from ending up in one of the vast cemeteries in Flanders or in a prisoner-of-war camp in Germany. And there we were, alive and drinking lemonade, as if the war had been a casual episode in our life, a kind of protracted toothache.

Having finished our lemonade, we went in search of lodgings. We checked into an inexpensive boarding house I knew, and in the evening I took Rato to dinner at Joaquina Cardosa's tavern. She recognized me and was glad to see me.

"You haven't been here for a while, Doctor. Have you graduated?"

"Not yet, Dona Joaquina," I said after we sat down. "But it won't be long."

"Well, it's about time! But, with that professor who flunks almost everyone..."

"Which professor?"

"A certain Salazar."

"Does he really flunk so many students?"

"As of late, it's been a massacre. The students complain a lot about him. It seems he once said in class that they ought be in the war instead of in Coimbra, fooling around and wasting their parents' money."

"Well said!" Rato exclaimed.

"The students didn't like it and some complained to the Rector. But it looks like the Rector and the Professor are friends, so nothing happened. The one who complained was the son of the secretary of a minister who's involved in politics in Lisbon. That's what I heard. It seems Professor Salazar's trying to denounce the deals the republicans cut so their sons wouldn't go to war. A student who used to come here even said the government only sent monarchists to war. It was a way of getting rid of them. If they died, so much the better. They wouldn't be missed here."

"Don't you believe that, Dona Joaquina. In the war there were both monarchists and republicans, and also those who were neither. And they all died alike."

"If you say so, Doctor... So, what will you have for dinner?"

I ordered rice with tomatoes, codfish fritters, and a jug of wine. Dona Joaquina went to the kitchen and I got to thinking about what she had told me about Professor Oliveira Salazar. If it was true, my chances of passing the exam were minimal. I knew nothing about his subject. I had the course readers at home, but I had not looked at them in two years, nor did I feel like doing so.

After the landlady brought us the food on two large plates and told us to enjoy our meal, Rato asked me, "Do you know if Fátima is far from here, sir?"

"Fátima?"

"Where Our Lady appeared."

"From what I've read in some newspaper, it's near Leiria.[28] Why?"

"I wanted to ask you a favor, sir."

"If I can do it... " I said, half guessing his request.

"When we was in the trenches, sir, I promised Our Lady of Fátima a huge candle, my size and weight, if I came back from the war alive."

"Can you tell me where you're going to find a candle weighing sixty plus kilos?"

"In a candle store, sir. When I told Vicência we was coming to Coimbra, she said I've got to keep my promise. She says broken promises bring bad luck. I even think that's why she didn't mind I came along with you."

"And now you have to keep your promise, or she'll nag you when we get back."

"That's about it, sir."

"Well, when she asks you if you've been to Fátima to keep your promise, you can just say yes," I said, probing his faith and cunning.

"Oh no, sir! That wouldn't do. She even gave me the money for the candle."

"Well, you can spend it on something more useful. You can buy her a skirt. You'll see she'll like it better than you keeping your promise."

"With all due respect, sir, I know you're not a religious man, but I think Vicência is right. If I made the promise, I got to keep it."

"But how do you know it was because of Our Lady's intervention that you didn't die in the war?"

"And do you know, sir? If it wasn't a miracle that saved us, can you tell me what done it?"

I did not want to argue about the role of chance in life. Rato was a guileless man. What good would it do to tell him I did not believe in miracles and even less in apparitions?

When it came to matters of faith, I thought everyone ought to believe whatever they felt like. If Rato believed he had been saved by Our Lady of Fátima, and if that made him feel better about himself and others, I would not be the one to destroy his illusion.

"Tomorrow we'll look for a candle store. But you'd better be prepared to carry it. I won't lay a finger on it."

"And that's the way it ought to be, sir. When you're keeping a promise, you're supposed to make the sacrifice. But if I was you, sir, I'd also buy a candle and thank Our Lady."

"I'll think about it."

We finished our rice and fritters, I paid Dona Joaquina and we went to the boarding house. The following day, instead of driving north, we would drive south.

Early the next morning Rato knocked on my bedroom door, eager to go looking for the candle store. After breakfast we loaded our luggage onto the automobile and went hunting for the store. But if there was one, we could not find it. In a town of revolutionaries, republicans, would-be republicans, anarchists, socialists, and communists, it was hard to find a store selling candles and devotional *ex votos* for keeping promises. Even so, Rato would not give up.

"Maybe we'll find one in Leiria."

And in that hope we drove to Leiria. We got there early in the afternoon, having stopped for lunch on the way. I parked at the foot of the hill of the castle. While Rato searched for a candle store, I went up for a walk among the ruins of King Dinis's twelfth century palace. Those high places overlooking the whole region did me a lot of good. I stopped at the colonnaded balcony to admire the landscape below, with the town in the background. I spotted my automobile in the shade of a tilia tree and saw Rato trudging toward it, bent over under the weight of an enormous candle. So he had found the store after all. I saw him set the candle down by the automobile and lean it against the door. He wiped sweat off his forehead with the back of his hand and looked around, trying to find me. I shouted, but he could not hear me because of the distance and the birds on the tilia tree. I walked downhill and joined him.

"I found it, sir!" he exclaimed. "It's three kilos heavier than me. But better heavier than lighter, so the saint won't take offence. The shop owner had dozens of candles. He said he's been selling lots of them on account of Fátima. Sometimes he runs out. He told me the revolutionaries tried to set fire to his shop. If you'd like to go there, there's lots of them to choose from."

"I thank you for your concern, but, kilo for kilo, I've got enough with what I've been eating. Did you ask at the store how we can get to Fátima?"

"The owner said there ain't no way we can get lost. And if we do, we just ask, everyone knows where Fátima is. Fátima is now more famous than Lisbon. There's automobiles and people coming and going all the time."

He set the candle in the back seat and we drove off to the little village where three shepherd children claimed to have seen the Virgin. It was not hard to find the road, choked with people and vehicles, mostly carts and buggies. At that time there were probably no more than five thousand automobiles in all of Portugal, which made it the least mechanized country in Europe. I parked under a holm oak near Cova da Iria[29] and Rato picked up the candle. When I saw him struggling – wax and wicker amounted to some seventy kilos – I offered to help, but he turned me down. At about fifty meters from the place where the Virgin was said to have appeared floating above a small holm oak, he was out of breath and had to rest the candle on the ground. I insisted on helping. Panting, he explained that he had to keep his own promise, or it wouldn't count. I argued the Virgin was unlikely to be angry if I helped him. He hesitated but finally decided that my help, though irregular, would not interfere with Our Lady's acceptance of his gift. We each grabbed an end of the candle and walked the remaining meters. The little holm oak had been chipped down to the bare trunk by pilgrims who believed in the miraculous power of its leaves and branches. A chapel was being built on that spot, but the door and the cornice still had to be put in. We placed the candle near the many others inside. Rato lit the wick and asked me to leave him alone to pray to the Virgin.

I moved away a few steps and looked around. There were hundreds of visitors. They were mostly women, who dragged themselves on their knees through the dust and the rocks covering the muddy ground. To avoid getting hurt, they wrapped their knees in handkerchiefs or cloth bundles. But I saw a woman with unprotected bleeding knees, holding a rosary and flanked by her husband and two small children. I asked the man why, and he told me she had promised that, if he came back from the war, she would walk to Fátima, and once there, crawl the remainder of the way on her knees. I thought Rato's wife's promise had been more reasonable. I asked the man which regiment he had been in and he answered, "The Santarém Regiment." [30] I wished him good luck and moved away.

Cova da Iria was a reddish rocky prairie, where a few scattered oak trees struggled to survive in barren soil. How was it possible, I thought, that the Lady should have appeared in such a place? Two years had passed since the latest apparition, during which the sun had reportedly seemed to dance in the sky, but people's faith had not weakened. On the contrary, it tended to grow stronger, even though the authorities and certain anticlerical organizations systematically discouraged such beliefs. All I knew about that place was what I had read in the papers. And that had not convinced me that what the shepherd children claimed to have seen – a young woman about fifteen years old, about a meter ten centimeters tall, who spoke Portuguese without moving her lips – was in fact Christ's mother, who died old, was of the average height of any Jewish woman of her time, and spoke Aramaic.

Either because it was very dry and hot, or because I was hungry, I felt slightly dizzy and had to sit down on a rock. I had left my jacket in the automobile and had my shirt sleeves rolled up. I felt an itch on my left arm and saw the scar of the bayonet wound I had got from a Boche had turned reddish. At that moment I feared the wound might reopen.

Having finished his prayers, Rato joined me and asked if I was feeling well. I told him the heat had affected me and I needed to drink something. We sat down at a roadside stall and ate some codfish cakes. Rato drank wine, but I chose lemonade. Later we walked around a while. The merchants were not wasting time. We saw a stall selling candles and wax *ex votos* such as legs, hands, arms, necks, stomachs, intestines, and other body parts. A lot more expensive than in Leiria, Rato commented, after asking about the price of a candle weighing at least sixty kilos. The merchant apologized, saying he had to pay for the transportation and for the work of setting up the stall.

Then we drove back to Leiria and I took Rato to see the Monastery of Batalha.[31]

"And they've already built a monastery to celebrate the battle? That was quick!"

"It's not the battle you're thinking of. It's a battle that took place many centuries ago. The battle of Aljubarrota."

"Oh, yes, I've heard about it. Wasn't that when a baker woman killed I don't know how many Spaniards with a baking shovel?"

"The same."

I explained that the Spaniards, who were then called Castilians, had invaded Portugal, and he said, "Like the Boche in France."

"Yes. Only there were no trenches and killing was cleaner then. The Castilians came over and then got kicked out. They didn't hang around to give us a hard time, like the Boche in France."

"The Boche was tough to beat."

"And so were we. Fortunately it's all over."

"Yes. For us and for them as died."

"Let's just hope it won't happen again."

IX

My mother, fretting over my melancholy, thought it would be a good idea for me to go to the beach for some rest and amusement. When I was young we used to spend a few days by the sea in Póvoa de Varzim, where an old classmate of my father's would find us lodgings. But after the man passed away and his family moved to Oporto, we stopped going. Those were joyful times, when I would run along the beach, build sand castles and swim, pretending to hold and protect an imaginary manuscript of *The Lusiads* in one arm, and struggle with the other to overcome the strong waves.[32]

I went along with my mother's suggestion. I bought swimming suits for Rato and myself. With their black and white stripes, they resembled prison uniforms and practically covered the entire body for the sake of decency. One morning we drove off in the Minerva headed towards Póvoa. The cold waters of the Atlantic did me good. After a dive and a few strokes, I lay down in the sand and managed to fall asleep, the sun beating down on me. We got quite a tan. Our dull white skin color from Flanders, where the sun barely shone for the duration of our stay, began to disappear. We felt like new.

When I got back from the war, I could never sleep peacefully in my own bed. I would wake up several times, sweating and terrified, imagining the exploding grenades and shrapnel, and feeling as if I were suffocating from poison gas. I would have to get up and drink water. On the beach, contrary to all logic, the sound of the waves breaking on the sand, which could have recalled the booming guns, actually made me feel as if I were on some enchanted island, convalescing from my battle wounds – Ulysses after the Trojan War. All I needed was my Calliope.

Rato had never swum in the ocean, but as a child he had learned to swim and dive in the Cávado River. At first he was afraid of the waves and hesitated when he saw me dive straight through them before they came crashing on the shore. He recalled his fright on our voyage to Brest and considered the ocean very fickle. I appealed to his pride, reminding him that for a Portuguese man, fear of the ocean betrayed his nation's glorious name. He would rub his mustache thoughtfully, take a few steps forward until the waves splashed around his shins, and stay put. One day, we went in at low tide when the sea was as smooth as a lake. I saw him splash around and swim in the still waters as if he were a child. He stayed in the water all morning long, swimming from the north end, where we had rented our tent, all the way to the south. I had to go call him to come out for lunch. He got out shivering, the skin on his hands and feet shriveled and his lips blue. He changed inside the tent and we went to a nearby restaurant. With the collard greens soup and a bowl of wine, his coloring soon returned to normal.

"You know, sir, the sea ain't that bad after all."

I told him it is only bad if we try to challenge it, and he agreed.

The following days, when we returned to Póvoa, Rato became less and less fearful of the waves and, before long, he was diving through them along with me. He even saved a little boy who had been carried away by a strong one. It was precisely this episode that led me to my Calliope.

Rato heard the boy yelling and saw him struggling in the ocean. Within six or seven strokes he reached him, held him under his arms and dragged him to the beach. The boy, who was about twelve, maybe a little older, had come to the beach with a woman we assumed was his mother, and a young woman I thought I had seen somewhere. The probable mother and the young woman came running from their tent and the little boy, frightened and choking up water, clung to them. A few curious bathers gathered around as some youngsters wriggled between their legs, trying to make their way through. We went back to our own tent to lie in the sun. We were uncomfortable in crowds. Since no one had drowned, the onlookers dispersed, disappointed. A false alarm.

I was lying face down in the sand staring at the scar on my left arm, which had practically disappeared since my trip to Fátima, when I sensed someone casting a shadow over me. I turned over and saw the boy's sister standing there. I looked at her somewhat surprisedly. Her white dress – back then at the northern seaside it was considered immoral for women to wear swimming costumes – was very fitted and she struck me as somewhat thin. Her nose was peeling and her neck and arms were sunburned. She protected her head with a small red cloth hat and her slightly long hair was tied back with a green ribbon.

"Pardon me, but they told me you're the one who saved my brother."

I sat up on the towel and saw her nearly covered knees – dresses were supposed to conceal anything above them – and looked at her, astounded. Could she be the young woman on the four cent coin, or was I hallucinating from the sun? Since she noticed I was perplexed, she added, "Forgive me, I may be addressing the wrong person..."

I finally reacted, still rather taken aback, and explained it had been my friend, not I, who had saved her brother. She turned to Rato who, noticing a female presence, nodded in acknowledgement. The young woman said, "I've come to thank you for what you did for my brother. If you hadn't come to his rescue, there'd certainly have been a disaster."

"Better tell your little brother," Rato said, "not to go into the ocean unless there's someone nearby to watch him. The ocean is dangerous when you try to challenge it."

"Yes, I'll tell him. It was our fault. Once again, I thank you."

"You're welcome," he answered.

"At your service," I added.

"That's very kind of you."

"Very kind of you to come and thank us."

She looked at me curiously, or at least that is how it seemed, smiled and went back to their tent, two rows in front of ours.

"That's a pretty girl," Rato commented, lying back on the towel, his hands behind his head.

"You think so? She seemed too thin to me," I said, trying to hide what I was really feeling and thinking.

"Well, French girls are thin too, but they sure are pretty."

That day we went to have lunch at another restaurant. The one where we had eaten twice before served bad wine, was crowded, and customers had to wait an eternity for a plate of roasted codfish or fried sardines. This new restaurant was more spacious and, from the looks of it, a lot more expensive. As we went inside, at a nearby table we noticed the young boy Rato had saved, his sister, and the woman we took for their mother. The two women greeted us with a nod. We responded with a slight bow and sat down at the only available table, off in a corner. We settled for some sea bass the manager said was just coming off the grill, and ordered a jug of white wine. Soon after, he reappeared carrying a bottle of wine with a good label. He explained it had been sent over by the ladies. I turned toward the table, nodding in thanks. The young woman, holding her fork, smiled at me.

They finished their lunch and stopped by our table on their way out. The lady reiterated her gratitude to Rato for having saved the boy. The young woman smiled at me again, in her long beige pleated dress and matching hat with silk flowers, like they used to wear in those days. I set down my fork, wiped my mouth with my napkin and stood up. Rato imitated me. I greeted the lady and introduced myself and Rato, not as Rato, but by his real name, Joaquim Domingues. They seemed charmed by our manners, or rather with mine, since Rato did not open his mouth, not just because it was full of fish, but also because being around such fine ladies made him reticent to speak without permission. The lady introduced herself and her companion, saying, "I'm Dona Generosa. This is my niece Aninhas, and this is Paulino."

After the introductions the young woman told us they would be holding her birthday party two days later at her aunt's house. It would be an honor if we would attend. And she handed me a card with the address. I thanked her for the invitation and said it would be a pleasure. They took their leave and we stayed, finishing our sea bass.

We went back to our tent on the beach and changed back into our swimming suits. Rato lay down in the shade to take a nap while I went for a stroll. Afternoon naps give me acid indigestion. Although swimming after lunch was normally forbidden, I recall seeing a lot of people in the ocean. I went walking along the beach, the waves lapping around my feet. Every once in a while a bigger one would splash my shins. As I felt the cold water and heard the waves breaking in the background, I was transported back to the trenches at Fauquissart. The sun beat down on my bare head. I rubbed it and thought I had forgotten my helmet in the shelter. One of the most serious mistakes you could make in the trenches, for which you paid dearly, was to forget your helmet. The swimmers' screams as they got drenched by the waves turned into those of the wounded, hit by mortar shelling. I felt my heart racing and the sweat running down my forehead blurred my vision.

"Are you all right?" I heard someone ask.

I let myself drop onto the beach. A wave broke over me and I got wet up to my waist. I rinsed my face with my cupped hands. Then I looked around to see who was talking. The sister of the little boy Rato had saved was bending over me with a look of concern.

"I thought I'd been hit with a shell fragment and had gone to heaven, where an angel welcomed me," I said.

"Unfortunately, as you can see, you're mistaken. This is not heaven, nor am I an angel."

"Excuse me for not getting up, Miss, but right now I just can't. I'm afraid my legs won't support me. And it's all because of the wine you and your aunt so generously sent over for our lunch."

"Well, that's not a problem. I can sit down at your side."

And so she did. The next wave soaked her dress and she did not mind at all, which made me think she was a highly unconventional girl.

"What a big coincidence finding you here!" I exclaimed.

"It's not a coincidence at all."

"No?" I said, surprised.

"I was watching you from a distance and I noticed something was wrong. You were leaning over and swerving as you walked."

"So, as if I were drunk."

"That's not what I thought. I imagined you were somehow indisposed, probably because you'd gone wading after lunch. That's why I came over."

"Today, two lives were saved. My friend saved your brother's and you, Miss, have saved mine."

"Were you really feeling that poorly, Mr. Vasques?"

"I believe I was. The effects of wine are unpredictable."

"You seem far too lucid for it to have been the wine. You wouldn't be hiding anything, would you?"

"Like what, for example?"

"An illness."

"I'm not sick, as far as I know. At least not since my last medical examination."

"So, if it wasn't the wine and you're not sick, what happened to you? Don't tell me you were hunting seashells and rocks and got dizzy all of a sudden."

"Well, that was exactly the explanation I was going to give you. What a shame you came up with it first."

We both laughed and then laughed even more when we were nearly drenched in a foamy wave breaking over us. The tide was starting to come in.

"Will you come along? It's starting to get dangerous out here," I said, standing up and offering her my hand.

She looked at me, entirely soaked, her legs stretched out on the wet sand, and answered, "I'll only go with you if you tell me what's really wrong."

"I'm certain you won't like it."

"How can you know?"

"There are a lot of things I don't know. But this, I do."

"What a mystery! Now I'm even more curious."

I held out my hand again to help her get up. She took it and we both stood up very close to each other. She was wet up to her neck, her damp dress clinging to her body, revealing the fullness of her breasts. She was about up to my shoulders in height.

"You're a tall man, Mr. Vasques," she said smiling.

"You don't need to call me mister."

I put my hand through her arm, on the pretext of steadying myself, in case I got dizzy again, and we walked southward down the beach to an area where the fishing boats lined up on the sand looked like tanks abandoned in no man's land. She kept me talking, wanting to know what had happened to me. I hesitated.

"If it's too upsetting, I understand. Mourning is hard, especially for someone close to you."

I really was going to have to tell her about the war. Otherwise, she would spend the rest of the afternoon dreaming up a story about me as a premature widower.

"My mourning is for a woman named Flanders."

"Flanders? That's an odd name for a woman."

Suddenly she stopped, pulling her arm away and

exclaiming, "What a fool I am! You're a Great War veteran."

"I told you, you weren't going to like it."

"Please forgive me for all the silly things I've said. I know very well what the war meant for those who went, and for those who never returned. And, unfortunately, there were a lot of them. A cousin of mine was killed on April 9, 1918. It was a terrible shock for the family."

We continued our walk. She did not put her arm through mine again, but walked alongside me, very serious, listening to what I had to say and questioning me now and again. I summarized my life in the trenches, and how lucky I was not to have been killed, in part because of Rato's intervention when he fired at the German who was about to slash me for the second time with his bayonet.

"Mr. Domingues is always in the right place at the right time," she commented.

"Yes, as I've told him time and again, he's my guardian angel."

"He saved my brother. So, he's my guardian angel too."

I stood there looking at her for a long time. I cannot remember if her expression was serious, amused, or ironic. Then I took her hands and kissed them. I recall her smile, like the sun, ocean, waves, lightness, and life.

We went back to the tents at sunset. Before saying goodbye, she reminded me of her birthday party two days from then.

"But if you want to come by tomorrow, I'll be around. Now you know where our tent is," she added.

I told her we probably would not be coming to the beach the following day, but that we would definitely be at the party.

"I'll be really upset if you two don't come," she said.

I went to our tent to find Rato, lying down on the towel, drying off. When he saw me, he got up and wanted to know why it had taken me so long. He had been worried that something might have happened to me without him there to protect me. I told him that Póvoa beach was not exactly the trenches with the Boche waiting to ambush, and that I did not need any protecting to take a stroll.

"Sir, the ocean is as tricky as the Boche."

He might have been right.

On the way home, along the dusty dirt roads between the towns of Barcelos and Braga, Rato, who had already forgotten his comparison between the ocean and the Germans, was now worried about the upcoming birthday party.

"Sir, I guess I'd better not come along."

"And why not? After all, you're the one the ladies are indebted to, not me. I'm the party crasher."

"I ain't got nothing fit to wear. My clothes are in a sorry state."

"Don't you worry about that. I'll lend you one of my suits. We've got to figure out what we're going to give the birthday girl."

"Do you have any ideas, sir?"

"Tomorrow we'll spend the day in Braga. Maybe we'll find something pretty and original."

"And if we don't, how about flowers?"

"You can make a bouquet from the flowers in the garden. Get Maria to help you. I've got to take something better."

"I don't get it," said Rato, crossing his arms and looking out the window at the corn fields we were driving by.

"What don't you get?"

"Just now, at the beach, you said, sir, that you thought the girl was skinny and a bunch of other stuff. Now you're all worried about what to give her for her birthday, as if it was a matter of life or death."

"I've thought it over, and I don't think this business of being skinny is too important. She's got a pretty smile and her eyes... Anyway, I'm talking too much."

"Sounds like romance to me."

"Don't be foolish. I don't even know who she is."

"Does it matter?"

"As a matter of fact, it doesn't. Personally, I'm more concerned with what she's like, with what she's made of. I couldn't care less whether her parents are rich or poor, or where they came from."

"I always thought the gentry worried about that."

"That's true. But not everyone in the gentry has been in the trenches and nearly killed by shrapnel, bullets, or the sharp end of a bayonet. The most important thing in life is to be happy, or at least to try."

X

The train we boarded in Brest stopped at the Laval station for about an hour. It was near daybreak. Members of the English supply service, or maybe hired civilians, were waiting for us with pots of steaming coffee which they served alongside the train. Since no one had orders to get off, every man leaned out the window to get served, tin cup in hand. They also issued each car a few more cans of corned beef and soup, crackers, and bread for the remainder of the trip. It was eight in the morning when the train started moving again. The landscape had changed somewhat. It seemed more populated. In the fields you could see old men, women, and children behind ploughs pulled by large horses. The adult men had either died in the first years of the war or were at the front.

The following morning we began to see the first troop cantonments, hospitals, and food and ammunition depots. These were wood and tin huts and canvas tents that extended for several kilometers. We were coming close to the great furnace. At three in the afternoon the train stopped at the station in Wizernes, a village near the Belgian border. We got off the cars exhausted, and had the battalion form up in marching order. I joined my platoon and the men looked ghastly. Nobody had shaved for over two days. The black stubble sprouting on our faces made us look unkempt and dirty.

With another battalion's marching band and an escort company, we marched fifteen kilometers to our cantonment site, a small village called Wismes, inhabited by old people, spinsters and children. The Headquarters paper-pushers had failed to do their job and, as we marched into the village, confusion reigned and nobody knew exactly where the men should be quartered.

"That's a swell beginning," I commented to the Captain.

"It's the usual Portuguese disorganization," he replied.

"The sharks run away from duty and the small fry have to fend for themselves as best they can. At Headquarters everyone is well lodged. What do they care about the rest!"

It was past midnight when we chanced upon a barn, or rather a hay loft, to shelter our company. I lay down on the hay and finally quit thinking about lodgings. The trip from Braga to Wismes was like Ulysses' return to Ithaca after the Trojan War. The only difference was that Ulysses had left the war behind and we were just arriving.

The next day, our battalion commander found billets for the officers with the help of the village's *maire,* a kind of mayor, while the barns were reassigned among the soldiers of the various companies. I was billeted in a small farm inhabited by an elderly couple, Monsieur and Madame Rolin. At first they were wary. The English, who had been there before us, had not left many pleasant memories. When I talked to them in French they became more responsive. They gave me their only free room, which had belonged to a grandson, missing in action in the battle of the Marne. The young man's parents had emigrated to French Africa on account of the war and were still there. Madame Rolin showed me the family photos. In one of them, colored by hand, was their young *poilu,*[33] smart in his blue uniform, with a rifle slung on his shoulder. Another photo showed his father and mother, dressed in white and wearing pith helmets, against a background where one could see a hamlet.

Rato, back to his role as my orderly, brought in my knapsack and suitcase. The house was small and the owners were people of modest means. Even so, I could not complain. Everything was clean and the kitchen, which had a good wood stove, was warm and relatively comfortable. It was nothing like the hovels where most people in Portugal lived. The blame for that, I thought, lay with the governments and with those of us who could change things but would rather maintain the *status quo,* out of self-interest or opportunism. Nothing had really changed with the switch from the Monarchy to the Republic.

Or maybe there had been a change for the worse: there were now more hungry families, more beggars, more misery, more people leaving the country for Brazil or the United States in search of better living conditions. Hail to the Republic! After all, wasn't the General Staff's scorn for the small fry the same as the scorn of the rich for the poor?

I spent a few evenings sitting by the stove with the elderly Rolin couple. They told me their life was arduous. They were too old to work their land and held on to it at great sacrifice. Before the war, their grandson, now gone, had been their crutch. He would take the horse and spend the whole day in the field, plowing, seeding, and harvesting. Without him, everything was a lot more complicated. Monsieur Rolin would go out with the horse but no longer had enough strength to hold the plow, nor energy to guide the animal. Plowing a field took much longer. Even so, the farm still produced some wheat, oats, beetroots, and potatoes. Enough to eat and sell the scant surplus to the Army.

They confessed they did not like the English. A bunch of heretics who didn't go to the parish church and ridiculed the saints. An English officer had been billeted in their home. He spoke French atrociously and was difficult to communicate with. He would walk in and out without paying any attention to them. On the very first day he pulled down a crucifix hung above his bedstead and stuck it under the bed, next to the chamber pot. That was offensive. The next day Madame Rolin put it back in place, only to find it next to the chamber pot again. Every time this happened she returned it to its place. It went on for about a week until the Englishman gave up.

Our battalion spent the month of May in Wismes. Everywhere the lilacs were in full bloom, and the exuberant spring made us forget the hardships of the trip and the reason why we were there.

A few days after our arrival, every man was issued a Lee-Enfield, the rifle used in the British Army, and the new

English helmet, shaped like a soup bowl and fitted with an anti-fragment rim. The Portuguese Expeditionary Corps had originally purchased seventy thousand helmets of extremely poor quality, and after a few soldiers had died from head wounds, it was necessary to buy another seventy thousand made of stronger steel. Nothing unusual about that deal. Someone had pocketed a few million. The men soon started using the helmet for washing and cooking potatoes. Not surprisingly, in a few days many were wearing soot-smudged helmets.

We put on our new helmets, shouldered our new rifles, and took up our training with arms drill, military gymnastics, and marches. We practiced for four hours in the morning and three in the afternoon. There was some difficulty in finding training grounds, as the village did not have any area large enough, and it was forbidden to use the planting fields. This situation gave rise to a few problems with the villagers. But the real problems had to do with complaints about theft. Chickens, eggs, potatoes, and other produce went missing, as the soldiers became increasingly fed up with corned beef and crackers.

Things calmed down when our battalion commander applied a few exemplary punishments. It also helped when the inhabitants of Wismes realized the Portuguese were religious, attended mass with great devotion, and left generous alms in the collection basket. After five in the afternoon, many soldiers volunteered to help with the field work and were given food supplies that complemented their meals.

We were stationed fifty kilometers from the battle front. On some days, when the wind changed direction, we could hear a distant cannonade rumble. Every now and then an airplane flew overhead. We got used to saying, "If this is war, we're just fine. Let's hope it'll always be like this."

Meanwhile, a number of officers and sergeants were sent to specialists' schools near Enguinegatte, twenty kilometers from Wismes. Without them, instruction became less intensive and discipline deteriorated. I went too, and for three weeks I was trained in machine guns, mortars, hand grenades, bayonet fencing, observation, communications, and trench maintenance. The instructors were Portuguese officers who had been recently trained by the English. We got back to Wismes and shortly afterwards followed with the battalion to Enguinegatte, where we would train our soldiers in those skills. The goal was to learn to kill effectively without getting killed or wounded.

Before leaving Wismes, I said goodbye to the Rolin couple. Madame Rolin gave me homemade cookies, which I shared with Rato. They praised him to the sky. During my absence he had come over every day when off duty to help with the farm work. In spite of speaking different languages, Rato and the Rolin couple managed to communicate with gestures and a few words. I thanked them for their kind hospitality and wished the best for them and their relatives, who some day would come back from Africa. The old lady made a point of kissing me and her husband embraced me. Might God and the saints keep me. They stood at the door, watching me walk away, with Rato walking ahead of me, carrying my gear to the company's assembly area.

If I remember correctly, we arrived in Enguinegatte on June 1st and took over the installations of a Portuguese battalion that had just left for the front. As we entered the cantonment, we marched past General Simas Machado, who watched us with some apprehension. Maybe he was wondering whether that bumpkin troop from Minho would be up to its task. The next day our battalion commander received a note signed by the General, demanding an explanation for the soldiers' lack of discipline during the march.

"This started badly and is getting worse," I commented to my fellow junior officers. "If the General had marched twenty kilometers on foot, instead of being driven around in an automobile, he'd know how hard it is to keep hundreds of men marching in formation."

"He's an idiot, like everyone at the top," Nogueira said.

"You fellows had better shut up," Coutinho whispered. "Somebody could hear and report you."

"Only if it's you," Nogueira replied.

"Me?" Coutinho retorted, offended. "I'm no snitch."

"Sometimes you sound like one."

"Come on, you two, knock it off!" I said.

Days later, our battalion commander was replaced, having been found medically unfit for active duty, probably thanks to some well-placed protector at the War Ministry. Although everyone wanted to pay homage to him when he was about to leave, many considered him stupid and incompetent, and he would not be missed. Before leaving, he issued a special order of the day, in which he praised himself and a few lackeys who had served under him. It was a patriotic speech, in keeping with the Republic's official line – widely aped by the present regime – dotted with clichés about the Fatherland, national heroes, glorious feats, valor, and greatness.

The new battalion commander turned out to be a martinet who tried to justify his appointment by keeping the battalion on a tight leash and extending training hours. The captains of the four companies protested and managed to convince him that such a regime would ruin the men's health, try the officers' patience, and fill up the Brigade Hospital with sick and crippled soldiers. The man finally came to his senses and calmed down in the following weeks.

In Enguinegatte, with Sergeant Rosado's assistance, I trained the thirty men under my command in handling a rifle, throwing hand grenades, bayonet fencing, wearing gas masks, and other similar subjects, not all of them terribly useful. Some soldiers received special training in firing the Lewis light machine gun and mortars. We exercised, practiced firing with live ammunition, learned to build shelters, went out on listening, reconnoitering, and combat patrols, and practiced reading topographic maps – in sum, everything related to trench warfare, which nobody knew anything about. But that situation was not to last.

In their free time after training hours the men washed their clothes, which were always filthy, played cards, and wrote or asked someone to write letters home. Letter writing became a profitable business. In our battalion – and I have no doubt it was the same in the others – over eighty percent of the men were illiterate. Other than the corporals and sergeants, the few soldiers who could read and write were engaged to do that job, at the rate of two packs of Abdulla cigarettes per letter. Father Cruz, our Chaplain, wrote letters only for soldiers who attended religious services regularly.

According to regulations, letters had to be censored by the platoon commanders, just in case they contained some classified information. It was forbidden to mention our positions, weapons, officers' names, troop movements, and a list of other topics which, if taken literally, would make it impossible to write an interesting letter. Reading one, we knew the contents of all the others because, except for a few details about an individual or his family life, all letters said about the same thing and had the same grammar and spelling errors. I recall a letter that went more or less like this:

dear maria today i thought id write you a couple lines so youd know im in good health thankgod but i got to tel you yesterday was one of my buddies birth day and i had a couple drinks and got a beer and wine hang over and i stil have a headache but thats all you can do to pass the time here cause if you dont you endup feelin sad for bein far from my family and so wif a couple of drinks every now and then we manage to put up with it with patience we sang all night but i only though of you today is sunday ill catch some sleep the news i gets from you makes me sad cant you write a letter without its about illnesses my life is sad enuf as it is i cant go nowhere and nobody don know when this war wil end its tuff and we need piece of mind like the lootenant sez we cant think about the boche nor the war dont you worry about me im very careful and theres no hankypanky not without we was to screw each other

or jerk of each other or stick it in a hole in the wal cause the french
women ran away cause of the war and them what stay behind is
old and toothles and so i sez goodbye i wont bore you no more say
hello to whoever asks about me and i hop your well and many kisses
to hour son and my mother and you can be sure everythin is goin
wel for me thats all for today love manuel

Officers' and sergeants' letters were not censored, but had to follow the same norms. When the mail arrived in small towns and villages, the common folk got together on the church square and the local bailiff read aloud letters when requested. He was also supposed to write their replies for free, although the soldiers' families usually rewarded him with a chicken or a basket of eggs. That was the way in our illiterate country, which neither the efforts of a few officials nor the eloquent lip service of all republican governments have managed to change, in spite of having created schools supposedly open to all. But the schools were not for everyone, and people knew that. Only the government seemed oblivious.

As letter writing became more expensive, both on account of the price of paper, envelopes, and stamps, and because of had to pay someone to write, many soldiers bought *cartes-lettres* or postcards depicting Flanders landscapes at the *estaminets*, which were cafés that also sold beer, liquor, and tobacco. Poking his tongue out of his mouth in an effort to concentrate, a soldier would scratch his name, or else ask a more or less literate comrade to do it for him. There were also *cartes-lettres* with pictures of children in ruffled dresses and holding a basket of flowers, *mademoiselles* demurely dressed and posing dreamingly, or others totally or partially undressed, winking naughtily at the reader. There also were pious *cartes-lettres* showing Our Lady of the Trenches, the Christ of Neuve-Chapelle,[34] or the bleeding Sacred Heart of Jesus. There was enough variety for all tastes and all addressees.

I wrote my parents and Libaninha several letters, and had

frequent answers from my parents, but none from my former fiancée. She had probably been forbidden to write me. My father commented on the estate and especially on current events in Portugal. Recurring themes were riots, street fights, and confrontations in Lisbon and Oporto, due to the food shortage, between the people and the forces of order, invariably resulting in dozens dead. In one of his letters he mentioned the euphoria sweeping the country on account of three shepherd children who said they had seen the Virgin floating above a holm oak in Fátima, a little village near Ourém. In the last paragraph of his letters, the handwriting became rounded. It was my mother's personal contribution, repeating recommendations and sending me kisses and regards.

In June our battalion bivouacked for eight days at the Marthes training camp. In addition to the usual drilling, the soldiers were trained in disassembling and reassembling the Lee-Enfield rifle, firing with live ammunition, running an obstacle course, and carrying out simulated trench attacks. The men were divided into small details and assigned to monitors, usually specialist sergeants. Among these a certain Sergeant Cacheira stood out, a thin, small, and tanned fellow, endowed with extraordinary agility, particularly in bayonet fencing. It was said that if the Allies had two hundred like him, the Boche would have run all the way back to Germany a long time ago. Being naturally skeptic, I thought Sergeant Cacheira, who certainly had never set foot in a front line trench, might be an excellent instructor, but no more than a mime.

At Marthes we trained in the morning, and in the afternoon we went on marches in the countryside, following itineraries set on maps. After eight days we went back to our cantonment in Enguinegatte.

Our boots became our worst enemy. Each man had received two pairs, since the boots brought from Portugal were all torn, their soles flapping after over a year's wear. During the waiting period between returning from maneuvers in Tancos and leaving for Brest, the soldiers had worn them in civilian life. The new boots, two or three sizes too big for most Portuguese feet, were also too stiff and heavy, which made walking uncomfortable. During the first marches, most got blistered feet, and at one point over two thirds of my platoon were incapacitated for military training. Rato was disabled after returning from the gas school in Mametz, or Mamey, as he called it. Since the officers' boots remained in good shape – because we never did anything, the soldiers used to say – we fortunately did not suffer from that discomfort.

As soon as the new boots were issued, our company was ordered to report the following day to the gas school located some five kilometers from the cantonment. Carrying full kit and rifles, happily unaware of what lay ahead, we hit the road flanked by fields of wheat and oats waving in the breeze. We were met by a cavalry second lieutenant specializing in gas warfare. He led one platoon at a time into a canvas tent where he taught us about the effects of toxic gases and the procedures to follow in case of an attack with mustard gas or some other gas, and the techniques for wearing the gas mask.

Tibães, one of the cockier soldiers in the platoon, quipped that Private Frossos's farts were probably more toxic than that mustard gas stuff, which, judging by its name, couldn't be all that bad. Everybody laughed, infuriating the cavalry second lieutenant, who bawled them out. They shrugged and piped down. Then he took us to a hut with our masks on. The doors were closed and tear gas was released. He then ordered us to take off our masks. We felt our eyes smarting, our tears started flowing, and everyone ran to the exit, seeking relief in the open air. If tear gas, which was harmless, had that effect, we could well imagine what mustard gas would do to us! Let that be a lesson, and let us remember to put on our masks at the slightest hint of gas. And if we left the gas mask behind, a bad idea, the alternative was to piss on a handkerchief or a piece of shirt fabric, and put it around our mouth and nose.

"What about the eyes, sir? Leave them unprotected?" asked Private Semelhe, who always had questions about everything.

"You can always ask a comrade to piss on you," retorted Tibães. The general laughter annoyed the cavalry second lieutenant and he dismissed us. Class was over.

We hiked five kilometers back to the cantonment in those British boots, and most men got blisters that burst and turned sore. The battalion commander gave us two days to recover. At that point the men hit on a method, supposedly quite popular among the English troops, for softening the boots: urinating in the boots and letting them soak overnight, so the leather would be more pliant the next day. Many tried it and it seemed to work.

Two days later, still not quite recovered, we had to trek back to Mametz for another training session, this time with the hooded mask for asphyxiating gas. The procedures were basically the same. The hood gave us a phantasmagoric appearance. It took us even longer to get back to the cantonment, stopping constantly because the men complained about their feet. The soldiers with the worst injuries just stuffed their boots in their knapsacks, or simply tied them around their necks like a huge necklace, and went barefoot, their feet wrapped up in rags. It was not a very dignified scene. Fortunately it was getting dark and we were spared having our warlike image ruined before civilians or English soldiers, which would have been very damaging for our soldiers' image. The next day over half of our men were out of commission, Rato among them.

"The English and whoever else did business with them should just shove those boots up their asses...," Rato would say, gazing at his feet covered with blisters, some of them burst. "They only give us what ain't no good."

After the battalion commander protested vehemently to Brigade Headquarters, two trucks drove up, loaded with new boots, also English, but much more pliable. Surely the paper pushers at the rear had been saving them for their own use. Our footgear problems coincided with the visit of Minister Afonso Costa, who paraded around the Portuguese sector in an automobile. He was received with military honors at the Portuguese Expeditionary Corps Headquarters. As the Minister reviewed the honor guard, a soldier, at attention and presenting arms, called him a son of a bitch. He pretended not to hear and went through with the review, but later the Republican National Guard,[35] which served as Military Police in Flanders, took the soldier away under arrest. It was found out later that he was court-martialed for treason and insulting a superior, and sentenced to death. The sentence was not to be carried out, however, because the government was deposed by the end of the 1917 and the new president, Sidónio Pais, commuted it.

In Enguinegatte, I was billeted at the home of the Gavroche family. It would be more precise to call it the Gavroche ladies' home, since at that point the family was made up of Madame Constance Gavroche, who owned the house, her elderly mother, and two children, a nine-year-old boy and an eleven-year-old girl. After my eight-day absence at the Marthes training field, the two ladies were happy to see me again. The same thing happened when I had to spend fifteen days at the machine gun school. Madame Gavroche's husband had been listed as missing in action in Verdun. It was not known whether he had died or been taken prisoner by the Germans.

The Gavroches lived in a comfortable, well-appointed house. They were small landowners and had a barn, a work horse, a cow, a few hens, and a dog. An English officer had been billeted there before me, and the complaints I had heard from the Rolin couple in Wismes were repeated. Madame Léonor Pigeard, Madame Constance Gavroche's mother, told me the officer would walk in and out, say *hello* or *good morning,* and nothing else. He could not speak French and made no effort to learn. On his last day, the daughter added, after collecting his belongings with his orderly, he said *goodbye* and not even *thank you,* as if they were obliged to have him in their home, or as if he were doing them a favor.

"Because, *vous comprenez, monsieur,* we did our best to please him and he despised us. *C'est pas juste.*"

The two women kept on complaining. Maybe they were trying to say they expected the Portuguese to be different. To show them we really were a different class of people, when I came home at night I would spend some time sitting with them by the stove. The children went to bed and I stayed with the two women talking about the war. They wanted to know what I thought. If the war was still going to last long. I knew only just as much as they did, but even so I reassured them. Now that the Portuguese had come to the front, the war would be a matter of two or three months, I told them. They were hopeful. They were fed up with the war, which had begun nearly three years ago, and had taken the lives of so many young Frenchmen. All the young women they knew were now widows, some of them even before getting married. There were thousands of young women who had suddenly become lonely.

The conversation would then turn to less gloomy topics. They asked me about Portugal, about what I did, what my parents did, and how come my country, which had no strong reason to enter the war, had decided to send its own *poilus* to fight the invaders. I told them about my interrupted studies, about my parents, our estate, and our house. They asked me about my fiancée, if she wrote me, if she was pretty. I was somewhat reticent about that, but since they insisted, I finally told them about my falling-out with Libaninha shortly before leaving for Flanders. The elderly lady was rather upset and suggested I should make up with *mademoiselle,* for it would be very hard for such a young and handsome soldier to withstand the war without having someone to love and think about during the more difficult moments.

As I said good-night, I thought no advice could be more sensible.

XI

Aninhas's aunt, Dona Generosa, lived on a street where most houses were owned by wealthy people, most of them foreigners. She was a spinster and usually had her niece and nephew visit during the summer. It was mid-afternoon when I parked near her house. Since Rato was five or six centimeters shorter than I, the suit I lent him was too long in the arms and legs, and he had folded the pants under with pins. Even so, he looked the perfect gentleman. We rang the doorbell and were met by a maid wearing a ruffled white apron. Not recognizing us, she went to get Dona Generosa, who came to greet us.

"Come in, come in," she said smiling, "we were beginning to think you weren't coming."

"Please forgive our late arrival," I said. "We came by way of Braga."

"Through Braga? I thought you were staying at Póvoa."

"No, we just come occasionally for the swimming."

"Oh dear! How tedious for you to have made such a long drive for a simple birthday gathering."

"Don't worry, it's a pleasure to be here." I followed her down a hallway, Rato trailing behind with the big bouquet. At the back of the house we came to a little garden where guests were seated on canvas chairs and wooden benches. Underneath a tent there was a table with several hors d'oeuvres, cakes, glasses, and drinks. Our hostess introduced us to Dr. Jaime Gouveia and Dona Leontina, the birthday girl's parents. He was around fifty and worked at the Santo António Hospital in Oporto. Dona Leontina was six or seven years younger. She had kept her figure and it was apparent she had been lovely in her day.

Next she introduced us to a friend of the family, Dr. Juvenal Pereira, a young physician and quite the dandy, fumigating the room with his cigarette; Miss Celeste, one of Aninhas's girlfriends from school; Mr. Valério Morgado and Dona Durvalina, the birthday girl's godparents and the proprietors of an estate in the Douro valley; and Miss Dulcídia, their daughter, an ugly young woman with fat lips. There were also a few children, including Aninhas's brother Paulino, but Dona Generosa wasted no time on them.

"Come along, dear, and accept these nice gentlemen's gifts."

She came over to us, extending her hand to Rato, who gave her the enormous bouquet. Her arms were full and her face was hidden behind the dahlias and zinnias.

"They're very beautiful, thank you so much, Mr. Domingues."

"Nothing is too pretty for you, Miss," Rato replied gallantly, which led me to jab him discreetly with my elbow. She laughed, giving me the opportunity to admire her perfectly straight white teeth, such a rarity among Portuguese girls. In order to greet me, she handed the flowers to her aunt, and gave me her hand, which I took gently.

"Thank you so much for coming."

"I wouldn't have missed it for the world."

"Another present?" She asked when I handed her the colorfully wrapped box with a red bow.

"Yes, another gift. Happy birthday."

"You shouldn't have gone to so much trouble," she said, accepting the present and placing it with the others on a small table in the shade of a flowering white oleander.

We joined the men. Dr. Gouveia was saying that Portugal's involvement in the war had increased the national debt and would probably lead to bankruptcy. The runaway inflation, shortages of essential goods, and the Spanish flu combined with malnutrition had caused the public health system to collapse. High mortality rates and emigration had left many small villages deserted, which meant a decrease in agricultural production and increasing unrest in the cities, seen in the prevalence of outrages, robberies, and pillaging.

Mr. Morgado added, "Inflation is so high that one silver escudo is now worth ten times more than its nominal value."

"What do you mean?" asked Dr. Pereira.

"What I mean is that our escudo is now worthless. If you can buy yourself a bag of peanuts, consider yourself lucky. But if you want to buy anything made of silver of equal weight, you'll need ten times the amount, if not more."

Everyone agreed the situation in the country was deteriorating. Some blamed the republican regime for allowing Portugal to fall into chaos, others blamed the entire situation. The point was, according to Aninhas's godfather, there was trouble everywhere. England, France, Germany, and several other countries across Europe were in no better shape. One simply had to be patient and wait for better times. As if testing my politics, Dr. Gouveia wanted to know what I thought of the Republic. I told him I didn't think anything about the Republic.

"So you have no opinion on something so important, Mr. Luís Vasques?"

Since I took a while to answer, he insisted I was among friends, all good republicans, although not all committed, so I shouldn't shy away from a good debate.

"Just take, for example, Mr. Morgado, my daughter's godfather and my great friend. He was one of thousands gathered at the City Council in Oporto on January 19 this year to support Paiva Couceiro and the Northern Monarchy.[36] The only reason I didn't participate was fear of reprisals at the hospital. Of course, no sooner had the enthusiasm for the Monarchy died down, repressed by the republican stronghold in Lisbon, we all became good republicans. What, after all, is the purpose of a Republic if not to work for the common good, no matter who's in charge, a king or an elected president?"

I gathered courage and told them my father had monarchical leanings, but I had not yet put a lot of thought into the matter, which to a certain extent was the truth. I had never been very political, unlike many of my classmates at Coimbra, future cabinet ministers. There followed some commentary on the general lack of interest in politics among the new generation, resulting from politicians' inability to communicate with young people.

"Politicians these days are pandering to the *sapateiro* movement,"[37] Mr. Morgado said, "as if the entire country were in agreement."

"The *sapateiros* are the most die-hard republicans around, and also the most committed," Dr. Pereira added.

"Not to mention the informers. They overhear something and immediately report it to the police."

"A lot of people have gone to prison on account of those characters."

"Well, do we have any *sapateiros* among us?" asked Dr. Gouveia. Everyone laughed.

At one point in the conversation, Dr. Gouveia wanted to know which one of us had pulled his son from the treacherous waves. I pointed to Rato, sitting upright next to me, his hair slicked back and his mustache curved upward.

"So, what happened? Tell us all about it," Dr. Gouveia insisted.

Rato, in his typical fashion, said that there wasn't much to tell. Nonetheless, given their interest, he more or less summarized the situation in the following terms:

"I was catching waves and heard a boy hollering. About ten meters out, your young man was struggling, trying to stay on top of the water. The ocean was rough, you had to be careful of the undertow. I got to him in about six strokes and dragged him out."

Mr. Morgado wanted to know if Rato was a fisherman.

"No, sir. I learned to swim in the Cávado River when I was a kid. I'm a day worker by trade which, as everyone knows, ain't really no trade at all. But I'm good with water."

"Good with water?" Dr. Gouveia asked, "What do you mean by that?"

"My father, may he rest in peace, he was a dowser and learned me the trade."

"What do you mean, a dowser?" Aninhas's father wanted to know.

"It's a way of walking around a field, looking for water with a rod."

"So you mean you can guess where there's water?" asked a skeptical Dr. Pereira.

"No, I don't guess nothing. Guessing is for witches. Or that's what they say. Where there's water underground, the rod starts to bend towards it."

The two doctors were not terribly convinced. Mr. Morgado, who was familiar with the method and had some faith in it, then asked, "And have you found a lot of water with that rod of yours?"

"Some."

"So, it works then."

"The dowsing rod never fails. If there's water, it says so. If there ain't, it's as quiet as can be. The thing is, a lot of times people want to dig a well where there ain't no water vein. So the rod won't bend. But if you go over water, it bends, unless it's real deep down. But in that case, the rod won't work. You have to use some sort of magnetic gadget I heard about in France."

"And you've been to France?" Dr. Gouveia asked.

"Yes, I have, with the Lieutenant here."

"The Lieutenant? So the two of you are in the military?" Mr. Morgado wanted to know.

Rato looked at me, trying to figure out if he had put his foot in his mouth. I took over, saying, "We were both in Flanders. Mr. Joaquim Domingues was my orderly. We came back in April this year."

Dr. Pereira, dandy that he was, wanted to know if we had liked France, if the food was good, and if the women lived up to their lively reputation. According to their questions and comments, it was quite clear that, as far as they were concerned, the Portuguese expedition in Flanders in the middle of the war amounted to no more than a free trip abroad at public expense. Well, it is impossible to reason with such ill-informed people, with little or no respect for the suffering of men who did their duty. I put an end to the conversation asking if anyone there had ever served in the military. Dr. Gouveia said he had served some time as a medical officer at the Lancers Regiment in Oporto. Dr. Pereira had never been in the military. I asked him why. After all, he was only a little older than I and it seemed strange he had not been recruited, especially since he was a medical doctor.

"I was discharged, diagnosed with a serious heart problem which prevented me from joining in any capacity."

I didn't want to start an argument, nor did I want to be rude. I felt like asking Dr. Pereira what kind of heart condition had kept him from practicing medicine in the military, but allowed him to practice in civilian life. Not only that but, smoking and drinking the way he did the entire time we were there, I could not imagine the particular nature of his serious heart disease.

"Adérito, my nephew, wasn't so lucky, he stayed over there after a bomb blew him to smithereens," Dr. Gouveia added.

"May he rest in peace," Mr. Morgado said, crossing himself.

"But tell me, what did you do, Mr. Vasques, before you were called up?" Dr. Gouveia inquired.

"I was studying Law at Coimbra," I answered. "I had one year to go."

"Law is a good profession. Especially now, with all this talk of politics, lawyers have it made. Their places are guaranteed in Parliament or the Cabinet."

"Ah, so we have here a future Member of Parliament or, who knows, maybe a Cabinet Minister."

"I have no political aspirations," I said. "My goals in life are fairly modest: graduate from college and help out in my father's firm. He's a lawyer too."

"So your father's a lawyer?"

"He has an office in Braga, but he's nearly retired, and spends most of his time at our estate on the outskirts of town, tending the vineyards, orchards, and rose garden."

"I imagine you have a fiancée..." Dr. Gouveia pried.

"Not right now. You must think it's odd for a man my age. The war kept me from such sweet pleasures for two full years. Now that I've got a gray hair or two, I'll have to spend some time looking for a fiancée, if there's still anyone available who'll have me."

"You'll find no lack of interest among the young available women, some of them from good families," Mr. Morgado added, probably thinking of his hideous daughter.

Meanwhile, the conversation turned once again to Portugal's economic crisis, in large part due to the country's involvement in the war, which had ruined the finances of all participating nations. I withdrew from the conversation, observing Aninhas out of the corner of my eye. She was engaged in a lighthearted conversation with other women, about the new fashion in autumn hats. She had a fine profile, like that of the woman on the four cent coin I had so often contemplated and caressed. At one point, our eyes met and we exchanged smiles, maintaining eye contact for a few seconds before turning away. She looked downward and I, back toward Dr. Gouveia, who was holding forth on the high rate of infant mortality due to malnutrition, lack of hygiene, and a scarcity of vaccines.

The conversation was interrupted when the hostess invited everyone to the table for cake. They handed out slices of king cake, tarts, little skewers of ham and cheese, soft drinks, and port wine. On the birthday cake, decorated with garlands and roses, TWENTY was written in chocolate. Aninhas did not blow out candles – they were not customary at the time – but she cut the birthday cake and handed each guest a slice on a little porcelain plate.

Dr. Pereira, the dandy, never left her side, maintaining a constant flow of compliments and whispers. I wondered whether he was courting her. It would have been perfectly natural. He seemed to be a friend of the family and Aninhas was obviously a good catch. Would I be able to oust this potential adversary? Was I brave enough to face yet another war, this time a battle of affections?

Once the cake had been eaten, Aninhas, at her aunt and godmother's insistence, opened the presents in front of everyone. She unwrapped a few books, mainly French novels, beautifully bound with engraved gold titles, a hat and parasol, a pair of gloves, earrings – likely the dandy's gift – two boxes of candy, and a necklace, my present. It was an emerald attached to a braided gold chain. When she opened the box and showed it to the ladies, they were all astonished.

"Is it real?" asked Miss Dulcídia, in a slightly envious tone.

"It can't be!" exclaimed Dona Durvalina, her godmother, "If it is, that necklace would've cost a fortune."

"I wouldn't say a fortune, but it certainly wasn't inexpensive," Dona Generosa added.

Aninhas looked at me disapprovingly and seemed embarrassed when the other ladies suggested she try it on. I remained silent, leaning against a wall with my arms crossed. Rato was sitting on a bench, sipping his drink, as I mused on how I had acquired that necklace.

"Mr. Moniz, I'd like something special, for a gift," I told the jeweler as I entered his store in Braga.

"I presume it's for a lady," he said, his hands spread out on the glass display case housing a collection of gold rings and earrings.

"You presume correctly," I answered.

"And how old might she be?"

"Twenty."

"Aha! So Mr. Vasques, you've finally decided to formalize your engagement to young Miss Libânia! It's about time!"

"No, Mr. Moniz. I guess you haven't heard we broke off our engagement two years ago and she married someone else."

"You don't say! How unfortunate. And here I go, putting my foot in my mouth. Pardon me, Mr. Vasques, for not keeping up and, of course, for being so rude."

He mumbled a few conventional apologies and kept talking, "So, if it's not for young Miss Libânia, pardon me, I mean Senhora Dona Libânia..."

"It's for another young lady. I won't tell you her name for the time being, because at this point, we're just friends."

"Just friends?" He said, somewhat confused.

"We met recently. But she's invited me to her birthday party and I thought you might have something on hand that I could offer her. I mean, something she won't think is too forward on my part, but at the same time, if she's not enraptured then, at least, I want her to be surprised."

"Let me see if I've understood. Mr. Vasques, you'd like to give the young lady a piece of jewelry that won't make her think, if you'll pardon me, that you're asking for a commitment, but something that will make her think that someday you might do so."

"Mr. Moniz, you are a very perceptive man."

"Well then, we understand each other. You've presented me with an unusual situation and I need to think it over. A ring isn't advisable. The young lady would most certainly think that a proposal is forthcoming. Which is not exactly appropriate. Earrings are given when the relationship is somewhat stable, and never prior to its beginning. In your case, in my modest opinion, it would be in poor taste to give her earrings. Not that I couldn't show you some beautiful pairs of the finest quality."

"I have no doubt, Mr. Moniz."

"But it wouldn't be appropriate to give her earrings. Let me see, what else can I show you? We could consider a brooch."

"A brooch?"

"Yes, a brooch. I have several in all shapes and styles, very tasteful."

"I'm not sure about a brooch... Actually, my mother often wears one mid-bust. But, I don't think so. We'd better look at something else."

"Allow me to suggest a wristwatch. It's the very latest thing: women's wristwatches in silver and gold."

"I'm sure she already has one."

"How about a necklace?"

"I like the idea of a necklace. Let me see your selection."

"Very good. Let's have a look at the necklaces."

Mr. Moniz turned around and pulled out a slender drawer from one of the shelves behind him. It had several compartments lined in red velvet where he stored dozens of necklaces.

"This merchandise is of the finest quality. We have simple gold necklaces, diamond necklaces, precious and semi-precious stones, as well as pearls. All you have to do is choose."

I looked at all those necklaces and could not decide whether Aninhas would like any of them. I certainly was not a jewelry connoisseur and I did not want to make a fool of myself.

"If it were up to you, Mr. Moniz, which one would you choose?"

"It's a hard choice, Mr. Vasques, first of all, because they're all beautiful, and second because, in my role as salesman, I might try to sell you the most expensive."

"And which one is the most expensive?"

"This one here, with the emerald."

"Very well, that's the one I want."

"Are you sure?"

"Yes, I am. Unless it's so exorbitant that I'd have to sell my automobile to afford it."

"No, you don't have to go to such an extreme. Besides, I'll sell it to you for a good price."

"I really appreciate it. It's just a shame there's no woman around who can model it for us."

"I can arrange that. Just wait a minute and I'll go call my Eulália. And in the meantime, please be so kind as to keep an eye on the store."

"Of course."

Mr. Moniz went to the back of the store and I heard him call Dona Eulália. A few minutes later he returned with his wife, an elegant woman, with a generous bosom, whom I vaguely recognized.

"Mr. Vasques here would like to buy a necklace for a very special young lady," he explained to his wife, "but he'd like to see how it looks, do you mind, dear?"

"Of course not. Let me try it on."

While Mr. Moniz fastened it around her neck, she looked at me, asking if I wasn't the attorney Dr. Vasques's son.

"Yes, Ma'am, I am."

"Goodness sakes, how you've grown. Why, you look like a grown man."

"Now, Eulália, he doesn't look like a grown man, he *is* a grown man."

"How silly of me! Of course he's a grown man. And how's your dear mother?"

"She's doing very well, thank you."

"Now then, here's the necklace," said Mr. Moniz, distancing himself slightly from Dona Eulália.

It was a lovely necklace, no doubt. It brought out the fairness of her skin and the emerald fit perfectly in her cleavage, like a pointing arrow. Dona Eulália turned slightly side to side and the emerald glistened. Mr. Moniz commented, "If you can extrapolate the model's proportions, it seems to me the necklace makes a perfect gift for a pretty young lady."

"And just what do you mean by the model's proportions?" Dona Eulália asked, somewhat offended.

"Just men's talk."

Mr. Moniz removed the necklace and sent her off. Dona Eulália took her leave, sending her regards to my parents, and went back inside. Then sold it to me for nearly half the price. As I left his store, the necklace carefully wrapped up, it occurred to me he might have given me such a good deal because of the dire economic situation. Or because he owed my father a few favors. He could never have sold that necklace at market price. Or could he? Then I remembered something my father used to say about hard times: when the poor get poorer, the rich get richer and people who work in luxury goods have their hands full. A necklace was certainly a luxury good.

And that is how I brought the necklace to Aninhas. I paid for it with the French francs I had saved from my salary in Flanders. While other officers spent their earnings on trips to Paris or other neighboring cities whenever they could get away, I would stay with my men, or else, if I ever indulged in an outing, I would go to Enguinegatte to visit Madame Constance Gavroche. When the war ended, to my surprise I realized I had hardly spent any of my earnings. It wasn't because I was thrifty or stingy, just oblivious.

With nearly twenty years' hindsight, I wonder about that remarkable decision to buy an expensive piece of jewelry for a woman I hardly knew. If I had told my parents, they would have called me a spendthrift. What if the girl already had a fiancé? And what if I decided I did not really like her after all? One simply does not offer a gift costing several hundred francs in those circumstances. Yet, it was one of the only times in my life I acted impulsively, with no regrets.

When we left the party, Aninhas accompanied us to the door and wanted to return the box with the necklace.

"I can't accept it," she said apologetically. "Just a bouquet would have been enough, like the one your friend brought."

"But don't you like the necklace?" I asked, disappointed by her refusal.

"I do, it's beautiful. But..."

"You've barely tried it on."

Aninhas shook her head, as if that were not what she wanted to hear.

"Mr. Vasques, you don't seem to understand. I wanted to invite you and your friend to my party, but not because I was expecting jewelry or anything like that. A present like this is for a close relative you're very fond of, either that, or someone very dear."

"Miss Aninhas, please accept the gift, and please accept my invitation to go for a stroll along the beach tomorrow. You can bring your little brother along, if you'd like."

"I..."

"If you'll excuse me?"

I took the box from her and removed the necklace. Handing the box to Rato, I went behind her and fastened the necklace around her neck, which was slender and slightly tanned from the beach. The necklace caused a very different impression on her than it had on the jeweler's wife. In order to look like her, Aninhas would have had to gain at least ten kilos. Nonetheless, I was charmed by what I saw and she too seemed pleased with her image in the entryway mirror.

"Tomorrow," I told her, "I'd like to see it on you. Around eleven o'clock, I'll look for you at your usual tent. And if you're not there, I'll search the entire beach to find you."

"And what if I'm not on the beach?" she asked, smiling.

"I'll search the entire town of Póvoa."

"And if I'm not in Póvoa?"

"Then there'll be nothing left for me to do but lament losing the woman of my dreams when she was so close by."

She blushed and I smiled, motioning to Rato, who gave her back the empty box. We both bowed slightly and went out to the automobile. As I drove off, she was still at the door watching us leave, one hand on her emerald and the other waving goodbye.

"She's a pretty girl, sir," Rato said. "I guess you couldn't go wrong asking for her hand."

XII

By late June our battalion commander announced that a few officers would be sent for a six-day training period in the trenches. Captain Rebelo, Second Lieutenant Nogueira and I were chosen from our company. We left early in the morning by truck. After picking up more officers at other cantonments, it dropped us off at the railway station in Aire-sur-la-Lys. Then we took a train, arriving at Brigade Headquarters by mid-afternoon. We turned in our marching orders, signed a pack of forms, received another pack to fill out during our six days in the trenches, and started out on foot toward the front lines. About an hour later, escorted by a guide, we arrived at the command post of the assigned battalion. The effects of the war were already apparent. The command post was in a house torn down by successive bombardments and propped up with sand bags. The major in command received us cordially in a cramped area piled high with weapons, ammunition boxes, ration cans, blankets, telephone wires, paper packs, orderlies, administrative sergeants, and officers. He offered us a drink.

Each of us was assigned to a front line company, but before leaving we ate dinner and were allowed to rest for a few hours in a nearby hut. Contrary to what we had heard from comrades who had already been there, the night was rather quiet. We neither saw nor felt the horrors of the nerve-racking shelling that usually left men wounded, crippled, or dead. Every now and then we heard an isolated shot, the detonation of a Very flare, or machine gun bursts lasting one or two minutes. None of that meant much, or meant simply that neither side had been ordered to attack the opposite trenches that night. Maybe an attack had been ordered in another sector. At least for the time being, we were lucky.

Shortly before dawn, an orderly woke us up and each of us went along with the officers and soldiers of his designated company. I reported to Captain Martins, who commanded my assigned company. He welcomed me to the front and ordered me to join the second platoon, commanded by a second lieutenant named Amorim.

Relief took place very early in the morning, according to regulations, to avoid surprises from the enemy. But since the Boche knew our regulations and our routine, nearly every day mortar shells rained on the communication trenches the men had to go through. Fortunately that morning the shells fell a few meters outside the trenches and nobody was hurt. Being wet behind the ears, I tried to hide my fear. Were it not for the twilight, I would have been embarrassed if the soldiers had seen me shaking and hopelessly trying to pull my helmet all the way down to my neck. I was surprised to find my comrades so relaxed. As they moved forward, loaded like mules with their weapons, ammunition, rations, blankets, and knapsacks, they laughed and told jokes in muffled tones, to prevent the Germans from hearing them and adjusting their sights to hit our path. Since it was strictly forbidden to talk during relief, Portuguese soldiers considered it a point of honor to disobey.

After posting the men who had come with us, Second Lieutenant Amorim guided me to a shelter, pulled a burlap curtain aside, motioned for me to walk in, and left. I found Captain Martins sitting on an empty wooden box, trying to fill out a pile of forms, and another second lieutenant lying in one of the bunks. The Captain lifted his eyes from the papers, yawned, and asked if I had already eaten. I said I had. A candle stump lit the shelter, called a dugout in the English military manuals, and an elephant by the Portuguese soldiers. It was a hole armored with iron and cement, and covered with bags of dirt and mud. It could resist rifle and machine gun bullets and light mortar rounds, but little else. If it were hit by a cannon shell or a heavy mortar round, that would be the end of the elephant and its occupants. Whenever you heard heavy mortar rounds whistling in the distance, you immediately ran out to find another place to die. It was safer outside than inside, in spite of the danger of being hit by shell fragments or buried under half a ton of dirt from a crumbling trench.

The Captain motioned me to a vacant wooden box. As my eyesight adjusted to the light, I noticed two bunks made of wooden slats nailed together, resting on four legs stuck in the dirt floor. A net served as mattress over which you placed a blanket. If you knew a horse handler in the transportation section, you could always get some straw to pad your bunk. But the comfort offered by the straw did not last long. A few days later the net was swarming with fleas. The rats, for lack of better food, ate the straw, leaving only the fleas.

Captain Martins explained that I was supposed to get some front line experience but would not yet have any command responsibility. I should try to see and learn as much as I could for when I came back with my men. As one of the first Portuguese officers to have a front line command, he had faced some initial difficulties learning from the English. In spite of having an interpreter, it had been very hard to figure out the orders and counter-orders, and to supervise all the activities required of trench defenders. Fortunately, those who came later would not have to go through that. He also mentioned I was very lucky to be attached to his company. At precisely that moment, a few hundred meters away, my comrades were being hazed. Even though hazing was formally forbidden, it was prevalent, particularly among soldiers and sergeants. He was against hazing newcomers. It was not only humiliating but also dangerous for front line security. Bullets and the mortar shells flying overhead were the best hazing a beginner could go through.

"You're lucky," the Captain repeated, striking a match to light his pipe. "It's rather quiet this morning."

While he spoke I felt something rubbing my legs.

"Is there a cat here?" I asked.

The two officers laughed.

142

"We've tried bringing cats in here, but they all run away. If they don't, the rats tear them to pieces."

"You mean..."

"Yes, that was surely a rat rubbing your legs. It can't be far. Raise that candle, Silva."

As the other officer lifted the candle, the Captain grabbed a bayonet and started searching the corners of the shelter.

"Here it is! The son-of-a-bitch's licking a can of corned beef someone left open. Silva, light this corner, will you?"

The Captain advanced very carefully, pointing the bayonet, and in a quick move, stuck it into the dirt floor. We heard a squeak as he lifted the bayonet, showing a huge screeching rat impaled.

"What shall we do with this one, Silva?"

"That's a fat one. It'll be great for breakfast."

"All right, hand it over to the cook."

I felt like retching.

"Don't tell me you're going to eat that!"

They burst out laughing and I realized they were pulling my leg.

The Captain put the rat, still squeaking and screeching, down on the dirt floor, held it under the tip of his boot, pulled out the bayonet and, as if he were killing an insect, crushed its head. The squeaking stopped.

"Silva, take this shit outside and throw it into no man's land. Otherwise his hungry relatives will soon be here claiming the corpse for a funeral."

Second Lieutenant Silva picked up the rat by the tail and walked out.

"Rule number one in the dugout," the Captain started, stretching out on the bunk and chewing on his pipe. "Never leave food or leftovers anywhere. When there's food, eat all of it and lick the cans clean. The rats haven't learned to open them, not yet, anyway. Rule number two: Never kill a rat inside the dugout. The blood will attract other rats. Rule number three:

143

Never go to sleep barefoot, and don't keep your hands outside the blanket, or you may wake up missing a finger."

He was exaggerating. In the absence of food or fingers, rats were more likely to go for your nose or an ear. Therefore, whenever I had to spend the night in a dugout, I left some corned beef in the can or a few crackers on the dirt floor. As long as the rats entertained themselves with that, they would not try their luck with some part of my body. I always got along with those animals, the only mammals, together with politicians and weapons manufacturers, who prospered, increased in number, and grew fat during the war.

Having disposed of the rat's body, the Captain invited me to visit the front line. It was a sunny morning and gunfire could be heard far away to the south. The Captain explained that it was a bad sign when the bombardment lasted several hours during the day. Either the Germans were preparing an offensive or the Allies were preparing a counterattack. No matter what, the result was always the same: thousands dead on either side. I asked him if there were plans for us to attack the enemy trenches.

"Not that I know of. I've been told we're here to hold this position. In fact, we have neither enough men, nor equipment, nor the training to attack the Boche position in front of us. To carry out an attack that might do some damage, we'd have to be two hundred thousand instead of fifty thousand. And most likely, we'd advance only a dozen meters, with heavy losses in men and equipment. This war doesn't have a military solution. If the politicians don't settle this by diplomatic means, we're going to spend a few years here exchanging shots and mortar shells."

I was devastated by what I heard. First, that the war would last so long. Second, that the Portuguese Expeditionary Corps was like a lone bean in a soup that could be cooked perfectly well without it. We were there just to hold eleven kilometers on a front that stretched for more than four hundred, from the sea as far as the Swiss border.

We crossed a trench and reached the second line. The Captain went up to a kind of roofless shelter serving as kitchen and chewed out the cook for making too much smoke. If the Germans noticed it, they would plaster the place with mortar shells. We went along another trench, past several sentry posts, and reached the first line, the trench facing the enemy. In between was no man's land, which our men had dubbed Afonso Costa Avenue. I tried to peek over the parapet and the Captain asked if I wanted to get a bullet between the eyes from some Boche sniper. Further down the trench we ran into a soldier standing on a wooden bench, looking through a periscope.

"Any news?" the Captain asked in a muffled voice.

"Nothing, sir," the soldier answered, with a Lisbon accent.

"Do you care to take a look, Vasques? Here you can do it in relative safety."

"Relative safety?"

"When you're in the trench, there's never a lot of safety. But it's safer to look through the periscope than to stick your head out over the parapet."

I stepped onto the bench next to the soldier, who showed me what to do. The periscope was a contraption made with mirrors that let you see what was going on in front of you, without attracting too much attention.

"What you see in the background is the enemy trench," the soldier explained.

"But it's really close!" I exclaimed, surprised.

"In this area, it's between eighty and ninety meters from where we are," the Captain whispered. "If we say something out loud, the Boche'll hear us and greet us with a round of mortar fire. Therefore, on the first line, we either keep quiet, or speak softly. But it's better to keep quiet. The Boche have invented a gadget that can detect a snore at less than a hundred meters, and a fart at less than eighty."

I took another peek through the periscope. No man's land was a greenish wasteland covered by mounds and holes,

145

which later I found out were craters made by mortar shells and grenades. You could tell the Boche trench because it was slightly raised, extending from left to right, and covered with barbed wire.

The Captain showed me a few more posts where, as a rule, there was a man on the bench, looking through a periscope, and another resting below. Every now and then they traded positions.

"Life in a trench boils down to this: watching, being watched, and avoiding danger. As you can see, except for occasional shots and mortar shells, we live a quiet life. On some occasions it even gets boring. But it's time for lunch, let's go eat."

We walked back to the dugout where we met the company's other junior officers. We sat on wooden boxes outside the shelter and the cook served us a meal that I never expected to eat there. Using aluminum plates, we ate a stew of pork and beans, accompanied by wine, plum jam on hardtack, and coffee. After eating I felt drowsy and requested permission to stretch my legs and take a nap. The Captain said no, and ordered Second Lieutenant Amorim to take me to inspect the posts, precisely to prevent the sentries from taking a nap. I thought that was cruel, particularly after eating pork and beans, but kept quiet and followed my comrade.

In some sections of the trench the men were engaged in repair work, an activity the English used to avoid post-prandial drowsiness. They filled bags with dirt, dug up or leveled out trench areas that had been wrecked the night before, replaced broken duckboard planks, and disinfected the latrines, which were a hole in a corner where two or three men could relieve themselves at the same time. Even after disinfection, and with the feces covered up with dirt, the stench remained. Actually, the stench was so generalized that you could say it was the nature of the trenches. During the night some men emptied their bladders anywhere, and the smell of ammonia impregnated nearly every corner.

The last stand-to-arms was at dusk, after dinner. The

men who had kept watch during the day were relieved. The officers' job was to make sure all the soldiers were present, and their weapons duly oiled and loaded. Amorim told me about a soldier who, after sundown, used to jump over the parapet and go for a walk on Afonso Costa Avenue. He always brought back something: a German helmet, a rusty bayonet, a mud-covered watch, unexploded grenades, shell fragments, anything that could be found on a battlefield. What was surprising, Amorim said, was that whenever they had to send a patrol into no man's land or up to the enemy trench, that same soldier would never volunteer and only went if he was forced to go.

"What happened to him?" I asked.

"About two weeks ago, he was asleep in a shelter with two other soldiers, and a shrapnel shell blew up above them. The shelter gave in and they were buried. We rushed and managed to dig two of them out. They'd swallowed some dirt but pulled through. But the soldier who used to walk in no-man's land alone, however, choked to death. Later we learned from his comrades he had been afraid to die in the trenches, which was why he would go into no man's land, where he could breathe freely. The poor devil suffered from claustrophobia."

We went back to the shelter and lay down on a bunk each. I took the Captain's, who used to take the first watch. We would be woken up by him and by another second lieutenant two hours later to go on watch. I was tired out and fell asleep at once, fully dressed and with my boots on. After two hours, Captain Martins shook me, I got up and he took my place. I went out in the dark with Amorim, who guided me through the labyrinth of the trenches. It was a starry night and my eyes soon adjusted to seeing the duckboard planks. The sound of crickets and cicadas came from no man's land. During our tour, we caught a soldier asleep. Amorim kicked him and the poor wretch woke up with a start, grabbed his rifle and pointed it in the dark, demanding the password. Amorim calmed him down, saying that if we had been Germans, he would be dead. The soldier snapped at attention and whispered, "Sir, for Lord's sake, don't report me. I just dozed off. I've already been reported to the Captain twice. The third time, he'll send me on the next patrol to the enemy lines, and I'll get killed for sure."

"If you know that, how come you fell asleep, you fool?"

"I... it was just two minutes, sir."

Amorim reported him, and the sleepyhead was sent on the only patrol that went out while I was in the trench. He came back wounded in a leg. It seems that while crawling in no man's land, he had accidentally stuck his own bayonet into his thigh. It was like scoring an own goal. Except for that incident, those six days in the trenches misled me to think that, if war was like that, nothing serious could happen to me. Trench life was unpleasant, but nothing that a healthy man could not put up with. I felt rather optimistic and did not know what awaited me in the following months. I simply had failed to realize that, if that sector was quiet, it was because Boche and Allies were massacring each other elsewhere. But things could change.

When my training was over, I said goodbye to my hosts and went back to my unit with Captain Rebelo and Second Lieutenant Nogueira. We were filthy and our backs were out from sleeping on boards with only a net for a mattress. The officers who had yet to be on the first line pelted us with questions. The Captain calmed them down, saying it was as easy as pie. When we met the next day, the men in my platoon also wanted to know what it was like. Without going into too many details, I told them it was like keeping watch on a pile of manure nobody wanted to steal. They laughed and seemed less apprehensive. Rato asked me privately if I had seen the Boche. I said I had not, but had smelled them.

"Smelled them? How come?"

"When the wind changes direction, the smell of their shit comes as far as our lines."

"And what is it like, sir?"

"Just like ours. Maybe not so strong, because they don't eat pork and beans, and take better care of their latrines."

XIII

The day after Aninhas's birthday party, Rato and I drove back to Póvoa. It was a rough trip from the estate because the roads were in such bad shape, so I decided to rent a room in Póvoa for a week. My parents had no objection, but were suspicious about my sudden interest in the beach. We got there just before ten o'clock. The manager of a restaurant we knew told me it would be hard to find a room so late in the season. Hotels and boarding houses would certainly be full and private homes would have been booked well in advance. We should have made our plans earlier. I was very disappointed. Nonetheless, he suggested I try the hotels and boarding houses. Maybe we would get lucky; someone might have left early. He gave me the name of several nearby establishments and we went out in search of rooms. There were none to be found.

"Now what should we do? Go home?" I asked Rato.

"It's up to you, sir. As far as I'm concerned, we should stay, even if we have to sleep in the open air. I told my Vicência I'd be at the beach for a week and, if we go back now, she'll make a laughingstock of me and send me out to hoe corn."

"Well, we can't sleep outdoors."

"For anyone who's slept in the freezing cold winter of Flanders, sir, sleeping on the beach in August will be like paradise."

"You know perfectly well we can't sleep on the beach. The north winds here are just as cold and hostile as the winds in Flanders."

"We could always sleep in the automobile."

"That makes more sense. But I don't think Aninhas would like to learn we'd spent the night in the automobile on her account."

"It's a sign of love, sir."

Rato was a such a joker. It was almost time for us to meet

Aninhas and we had not figured out what to do.

"If I could at least come up with the name of a Coimbra classmate living here in Póvoa, maybe he'd be able to get us out of this predicament."

"Can't you think of anyone, sir?"

"Yes, I do recall one fellow, but I have no idea where he lives. What was his name? Brás? Vaz? You see, I can't even remember his name. The war has played havoc with my memory."

"Speaking of the war, sir, I just remembered someone who could get us out of this fix."

"Really? Who?"

"Do you remember Apúlia, sir?"

"Yes, I remember him."

"Well, he was married to a girl from Caxinas, a town just nearby. He used to talk about Póvoa a lot."

"But isn't he from Apúlia?"

"Exactly, but he came here to work with the fishing fleet, married a girl from Caxinas, then went to serve his two years in Flanders."

"Well then, he probably lives around here."

"That's for sure."

"All right, let's find him."

We went back to the automobile and headed for Caxinas, a small fishing village nearby. But along the way, I began to have my doubts.

"We've got a problem, Rato. I don't remember his real name."

"I always heard people call him Apúlia."

"Sure, that's his *nom de guerre*, usually based on where a man's from. But how many fishermen must there be in Caxinas from Apúlia and who served in Flanders? Five? Ten? Fifteen?"

"There could be a lot. But he was the only one I knew in our platoon."

I parked next to some wooden huts, not far from the

ocean, and asked a few kids mending fishing nets if they knew a fisherman from Apúlia who had been in the war. One of them with a runny nose answered in his singsong northern accent that he knew him and would take us to his house. He took off ahead of us and we found ourselves hard-pressed to follow him through the labyrinth of fishing huts.

"That snotty kid is slipperier than a Boche," Rato commented as he huffed and puffed at my side. We thought we had lost him and were completely disoriented, but the kid reappeared, standing near a hut, and waved us over.

Rato said, "He must've gone to tell Apúlia we was coming."

"Let's just hope he won't run away, thinking we're the police."

"After a man's been in Flanders, sir, he don't run away from nothing, not even the Devil himself."

"Well, I'd sure run from the Devil."

"It's right there," the kid said, pointing to what was probably the most miserable of the huts.

A woman with two children stood in the doorway, eyeing us warily.

"I don't think it was such a good idea to come here, sir," Rato whispered.

I took a deep breath and approached her.

"Good afternoon, Ma'am. Is this where Private Apúlia lives?"

"This is Manuel Santos' house. He's from Apúlia, but I don't know if he's the one you want."

"Manuel Santos? Exactly!"

The name had come back to me. I had written and read it hundreds of times, along with the names of the other men in my platoon, on orders, payments, reprimands, messages, passes, permits, reports, censored letters, and everything military bureaucracy came up with to help us to pass the long, boring hours in the trenches. Junior officers, instead of carrying out orders, would fill out papers for senior officers to justify their staying behind the lines.

"Are you the police, sirs?"

"No, Ma'am, we're his comrades."

"*Com* who?"

"We served with him in the war."

"Oh! I see. And what do you want with him?"

"We'd like to see him. Is he around?"

The woman pointed inside the hut.

"Could you call him?"

"You'd best come in, sirs."

We took off our hats and went in. She followed and shut the door behind us. With no windows, it was really dark inside. From over in the corner of that one-room hut, we heard coughing.

"Who's there?" someone asked in a weak voice. "Is that you, Avelina?"

"There's some gentlemen here wants to see you," the woman answered.

"Gentlemen? Who?"

Rato approached him, saying, "It's me, Rato."

"Rato?"

"From the Army."

"Rato? What are you doing here?" the fisherman asked between coughing fits.

"I'm here with the Lieutenant."

"The Lieutenant?"

"Yup. We come to pay you a visit."

My eyes were getting used to the dark and I began to make out my surroundings. Apúlia was lying down on a cot over in the corner, all wrapped up in a dirty blanket, looking like he was going to catch his death of cold. The place smelled like rotten fish, urine, and fever. It was strewn with fishing gear, an old chest with saints' images on top of it, a pile of dirty clothes, kitchen utensils, a few wooden stools, a fireplace with two metal

152

pots and a few sticks of firewood. There was no fire. If that was Apúlia's house, which it apparently was, we had certainly come knocking at the wrong door.

"How are you doing, Apúlia?" I asked him.

"Sir – beg pardon, I can't get up. I've been praying a lot for Our Lady of Guidance to give me strength, but she must think I'm a terrible sinner, so here I am, an invalid."

"What happened?"

"When I came back in April, I was real weak. I'd got pneumonia or something and I was spitting blood. The wife here, she told me to go to the doctor's. But I wanted to go out to sea. It'd been such a long while since I'd set foot on a fishing boat. A man takes to fishing just like hunting. Same vice. Once you're caught, you're done for. Ain't no cure. I asked one of the ship owners for work, and he got me a job on a boat. I was real happy. But so weak, I couldn't row, couldn't pull in the nets. So the skipper let me go. I got worse and went to see the doc. He told me I got TB. Told me to stay in bed, gave me cough syrup. And here I am. Can't do nothing. Just spitting blood."

We didn't know what to say. On the dirt floor next to the bed, there were some rags, stained with dark spots, probably from spitting.

"But how'd you find me?"

"I come with the Lieutenant to spend a few days in Póvoa and, since we knew you lived here in Caxinas, we thought we'd come pass the time."

"Well, I'm grateful. If I was having a better day, I'd take you out and around. We'd make you a big fish stew."

"We'll save it for next time, Apúlia," I said. "We'll come back when you're feeling better, and then we'll gladly join you for fish stew."

"All right then, it's a deal. I'll get you the best fish off the boat. After all, if it wasn't for you, sir, most of our platoon would be buried over in Flanders."

We stayed a little longer, talking about the war. But since

he coughed so much every time he tried to talk, we told him to get well soon and took our leave. When we got outside, I asked his wife about their finances. She told me that ever since he had been bedridden, some three months now, they had been depending on charity from their relatives and neighbors. I asked if he was taking the medicine the doctor had prescribed. She said he had at first, but then it had run out and they couldn't afford to buy more. Besides, she said, he didn't think it was worth going into debt at the pharmacy on account of medicine that wasn't really doing any good. I was very disturbed and I told her she had to give her husband the medicine if she didn't want to be a widow. Also, she'd better call the doctor to check up on him. She said no doctor wanted to visit them, even if they could pay.

With that, I made a decision.

"Rato, give me a hand."

I went back inside the hut, "Apúlia, we're taking you to the hospital."

"The hospital? What the hell for?"

"Put on some pants and a clean shirt."

"I'm staying put."

"It's an order."

"An order? Ain't we out of the Army now?"

"I'm not ordering you as your superior, which I no longer am, but as your friend. Come on, get up."

"If I got to die, I'd rather die at home."

I raised my voice, alarming his wife and children, who were coming back into the hut.

"So, I spent two years trying to save your hide and now I'm going to leave you here, dying like a dog? After all we went through in the war, you want to die here in this hut?"

Between coughing and choking, he said it was his house.

"If you stay here without getting any care, it won't be for long."

154

"Oh, Manuel! Do what the gentleman says," his wife pleaded.

She came over and helped him put on a pair of pants and a checkered shirt. She put on his boots and tied them up. We led him out to the automobile, his arms around our shoulders, and put him in the back seat. As we were doing this, the young boys working on the fishing nets started poking around, trying to figure out what was going on.

I headed back to Póvoa and, getting directions here and there, managed to find the Catholic Hospital. I spoke to the physician on duty, urging him to take good care of Apúlia, who was a war hero and deserved the best. The doctor shrugged his shoulders and took off, saying it was his lunch hour. We left Apúlia in the care of two nurses, in whose hands I pressed a five escudo bill, making it clear that if they took good care of the patient, there would be more to come.

As I left the hospital, somewhat disoriented, I asked Rato what we should do. We had not found lodgings and I was late for my meeting with Aninhas at the beach.

"Right now, sir, we better go eat. We won't find Miss Aninhas at the beach anyway."

"You're right."

We went back to the automobile and parked near our usual restaurant. The manager asked if we had found a place to stay. He could tell by our lack of enthusiasm that we had not. He recommended grilled squid, with potatoes and bell peppers. As he served our wine, I asked him if Dona Generosa had been there with Aninhas and the boy. He said no.

"Maybe they'll be around," I speculated.

"It's not likely," he warned me. "It's past one thirty. But you gentlemen could pay them a call at their house, which is right nearby. I can get one of the boys to show you the way."

"Thank you, but it's not necessary. We know where they live."

"Is that so?"

155

"Yes, we were there yesterday."

"Oh! Then you were invited to Miss Aninhas's birthday party."

"Yes, we got lucky. It was a nice party."

"I'd guess so. They did the right thing, inviting you. After all, you saved the boy from drowning. If you'll excuse me, I'll go get you some bread to keep you busy while the squid's grilling."

When we finished the squid, which Rato had not particularly enjoyed, we headed to the beach. I told him to take a walk and I went over to where they usually settled. I found Dona Generosa in the shade, working on her embroidery. Aninhas's brother was playing in the sand with another boy. I greeted Dona Generosa and asked about her niece.

"It's about time," she said, ignoring my question.

"I'm terribly sorry, Dona Generosa, but a couple of unexpected problems prevented me from getting here sooner. At any rate, I was hoping to find you all at the restaurant."

"Sit here in the shade," she said, pointing to a canvas chair. "We didn't go to the restaurant today. There was so much food left over from the party that we've brought things to snack on here. These aren't times to be wasteful. In Lisbon, people are killing each other over a scrap of bread."

"You're right, Dona Generosa."

"Now, you see here, Mr. Vasques; we were very upset this morning. We thought something might have happened to you. The roads are so bad, and there are thieves all over the place... Aninhas was very distraught, wandering, looking all over the place for you. She didn't even go to the baths."

"I'm very sorry. Unfortunately, I couldn't let you know what was going on. I was out looking for lodgings so that we can stay here for a few days, but I didn't find anything."

"So, you're planning on staying a while?"

"Yes. The coming and going is tiring, lots of time on the road. But it seems we have no choice. There's not one room to be had in Póvoa."

156

"Have you tried Vila do Conde? It's a small village about fifteen minutes from here."

"Vila do Conde? I didn't think of that. But, Dona Generosa, do you think there are rooms available there?"

"I'm certain of it. They have several hotels and boarding houses. Since the village isn't that close to the beach, they don't get as booked up. Summer people like to stay closer. But since you have an automobile, it won't make any difference."

"Thank you, I appreciate the suggestion."

"You don't have to thank me. If I were you, I'd worry about my lodgings later. Right now, I'd go find Aninhas. She may not still be worried but, by now, she'll be disappointed."

"Disappointed?"

"After the party last night, she was so happy. I asked if it was because the party had been a success. That was one of the reasons – not the only one. Never mind, I'm babbling, it's women's talk. All the same, between the two of us, if you're really interested in her, Mr. Vasques – which I assume you are, otherwise you wouldn't be here asking about her – I was just going to say, you can be sure of one thing: she's a fine young lady. And nothing would make me more unhappy than to see her dejected. This morning she got herself all dressed up, as if she weren't coming to the beach at all. She even wore the necklace you gave her for her birthday, Mr. Vasques. I'm certain she got herself primped up for you. Since you didn't come, it's natural that she's disappointed."

I confessed my good intentions regarding her niece, although it was too soon for a declaration, since we hardly knew each other. That was the reason I was planning to stay in Póvoa for the following few days, so that she and I could get to know each other better. I was certain of my feelings for Aninhas and was hoping she wasn't indifferent to me.

"But, Mr. Vasques, I'm not the one you should be telling all this, not that it displeases me. Go find her."

I stood up, looking up and down the beach and, per-

157

ceiving my hesitation, she added, "Aninhas went off with a girlfriend to see the boats. If you head in that direction, you might find her."

I thanked her for the information and walked southwards down the beach toward the fishing port. I took off my shoes and socks so I could walk faster, digging my toes into the coarse sand.

The waves came breaking at my feet. I had to roll my pants up to my knees so they wouldn't get wet. Although the water was freezing cold, it felt great. Because of constantly wearing military boots the previous three years, my feet felt as if they were made of wood. The salt water had begun soaking through my crusty skin, which after several days at the beach, was like that of a child.

I reached the boats. Quite a few of them were beached, and off in the distance, walking towards me, I saw a man in a hat with a woman on either side. Right before we passed each other, I was surprised to see it was Rato, with Aninhas and Celeste, a friend of hers I recognized from the birthday party. Rato was explaining something to them with grand gestures. I stopped, waiting for them to reach me.

"Luís!" Aninhas exclaimed.

"Sir!" Rato cried out.

"Ladies," I said, "you should be careful of this man. Not only is he married with children, but he's a Don Juan who's left many women in France pining for him."

"Ain't no need to exaggerate, sir. Besides, I'm an honorable man. I ain't never once stolen another man's woman. I only come to the aid of women not spoken for, or who've lost their man."

The two young women laughed. When I saw Aninhas, the necklace I'd given her defining her neck and cleavage, I wanted to get down on my knees right then and there and tell her she was the woman of my life. Instead, I apologized for my tardiness and, when I was getting ready to explain what had happened, she interrupted, saying, "Mr. Joaquim Domingues has already told me everything."

"I just happened to run into these young ladies when I was walking along the beach," Rato began to explain. "One of them was sobbing like a baby. She was very riled because you didn't come to the beach, like you said you would, sir. In order to patch things up, I told her what had happened. Miss Aninhas was so touched she even wants to go to the hospital to take flowers to Apúlia, even though I told her that ain't really what he needs."

"Except for the crying, that's more or less what happened," Aninhas confirmed.

We walked back to the tents, where we left Celeste to keep Dona Generosa company. Rato went to a tavern across the avenue to have a cool drink with drop of brandy and I finally had Aninhas to myself. She suggested we take a walk along the beach northwards, and so we went, side by side. I was carrying my shoes and still had my pants rolled up, and she was holding her hemline in one hand and her hat with the other so it wouldn't fly away. The wind came up and the ocean started getting rough. It was bad for fishing, she said, and worse for swimming.

"But perfect for strolling," I added.

"That depends. It's dreadful for hats. If the wind blows mine away, promise you'll go get it, no matter where it goes?"

"I promise."

"Even in the ocean?"

"Even in the ocean. I just can't promise I'll come back."

"Why not?"

"I'm a terrible swimmer. You'll either lose your hat in the waves, or I'll drown. And so, Miss Aninhas, you'll most likely end up without a hat and without a...."

I couldn't find the right word, and she cut me off, "Sweetheart?"

We held still, facing each other with the foaming waves

breaking at our feet. The vacationers in the nearby tents seemed to ignore us.

I looked at her for a few seconds and said, "Yes, sweetheart."

She smiled, let go of her skirt, gave me her hand, and we continued down the beach.

XIV

The evening I returned to Enguinegatte from my front line training, the two ladies of the house seemed very happy to see me. They even hugged me as if I were a son, a brother, or a husband returning alive from a major battle. After embracing me, Madame Gavroche, noticing my muddy, greasy uniform, and sensing my stench, insisted on drawing me a bath. She heated water on the stove and lugged several pails upstairs, where there was a partition enclosing a huge brass bathtub. When it was about half full, she checked the temperature with her hand, added some cold water, and ordered me to take off my clothes so she could wash them. I told her not to worry, since Rato, as my orderly, would take care of it. But she, who was certainly familiar with that kind of situation, said it was women's work, at least in wartime, and that it would be an honor for her to do the laundry of a hero returning from the trenches. I liked the compliment, even though I did not exactly feel like a hero. I felt tired and wiped out from lack of sleep. Maybe it was my distracted expression that led her to want to do something for me.

It was only after I had stripped down to my underwear that I realized how dirty and smelly I was. I took off my yellowed undershirt and long johns and climbed into the bathtub. The water temperature was pleasant, and instead of starting to scrub myself, I closed my eyes and fell asleep with water up to my shoulders. Suddenly I woke up, startled by a thundering noise. Had I dreamed that I was in a bathtub when in fact I was in a trench under enemy fire? No, it was Madame Gavroche banging on the door. She asked from the outside if everything was all right. I said it was, but she probably did not understand and asked if she might come in. I was a little disconcerted. After all, I was stark naked in the water. While I hesitated, she just walked in, modestly averting her eyes, and picked up the clothes scattered on the floor. She apologized for having entered. She had been worried because I was taking so long and was so quiet. When someone takes a bath, you usually hear the water splashing. She thought something might have happened. She knew of cases of people dying in a bathtub, either from of a heart attack, or from falling asleep and drowning. Bathtubs could be very dangerous.

"No more so than the trenches, Madame Gavroche," I said, grabbing the soap and scrubbing myself furiously.

She came over, still averting her eyes, and stuck a hand into the water.

"It's almost cold, Monsieur Vasques. I'll bring you another pail."

"Please don't bother. I'm almost finished, and the water's fine."

"When you finish lathering your hair, call me. I'll bring clean water for you to rinse. There's no point in sticking your head into that dirty water."

She walked out, holding my bundled clothes at arm's length, her nose wrinkled and her head turned away, as if carrying an armful of manure. As I lathered my head, ears, and neck, I noticed some lice floating on the water. I had certainly caught them from the bunks in the shelter. I had been itching the last few days, but it had not occurred to me that I might be infested with parasites. I submerged for a few seconds, trying to drown the lice. Madame Gavroche walked in and was startled to see me underwater. Thinking I was drowning, she rushed over yelling and grabbed my arms to pull me out. It was so unexpected that I ended up swallowing water filled with filth, soap, and lice. But just like Rato would say when he found a stewed fly in a corned beef can, if I eat him, he can't eat me, and so that gulp of bath water had no effect on me.

Madame Gavroche's reaction was more problematic. When she pulled me out, I swallowed more water and started coughing, and she thought I was really drowning. It would have been silly to try to explain I was just trying to get rid of the lice by drowning them. While she helped me out of the bathtub I thanked her for trying to save me, and stood up, naked and helpless, dripping all over the floor, and waiting for her to hand me a towel. She gave it to me without any embarrassment, this time facing me as if she saw naked men on a daily basis. I tied the towel around my waist and she grabbed another and applied herself to drying my head, shoulders, arms, and back.

"You really must be more careful in the bath, Monsieur Vasques. Wouldn't it be a shame to drown in the bathtub like a cat, instead of dying in a trench like an *enfant de la patrie*?"

Finally she handed me the towel and told me to finish drying off. Dinner was almost ready and I shouldn't take too long to get dressed. I protested. After all, Rato was responsible for fixing my dinner, since he knew when I was coming back.

"I sent him away. The poor man was so tired because of so much marching yesterday."

"And where has he gone?"

"To join his comrades, I suppose. While Monsieur Vasques was at the front, he came here every day after work and helped us with the harvest. But do finish drying off, we'll talk later."

I shaved, put on a clean uniform and my spare pair of boots, duly shined by Rato, and went downstairs to the dining room. I could smell roast chicken, served with potatoes and green salad. After a week eating corned beef, rock-hard crackers, and the pork and beans stewed in a hurry by cooks perennially afraid the Boche might see the smoke and blow up the kitchen, that dinner was a royal banquet. The two children asked questions about the front.

"How many Boche did you send to hell?" François asked.

He was disappointed when I told him I had not even seen a single one.

"Daddy killed seven with one blow," he said, picking at a chicken wing.

"Yes, like the valiant Little Tailor," added his sister, sitting next to him.

"Your father was a hero," I said, with a twinge of irony they did not catch.

There was a moment of silence and Madame Constance, probably upset, went to the kitchen to check the pans. Madame Léonor Pigeart, sitting at the head of the table, commented, "My daughter hasn't recovered , since her husband disappeared at the front. Mourning's a way of weeping for our dead ones. It's a way to honor and respect them, but it also helps us recover the sense of life, which doesn't end when a loved one dies. My daughter's not yet been able to mourn her husband the way he deserves, maybe because she doesn't really believe he's dead. But we all know he's dead and buried in some mass grave somewhere in Verdun. There are many widows in Enguinegatte. Although they've not forgotten their husbands, they've mourned them and their life goes on."

"Time," I said, "cures everything."

"It also kills," the old lady said.

Madame Gavroche came back to the dining room with a bowl of strawberries and handed them around. We drank the coffee I had brought, much better than what they could buy at French stores. Since I was so tired, I answered a few more questions about the front and went to bed. I must have fallen asleep at once, for I woke as if I had been lying down for just a second, but the sun was already high in the sky. At that point I had not yet developed sleeping problems.

It was Sunday and our battalion was on furlough. I spent the morning resting. I read the letters accumulated during my absence and wrote my parents. Rato, sent away by Madame Gavroche, did not show up. In the afternoon I walked to the barn, located on a nearby farm, where my platoon was billeted. Some of the men were asleep, others were doing their laundry. I found Corporal Fontes shining his boots and asked him where the others were. They had left after lunch to go to a soldiers' *estaminet* named *Bourriquet* to drink and play cards. Rato would surely be there. Instead of going to the *Bourriquet,* I went to the *Gentillet,* a slightly more presentable *estaminet* frequented by officers. It had a piano, and the drinks were a little more expensive, to discourage common soldiers. I ran into Nogueira and Coutinho. Nogueira, who had been to the front with me, but with another company, had come back discouraged and full of horror stories. Coutinho cheerfully mentioned that our battalion would leave for the front in a couple of days.

"So soon?" I found that strange. "But the men aren't ready yet. Most of them have never set foot in a trench."

"We're going to provide support for an English battalion for three days," he explained. "It's a way for the men to get some practice, before the General commanding the 2nd Division sends us to guard a sector by ourselves. The English want to withdraw as many men as possible from defensive positions in order to use them in a large-scale offensive that's supposed to bring the war to an end. The idea's for us to replace them in some sectors at the front."

"Can you fellows speak English?" I asked.

"Not a word," Nogueira confessed. Coutinho just echoed him.

"That's going to be a pretty scene."

"They say we're going to get a few liaison officers who can get by with some Portuguese. Our company will get a fellow from Bristol who spent two months in Lisbon."

"He must be able to say at least a few words," Nogueira said.

"Sure. *Fado, ginjinha,* and Intendente *putas,*"[38] Coutinho replied. Nobody thought that was funny.

"Maybe we can communicate in French," Nogueira suggested.

"Let's hope so, but I doubt it," I said. "It's unusual to find an Englishman who can speak French. At least that's what the locals say."

We were sitting at a table with our glasses of cognac. There were three other tables with officers from other companies. Those nearest, who knew us, wanted to know our opinion about the trenches. Nogueira told his horror stories again. I tried to play it all down, saying that, in spite of rats the size of cats, bad food, and booming heavy guns that didn't let you sleep, there was nothing we couldn't put up with.

"Another cognac, monsieur?" asked the young woman who was waiting on the tables.

It was only then that I noticed her. She was tall, with crystalline blue eyes and blonde braids that would have made Rapunzel jealous.

"*Oui, merci,*" I answered, momentarily shocked by such perfection.

My comrades smiled. After she had left, Coutinho commented, "Her name's Gisèle. She's the battalion's mascot."

"Mascot? I thought our mascot was that dog we brought over from Braga," said Nogueira, who seemed to know as little as I did.

"Right, and it still is," said Coutinho. "But now we have two: Gisèle and the dog. Lots of fellows have been dreaming of her. Her admirers bring her gifts she never accepts: flowers, chocolates, sweets, perfumes, hair ribbons, whatever. Some say she's as cold as ice."

"She doesn't strike me that way," I said. "I got the impression she's kind, and she's got a charming smile. If she really were so cold, you'd notice it."

"Monsieur, your cognac."

She had come over and placed the snifter with the brownish liquid on the table.

As she went to wait on another table, Coutinho told us she was the eldest daughter of the landlady, a widow who worked in the field with her other children in the afternoon, leaving Gisèle to wait on the clients. It was said that the mother warned the daughter to pay no attention to the military. In the evening the mother took charge of the *estaminet* to prevent some of the bolder officers' advances.

The next day after work I went back to the *estaminet*. The landlady was at the counter. I asked for a beer and struck up a conversation. If you have your eyes on the daughter, the trick is always to get on good terms with the mother. She told me she was impressed by the Portuguese officers' gentlemanliness. They knew how to drink and to behave themselves. Which was not the case with English officers, who got drunk all the time and made trouble. It was not unusual for the Military Police to be called in to restore order. Besides, they were rude to women. She confessed that on several occasions they had tried to rape her and her daughter, and that the Enguinegatte *maire* had suggested they should close the *estaminet*. But she could not afford to. The *estaminet* was the family's main source of income, even though they did not make much money on the English, who only drank beer and whisky, and after getting drunk often left without paying. But that was preferable to watching them start fights. The Portuguese, despite insisting on wooing her daughter, which she could not blame them for, but felt obliged to prevent, were much more pleasant and respectful.

"Well," I said, "at least with us you need not fear the worst. As a matter of principle, we Portuguese won't do anything that a woman doesn't want."

She laughed and I went on, "But you'll understand, Madame, that a charming young woman like your daughter is a constant temptation for the officers who come here. I, for one, am very happy to see her. In wartime, seeing an angel every now and then makes a man think life isn't just a valley of tears."

Gisèle, who had come over carrying some dirty glasses, overheard my last words and said, "You're very kind, Monsieur."

"*Les portugais sont toujours gais,*" I added.[39]

Later, when the war was over, I found out she had been engaged to a Portuguese captain. Apparently she died in childbirth and he went around boasting he had hitched up with a baroness and knocked her up. But we all knew she was a tavern keeper's daughter who, when it came to looks and kindness, was just as fine as any noblewoman.

It was a great pleasure for me and my comrades to go to the *Gentillet* for a drink. Unlike other establishments that prospered near the front, the *Gentillet* was one of the cleanest, had impeccable morals, and served an acceptable cognac. I got to know many such places that served poor wine and had a bad reputation. The owners – oddly enough, they were nearly all women and raked in a fat profit by selling not only cheap wine to the ever-thirsty soldiers, but, depending on their the mood, sexual favors as well. At those bars one would often see men lined up with their flies unbuttoned, waiting for their turn. I made such places off-limits to my platoon, but to no avail. I once spotted Rato in a line and told him that if it happened again, I would fire him and appoint someone else as my orderly. But my warning went unheeded.

The officers were usually more discreet. Either they were lucky enough to strike an understanding with a lady at the house where they were billeted, or, for a few francs, they could relieve themselves in one of the many brothels in Bétune or Aire. I never went to brothels much. In Coimbra, dragged by classmates, I called on a prostitute known as the law tart. There was also a medicine tart, a philosophy tart, and a theology tart. It was there that law students lost their virginity or dealt with their unrequited love. That is not to say they did not see other prostitutes. I had a bad experience and could not even do what I was supposed to do. The lady in question, a toothless scarecrow as skinny as a stray she-dog, could do nothing to make me leave that place satisfied and triumphant.

But I do digress. At this rate, I'll be finishing this memoir by the Twelfth of Never.

The days I spent in Enguinegatte before returning to the trenches were very pleasant. The weather was splendid, the fields were covered with flowers, arms drill was kept light so the men would not get too tired, and the sound of war was a distant rumor. Madame Gavroche covered me with attention. Although Rato was responsible for my meals and clothes, she took over those tasks. He kept busy doing repairs around the house and the barn, and helping out in the field. The two children followed him around and taught him French. He repeated words and phrases and managed to make himself understood, at first only in the so-called *pas compris*[40] pidgin. One day, however, I was impressed to hear him talking to Madame Gavroche in a medley of Portuguese grammar and French vocabulary.

In the evening, after dinner, Rato would ask for permission to retire to the barn at the farm next door, where our platoon was billeted. Madame Pigeard would go to bed, the children in tow, and I often stayed in the living room talking to Madame Gavroche. She was a plain woman, not used to books, but much more educated than a wealthier Portuguese woman of higher social standing would have been. In Portugal, a woman of her social class would be illiterate. Madame Gavroche read the newspaper once a week, was relatively well-informed about important current topics, and made very reasonable comments about politics and the way the war was being conducted. That gave us something to talk about in the evening.

She was about ten years older than I, maybe about thirty-four or thirty-five. From the framed photographs on the walls one could see she had been a beautiful woman. Some features from that past beauty were still visible. Her long, wavy hair, blue eyes, smooth white skin, her elegant figure and bearing made her very attractive. From what she said about her husband, she had been happy with him. But the farm did not produce enough, the animals did not thrive, and the children were growing up wild. François, in particular, needed a strong male voice and an occasional ear-pull to make him toe the line.

I reminded her that Rato was lending them a hand. She agreed, but was sorry it was for such a short time. Some day we would leave and they would again be left without anyone they could count on. She criticized the war, the Boche, and Kaiser William, that mad tyrant everyone in Germany worshipped like a god. She criticized the politicians who could not put an end to the war, and those incompetent generals who could not win it.

"It's the people who really suffer, Monsieur Vasques, and it isn't their fault."

She regretted that the war was destroying millions of lives pointlessly and she suggested matters should be settled in the old way, by a duel. Kaiser William's generals on one side and the French generals on the other. She did not mention the Portuguese generals, either because she forgot them, or because the number of men they commanded did not quite entitle them to take part in the duel. I thought that was too bad. It would have been a way to get rid of a bunch of incompetent parasites.

Madame Gavroche still hoped her husband would return some day. She believed he hadn't died, surely he'd been captured and would be in some prison in Germany. However, I knew war prisoners usually sent news through the Red Cross about a month after being captured. If that was not the case with her husband, it was because he was dead. She must have known too, but she kept on deluding herself with other explanations. Maybe he was sick, or blind, or deaf, and couldn't write.

One evening, she joined me in half a glass of brandy. She talked about her husband, about how they had started dating at a church dance, how they became engaged and got married. He was a rather shy boy. They had been in school together, and when they got married, he moved into her house. He also had some property inherited from his parents. Before the war, life had been going well for them. They worked hard and were considering sending their children to study in Lille or maybe even in Paris. But the war had ruined all their plans.

"And what about you, Monsieur Vasques?" she asked.

"Because of the war, I had to leave the university, I lost my fiancée, and I'm far from my parents."

"What happened to your fiancée?"

"Nothing that I know of."

"Well, then?"

"She broke off our engagement."

"Don't let that bother you, Monsieur Vasques. I'm sure you'll meet someone worthy of your affection."

XV

While we were at Póvoa de Varzim, either there were cold northerly winds or else the ocean was so rough it was impossible to swim, or both. Aninhas and I took long walks along the beach, arm in arm, talking at length. I learned more about her in those three days than I had about Libaninha in nearly three years.

Libaninha and I had never talked very much. She was not interested in what I could have told her about my studies and I, for that matter, was far less interested in what she had to tell me about dresses, hats, and family upheavals. When I asked her about Brazil, where she had lived until she was fifteen, she either did not answer or changed the subject. Generally speaking the dating and, later, the engagement were restrained. We maintained both our distance and the social norms. In those days, people got married before they got to know each other. When their parents would allow them a few moments alone, young couples exchanged common pleasantries, and stolen kisses. And in the extremely rare event that a couple escaped the constant vigilance, other things might happen. But that is not relevant here, at least not right now.

Aninhas, without stepping outside the moral boundaries of that period, let me get to know her, and I, who almost never told anyone what was on my mind, found myself telling her practically my life story. When I told her about Libaninha and the broken engagement, she promised if she were ever to become engaged, nothing could make her break it off. I took her hands and kissed them. Soon afterwards, however, I was not so sure that she too, if faced with an obstacle, would not act just like Libaninha. But that is what makes love so disruptive and so exciting, all the suspicion and doubt.

One afternoon, we went to visit Apúlia in the Catholic Hospital. They told us at the reception the patient had been released the previous day. I thought that was odd, given what a bad state he had been in, and I asked to speak to a doctor. A nurse appeared, one of the two I had tipped when Apúlia had been admitted. I asked her why Manuel Santos had been sent home. She explained it had been Dr. Baldeia's orders.

"But is he better?" I asked.

The nurse burst out laughing, revealing her crooked teeth, stained yellow from the cigarettes she undoubtedly smoked on the sly.

"Better? He's terminal. We sent him home to free up a bed."

"Terminal? And how, if you don't mind telling me, Nurse, do you know?"

"Because the doctor said so."

"Let me make one thing very clear: we're not leaving until we've seen him."

"The doctor isn't here yet."

"We'll wait."

"Well then, you're going to have to wait a long time."

"Doesn't he have a schedule?" Aninhas asked, joining in the conversation. "If it's not his day off, he has to be here, either that or someone has to take his place. Who is in charge today?"

"Dr. Baldeia."

"So, where is he?"

"I'm not authorized to provide that information."

"Listen here, it's not hard to find out," said Aninhas.

She took me by the arm and turned on her heel. At the front desk, she suggested we talk to the director of the hospital.

The director, after Aninhas introduced herself, was fairly polite. He knew Dr. Jaime Gouveia, her father, by name. I explained why we'd come to the hospital. He called an orderly and told him to go find the doctor. The man came back shortly after and told the director that the doctor was not at the hospital. One of the nurses on duty mentioned he might be at home. The director called his house and, an hour later, the doctor saw me in his office while Aninhas and Rato waited outside in the hallway.

He was quite irritated at having been summoned by the director. I thought it had probably interrupted his afternoon at the beach.

I started by asking him why he had discharged the patient. He explained that the hospital was no boarding house. For terminal patients, it made no difference whether they died at the hospital or at home. I asked if they had tried to cure him. He told me they did everything in their power to take care of their patients. In other words, I said to myself, nothing.

"I'd like to know what type of treatment he received."

"Well, you can't. It's none of your business. To the best of my knowledge, you are not a relative of the patient."

"I was his superior in the war and it is my moral responsibility to make sure he's properly taken care of."

"That has nothing to do with me. The war's over and, as you so appropriately put it, you *were* his superior. In other words, that is no longer the case. And, even if it were, it wouldn't change anything. So, if you'll excuse me, I'm very busy." He waved me out.

"Listen here, you moron!" I shouted, banging my fist on the desk. "You'll send an ambulance to the home of Private Manuel Santos and bring him back to the hospital right this minute, or I'll take care of you myself. Is that understood?"

The doctor flushed and, without standing up, said disdainfully, "And just who do you think you are, barging in like this, giving orders and threatening me. This is not the Army. You get out of my office." He pointed to the door, which opened at precisely that instant. It was Aninhas, peering in, and right behind her, Rato, both of them alarmed at the hollering.

"Let's go," I said, "there's nothing more for us to do here."

We left the hospital and, back in the automobile, I told them more or less what had happened. Apparently, the doctor had sent Apúlia home to free up a bed.

"But is he better?" asked Rato.

"No, he's dying."

After a few moments of silence, Aninhas said, "But how does the doctor know he's going to die? Is he some kind of a seer?"

"He may not know the exact date but, based on the patient's symptoms, it's certain he doesn't have long," I said, as I turned onto the main avenue running along the beach.

"If you'll pardon me, sir – and you too, Miss Aninhas – I don't think the doctor even looked at him. Poor folk, when they go to the hospital, that's what happens. They send them right home. They don't want poor folk around there. I know, because I seen it happen, that's why I'm telling you. At hospitals, why, they only take care of rich folks, or folks they know, or finaglers."

"Long live the Republic," I cried out. "Long live the Republic of the privileged! Long live the Republic of the poor and the miserable, who are increasingly poor and miserable!"

A few summer people who noticed us driving by stared indignantly. They must have thought I was either drunk or an anarchist.

I headed toward Caxinas to find out how Apúlia was doing. I even forgot those surroundings might shock Aninhas. About half way there, she suggested we stop and reconsider our plans. I pulled over, near the retaining wall running along the ocean, and she said, "Maybe we could get Apúlia into the Santo António Hospital in Oporto or, even better, the sanatorium for tuberculosis patients, at Francelos beach."

"I was thinking of taking him to Braga, although we'd run the risk the same thing would happen there."

"It's likely. That's why I think either the hospital in Oporto or the sanatorium at Francelos would be the best. I can

175

call my father. Or maybe Juvenal. Yes, I think that's better, his specialty is infectious diseases. He can help us."

"Who's Juvenal?" Rato asked.

"The doctor who was at my birthday party. You two must remember him."

"Oh, yes, the dandy," I recalled, thinking, *who spent the whole time courting you.*

"The dandy?" she asked.

"You know, the one with the Charlie Chaplin mustache," Rato explained.

"No more dandy than the two of you."

"He's no match," Rato shot back.

"He's usually on duty at the Francelos sanatorium and I'm sure, if I put a word in, he'll do whatever he can to make sure your comrade gets checked into a hospital and is well taken care of."

"Didn't I just tell you," Rato called out from the back seat, "in this country, you have to either be rich or a finagler."

We headed for the telegraph office, where Aninhas sent a telegram to the dandy, saying more or less the following: "Tuberculosis patient in Póvoa. Hospitalization urgent. Family friend. Ana Gouveia."

I asked if it wouldn't be easier to call. She thought not. Dr. Juvenal Pereira never stayed in one place for very long. Furthermore, she didn't know for sure where to call, it could take hours for them to find him and get him to the phone, or give him the message. The telegram would go directly to the sanatorium and they'd make certain he got it, or else tell the telegraph messenger where to find him.

In case he replied, Aninhas suggested we go to her aunt's house. We found Dona Generosa, back from the beach, embroidering, with Paulinho keeping her company, reading out loud from an Emílio Salgari adventure story. Aninhas told her aunt what had happened, and Dona Generosa thought Aninhas had made the right decision to contact Dr. Pereira. In the meantime, she invited us to drink some lemonade and snack on homemade cookies the maid had just set down.

It was near dinnertime and we decided we had better go. Given how late it was, there would probably not be any news. We took our leave and drove to Vila do Conde, where we had managed to find a hotel. We did not have our dinner there because they had a terrible cook, instead we went to a tavern down the street. The owner, a fat middle-aged woman, told us they were serving lamprey eel rice. Since we had never eaten that well-known delicacy, we went along with her suggestion. When she brought us the steaming platter, at first glance we saw it was very much like the chicken blood rice dish we were familiar with. The difference being in the flavor, and the price.

That night I tossed and turned. I could feel the lampreys swimming around inside me. I dreamed of the terrifying bloodsucking mouths in the serving spoon. The brown-blooded sauce swarming with rice and chunks of lamprey brought back images from the trenches, where pieces of human bodies got mixed up in the mud. Among the pieces, I recognized Apúlia's head, vomiting huge clots of dark blood.

I have never eaten lamprey again.

The following day, we went to a café near the beach where we had agreed to meet Aninhas. I had barely stepped inside and I was already furious. Aninhas was sitting at a table with Dr. Juvenal Pereira. Just seeing her might have cheered me up, except that he had his hand on hers and was whispering to her – God only knew what – his lips practically inside one of her ears. As soon as I approached, the jerk moved his hand. I acted as if I had not noticed anything. Rato was waiting outside.

"Good morning," I greeted them.

"I have good news. Dr. Juvenal Pereira, who was at my birthday party..."

The jerk stood up slightly and extended his hand, "It's nice to see you again, please, have a seat."

I sat down, having returned the greeting.

"What would you like?"

"I already had my breakfast at the hotel."

"So you're staying around here?" he said, somewhat taken aback.

"No, I'm over at Vila do Conde."

"Oh! I see. Anyway, not too far away."

Aninhas was effusive, smiling from ear to ear, as if she had a pencil in her mouth, holding her grin in place. I had no idea as to the nature of their relations. Were Aninhas and the young doctor relatives, friends, former sweethearts? I could not erase the memory of his hand on hers and, at that point, I could not have been further away from my goal, which was to get Apúlia into a hospital.

Dr. Pereira filled me in, "I got the telegram yesterday late afternoon, as I was getting ready to leave the sanatorium. For some reason, the deliveryman couldn't get it to me any sooner. If he had, there would've been time to call an ambulance to transport the patient."

"Typical incompetence," I commented.

"That's the way this country is. But all's not lost. The ambulance will be here at around ten o'clock. Since it's tuberculosis, there's no urgency. He'll be very well looked after at the sanatorium. There's better hygiene, excellent lung specialists, and expert care for TB patients. We've saved the lives of many. Let's hope the bacteria hasn't spread too far, otherwise, treatment is virtually useless."

I thanked the doctor for his efforts. He said if anyone was to be thanked, it should be Aninhas. Then he smiled at her, which put me in an even worse mood, my jealous suspicions gnawing away at me like bacteria.

"Well, I guess we should be on our way," suggested the dandy. "I'd like to have a look at the patient before the ambulance gets here."

We stood up, he paid the bill and we left. Rato joined us and we got in my automobile. The doctor's was nearby. I was still thinking Aninhas would ride along with us, but she chose to ride with him. That's when I started believing I had a real rival on my hands. Rato noticed the heavy atmosphere during the ride and, with his customary frankness, asked me, "A bit jealous, sir?"

I banged the steering wheel and swore. "Yeah, that's it. You can clam up now." And he did.

Back at Apúlia's shack, we went through more or less the same routine as the first time. Apúlia, spitting blood, refused to go to the hospital. Dr. Pereira checked him out, listened to his lungs and chest, and told the stretcher bearers to put him in the ambulance. Aninhas was moved by the miserable conditions of their shack. She promised to return with groceries and clothing. I tried to give the woman two twenty escudo bills, but she would not take them. She told me she still hadn't spent the money I'd left for them the last time. But I did not recall having given them any money on the previous visit.

When we got out to our automobiles, the doctor told us not to worry about Apúlia. He was in good hands and we could only hope the treatment would be effective.

"So, you won't send him home like as did at the Catholic hospital, where the only thing Catholic about it is in the name?" I asked warily.

"We'll only send him home when he's well enough to leave the sanatorium."

"And, what if he doesn't get well?"

"Then, he may have to go to a different sanatorium, in the south. The humidity here in the north is terrible for people with lung disease. At any rate, we don't know for certain whether or not he's got tuberculosis."

"A doctor had told him he does."

"Maybe. But we can only know for sure when we get the results of the blood test. Tubercular bacteria are relatively easy to identify under a microscope."

He dismissed the ambulance, shook my hand, ignoring

Rato who was standing right next to me, and got into his black Fiat 501. Aninhas got in next to him, saying goodbye. Rato and I stood there once again, surrounded by street urchins, staring at the automobile speeding off towards Póvoa.

"I've got a sneaking feeling you've just lost your sweet-heart, sir."

"Rato, you can't lose what you don't have."

I got in the Minerva, started her up and called Rato, who was still handing out one cent coins to the boys, "Come on, let's go pick up the suitcases at the hotel. We're done with the beach."

So that was how our days in Póvoa came to an end. Within two hours we reached Braga, where we had lunch. We made the trip in silence, with the top up, to protect us from the sun. Anything Rato might have said would only make me feel worse. Since he had figured that out, he remained silent.

What bothered me most was thinking about the promises we had made, apparently erased from Aninhas's memory. Although I had not been open with her about my goals and feelings, it would not have been hard for her to figure them out, especially not for a young woman like Aninhas. Based on what I had seen, the only conclusion I could draw was that I had misjudged her feelings for me. I saw myself playing the role of substitute suitor. The bourgeois young woman had found herself some entertainment to help pass the time on the long days at the beach. And, innocent fool that I was, I took on the role splendidly. It was my own fault.

After the collard greens soup and while we waited for our codfish and potatoes, Rato invited me to come along with him that afternoon to a street he knew near the Cathedral. I figured out what he had in mind and refused. That was just what I needed, to go drown my sorrows in the arms of some toothless broad. He insisted, saying I should trust him. He knew a very nice woman in Braga who had two nieces that often entertained gentlemen, very discretely. It was slightly pricey, but

180

worth it. Even so, I said no. Just because they were expensive, it didn't mean they were any healthier or more presentable than the rest of them. Not only that, but I was against the sexual exploitation of women.

"But, sir, it ain't us who's doing the exploiting. They're the ones exploiting us."

He insisted on the cleanliness and decency of Dona Felisbina's nieces and how much good it would do me to forget about everything at Póvoa. He was being so insistent – meanwhile we had eaten the codfish with potatoes – that I began to suspect his interest had more to do with his own needs than with my consolation. I finally gave in, but on condition that I could first take a look at the girls, and get out of there if need be.

"Oh, you can have them both together if you like, sir. I mean, if you think you've got enough rounds in your rifle."

"You'll have to help me with one of them."

"Don't worry about that. You can have the two of them to yourself, if you'd like. Ain't nothing wrong with their aunt, either."

"I didn't know you liked older women."

"You don't seem to mind them neither, sir. But if you prefer the aunt, I don't mind. I can take care of the girls."

"What do you mean by that?" I asked, in a slightly grievous tone, suspecting he was referring to my relationship with Madame Gavroche.

"Please, sir, don't take offence, I don't mean nothing. To each his own."

We finished the potatoes, drank the entire jug of *vinho verde*[41] and headed off toward the Cathedral. It was a scorching hot afternoon and there was no one in the streets. We approached an old building and Rato rang the bell. We waited for five minutes.

"Maybe nobody's home?"

"In this heat, they may have gone to the beach," I ventured.

181

"Or to the mountains to visit relatives."

"Who's there?" We heard someone call from above. We looked up and saw a girl standing on one of the second story balconies.

"It's me, Joaquim Domingues."

"Rato?" the girl asked, incredulously.

"Yes, it's me."

"They told us you'd been killed in the war."

"That's just gossip."

"You've got a friend with you?"

"If there's room..."

"Where there's room for one, there's room for two. Just a minute, I'll go tell my aunt."

"The girl's cute," I said.

"She's cute and very sweet," Rato added, sitting on the doorstep.

We waited for a few more minutes. Since it was a narrow, shady street, shaded from the sun, we were able to cool off from our walk. We had taken off our jackets and were just in our shirtsleeves.

"The canons from the Cathedral, this is where they take care of their needs," Rato explained in a muffled voice. "Very demanding clients. As for disease – you don't have to worry about a thing."

"And how do you know?"

"I found out from our Chaplain, Father Cruz. You must remember, sir, I used to help with Mass at the barracks. One day the Padre asked me to go with him. I think he was afraid of a certain sergeant, a fellow what wanted to settle some card debts. Seems the Padre squealed on him to the Colonel and the fellow wanted to get even. Dona Felisbina and her nieces liked me and told me I could come back whenever I liked, their door was open. Told me I could bring a friend, but not just anyone. Had to be a good sort of folks. On account of the hygiene and to avoid scandal. The priests, they're usually quiet types, don't cause no gossip, but they can't give the gals everything they like and want. So every once in a while, the gals don't mind seeing fellows a little less saint-like."

Someone pulled a wire to release the door latch and we finally went inside. We walked upstairs to the second floor and Dona Felisbina came to greet us, flustering about, issuing thousands of apologies over the delay. They weren't counting on any visitors on such a hot day. The priests had apparently gone swimming, and she and Inocência, one of her nieces, had taken the opportunity to rest. When Rato asked about Virtuosa, Dona Felisbina said she was in Montalegre, visiting her family, and was going to get married at the end of the month to a distant cousin just back from Brazil, a man who'd made a lot of money in the Amazon. He'd heard Virtuosa was at school in Braga and wanted to meet her. He spoke to her parents, they wrote Dona Felisbina, and Virtuosa went to meet him. He fell for her, such fine upbringing and delicate manners. And so he'd asked her to marry him right away. Lucky for her. And for him too. No Brazilian woman could make him as happy as Virtuosa would.

And with the explanations out of the way, she led us to a salon where her niece was sitting.

"This is Inocência, my niece."

We sat on the empty sofa, opposite a table laid with a steaming tea pot and four cups. Dona Felisbina told us the tea was excellent for alleviating the heat and quenching thirst. Rato was not convinced and asked for some lemonade, if possible. Inocência got up and went to get it. She came back a little while later with a huge glass of sugar water and a slice of lemon on the rim.

Dona Felisbina asked us questions about the war and I realized she was an unusual woman, whose exposure to the priests had done her good. She was probably close to fifty, wearing a dark dress and with a large gold crucifix around her neck, undoubtedly a gift from some canon.

"But what brings you here?" she asked at one point.

"The Lieutenant here's got a few some problems in his love life," Rato explained.

"Poor boy!" Dona Felisbina exclaimed. "We can't cure that. But we can ease the pain. My niece Inocência will be happy to take care of you, Lieutenant, if you'd like."

The girl smiled at me. She was lovely, with straight white teeth, long light brown hair and light skin. She was wearing a pearl colored dress that made her look as fresh as a teenager.

"If you'll excuse me, I have to go," said Dona Felisbina. "If Mr. Joaquim Domingues could accompany me, there's a leaky faucet in the kitchen. Maybe you could fix it."

"It's my pleasure, Ma'am." Rato answered.

The two of them left and I was alone with Inocência. She sat down next to me on the sofa, saying, "You shouldn't get upset with these disappointments in love, Lieutenant. A handsome man like you can have any woman he wants."

"You think so, Miss?"

"I'm certain."

She came closer and kissed me on the mouth. She had thick, soft lips. I started kissing her back and was surprised to feel her tongue between my teeth. I touched it with the tip of mine and found it pleasant. She drew back a little, smiling, and asked if I'd like to go to the bedroom where we'd be more comfortable. I nodded in agreement and she led me inside the house. In the hallway we heard whispering voices. Probably Rato, trying to fix Dona Felisbina's faucet.

Once inside the bedroom, in the cool darkness, Inocência helped me take off my shirt and pants, then undressed and lay down on the bed, inviting me to join her. Then, very politely, she confessed she was a virgin and would like to remain so until she got married. I grimaced in disbelief. How could a prostitute be a virgin? She understood my doubt and assured me she really was a virgin. Because pregnancies were so inconvenient, her aunt had told her she should never let a customer touch her pussy with his member. If he didn't want to respect that, he should leave.

"And so what are we going to do?" I asked playfully.

"There are other things we can do," she answered naughtily.

To prevent this from turning into the erotic memories of a Casanova who I have no intention of becoming, I will interrupt this narrative. I will only say, to conclude, that Rato and I went home late that afternoon relaxed and nearly happy. Aninhas was a vague image among waves breaking on the beach.

XVI

In mid-July our battalion received orders to leave Enguinegatte and move on to the front, where we would be inserted in front-line English units to acquire some experience. As
we said goodbye, Madame Gavroche's mother gave me a small
Jeanne d'Arc medal to wear on my chest. It would protect me,
she said. Her daughter wiped a tear with her apron. I was one
more soldier she saw leaving and who most likely would not
return. She made me promise to visit her if I went on leave.
They would always keep their home open for me and Rato. I
said it might be difficult, especially considering that, as soon
as we left, other soldiers would be billeted with them. She said
she hoped not. We, the Portuguese, would teach the Boche a
lesson and bring the war to an end.

My knapsack was packed full with cheese, salami, and
crackers, and if I had not protested about the weight, they would
have loaded me with jars of preserves and pots of marmalade.

Our battalion was transported by British military trucks
as far as Sally-sur-la-Lys. We arrived late in the afternoon and
the company officers saw to lodging the men. Everybody slept
as best they could, wherever they managed to find a spot. Since
it was hot, any odd place, as long as it was reasonably quiet,
sufficed to spread out a blanket and try to get some rest. We
would never again enjoy the lodging conditions we had in Enguinegatte. War was about to begin in earnest for us.

The next morning the Major ordered officers and sergeants to leave for the trenches, to reconnoiter the subsector
each company would occupy. We were guided to the lines by a
first lieutenant named Peterson, who had reported to Captain
Rebelo as our liaison officer.

The Colonel in command of the English battalion we
would join ordered us to have our men ready to occupy the
trenches that afternoon, fully equipped and divided into small

detachments. Captain Rebelo asked him if it would not be less risky for the men to enter the lines before dawn, rather than before nightfall. The Colonel answered that it was necessary to vary the schedule to avoid artillery attacks. But the Boche, either because they had spies among us, or because they paid attention to what went on opposite them, found out about the schedule changes. As soon as we started occupying our subsector, they began hitting the communication trenches with heavy mortar fire and gas grenades. It was the first time we had to wear our gas masks in actual combat. Seen by the light of the stars and the bursting shells, we looked like a ghost army. Fortunately, nobody was wounded and the men were posted without major problems. The English guides made sure nobody got lost or took a wrong turn in the maze of the trenches.

Having posted my men, I walked to the dugout assigned to the company officers. Captain Rebelo and Second Lieutenant Nogueira were already there. By that time the bombardment had let up and the shells were falling far behind us, in the cantonment area. So much the better, I thought.

As I walked into the dugout, the Captain, sitting on a wooden box and writing the day's report by candlelight, asked me how my men were holding up.

"Enthusiastic," I said. "It's all news to them."

"Any danger someone might get scared shitless and run away?"

"I doubt it. I even had to chew out a few for trying to peek over the parapet into no man's land."

"They don't know the risk," Nogueira said.

"My only concern is that someone may start smoking and get spotted by a sniper."

"It won't be for lack of warning."

The Captain seemed proud. After so many long months, he said, we had finally managed to train the men entrusted to us, and now they were in the front line, as combatants in the cruelest and deadliest war in memory. Our negative feelings regarding Portugal's entry into the war vanished momentarily. That night we were convinced that our participation could be decisive to end the war. The Captain recalled the battle of Thermopylae, a narrow pass where a handful of Greeks had heroically resisted the advancing Persian armies. I was tempted to remind him that resistance had been useless, for in the long run the Persians had broken through, wiped out the Greek defenders, and taken Athens, which had been evacuated. But I did not want to ruin the moment, so I kept quiet. On that evening of patriotic pride, none of us could imagine that the Portuguese sacrifice would be just a drop of blood in the great slaughterhouse of Flanders.

Nothing noteworthy happened during those three days. We followed our instructions to the letter, and the men, maybe because it was their first time in the trenches, carried out their orders rigorously, from cleaning and maintenance to keeping watch. Nobody got killed or wounded. Occasionally, a few shots coming from the enemy side reminded us that we were at war. The quiet, however, caused many of the men to get the wrong idea about what was actually going on. Having heard the trenches were a slaughterhouse and now confronting that enormous silence, they concluded someone had been exaggerating. I must confess I thought so too. That attitude led us to lower our guard and to act recklessly, and we paid dearly for it later.

We received our orders in English directly from the commander of the English battalion in which our company was inserted, and Lieutenant Peterson translated them into French, either in writing, or by phone, or in person. We agreed we would write our reports in French and he would translate them into English. As it turned out, Coutinho had got it all wrong: Lieutenant Peterson was not from Bristol and had never been in Lisbon. All he knew about Portugal was port wine.

We were posted between two English companies and the men lived side by side without any problems. Basic communication problems were solved by the so-called *pas compris* pidgin, with gaps filled by universally understood gestures. During my rounds I saw soldiers from both countries swapping cigarettes, since theirs were better than ours, heating corned beef over the brazier, and drinking from the same bottle. The Tommies preferred our bagaço[42] and we preferred their whisky. They were more disciplined than we were, except when they drank too much. Then they became rude and xenophobic, displaying considerable animosity. On such occasions they showed their feeling of superiority toward us Portuguese, citizens from what they considered an insignificant country. But we could not complain, as they also despised the French, who had not been able to defend themselves from the invading Germans, as well as their Scottish and Welsh neighbors, and above all the Irish, those Catholic swine.

Despite that flaw, during the three days of our trench training, the Tommies, from the officers down to the last private, were very cordial. On the first night, Lieutenant Peterson brought a bottle of whisky to our shelter. I opened my knapsack and passed around Madame Constance Gavroche's treats. I do not really like the taste of whisky, because it does not agree with me. Lieutenant Peterson drank it with the same abandon Captain Rebelo drank bagaço.

To make friendly conversation, the Captain asked Lieutenant Peterson how he'd got into the war. He told us he'd volunteered in 1914. He'd lied about his age and was enlisted. His parents were afraid he might be punished, so they did not protest, and he departed for France with the first contingents.

Captain Rebelo wondered why he'd volunteered, and he confessed it'd been a dumb thing to do. Stupidity fed by pro-war propaganda. Also, the patriotism he'd been bombarded with at school, at home, on the street, and from the newspapers. That was the only way to explain how he'd volunteered for that carnage.

"Do you regret having enlisted?"

He said he didn't. If he hadn't volunteered, he wouldn't have gone to war in 1914 because he was under age, but in 1915 or 1916 he'd have been drafted, willingly or not. Most of his comrades had been killed in the first combats. He considered himself a lucky man.

While the bottles made the rounds, he told us about the battles he had been in. He had not suffered a single scratch, but out of his original regiment, only he and a doctor were still alive. The doctor lost a leg when his hospital was shelled and was then sent home. At the battle of Ypres, there were seven Englishmen for each German, or at least that's what they said. The generals were optimistic. They said the war would be won in a matter of days.

"And we're still here. Every day we sink a little deeper into the mud, and we can't figure out why we can't break the enemy lines and end this war," he said.

Nogueira asked him how he had made lieutenant, having left England as a private. He explained it had been sheer luck, and also because the Germans had wiped out the noncoms in his platoon. Since he was the private with most formal education, they'd made him a corporal, then a sergeant, and finally, an officer. During the three years of war he learned French with the civilians and the *poilus*. Then, when the Portuguese arrived, he was appointed interpreter and liaison officer by General Hacking, who commanded the Eleventh British Army Corps in which the Portuguese Expeditionary Corps was inserted.

He intended to learn Portuguese and, after the war – if it did not last twenty years and he managed to survive – he would go to Portugal. Other military men who had been there before us told so many wonderful things about the country – the sun, the good wine, the brunettes, the fado – that he was considering setting up an export business. He'd even written about it to his father, who was a businessman in York and thought it was a good idea.

On the last day we exchanged addresses and Lieutenant

Peterson promised to contact us when he came to Portugal. He has yet to do so, either because he changed his mind about the wonders of this country, or because he died in the months that followed, killed in one of the senseless attacks ordered by Marshal Sir Douglas Haig, Commander-in-Chief of the British armies, and one of the most incompetent generals sent to Flanders by the English government.

The heat of summer practically dried up the trenches. On the one hand, it got rid of the mud and dampness, but on the other it made the churned-up dirt let out an intolerable stench of decay. Lieutenant Peterson explained that thousands of bodies had been buried there since 1915, because the constant shelling had made it impossible to remove them for proper burial in a cemetery. So it was not surprising, when dirt was shoveled out in digging a funk-hole or opening a new trench section, that we found the remnants of a foot, or a hand, or a head with hair still on it. In his opinion the rats had become real guardians of hygiene, because they gnawed the bones clean and thus prevented an epidemic. I, on the contrary, thought the rats, despite being filthy, would not eat rotten flesh. Otherwise it was not possible to understand how, two years later, that repulsive odor was still there.

During my rounds in those three days and nights in the front line, I noticed the men's morale was still high. Once I found Rato on duty at a watch post, standing on the fire step and peering into no man's land through a periscope. Even though he was my orderly, he had to do at least one turn of sentry duty. Private Frossos was resting next to him.

"How's everything?" I whispered.

"Same as always, sir," Rato answered. "No news. And I used to think you couldn't get bored here! So far I ain't seen a single Boche. I wonder if they're really over there. I reckon they gone away and we think they're still there."

"We can make a test."

"Like what, sir?"

"You climb on the parapet, light a cigarette, and wait to see what happens."

"You're pulling my leg, sir."

"Are you afraid?"

"No. But I ain't stupid either. If they're there, they'll shoot me dead."

"But maybe they're not. Never mind, I've another idea. Let's stir them up."

I climbed on the fire step, and cupping my hand in front of my mouth, yelled:

"*Boche de merde! Allez-vous en, chez vous! Vos mères? Elles ne sont que des putains! La victoire est à nous! Vainqueurs de cette guerre, on ira en Allemagne. C'est vrai! Il faut y aller pour enculer vos mères et vos fiancées!*"[43]

Pretty soon we heard shouting in German from the other side and a machine gun started firing. Bullets flew over our heads and ended up buried in the parados, the trench wall behind us. A Vickers, manned by an English team, fired back for a few minutes, and finally both sides went silent again. There was no point in wasting ammunition on account of a few insults, particularly during the night. And if they had been shouted during the day, common sense would have dictated that we should run away before a mortar shell turned us into mincemeat.

"There they are," I said. "Alert and ready to wipe us out if we give them a chance."

"Sure, just like us."

As I walked away, I told him not to serve me that lousy bacon and eggs for breakfast, it ruined my stomach. After all, I was no Englishman.

"And what shall I bring you, sir?"

"A mug of black coffee and bread, if there's any. And no butter, do you hear? Lieutenant Peterson told me he got wind that, because of a milk shortage in England, they're using the fat from corpses to make butter."

"From corpses? So now they're using even dead people?"

"Well, I guess he didn't mean people. Probably dead animals. Even so, we'd better not take any risks. We just don't know what kind of animals they may be using."

"No butter, then."

"Any mail from home?"

"Yes, sir."

"What's the news?"

"The wife says the child was born. A girl. She nurses well, and that's what counts. The other kids are all right. Delmiro, the eldest, is working at your father's estate, sir. The schoolmistress wouldn't take him, said we should've signed up at the beginning of the year. We'll see if he can do it in autumn. But if you want to know what I think, sir, I think that's a waste of time. That boy ought to start learning a trade. Letters and books don't fill nobody's belly. And, like Father Ruas says, they may make a good Christian lose his soul."

I told him Father Ruas was mistaken. Portugal was a land of illiterates, and that made us the most backward country in Europe. Besides, as he probably knew, you can never learn too much. Rato argued that might be true, but he didn't see much difference between the Portuguese and English soldiers serving in the trenches. I said there was an important difference: it would be hard to find an English soldier who couldn't write a letter, whereas most Portuguese privates had to ask the Chaplain or a noncom for help.

"Maybe the Tommies can write, sir. But when it comes to working, we're a lot tougher. Even though we're smaller than them. When they grab a shovel or a dirt bag, they gripe about it. 'Cause if you ain't used to it, your hands get calluses from the shovel, and the dirt bags ruin your back."

It was not quite fair to call the English lazy. There were bums on all sides, and we had a few in our platoon. Like Private Frossos, lying down nearby, who did not even budge during

193

the shooting. He would spend most of the day snoozing, even when leaning on a shovel handle or against a trench wall. I had to discipline him several times when I caught him asleep on duty, but it was no use. Later, on the day of the battle, he dispatched several Boche with an ordinary rifle from a distance of two hundred meters, saving the comrades who were with him. Then he fell asleep again and only woke up when his ship docked at Alcântara Pier. According to Rato, he then walked straight to the Alfama district and popped into bed with the first toothless whore he found. Then he took her to Braga and married her. He once came to see me at my office, right after the 1926 revolution, on account of some inheritance issue. He told me his wife had died from consumption, leaving him with two girls as pretty as the moon. He asked me how much he owed me and I told him there was no charge. A few days later he brought me a ham.

One night, in October or November, I found Private Frossos asleep on sentry duty. Without waking him up, I took his rifle and hid it in the bottom of the trench. Then I shook him and asked him about his weapon. Wiping his eyes on his dirty sleeves, he said that either a Boche had come by and taken it, or, more likely, some son-of-a-gun of a buddy had pinched it to sell it on the black market.

I gave him back his rifle, chewed him out, and ordered him to stay alert, or he might really lose his rifle and spend the remainder of the war in jail.

"It might not be such a bad deal, sir," he said, poker-faced. "I'd be rid of trench duty and could sleep all the time."

What else could I do if not laugh?

When our first front line stint was over, we were relieved by an English battalion. As I said goodbye to Lieutenant Peterson, I asked him what he thought of our men's performance. He said it was excellent. They were disciplined, hard-working, fearless, and tough. Very tough. If he had to criticize anything – which he insisted he did not – it might be about cleanliness. A certain carelessness about personal hygiene and in disinfecting the latrines had been noticed. He said that sometimes he had the impression that, instead of gas grenades, we had been shelled with grenades *pleines de merde*. We both laughed. I wished him best of luck for the remainder of the war and the rest of his life, and told him I would expect a visit from him. He said he'd be leaving for Ypres at the end of the month. The British Army was preparing the summer offensive and would only stop in Berlin. As he said this, we both grinned. He did not trust Marshal Sir Douglas Haig, and was afraid the offensive might turn into another carnage with minimal results.

"This must be the most expensive piece of real estate in the world!" he cried, spreading his arms wide. "According to statistics, a hundred twenty three point two men have died trying to defend every meter of terrain, with a hundred thousand pounds of military equipment now used up. The total amount spent on all of Flanders would be enough to feed the whole needy population of Europe for fifty years."

XVII

In the weeks following those days at the beach, I spent my time buried in the readers for the political economy course, one of the required fields for the law degree. The examination was to be in mid-September and, if I wanted to pass, I still needed to memorize the main points of pages and pages of material. Given that I had attended so few classes, I had no idea what was important and what was superfluous. But since I was well aware that those professors at Coimbra usually included in the examinations what the Devil himself could not have remembered, the best thing to do was to study it all.

I would get up at eight, eat breakfast with my parents and remain in the study until my mother called me for lunch. After I returned from Flanders, my father gave me permission to use the study, which until then had been reserved for him alone. I used to study in my bedroom, where I had a small desk, but the study was more comfortable, furnished with overflowing bookcases – many legal treatises – and a huge mahogany desk, two sofas and an armchair. While I plowed through my readers, my father sat in the armchair, reading the newspaper, and every once in a while he made a comment or read me a paragraph.

Around that time, newspapers were filled with articles about António José de Almeida's victory as the President of Portugal, and about the looting of stores due to food shortages. The war had been over for almost a year and the country was submerged in a political, economic, and social crisis. The Treaty of Versailles, signed in June of that year, had required Germany to pay the Allies heavy war compensations. My father would shake his head, wondering how Germany was going to pay, since the country was bankrupt. The Allies' demands, especially those imposed by France and Great Britain, were so disproportionate they just might lead up to another world war. My father doubted the Germans were prepared to starve to death to pay war compensations. And now, with almost twenty years' hindsight, I believe his concerns may come to pass. Hitler has taken advantage of the people's frustration to rise to power and to remilitarize the country. When the Great War ended, few people would have doubted it was indeed the war to end all wars. That was what I thought, anyway, and that was how I minimized the damage and misery it caused. My own sacrifice and that of the millions of other men who fought in the war was the price of peace. Now, sitting in the same chair where my father used to sit, when I read the newspaper I get the feeling our sacrifice may have been in vain.

Since the muddy mess of 1918, the world has been preparing for something much worse. Even though Hitler talks peace, he is arming the country to the teeth. It seems as if the English and the French, the only ones who would be able to confront him at this point, are trying to involve him in negotiations, maybe because they believe he would not dare start a war. He says yes to everything, meanwhile snatching up – peacefully, he claims – the neighboring regions. First it was Rhineland, then Austria, and soon it will be Czechoslovakia if the alarming news is true. In Spain, as if expunging a scourge, Franco has been exterminating what he vaguely calls "the Reds," meaning anyone and everyone who disagrees with the fascists, nationalists, totalitarians, and the rest of the backward think-ing. Mussolini, acting like some kind of vaudeville emperor, has annexed Ethiopia and struts around like a peacock alongside Hitler in Berlin and Rome. Not to mention the Japanese, who have rediscovered their aggressive samurai instinct and invaded China.

But by the end of August 1919 I was not thinking about war. My biggest concern was to pass the examination in Political Economy, register for my last year at university, and graduate. I was sick and tired of the rumble of cannon. That was the rea-son I applied myself so arduously to reading and underlining all those readers. When I had any doubts and my father was nearby, I would ask him. From his vast encyclopedic memory he could cite examples, cases, and details.

My father would usually go out midmorning to supervise the day workers, and we saw him again at lunchtime. In the afternoon, I would go outside for a short walk to aid my digestion and then go back to the study. And later on, after tea, I would go out again for a ride on Ruddy. I usually had tea with my mother. My father only drank tea when he was sick and bedridden.

My mother used to ask me about France or else she would talk about what was going on with our relatives and friends. Uncle Alcides, her brother, was sick; Dona Isilda had died of a stroke; Gaudêncio had stolen a cartload of potatoes from his employer; Old Felício was asking to have his lease lowered on account of expenses, since his son had got an underage girl into trouble; Benito had smacked Lateiro with a hoe over water rights; Aprígio had emigrated to Brazil; Milomes was to be a father for the seventeenth time.

At one point, she wanted to know what Rato and I had been doing at the beach. I told her, skimming over the details, about Rato having saved the boy from drowning, about the birthday party for Aninhas, the boy's sister, and about Apúlia's situation. She wanted to find out more about Aninhas, but I was very vague.

Around that time, a letter from Aninhas arrived. My mother brought it to the study one afternoon. I stared at the handwriting on the envelope for a few moments.

"Well then, aren't you going to open it?"

Since I did not react, she added, "I'll leave you alone."

I emerged from my lethargy, "No, Mother, you can stay. I just wasn't expecting a letter."

"I saw the name, Ana Maria Gouveia. Is that the girl you met in Póvoa?"

"Yes, she is."

"Are you sweethearts?"

"No Mother! What an idea!"

"Well, you're friends, at least..."

"Maybe so, maybe not."

She ruffled my hair as if I were still a child and said, "I'll leave you to your letter. And try to make up your mind. When a man doesn't know whether a girl's a friend or a sweetheart, she'll probably end up as neither."

I did not read the letter. At least not that day. I stuck it between the pages of my reader and went back to my studies. At tea, my mother asked if there was good news in the letter. I told her the news was neither good, nor bad. She wanted details. Nothing special, I answered. She did not insist, maybe suspecting I had not read it yet after all.

"What's this all about, Luís?" she asked suspiciously, stirring the sugar in her tea.

"Nothing, Mother."

"Have you seen Libaninha?"

"Why, didn't she get married?"

"Yes, she got married. But, I thought you might have run into her on one of your outings."

"No, I haven't seen her."

"They say her relations with her husband aren't the best. I've heard that, in an argument with her mother, she told her you're the man of her life and she only married the other man because they made her."

"If indeed someone told you that, it's probably a lie. How can anyone know what was and what wasn't said in someone else's house?"

"You're forgetting about the servants. They're an excellent source of information."

"I haven't seen any of the Azevedos' servants around here telling you what's going on at their home."

"Not me. You may not know it, but our maid, Maria, is Benvinda's goddaughter, the Azevedos' longtime maid. Every once in a while, the two meet at the market and the old gal talks a lot."

"Oh Mother, you shouldn't pay attention to servants' gossip."

After tea that day, I mounted Ruddy and rode off to the village. The corn was nearly ripe in the fields and the grapes, within a week or two, would be ready for harvesting. Right around then my father was overseeing the cleaning and disinfecting of the wine press, the barrels and containers. I offered to help several times, but he said it made more sense for me to study for the exam. I'd have plenty of time to take over the work on the estate when God, Providence, or whoever was running the show called him to settle his final accounts.

Riding Ruddy those early September evenings, with the soft sunshine rendering the landscape green, yellow, and red, I felt safe and at peace with the world. In contrast, the grayness of the trenches was engraved in my memory as the color of suffering and death.

Occasionally I would meet Rato strolling home, or else, outside Bigarrilha's tavern, quenching his thirst with other day workers. Sometimes I dismounted and joined them, accepting a swig from Rato's bowl. They often drank a sort of thick, dark wine. On one of these occasions he seemed somewhat downcast, so I asked him if everything was all right. He told me yes, under the circumstances.

"The circumstances?"

He did not want to talk in front of the others at the tavern. I accompanied him on his way home, holding Ruddy by the reins. I insisted he tell me what was bothering him.

"I don't belong here, sir," he blurted out.

"What do you mean you don't belong?"

"Just that. I don't belong here. I waited so long to come back from the war and now that I'm here, all I want to do is go away."

"But why? Are you having problems with Vicência?"

"It's not that. She's a fine woman. Hard working, a good mother, honest. But she ain't got no idea what we went through over in Flanders. She thinks we spent the whole time

200

having fun. That we didn't do nothing at all besides eating on the government's money, sleeping and going on outings. But that ain't the only reason I want to get out of here."

"Go on."

"It's on account of everything. Cheap little country. The others what didn't go to war, they look me over like I was some kind of beast with seven heads. No work to be had except for wage labor, slaving away in the fields from sun up to sun down. And if a body finds work, the pay's not even good enough to buy food. From what I've been hearing, one of these days even with money there won't be nothing to buy. Everyone'll probably die out, starve to death. So that's it, and other things too. I'm wasting my time here."

I did not want to argue with him. What he said was true. The lack of understanding regarding the war veterans contributed to their increasing sense of alienation. There was so much misery among those who had little or nothing to call their own that thousands of Portuguese were abandoning the country in search of a better life. If it kept up, before long the entire country would be vacant. Except for the landowners, left on their own to work the land.

"Where are you thinking of going?"

"To Flanders, sir. There must be plenty of work there, now that the war's over."

"And have you thought about how you're going to get there?"

"I'll go by train. The money you gave me, sir, for when I went along on your trips, should be enough for the ticket."

"I'm sure it won't be. But we can figure that out. My savings from Flanders should be spent on something besides necklaces for people that don't deserve them. Still, what worries me is that you might get there and not find any work. The French are mistrustful and I think they've got worse since the war. I don't see them running the risk of hiring a stranger and putting him up."

"There must someone in the villages and towns we marched through that remembers the Portuguese."

"Maybe so, maybe not. Besides, I doubt all of us made a good impression on the French."

I thought for a few more minutes while we walked along the dirt road. Ruddy had gnawed the vines off a wall and was chewing them as if they were an unexpected delicacy. I remembered Madame Gavroche. I thought about writing her to see if she would consider hiring Rato, to find out if she needed another pair of arms to work the farm. Or she might have information about work elsewhere. I explained my idea to Rato and he was enthusiastic. As soon as I heard back from her, I would tell him. In the meantime, he should go talk to my father. It was getting near time to harvest grapes and there was a lot of work to be done. He said he didn't know if that was such a good idea.

"Why not?"

"For the time being, I'm doing day labor for Senhor[44] Arnaldo over at Quinta de Santa Madalena, and he might not like it."

"What? What does that have to do with anything?"

"Well, you know, sir, when it comes to things like this, bosses can be really... What's it called?"

"Touchy?"

"Yeah, that. Especially after what happened."

"What happened?"

"Weren't you going to marry his daughter, sir?"

"Yes, but what does that have to do with you?"

"If I stop working there to go work at your father's Quinta de São Francisco, it's like I'm crossing over to the enemy."

"That's absurd! Senhor Arnaldo must know by now you and I were at war together, and we're friends."

"Oh, he does, and I can tell you one thing, he sure doesn't like it."

"What the devil! I'm the one who should be angry at

202

those people. I'm the one who was ill-treated. But I sure as hell won't waste time thinking about it."

"Right. But ever since Libaninha's been mad at her husband, Senhor Arnaldo and Dona Eleutéria have been real worried. They're afraid their girl will get ideas and try to send a message."

"To me?"

"Well, certainly not to me."

"But do you think she..."

"I wouldn't put nothing past her. A few days ago, I was detasseling corn in their fields, she came over and started asking me questions about you, sir. If you'd had a sweetheart over in France, if you've got plans to marry, if this and if that. I told her I didn't know nothing. She started yelling at me. Called me a liar, said she was going to tell her father not to give me no more work. I put on a real show, kneeled down before her, clinging to her skirt – even got a glimpse of those pretty thighs of hers – and carried on about all my hard luck, my litter of starving kids, begged her not to tell her father nothing, said I'd tell her everything she wanted to know."

"And what did you tell her?"

"A whole bunch of hogwash, sir. That you'd found yourself a real rich, real pretty baroness living in a castle and that you visited her every single day; I told Libaninha you'd drive around the trenches in the baroness's automobile and all the generals was envious; that you'd gone to Paris with her lots of times and that she took you to fancy places where you and her drunk lots of champagne. And then, when you came back, she came here to Oporto to visit and you're about to marry her."

"You're a real rogue..."

"Well, all I can say is, after all that talk, she never once come talk to me again and I ain't seen her husband around. Some say they've patched things up."

"Well, good for her."

We had reached the door of Rato's house and I added,

203

"Still, do what I've suggested. Go see my father. He'll give you work for sure, and he pays better too. If Senhor Arnaldo gets mad, that's his problem."

The letter I had to write Madame Constance Gavroche reminded me of another one I had put between the pages of my reader. I read it that day, or probably the next, lying in my bed, right before turning out my lights, just like I used to do in the trench dugout, reading letters by candle light. Mail was handed out during the day and most men read it as soon as they could. I liked to keep my letters in the pocket of my tunic, to put off the pleasure until nighttime, lying on my bunk. It was almost always letters from my father with a few lines added by my mother. She never wrote me a letter of her own. It was not as if she did not like to write – barely a day went by that she did not write to an aunt in Brazil, to her brother Alcides in Lisbon or to old school friends. Maybe she thought since my father signed the letters "your parents," they would give me more courage.

Aninhas's envelope was long, and the stamp with the scythe-holding goddess Ceres was postmarked Oporto. All the stamps at the time pictured that goddess, the only difference among them being the color, which varied according to their value. Every single letter I received from Portugal while I was at Flanders had stamps with her image. The goddess Ceres became the goddess of family, of good or bad news, of hope, of everything we all longed for. The republicanoids identified the goddess with the regime, she was the goddess of the Republic. This was in contrast to the woman a few shepherd children claimed to have seen in an apparition at Fátima. But the woman from Fátima had no stamps in her honor, at least not for the time being, so for the simple soldiers, the goddess Ceres and the apparition from Fátima became one and the same. It was not unusual for them to cross themselves while holding the envelope, and to kiss the stamp as if it were a holy card.

I slit the envelope with a paperknife and took out the letter, folded in three, and written in round symmetrical handwriting. I cannot transcribe it because I have lost track of it. It is probably among my course readers, in the trunk in the attic where I store papers and old books. Since it would take me ages to go look for it now, and there is no guarantee I would find it, I will summarize it.

I remember she addressed me as "dear Luís," which was a good start. Then she wrote she had been very worried about me and that was the reason she was writing. She had a vague idea of where I lived and hoped that the letter, even without the full address, would reach me. She confessed she had been mystified by my sudden departure from Póvoa, since I had left no word. In the days following Apúlia's internment, she had walked the beach looking for me, and had asked at the restaurant. When she could not find me, she decided to telephone the hotel in Vila do Conde and that was how she found out Rato and I had left. She was very worried and, at the same time, thought perhaps we had left so suddenly on her account. She thought about it for a few days, wondering what she might have done wrong and was having a hard time figuring it out. She also said her aunt was very upset. Dona Generosa did not think it becoming of a gentleman, and she had considered me as such from the day she had met me. Aninhas told her aunt maybe I had left for something very important and I had not had time to tell. She went on to say the remaining time in Póvoa had been extremely dull. The ocean was always rough and it rained constantly. Her friend Celeste, who had been staying with her family in Póvoa, had gone home to Matosinhos, so Aninhas was alone. She said she had missed me a lot, and now that she was back in Oporto, she feared she had lost me forever. She begged me to write and explain what had happened, so that she could stop worrying and make amends for any offense she may have inadvertently committed. She ended the letter confessing her affection for me and her hope that she would see me soon. In the post script, she told me Apúlia had been placed in the sanatorium at Francelos, and praised my efforts to help the unfortunate man. If he were to regain his health – and he would, God willing – it would be thanks to my determination.

I read the letter three times that night and several more the following day, searching for any hint behind those words to confirm my jealousy. I could find nothing more than a letter from someone who cared about me, and who was worried about my ungentlemanly departure and my silence.

I decided to send her a brief response, thanking her for her concern, which was unnecessary. Everything was fine with me, with my family and with Rato. I had to study for an exam and that was one of the reasons I had come home precipitately. The other reason was my having sensed, the day her doctor friend had gone to pick up Apúlia, that Rato and I were in the way and probably an inconvenience. When a person gets in the way, it means he is out of place. I signed my full name, put the letter in an envelope, embossed with Quinta de São Francisco, and put it on the tray of outgoing mail. On top of it, I set another to Madame Gavroche. The mailman usually came after lunch, and he would take them. Two days before I departed for Coimbra, I received another letter from Aninhas. It was substantially shorter. It said more or less the following:

Dear Luís,

It had occurred to me there must have been a misunderstanding. I blame myself entirely for causing it and making you suffer! All there is between Dr. Juvenal Pereira and me is friendship. We've known each other since we were children. He has a fiancée and is to be married in the near future. But even if it weren't so, I want to tell you that you're the person I've given my heart to and I had hoped that you would accept it, as I have accepted yours.

From someone who will never forget you,
Ana Maria

The first time I read the letter, I wanted to beat myself up for having been so stupid. I had found the woman of my life and had started ruining everything with jealousy, suspicion and doubt. That is the price, so say the experts, of love.

The exam was to be on Monday morning and I had planned on leaving on Sunday. I decided to go instead on Saturday, to stop in Oporto along the way to set things straight. I drove to Braga, left the automobile in a garage for an inspection and took the train. If I had written to tell her I was going to Oporto, the letter would not have arrived in time. A telegram would have been too brief and might have made Aninhas's parents suspicious or uneasy. Besides, I wanted to surprise her.

On the way to the railway station, I reread her letter. I had brought along the readers on Political Economy, intending to go over them, but I did not take them out of my bag. At that point, love and happiness was more important to me than law and whatever my professional future held. Since I did not have a photograph of Aninhas, I looked for the four cent coin in my pocket and lingered over the bust of the young woman, caressing it.

When I got to the station, I hailed a carriage, giving the driver directions to their house and, within fifteen minutes of winding through several streets, I was in front of a building down by the river. I paid the driver and rang the bell. A young boy appeared on the balcony and looked down at the street. It was Aninhas's brother.

"Hello there, Paulino."

"Senhor Luís! What are you doing here?"

"Is Aninhas home?"

"No, she went out with a friend. But wait there. I'll go tell my mother you are here, sir."

"No, you don't have to do that."

But the boy had already gone back inside.

In a few minutes, I heard the door open. I went in and climbed the stairs to the first floor where Paulino and Dona Leontina were waiting for me.

"Senhor Luís, to what do we owe the pleasure?"

I greeted mother and son, explaining I was on my way to Coimbra, so I'd decided to stop to call on Aninhas. But, apparently I was out of luck.

"Unfortunately, she's not home. She left right after lunch. She went to the movies with Celeste and will only be back for tea."

"Do you know which movie theater? Maybe I can meet her there."

"She didn't say. There are three or four she may have gone to."

"Aninhas said she was going to see a Charlie Chaplin movie," Paulino piped up.

"That doesn't help much, all the theaters could be showing a Chaplin movie."

"But why don't you come in and wait until she comes back? Have you had lunch yet, Senhor Luís?"

"No, I haven't had the chance. The train left Braga before noon and I confess, I forgot to eat."

"Well then, do come in. Clorinda, our maid, will fix you something."

"I don't want to be a bother, Dona Leontina."

"It's no bother. While you eat, we can chat."

And it was there at the table, surrounded by codfish cakes and little skewers of ham, that Aninhas found me.

XVIII

After the three days in the trenches under the orders of an English battalion commander, our company withdrew during the night to Sailly-sur-la-Lys. We slept as best we could in Bac-St-Maur. Having spent the preceding nights under the worst conditions imaginable, the straw awaiting us in the barns of the partially destroyed farms felt as cozy as a bed with fresh sheets and a good blanket.

The following afternoon we left for a new cantonment, where we were to stay for about two months. According to the movement order from Brigade Headquarters, our cantonment was located in l'Épinette. But since this place did not appear on our topographic map, we got lost on the trails and roads of the region. The civilians we ran into could not guide us, either because they were unfamiliar with the area, or because it was too complicated to give precise directions. It took us seven hours to get to our destination, instead of the two it would have taken if a simple sketch had been attached to the movement order. After three exhausting days in the trenches, we had to waste one more day for no good reason. At some point during the march I overheard Private Tibáes grumble we were so lost we would end up crossing the enemy lines and find ourselves in Belgium.

It was midnight when we finally arrived in l'Épinette, after walking in circles over half of Flanders, cursing the clerks at Brigade Headquarters for their incompetence. But we were just letting off steam. Eventually we would get used to figuring things out for ourselves when the pen pushers at the rear failed to carry out their duty for those of us at the front. That is the way of war: those who give orders stay behind, watching those who carry them out die. On that day we started hating the administrative clerks and the top brass, and our hatred increased steadily even after the war was over.

Conditions at the l'Épinette cantonment were awful. The town was overcrowded with soldiers, mostly Portuguese, and with refugees from the front line villages, many of them forcibly evacuated. The villagers insisted on not moving too far from their properties. Since most houses had been destroyed by enemy artillery, they stayed in nearby villages that had suffered less damage. Every day they set out in their carts to work in the fields near the trenches. German cannon fire, which could reach Paris, located at fifty kilometers from the most advanced front line point, could shell that area much more easily. Besides, airplanes sometimes dropped bombs to terrorize the population, causing more psychological than destructive damage.

Nogueira and I were billeted in a farmhouse, together with thirteen civilians, women and children. More than half were relatives of the farm's owner who had escaped from Neuve-Chapelle, where the ruins of their houses now sheltered soldiers from both sides. Two women without family ties were being sheltered in exchange for helping with the farm work. They had lost their families and possessions. One of them fell in love with Nogueira.

The landlady, a certain Eveline Pinat, was a fiftyish miser who exploited both her relatives and the women in need of shelter. The *maire* had forced her to billet the Portuguese officers and, even though we were far more profitable than any other guest, she eyed us with suspicion.

It was virtually impossible to get decent living conditions in the house. The landlady gave us a little back room with hardly enough space for two small iron beds. Nogueira's orderly and Rato fixed the room as best they could; nonetheless, I missed the Rolins' house in Wismes and Madame Constance Gavroche's home in Enguinegatte. But Captain Rebelo said we should count our blessings for having a bed and a roof over our head right in the middle of the war zone. Millions of men were in a much worse situation in the trenches. It seemed to me that the closer we got to the inferno, comfort decreased and fear increased. In that place we were all cowards.

Our battalion would remain cantoned in l'Epinette from late July to late September, as a reserve of the Portuguese Expeditionary Corps. Thus, although our going to the front line was postponed and we did not have garrison or defense duties, we often went to the trenches for training and repair work, where we were shelled and attacked by assault troops.

On the last day in July, when we were at the training field in Pacaut, we heard that the so-called battle of Passchendaele had begun in a region north of our position. The English, with the biggest army ever seen, were about to try to break through enemy lines and determine the fate of the war. They advanced half a dozen kilometers, lost a hundred thousand men, and abandoned the living, stuck in the mud. In ordering the attack, Marshal Sir Douglas Haig had forgotten to look at the sky, thus missing what any peasant would have seen, namely that on the day set for the beginning of the offensive and on those that followed, it would rain cats and dogs, and consequently the conditions of the terrain in Flanders would be fatal for any army's advance.

The Pacaut training field also turned into a muddy bog, replicating in miniature what was happening at the front. Rain and mud notwithstanding, instruction went on. We spent those days drenched. At the command posts, with their dry feet on Persian rugs and carpets, the top brass imbibed cognac and gave orders by telephone. At the end of the day, soaked through, we would slosh our way back to the cantonment in our mud-caked boots. The men flopped down in the barns and some, too worn out to change their clothes, got sick. When the war was over many would go back home suffering from tuberculosis.

The girl who had fallen in love with Nogueira – or he with her, I can't remember which – was named Bathilde. She was one of the refugees from the destroyed village of Neuve-Chapelle. She had lost her parents, siblings, and fiancé. Our landlady knew her and took her in. She worked in the kitchen. She was probably around twenty-two years old and had a country girl's round, ruddy face. She kept her blond, thick hair in two braids that gave her a playful look. A Portuguese girl of the same station would have worn a headscarf, a thick shawl over her protruding breasts, and a black skirt dragging on the floor, so as not to arouse men's lust. Despite her misfortune, that girl was cheerful, enjoyed singing, and often exchanged jokes and pranks with us. Maybe that was why Nogueira fell in love with her.

We slept in the little room Madame Pinat had given us, but I was alone most nights. Shortly after the living room clock struck twelve, Nogueira would slip into the girl's little room, next to the kitchen, and stay there until a little before dawn. Since she was first to get up to put the kettle on the fire, they ran little danger of being caught by the landlady, who slept on the floor above and only came downstairs when the sun was high in the sky. She took her time saying her morning prayers for the end of the war and for the souls of three generations of dead relatives. Her litany worked like an early alarm clock for me and surely also for the two lovebirds.

One night, when we were both in bed and Nogueira was waiting to go to Mademoiselle Bathilde's room, I commented that, if he did not put an end to that affair, he might become a father. It was one thing to visit a whore, pay her, and be free of any obligations, and quite another to frequent the bed of a single young woman from a good family and have to assume paternity if things went wrong. It would be very hard for him to shake that off. He would have Madame Pinar after him, as well as the village *maire*, our Major and, in all likelihood, the General. The affair might turn into a diplomatic case, with marriage as the only solution. Nogueira laughed it off and said, "Don't worry, Vasques. We're careful."

"Careful? I wonder if you can be careful enough to avoid what I've just told you."

"What do you know about that?"

"I know what I see."

"We're talking past each other. I guess you didn't quite get what I meant by careful."

"If you could clarify it..."

"You don't mean you want me to explain it to you!"

"You're beginning to get on my nerves. Is there some secret I don't get?"

"It looks that way."

"Well then, shoot."

He was lying on his back and turned to me, winked, and said, "When I came over, I knew what every man more or less knows about life."

"About life?" I said.

"About sex, damn it!"

"All right, you could have said so. Go on."

"For me, sex was – how can I put it – sticking my prick in, pumping it until the woman started calling her mother, and coming. But Bathilde, who is no whore, since she even used to have a fiancé, has shown me that sex is a lot more than that. Sex is an art. The art of pleasure."

"*Ars Amantis.*"

"Airs what?"

"That's the title of a book by Ovid on the art of loving."

"Did you meet that Avid?"

"Ovid. No, I didn't. He was a Latin poet who died more than a thousand nine hundred years ago."

"That's a heck of a long time. I can't believe they talked about sex when that fellow was alive."

"They not only talked, they also practiced it. The Romans knew how to enjoy it, without prejudices and with no fear of going to hell."

"Oh well. They were pagans."

"You don't have to be a pagan to practice the best sex possible. Take your French girl. She must go to mass every Sunday, and nevertheless... But you haven't yet explained what you do to avoid becoming a father."

"It's very simple. She says I can do anything I want, except come inside her cunt."

"But then you don't finish off."

"It depends on how you look at it. I pull it out before I come. If I get too excited, then she tells me to pull it out. And then she takes care of me."

"How so?"

"She grabs my prick and sucks it until I come."

I was flabbergasted. Obviously, reading a few passages of *Ars Amantis* in Latin on the sly at school had not helped me much. I still had a lot to learn. Maybe that technique, if implemented in Portugal, might drastically reduce the birth rate among the poor. But I cannot see how that could be done, given our people's moral prejudices and the Church's thought control.

Nogueira's affair with Bathilde lasted until September, when our battalion left for the front line for good. He even went back to visit her twice more, but the idyll was over. There were other officers billeted at Madame Eveline Piñata's home, and the two lovebirds could no longer get together without arousing suspicion. The second time she did not show up, and Nogueira was rather annoyed, as he had scrambled to get someone to loan him a horse. Then he found out she was involved with a sergeant from another battalion. He spent the remainder of the war nursing a broken heart and badmouthing French women, a bunch of whores who went to bed with the first man that came their way.

Nevertheless, young women like Bathilde, who were favored by the sergeants and some officers, were not as frivolous as Nogueira made them out to be. It is true, however, they often competed with the professional prostitutes who set up shop in the back room of the *estaminets* and were sought after by the soldiers.

We did not rest in l'Epinette for very long. In early August our company marched to Neuve-Chapelle to do some trench repair work. During the night the Boche shelled the communication trenches, the parapets, the chevaux-de-frise and the shelters, and during the day we shoveled it all back into place. Shoveling and shelling, shelling and shoveling. It was hard, dirty work. In the preceding weeks the trenches had been flooded by the heavy rain and now had to be drained with pumps borrowed from the English. In the front line, the water was drained straight into no man's land. The men draped the hose over the parapet and pumped away at the bottom of the trench. Through the periscope we could see the Boche were doing the same. Rain was for everybody, and no man's land was like a big whore into which both sides relieved themselves.

In some places in the trenches the duckboard was in bad shape due to the dampness, the poor quality of the wood, the constant use, and the shellings. Often a plank gave way under a man's weight, leaving him stuck in the mud up to his knees. Freeing him was hard, since two men were needed to pull him out, and frequently all three ended up trapped and had to be pulled out by half a dozen men using a rope. Things would get rough when the Boche, sensing the commotion at a certain point, launched a mortar barrage. Then the only thing to do was to dive into the mud to avoid the shell fragments whizzing all over. That happened to me once right after a plank broke underneath me. Rato and Apúlia were trying to pull me out when we heard the whistle of a mortar shell. I barked an order and they threw themselves flat onto the mud. When the danger was over, and with the help of other soldiers, we managed to get out, duly camouflaged with mud. As he wiped off his eyes with his fingertips, Rato commented, "This mud smells like shit, sir. Someone must have crapped here."

"You're right. The crappers are the politicians, and the war is their shit."

"Excuse me, sir, but this shit is for real," he said, shaking off his hands and splattering his comrades, who complained aloud. "Some guys don't know where the latrine is," Apúlia said, wiping mud off his nose.

215

Five days later we returned to l'Epinette, filthy and worn out, the soldiers from shoveling dirt and pumping water, the officers and sergeants from giving orders. Some may say there is no comparison between giving orders and pumping water or shoveling dirt. And it is true. There is no comparison between the two jobs. But I am not the one who made this world of masters and servants, generals and colonels, colonels and majors, majors and captains, captains and first lieutenants, first lieutenants and second lieutenants, second lieutenants and sergeants, sergeants and corporals, corporals and privates. My job, I was told, was to take orders and have them carried out, not to carry them out myself. If the order was to have a parapet repaired, my duty was to lead my men to the parapet and make sure that they, and not I, repaired it according to regulations. A shovel was not part of an officer's kit. It would have been considered a serious offense if I had grabbed a shovel and started digging side by side with my soldiers. An officer's digging was of another kind. Almost every officer dreamed of digging a niche for himself in the rear, or, with a little bit of luck, in Portugal, out of reach of the big guns.

None of this means that I, being an officer, did not get tired, or that it was easy for me to watch the soldiers working hard. How many times did I have to hide my fatigue to set a good example! The fact is that after a day's work, the thirty soldiers under my orders were free to mind their own business. As the officer responsible for them, I had to turn my attention to the piles of forms to be read and filled out, which came from the most unexpected departments of the Battalion, the Brigade, the Division, and General Headquarters. There were service orders, memos, inquiries about equipment checks, requisitions to be done over and filed again because they had not been filled out according to regulations, reports to be written, and piles of letters – in illegible scrawling, fanciful spelling, and convoluted syntax – to be censored. Only someone unfamiliar with the obsession with paperwork – endemic to the Portuguese

Expeditionary Corps and slowing everything down to a snail's pace – would be surprised at what happened on April 9, 1918. The republican toadies, who have scribbled and babbled so much nonsense about the La Lys disaster, have unjustly blamed the Portuguese soldiers for being poorly trained or for running away like cowards instead of facing the enemy. But the Portuguese soldiers were in no way inferior to others fighting on the Western front. Quite to the contrary, their preparation was apparent in the intensity and variety of military training each man had received.

I am completely convinced that the main cause of the disaster, besides the fact that the troops were worn out and in urgent need of being relieved at the front, was the High Command's obsession with paperwork. In the trenches I lived between two fronts: the Boche and the bureaucracy. The former only troubled us sporadically, whereas the latter demanded a mountaineer's endurance and an angler's patience to avoid perishing in a flood of paper.

XIX

I have not written about the present for quite some time now. I take refuge in the past, not only to exorcize my demons, but also because the present holds no pleasure for me. Twenty years after the Great War, Europe is now getting ready for another conflict. The sanctions the Allies put on Germany were for naught. Or if they had any use at all, it was to put us in our current situation: a Germany eager for revenge, armed to the teeth, and blindly following a crazy tiger. Salazar, as meek as a priest, spends his time stroking Hitler, while reinforcing our old ties with the English. This time I have no fear we will make the same mistake the republican government made in 1916, taken in by the rhetoric of Afonso Costa and his minions, who did everything they possibly could to make Germany declare war on Portugal. Salazar is too smart to fall into that trap. I firmly believe he is not, like Afonso Costa and his cronies, driven by political ambition or money to be deposited in Swiss bank accounts in order to live like a pasha after the war ends.

It is unbelievable how a man like Salazar has got as far as he has with no personal ambition whatsoever. He made it to the top without doing anything to get there. They say that as soon as Portugal gets straightened out, he will quit his position as Prime Minister and go back to his professorship at Coimbra. But with all the clouds gathering on the horizon, I doubt that will happen any time too soon. And if Portugal intends to survive a possible war, it might not be so bad to have Professor Salazar at the helm.

I am not here to defend him. I have been very disappointed in his style of governing. He has an iron fist and is intransigent in dealing with the opposition and with his critics, both of which are legitimate and healthy in a democracy. The truth is, he put an end to the freeloading caused by the republican leaders' being more concerned with their own welfare than with the country's. But that is not enough to make Portugal a country of prosperity, emancipation, fraternity, and liberty. To hell with equality. We are all born different and we will never be equal. Anyone who says otherwise is either a demagogue or a fool. I do not say this to justify my position in society, and much less to defend my genteel background as a country squire with slight traces of blue blood – or so say the parchments – from the Goths, those distant relatives of the Boche. Real nobility is not inherited, it is earned, and it is found in the strength required to defend truth and justice. I may have inherited my father's ring bearing our family's coat of arms, this estate, this mansion, and our family names. But I would be no better than a scoundrel if I were dishonest, if I were to limit the freedom of my fellow man – whether or not he be a simple day worker – if I were not just, if I were unable to control my passions, my fears, and my anger.

I am forty-four years old and I believe that, although I am not a scoundrel, I have not been a just man. I am not aiming for sainthood. I do not go to church regularly and my faith wavers aimlessly. Saints confuse me. Sainthood is a kind of insanity, a kind of incurable schizophrenia. Generally speaking, I do not think founders of religions are very nice people. Mussolini, Lenin, Hitler, and Franco are the religious founders of our century – godless, but with the same fanaticism and the same intolerance. And these new religions, I fear, will be far bloodier than any that have been fighting each other in the name of faith for the last 1900 years.

Father Ruas considers me a pagan, an apostate, a heretic, an impenitent, and all kinds of other ugly names that would have seen me tossed to the flames when the Inquisition reigned. Now someone else rules and, if there are no flames, there are the political police, suspicious of everyone who makes any move away from mediocrity, behaves in any unusual manner, or makes less than enthusiastic remarks about the so-called national reconstruction. Father Ruas is not a bad person and I usually invite him in for a luncheon with everyone else in the local Easter procession. Aninhas enjoys it and so does the maid. The children love having all those people over. And ever since he joined the seminary, Pedro almost always participates in the procession. Father Ruas has put him in charge of collecting alms for Saint Peter. The gravedigger used to carry the alms bag, but since the bag seemed to contain a steadily decreasing amount from year to year, Father Ruas, suspecting the gravedigger of filching, took away the privilege and bestowed it on my son. In fact, the bag has gotten heavier by the end of the parade, which seems to confirm Father Ruas's suspicions regarding the gravedigger.

Pedro is very proud of himself, all dressed up in the white surplice, walking alongside Father Ruas behind the cross and the bell ringer. He takes the saving of souls very much to heart, and has told me that, when he is ordained, he is going to save mine. I laugh and ask him precisely how he plans to do that.

"With a lot of prayer," he says. And also, he adds, with a lot of conversation. For the time being, he acknowledges he does not have the rhetorical expertise to counter my arguments. But when he studies philosophy and theology, he will turn my point of view upside down and convince me of the true road to follow, with the grace of God.

My son's vocation is strange. I did nothing to encourage it. I actually think he will eventually come to the conclusion there are other paths to be taken. I do not look forward to having a son who pays more credence to priests than to his own father's advice. Nonetheless, my son Pedro is a wise young man. What can a skeptic like me have to say to him?

To go back to Professor Salazar. In 1919 he was Professor of Political Economy and Finance at Coimbra. He made it possible for me to take the special examination in September. When I arrived at Coimbra by train after a stopover in Oporto to see Aninhas, I thought I would be the only one taking the exam. There were thirty more classmates in the room, all of them war veterans, except for a few chronic numskulls, trying once again to pass without having cracked open a reader. At the time, professors would traditionally pass two or three of them so the university system would not get clogged, even if they knew nothing at all about the topic. It was like some sort of unofficial amnesty. All the students had to do was to show up at the exam, fill in their name and sit through the regulation time period, pretending to write. The professor would give them a seven or an eight, they would proceed to the oral exam, where they would make a few bogus comments and they would pass with a ten. The problem was that almost everyone in that exam was in the same situation, not because they were numskulls, but because they had been forced to interrupt their studies to fight for their country, and very few of us knew much about the reader's contents. We had had neither the time, nor the inclination, nor the willingness to study seriously. After returning from war, the first thing you want to do is to live. *Primum vivere, deinde philosophare.*[45]

To everyone's – or almost everyone's – satisfaction, Professor Oliveira Salazar gave us a high enough grade in the written exam to pass on to the orals. The grades came out the next day, which was very unusual. The man must have spent the entire night correcting the exams. I got a nine – not one of the worst in the group, perhaps because I had managed to study a thing or two. The only students excused from the orals were the numskulls, whose grades were below seven. They would have to try for the amnesty the following year, when there would be fewer candidates.

The oral exam was set for three days later. It started at nine o'clock and they called my name at around eleven. I sat down opposite the examiner's desk, which stood on a dais. Professor Salazar was accompanied by an assistant who called out the names, jotted down the whispered grades, and then calculated the average. Every once in a while he would whisper some additional information about a student. The professor was the Grand Inquisitor. He showed no signs of recognizing me, perhaps to look more formal in front of the other students. He asked me if I had prepared some topic on Political Economy that I would like to talk about. I told him I had prepared myself to talk about taxation.

"And what do you have to say about it, sir?"

I parroted whatever I remembered from the reader, stressing a few concepts I had memorized. He seemed relatively satisfied and, when I was about to stand up, he said he would like to speak to me after the exam.

I sat in the back of the room, observing the other students' exams. The whole thing really got on my nerves. It all seemed so childish. Maybe the war had hardened me too much. The academic procedures all looked like child's play compared to the tragedy of killing and dying. I was so fed up with the whole thing that I finally left the room. I was not going to wait for the professor. If he wanted to flunk me, I could not have cared less. I decided to head for Oporto immediately, where Aninhas would be waiting for me. At that moment, she was the most important thing in my life. Nevertheless, I doubted he would fail me. I had got a nine on the written exam and I had not said anything nonsensical in the oral. It would have been unfair to flunk me. And the professor was not known for being unfair. He used to boast in class that he never had been.

It was lunchtime and I decided to eat at Joaquina Cardosa's tavern, still not crowded because most students were on vacation. While I deboned my mackerel, I thought about what had happened in Oporto at the Gouveias', before I caught the train to Coimbra.

When Aninhas got back from the movies, she had been quite surprised to see me chatting animatedly with her mother. She would never have expected to find me there. She acted as if there had been no misunderstanding between the two of us and seemed happy to see me. Since it was almost time for me to go back to the railway station, she offered to accompany me.

We would be able to talk in privacy. Once on the street, she suggested we walk, since the station was not far off. We walked side by side along the promenade by the riverbank toward the Dom Luís bridge, lit by the setting sun. It was a very pleasant afternoon and, maybe for the first time since returning from Flanders, I felt at peace with myself and with everyone else. At one point, I stopped to look at the rabelo boats, loaded with barrels, probably still empty, moored near the warehouses on the Gaia bank.[46] It was nearly time to harvest the grapes and the companies were sending their boats upriver with the empty barrels to be filled with young wine. I leaned on the stone wall next to the river and felt Aninhas put her hand over mine. I looked at her. She smiled at me, I smiled back and everything between the two of us was settled without a word spoken. To this day, we have never once referred to the dandy doctor. At the station, before boarding the train, I embraced her. She held me close and, before letting me go, made me promise to never again doubt her love.

"When you come back from Coimbra, stop by Oporto. We can spend the day together."

"I don't know how long I'll be there."

"Then write me."

"I'll most likely get here before the letter."

I kissed her hand and boarded the train. I sat in the middle of the car, facing backwards, next to a window. Aninhas stayed near the tracks, smiling at me until the train headed into a tunnel. That was when I realized she was indeed the same girl I had seen in Campanhã two years before, on the trip from Braga to Lisbon on the way to the war. She was wearing the same pink dress and a hat with a green ribbon.

Once, when I brought it up, she told me she had gone to see off her cousin, who was an officer in one of the regiments from Braga and was headed for Flanders. She did not remember me, nor that we had looked at each other and she had smiled. She remembered the soldiers who filled up the cars. To her, they all looked alike, with their grey caps and uniforms, their mustaches and their sad expressions.

"But I don't have a mustache, and I didn't back then, either," I countered.

"If I really did look at you and smiled, then that must have been the reason. I don't like men with a mustache. All that hair on their lip, isn't it bothersome?"

I took advantage of my days in Coimbra to prepare for the oral examination and to find a place to live the upcoming term. My parents did not like me to live in student boarding houses, mainly filled with anti-monarchists, leftist extremists, anarchists, or sympathizers of secret society. In general, the republicans were the arrogant loafers that have put this country in the situation it is in today. From the time of the assassination of the King and the Prince Royal, through the 1910 coup d'état, including all of the revolutions and counter-revolutions that beleaguered long-suffering Portugal until 1926, when General Gomes da Costa finally decided to put an end to the mayhem and the republican tricks and pranks by setting up a dictatorship.

Professor Salazar, who has been persecuting the republicans, actually owes them his position. As I have mentioned, if it had not been for the republican upheaval and the ensuing chaos, there would never have been the march on Lisbon lead by General Gomes da Costa, who then handed over the reins of this wild horse of a country to Professor Salazar. Republicans opposed to Salazar claim his regime was born from an illegal coup, that of 1926. Well, how about the October 5, 1910 coup, was it legitimate? All revolutions are illegitimate in relation to current law. But without revolutions, we might still be paying tribute to the King of León.[47]

I kept pretty much to myself those days in Coimbra. My former classmates had already graduated and were practicing law all over Portugal. And those who had been mobilized like me were probably resting from the hardship of the war. Coimbra in September, in spite of the examinations, is a no-man's land and the yellowing leaves on the poplars lend it an air of having been deserted.

In my search for rooms, I called on a former landlady, an illiterate elderly woman who talked like a lawyer and owned two floors in a dilapidated building. Without going overboard, which was not her way, she seemed glad to see me alive and well, although thinner. She told me that unfortunately she could not rent me a room. They were all reserved. If I had spoken in June, there still would have been time. As things stood, I would have to make some other arrangements.

I walked all through the streets and alleys surrounding the university in hopes of finding a room available. On the evening prior to the examination, I had dinner at a Joaquina Cardosa's tavern and asked her if by any chance she knew of someone who had rooms available. Dona Joaquina said a good friend had asked if she knew of any decent student looking for rooms. Dona Joaquina's friend was a widow whose husband had been killed by poison gas in Flanders, and she needed to rent out one of the rooms in her house to make ends meet. But she didn't want to rent to just anyone. She knew students were usually noisy, stayed out late, and generally misbehaved. Nonetheless, Dona Joaquina went on to explain, since she knew I was a good student and, above all, a gentleman, she'd be more than happy to give me her good friend's address so I could see the room. I'd be very comfortable there. It was a fine family and I'd feel at home.

She gave me a scrap of paper where I took down her good friend's name and address. I thanked her and served myself from the platter of mackerel tails and rice mixed with collard greens she set down before me. After dinner I walked to her friend's house, pulled the bell wire, and a woman, about thirty years old, appeared at the window. I asked if that was where Dona Maria das Dores lived. Yes it was, and I was speaking to her. I told her Dona Joaquina Cardosa had sent me there, since I was looking for a room to rent. She looked me over, sizing me up, and told me to come in. She came to the stairs as I reached the top, and she looked me over again, like an officer inspecting a soldier's uniform on parade and, having found nothing wrong, she invited me in to show me the room and discuss the rates.

The room, with a view to the Mondego river, seemed excellent. There was a wrought iron bed with a white linen bedspread that gave it a homey atmosphere. I let her know I liked it. The only thing remaining was to find out if I would also like the price. She did not want to tell me right away. Instead, she guided me through the areas I would be sharing with the family, including a room that served for living and dining, a kitchen, and the water-closet. I found out, much to my consternation, that I would have to bathe in my room using a wash-bowl. At that time bathtubs and showers were, if not unheard of, at least unusual in most Portuguese households, and considered frivolous, used by people of questionable morals.

I indicated I was slightly disappointed there was no bathtub or shower in the house. I thought that might prevent her from charging an exorbitant price. Back in the living room, we sat in armchairs and discussed the particulars. She rambled on about her economic hardship since her husband's death, a sergeant of sappers in Flanders, and therefore my former comrade, and finally stated a price that I found affordable.

If I wanted to eat at the house, instead of having to go out to eat lousy food in any old restaurant, at the risk of getting sick, she would be happy to cook for me. I weighed her suggestion, taking all my expenses into consideration, and realized it was worthwhile. Besides, my mother would be pleased to know I was taking my meals in a household. Not to mention I would probably spend less money in the long run.

"Even at my best friend's restaurant," Dona Maria das Dores explained, "I know what they cook. They use all the cheapest ingredients. And everything cheap is either bad or rotten. If the government knew what goes on inside those kitchens, they'd shut down most of the restaurants in Coimbra. Mark my words, sir. They're ruining our students' health."

I told her that, no matter how bad that food was, it couldn't be any worse than what we'd eaten in Flanders during the war.

"So you were in the war, sir? My dear husband, poor soul, was there too. He was a sergeant. He was gassed and never came back."

She took a handkerchief out of the sleeve of her dress and blew her nose. I offered my condolences and made a brief comment on the horrors of trench warfare. She confessed she had never recovered, not since she had learned of her husband's death. She had two children who were spending a few days with their grandparents outside of Coimbra, near Condeixa. She got no help from the government and she had to make do.

I decided to pay the October rent in advance. She did not want to accept it, saying she trusted me, but just to make sure, I left the money on the table. I did not want to get there in October and find out the room had been rented to someone else. With those Coimbra people, you could never be too sure.

Once we had ironed out the details, she saw me to the door with a big smile that I remember well. There was something sort of artificial about it, not that I mean to criticize, for everyone tends to smile at people they have just barely met, not just to be polite but also because they are needy. I went away feeling sorry for the woman.

The next day after the oral exam, while I was lunching on cod fritters at the tavern, Dona Joaquina Cardosa asked if I had seen her friend about the room. I told her I had, and that we had worked out an arrangement.

"Well, that's very good. You'll see, sir, you won't regret it. My friend is a fine woman and she'll treat you like a king."

"There's no need for that, Dona Joaquina. Besides, the monarchy is over and done with."

"We don't know that for certain. Just yesterday I overheard two customers saying the restoration is upon us."

I did not answer. There were people who believed in King Sebastião's return.[48]

Having eaten the cod fritters, I went back to the boarding house to pick up my travel bag. As I walked toward the railway station, an automobile pulled up next to me and someone called me from inside, "Mr. Vasques, if you don't mind, sir."

Stopping, I recognized Professor Oliveira Salazar sitting next to his assistant, who was driving. I approached, somewhat uncomfortable at the chance meeting. I had not been very polite.

"What happened to you?" Professor Salazar asked.

I decided to make up an excuse, "Unfortunately, the oral examination took longer than I was expecting and I had to leave. Please excuse me, Professor, but I can't miss the train back to Oporto."

"And what about your grade? Didn't you want to know what you got?"

"Yes, of course, I did, but I ran out of time. And now, please excuse me, Professor. I had no intention of being rude. It's just that, I really cannot miss the train..."

"Get in, we'll drop you off at the station."

I got into the back seat and the assistant headed off towards the station.

"So, what's so urgent in Oporto?" the Professor asked, turning to look at me.

I hesitated. What could I tell him? That I had an uncle about to die? I decided to tell him the truth, "It's my fiancée. She's waiting for me."

"That's a good reason. But don't get too carried away. There are more important things."

I grimaced in disagreement and he added, "Your career, for example. Mr. Vasques, are you or are you not planning on becoming a successful lawyer?"

"I've been thinking about that. For the time being, I

plan on graduating, more to please my parents than for myself. Then we'll see."

"You're not an ambitious man, Mr. Vasques."

"Once you've lived through the war, Professor, ambition falls by the wayside."

"You didn't die, young man! You have your whole future ahead of you."

He paused, turned back around to face forward, and continued, "When I spoke to you in July, I thought you would be a good candidate for the Portuguese Catholic Center. I was going to invite you today."

"I appreciate your having thought of me, Professor, but I cannot accept. I am not a believer."

"What nonsense. You're baptized, aren't you?"

"Yes, but..."

"You had your first Communion and you went through Confirmation?"

"Yes."

"So, you are a believer."

"No, I'm not, Professor. After the war, sir, or maybe during the war, my faith was seriously shaken."

"That's a phase. I went through it too. I've had my doubts, just like Saint Thomas and Saint Augustine. You'll see that in one or two years from now, you'll come back to the bosom of the Church with your heart and soul. Only the Church can save us. I had a crisis of faith before I did my doctorate. But thankfully I came to the conclusion that God is not negotiable. To doubt is to put our very existence on the line, like Descartes did with his methodic doubt."

I decided not to argue with Professor Salazar. It was not worth it. Besides, perhaps he was right.

"Well, then, do you accept?" he insisted. "Think about it, it could be good for your future. As a member of the Center, you'd have the chance to do something for your country, which has suffered so much at the hands of incompetent opportunists."

"Does the Catholic Center have a political agenda, Professor?" I asked.

"No one involved with the Center has political aims, if that's what you want to know. The goal is to protect and defend Catholic values and the Christian roots of our civilization."

"I don't know, Professor. Next year, if all goes well, I'll graduate and go back up north. I'm through with fighting."

"You're mistaken, Mr. Vasques. War is the natural state of man. Man is in constant conflict with others and with himself. As a future lawyer, you'll be in conflict with truth and with lies, with justice and injustice."

His assistant parked the automobile at the station entrance and I readied myself to get out.

"Think about what I've told you and write me in a few days. I'd like to be able to count on you when classes begin. The Center needs people like you, with experience in the trenches and who cannot abide the way things stand right now in Portugal."

I thanked him for the ride, grabbed my bag and got out.

"Enjoy the rest of your vacation," the Professor said as I closed the door behind me. Then he added, "You didn't ask me what you got on your oral examination."

""I forgot, Professor, but if you don't mind telling me, sir, it would certainly be a relief."

"You got an eighteen. Take care and don't forget what I told you."

The automobile took off and I went to buy my ticket to Oporto. While I sat on the train, I mulled over the eighteen and wondered whether it was on account of my knowledge of Political Economy, or if it had been a prodigal gesture on the part of Professor Oliveira Salazar, known in Coimbra for being miserly when it came to grading and to giving handouts to the blind lingering around the Old Cathedral Square.

XX

Our orders to move on to Sailly-sur-la-Lys arrived in mid-August 1917. We had been assigned six days' training in the Boutillerie subsector, which belonged to Fleurbaix. Since nothing serious had happened up to that point, the men carried out their duties in a relatively relaxed mood, keeping watch on no man's land, patrolling the trenches, cleaning up and doing repairs, playing cards, eating, and sleeping. Rato took advantage of every free moment to play cards for money and, after cleaning his comrades out, he proceeded to take their cigarettes, combat rations, *cartes-lettres,* and devotional or personal objects.

At seven in the evening on our third day in the front line, after we had dined on English fare, enjoyed by gluttons and scorned by those with a sensitive stomach – corned beef, crackers, and marmalade – the Boche started bombarding our subsector. The shelling went on until we started thinking we would all die in that place. Since the telephone lines had been destroyed, Battalion Headquarters started sending runners to the companies, with orders for us to be on the alert because an enemy raid was likely. I was in our shelter with Captain Rebelo and Nogueira when a runner delivered our written orders. The Captain burst out laughing.

"Is it possible those blockheads at Headquarters haven't figured out there's an attack going on?"

"Maybe they'll only notice it when a shell lands on them," said Nogueira.

At midnight sharp – the Boche were like clockwork when it came to timing – the soldiers on watch on the parapet noticed something moving in no man's land. They sounded the alarm, our light machine guns fired for about ten minutes, and then there was silence. The attackers had either retreated or died. The general opinion was that they had come to test us, and then withdrew. In spite of the intensity of the bombardment, our casualties amounted to only a few light wounds caused by shell fragments, plus a lot of fouled trouser seats. At morning stand-to, some men stank as if they had fallen into a latrine, and I had to order them to wash themselves in a water-filled shell hole nearby.

Though memorable, the first raid was not exactly unexpected. Unlike our voyage from Lisbon to Brest, when the men had panicked in a storm, during that first raid they remained relatively calm and did not leave their positions. They endured it in silence and exorcized fear as best they could, either praying to their favorite saints or to the souls of their deceased relatives, or fouling their trousers. And those who did the latter were not necessarily the most cowardly. It was the kind of thing that could happen to anyone. Sergeant Rosado was one of those who at least got his pants wet. There were no such incidents among the officers. That does not mean we were not, at least figuratively, scared shitless. However, each one of us handled it as discreetly as possible. The Captain, who commanded the company and set an example for the rest, stayed in the shelter, nipping on a bottle of bagaço and telling jokes about the politicians, those opportunists who were filling their pockets at the expense of the poor devils who got themselves killed in the trenches. Coutinho, stretched on a cot, wearing his helmet just in case a splinter from the ceiling might ruin his hair – smoothed daily with a generous handful of pomade – listened to the Captain's jokes while mentally saying his rosary, counting off the Hail Marys on his fingers. The Captain did not notice, or he would have chewed him out, all the more so because Coutinho enjoyed passing himself off as an anticlerical atheist.

Nogueira and I could not stand being in the shelter, which we considered more dangerous than the open air, and so while the bombardment lasted we went around inspecting the posts. Every time I felt a mortar shell coming, I threw myself down on the duckboard, my chin glued to the planks. Rato, saying he did not wish to leave me alone, although I suspected it was the other way around, stuck to me as long as the shelling lasted.

"We're all going to die here today, sir!" he said, crouching as a shell whistled by and burst on the second line.

"That won't happen," I said, trying to calm him down. This is just the beginning of the war for us. It's going to last, Rato, and we'd better get used to it. The war's likely to get a lot worse than this."

"If I get out of this alive, I'll go to Fátima."

"To Fátima?" I asked, not understanding what he meant.

"To the place where the Virgin appeared."

"Do you really think she appeared?"

"I truly believe she did, sir. That's what they're saying. The wife, when she sends me letters, she talks about nothing else. They say the Virgin appeared to three shepherd children somewhere in Leiria, and told them we ought to repent for our sins, pray the rosary, and do penance."

"And you don't think we're doing enough penance as it is?"

Before he could reply, a shell burst a few meters from where we were, momentarily deafening us and splattering us with mud.

Two days later the Boche started bombarding our sub-sector again. Exactly two hours after that, the cannon fire and the shelling stopped, and our first line was attacked by assault troops. Our peasant soldiers defended themselves as best they could and succeeded in repelling the enemy. Upon hearing the alarm whispered down the line defended by our company, all the officers and sergeants rushed out of their shelters and joined the soldiers. Taking advantage of the lighting from Very flares being fired at regular intervals, we emptied our weapons into no man's land, even without glimpsing a single target.

After the shooting, we found out the company on our right, which had taken the brunt of the attack, had captured three Boche soldiers. I saw them the next morning, surrounded by our gawking men. The three were sitting, smoking very calmly. They had blue eyes, almost angel-like, and the skin on their faces was ruddy from having spent too much time in the sun. One of them seemed much younger than the others. I asked them their names in French, but they did not seem to understand. They must have been privates, as they had no insignia of rank. If we wanted to find out something useful about the enemy, those three would not likely be of much help.

Rato saw them too, and as we walked back to our shelter, he commented, "So that's what the Boche look like! I thought they looked different."

"What did you think they looked like?"

"I don't know. Maybe more threatening. After all, sir, those fellows are almost like us."

That same morning we checked the casualties and damages. On our side there were ten dead and twenty-two wounded, a few seriously. As to the enemy, we found no casualties in our trench, nor nearby. We did find blood and footprints that were probably Boche, and which the Captain, in his report, suggested were an indication that the enemy had suffered heavy casualties. I thought that, according to the law of probabilities, the thousands of rounds we had fired into no man's land might have hit someone. But if there were casualties, they certainly were not left behind.

What was certain was that the enemy had managed to penetrate our lines and inflict casualties. How that had been possible was something we ought to determine to make sure it would not happen again. How they had been able to approach the parapet, cut the barbed wire, jump over the chevaux-de-frise, penetrate our trench, massacre ten men and wound another twenty-two, without leaving behind a single wounded or dead soldier, after we had blasted the whole area in front of us, was definitely food for thought.

Rato could not figure out how they had approached

without being noticed. I made a couple of guesses, "Either they're better than we are and have more experience in making war, or we were asleep on duty and this is the result of our carelessness."

"Maybe it's both, sir."

"In that case, if we're not careful, we'll all die here. They are testing us and I suspect they already know what's going on. I'm quite sure we haven't seen the end of it."

"Do you think they're going to attack again, sir?"

"How many times have they attacked us?"

"Twice."

"The first time they were just reconnoitering. The second, they were testing us. The third, they'll break through and wipe us out."

"Well, sir, since we've arrived in France, the men have lost about five kilos each. If the Boche wait too long, by the time they get back they'll find a pile of skeletons instead of Portuguese flesh."

While we talked, shelling started again, this time with heavy mortars. I saw it was twenty-four minutes past ten in the morning and thought my watch was probably slow in relation to the enemy's. Anyway, if night shellings are appalling because you do not know exactly where the danger is coming from and where to take cover, during the day the smoke, the shell fragments and the destruction all around us can cause nearly unbearable despair.

During this third bombardment a shell fragment cut off the right hand of a second lieutenant from the second company. I saw the poor wretch being carried away by stretcher bearers toward the first aid post, his stump wrapped up in a bloody rag. For him the war was over. And if he did not recover from the mutilation, the cemetery awaited him, not far away, already filled with hundreds of Portuguese crosses, even though we had barely joined the war.

At lunchtime the mortars ceased firing and Rato managed

to bring me an aluminum can with hot soup. I could not eat and said he could have it. I did not have to say it twice before he sat down on two sand bags by the entrance of the shelter, the can on his knees and a soup spoon in hand. The sky might come down in a firestorm and set the world ablaze, but Rato would never lose his appetite. I envied him.

That night the Boche attacked again. They attacked one of the posts, but since we had doubled the sentries, the alarm was sounded at once, the men came to the parapet and fired at will. The Very lights we fired right away made it possible to locate some targets. But when the Boche saw the light and felt the bullets cracking past their ears and the hand grenades going off, they withdrew. We spent more ammunition that night than in the entire month following. We were angry over our casualties.

"These *Freets* are a bunch of cowards," Rato said, re-loading his Lee-Enfield, chewing up the word *Fritz*, another nickname for German soldiers.

That was the last night we spent in the trenches, since the next day we were relieved by an English battalion, although, due to a delay, they only arrived at ten in the evening. Our state of mind contrasted with the silence of the weapons. All we wanted was to be as far from that place as possible. Let that be called fear, or survival instinct. During those days under real fire, when I might have been one of the dead or wounded, I understood why so many men would do anything to avoid getting into a trench, or to get out of it. Trying to find a way out of the war – even though it was much criticized – was on every man's mind, from the lowest private to the Major commanding our battalion. What were we doing there? What ideals guided us? In whose name were we fighting? To defend what? There was no answer to these questions, in spite of the propaganda sent to us by the republican paper-pushing bureaucrats. Never having been in the front line, they tried hard to convince us that we were defending Portugal's interests, when in fact we were fighting for the usurpers who had staged the 1910 rebellion, supposedly for the people or in its name.

Having been relieved by the English battalion, we withdrew to Sailly-sur-la-Lys, where we bivouacked among the ruins. A day later, while we were preparing to go to the cantonment at l'Epinette for a few days' rest, we were ordered to fall in. General Simas Machado, who commanded the 2nd Division, had come from Headquarters, very far from the combat zone, to review the battalion and congratulate us. We formed up along the road and the General reviewed the men, one by one. After six days in the trenches we looked our worst, and the heat made our uniforms stink like a gutter. The review went slowly and the soldiers' faces showed they were fed up, and all they wanted was to see the General leave, so they could stand at ease.

But the General greeted each officer personally and made a speech praising the battalion's good performance against enemy attacks. It must have been a beautiful speech, unfortunately heard only by those who were about five meters from him. The soldiers, at attention and fully kitted, had to put up with that rigmarole without benefiting from it. Dark clouds were gathering overhead and we realized that if the General did not shut up soon, the rain would catch us right there, which it did a little later, on the road to l'Epinette, where we arrived, drenched, after nightfall.

I must acknowledge that our first stay in the front line was rather lively, not at all boring. Between the dead and the wounded, our battalion lost the equivalent of a platoon. In that war, that was no more than a drop of mud.

We spent almost the entire month of September at the l'Epinette cantonment. We kept busy training in trench defense – what training we had gone through had clearly proved insufficient – and sometimes we went to Neuve-Chapelle to repair and rebuild trenches. On such occasions the companies left at dawn and came back in the afternoon.

Even though it rained often, the temperature was still

mild and, after our baptism by fire, the weeks spent in l'Epinette afforded us some rest. We put on some weight and regained some color. A few of the lightly wounded came back from the field hospitals and were enthusiastically welcomed by their comrades. But they were not particularly happy with such merrymaking. They had thought their wounds would be their marching orders home. However, since the doctors thought otherwise, there they were, back on duty to defy death again.

In early September, I received a *carte-lettre* from Madame Constance Gavroche, complaining I had not kept my promise to visit them. They missed me and Rato. Their doors were always open to us. We could stay in their home as long as we wished. At present they had nobody billeted with them.

I decided to accept the invitation. I needed to leave that place for a few days, to get away from the rumble of guns, the mud, and the latrine stench. I went to see Captain Rabelo and requested a five-day leave. He watched me with the sarcastic grin he always had for his subordinates and said, "There's some French woman involved, I presume."

"French women," I said.

"Well, Vasques, isn't one enough for you? I didn't know you were a ladies' man."

"It's a family, Captain. I owe them a visit. And since the company can do without me at present..."

"I'll talk to the Major. But I can't promise you anything. I, too, would like to have a few days' leave to go to Paris and screw a baroness, but I have to stay here, putting up with you fellows and with those sons-of-bitches from Headquarters trying to drown me with paperwork.

"Wouldn't it be better to fill out an application?"

"You write your application. But you know nothing happens unless someone puts in a word. Paperwork stalls the machinery, but without paperwork the machinery won't function. Try to understand the contradictions of those office rats."

"May I fill one out for Rato too?"

"C'mon now, Vasques, you know very well officers aren't entitled to an orderly when they go on leave."

"It's not for me, sir, it's for him. The man needs to get out of this place for a few days."

"You don't seem to realize the implications of what you're saying, Vasques. You know very well that leaves for other ranks have been cancelled. And we can't set a precedent. Otherwise, every man in our company would demand, for the sake of fair treatment, a leave to go and do whatever he liked. And that would be chaos."

"In that case, I won't insist, sir."

A few days later, when I had already lost hope of getting a leave, the Captain called me to say he had a mission for me. I was supposed to go to Enguinegatte to bring twenty-four replacements to l'Epinette. They came from the Reserve Depot to replace the casualties from the last attack. He had found out about the mission in a meeting with the Major and had remembered my request. He had talked to the Major, who authorized him to send me to fetch the men, taking along a sergeant or someone I could trust. It was not exactly a leave, but I would be able to spend a day in Enguinegatte. And with the weekend, that would add up to three days.

"I owe you one, sir."

"Two. I want two bottles of old bagaço. All we have here is rum, whiskey, and some awful cognac nobody can drink. I feel better getting drunk on our own stuff. At least I know what I'm drinking."

"Or you think you do."

"There's no such thing as fake bagaço. Didn't you know that? Either it's bagaço or it isn't. If it isn't, it smells different."

"I've never had a very good nose."

"Well, you'd better get one, Vasques. One of these days we'll be attacked with mustard gas, and if you don't have a good nose, you'll choke to death without knowing why."

On the day it was announced that Colonel Gomes da

239

Costa had been promoted to General and appointed Commander of the Minho Brigade, to which our battalion belonged, Rato and I got on a *decauville*[49] to go as far as Enguinegatte. We packed our knapsacks with some clothes and left our rifles in l'Epinette. Following regulations, I holstered my pistol. Rato did not need a weapon but I knew he carried his clasp knife. He said it was for peeling fruit, but I doubt he ever peeled a single apple. When canned fruit was issued we ate it by taking the pieces to our mouth with a bayonet.

We got off the *decauville* and hiked about two kilometers to the Gavroche farm. The village seemed emptier than when our battalion had been billeted there. The Portuguese units, having received their preliminary training, were now at the front or very close to it. All that was left was the cantonment of the Brigade's Reserve Depot, where we fetched newly-arrived soldiers to fill gaps. As of December the government stopped sending replacements, and some say that was one of the reasons for the disaster of the Portuguese Expeditionary Corps. But since in September 1917 there were still some reserves, on Monday I would take charge of our twenty-four replacements. It was still Saturday, however, and we had almost two full days to rest, eat well, and enjoy the company of pleasant people who liked us.

We found Madame Constance Gavroche, her mother, and her children digging up potatoes from a vegetable garden next to their house. They stopped working and ran over, happy to see us again. We exchanged greetings and, to be hospitable, they offered to walk us to the house, but we would have none of it. We left our knapsacks on a wall and got down to helping them with their work. That was the first time my spoiled country gentleman's fingers handled potatoes plucked fresh out of the earth.

XXI

Since it was fairly late by the time I arrived in Oporto from Coimbra, I decided to spend the night at a boarding house near the railway station. I could not sleep much because of the crowd of drunks and prostitutes loitering in the street. Lying in bed, I could hear them laughing and shouting, swearing, spitting and heaving. I felt very alone. I could have wandered around town, found a tavern to drink a tankard with the local drunks, or paid a tart for a half hour of pleasure. Instead, I stayed in bed in the laundered sheets, which smelled of the mildew typical of a city that was grey and damp most of the year. In the middle of the night I heard the landlord, who doubled as receptionist, sending away a purported couple longing for two hours of shelter.

"This here is a respectable establishment!" I heard the man saying. "Go take care of your business behind the church. It'll be cheaper and you can always count on the bishop's blessing."

I wondered if the man had sent the potential clients away on my account, just to prove the place really was respectable, which in fact it was not, except for the likes of well-dressed clients like myself. Actually, if he had let them stay the night I might have forgotten my own loneliness while I listened to their maneuvers in the room next door.

The boarding house was once again silent, but the clamor in the streets continued. By about five o'clock the voices became intermittent and I started hearing the garbage carts and the vendors on their way to market. I looked for the four cent coin in my wallet and rolled it through my fingers. It began to get warm and before long, the woman on the coin started giving off heat. I wished Aninhas were there with me. Well, perhaps not exactly in that bed in that dismal boarding house. Maybe at the beach, sitting in the sand with my head resting on her breast, she would be caressing my face and hair with her long fingers, while I covered her soft white arms with kisses.

I left the boarding house around seven. Having asked the receptionist to store my bag, which I would pick up before catching the train to Braga, I decided to walk to Aninhas's house. Since it was too early to go knocking at someone's door, I bought a newspaper and went into a bakery to have breakfast. The main stories in the paper were about the peace treaty with Austria and the National Cooperative Congress taking place in Coimbra. I started wondering whether Professor Salazar was a member of that organization.

At about nine thirty, having read the newspaper from beginning to end, including the advertisements, I left the bakery and started walking back towards the river. It was a grey morning. Clorinda, the Gouveias' maid, greeted me from the balcony. She said the doctor had already left for the hospital and Dona Leontina had gone to the Bolhão Market with her children. She suggested I try the Café Majestic first, since they usually stopped there for a glass of milk. I thanked her for the information and asked her, in case I didn't run into them, to let Miss Aninhas know that I'd call again after lunch. The maid promised to give her the message and I walked back into town.

In a little over fifteen minutes, I walked into the Majestic. I looked among the crowd of middle-class customers drinking their morning coffee while reading or chatting, but I did not see them. So I walked up the street, swarming with carriages, automobiles, and people. When I got to the Bolhão Market, I realized that looking for Aninhas among that bustling crowd would be like searching for a needle in a haystack. Besides, all of the women were wearing hats that hid half their faces, making the endeavor even more complicated.

As I walked through the stalls, the lady vendors, in their piercing Oporto accents, tried to force upon me a basket of freshly laid eggs, a crate of grapes just harvested from the Douro vineyards, a string of onions still smelling of dirt, or a bundle of collard greens so tender I'd want to bite right into them. I stopped at a flower stall and asked the vendor, a chubby, ruddy woman, to make up a bouquet. She asked me if it was for a funeral. "No, of course not," I said.

"It might as well be though, the way old people around here's dropping like flies. And now, with the Spanish flu, it's both the old and the young."

And if it wasn't to honor some corpse, why did I want the flowers? "To give to someone," I said. But the woman was not satisfied. She needed to know if they were for a gentleman or a lady.

"A lady," I said, irritably.

The interrogation did not stop there. The woman needed to know the lady's age, if she was married or single and what my relationship to her was. Because, she explained, it makes a difference whether you're giving flowers to your mother, grand-mother, sister, godmother, aunt, wife, fiancé, or girlfriend.

"They're for a lady friend."

"Oh!" she exclaimed, winking at me. "I'll say, it's the first time anyone's ever asked me to make up a bouquet for a lady friend. I've got a lot of customers what come to buy flowers for a lady friend. Oh yes, sir, I've been in this here business for a long time. But they just ain't got the gumption to say so. Most often they say the flowers are for a mother's or a wife's birthday."

I did not understand right away what she was getting at. I thought it strange the woman would say her customers were too embarrassed to say the flowers were for a friend, but while she made the bouquet I realized that "lady friend" might also mean "mistress." The woman thought the flowers were for a woman, quite likely married, with whom I was having an affair. Just as she was handing me the bouquet, mostly of red roses, I heard a feminine voice almost whispering in my ear, "Are those flowers for a secret sweetheart?"

I turned around and saw Aninhas smiling at me. I handed her the flowers and said, "The sweetheart is no secret, it's the admirer who is."

243

She accepted the bouquet, saying, "Tell the secret admirer I was really touched by the bouquet and I'll meet him at the exit in ten minutes."

And she disappeared into the flurry of customers around the flower, fruit and vegetable stalls.

The vendor, who had smiled with rapture throughout the scene, made a point of telling me I had not yet paid for the little bouquet. "That'll be five cents," she said. I went through my wallet, but found only those huge silver one escudo coins, whose monetary value at that point was half the value of their weight in silver – the irony of inflation – and a few bills. The woman took one of the coins and gave me the change, adding, "Thank you very much, and let me tell you, sir, your lady friend's very nice and very pretty. But don't you slip and let her husband catch on. Sometimes them things can go wrong. And you're very young, sir. Don't neglect her, but be discreet. A jealous husband, if he suspects something's going on, well, he might just kill you. Here in Oporto, let me tell you, it happens all the time."

"Thank you for your concern. There's no need to worry on my account. She is not married."

"Not married? But, sir, didn't you say she's your lady friend? Or the flowers ain't for her after all? Now I'm confused."

I was not about to tell my life story to a flower seller, and since a nearby woman then asked for a half dozen gerberas and some carnations, I took the opportunity to make my way to the exit. Still, I heard the vendor call out, "Come back soon!"

The market had exits onto several streets and I wondered which one to choose to wait for Aninhas. In a situation like that a telephone, obviously wireless, would have come in handy. The Americans had used field radiotelephones in the war, but those were too heavy. Maybe someday someone would invent one small enough to be carried around in your coat pocket. Take clocks, for example. The first ones, made over three hundred years ago, were the size of a wardrobe. Nowadays, however, people go around with watches on their wrist or in their pocket.

I waited near the exit that seemed most probable, but as it turned out, I was wrong. Aninhas went out a different one, with her mother and brother.

"Luís!" I heard someone cry out from a carriage making its way slowly down the street. The coachman stopped the horses by the curb and I saw Aninhas with the bouquet, Dona Leontina, and Paulino.

"Please get in," Dona Leontina said.

"Unless you want to jog along after us," Aninhas added, smiling teasingly.

I got in the carriage and sat down next to Paulino, facing Aninhas. The driver started the horses and off we went. When the carriage bumped, our knees rubbed against each other. The red roses in her lap contrasted strikingly with her cream colored dress and hat. I watched her as she caressed the petals dreamily. Although we were entertained watching the hustle and bustle in the streets, every once in a while our eyes met and she smiled at me.

When we got onto quieter streets, Dona Leontina asked me about my stay in Coimbra, and my exam. I told her in not much detail what I had done, omitting my conversation with Professor Salazar and his invitation. I wanted to think about it and get my father's advice.

The driver stopped at a bakery and Dona Leontina went in to buy cakes for the afternoon snack. When we were again on our way, she invited me to lunch but I did not accept. I wanted to take Aninhas out to a restaurant, if Dona Leontina would allow it. She hesitated at first but, since Aninhas looked at her imploringly, she ended up agreeing. We would naturally be more comfortable talking over our affairs, she concluded. It was, after all, best to get things settled, and if we so decided, to formalize the courtship. Aninhas tried to protest, but she

245

continued, "You know very well, Ana Maria, whether you like it or not, this is the way these things are. I'm certain Mr. Luís Vasques is a gentleman. That's why I'm saying this. Otherwise, I would keep quiet. Mr. Vasques, to avoid misunderstanding, it's best you speak to my husband and tell him your intentions regarding Ana Maria. Not to ask permission to be sweethearts and, much less, engaged. It's too soon for that. But some kind of commitment of good faith."

Since Aninhas did not answer her mother, I assumed she was in agreement. As for me, I had no reason whatsoever, at least not then, to come up with a response. So I remained silent, which, in such circumstances, is always the best approach.

The driver stopped the carriage in front of the Gouveias' house. Dona Leontina paid the fare – I did not insist because it might have been misunderstood – and invited me in. In spite of their protests, I carried their shopping bags and parcels up the stairway and handed them to the maid. The first time I had been there, about a week prior, I had remained in their dining room, where they had offered me a small meal while I waited for Aninhas. This time Dona Leontina suggested that Aninhas show me around the house. I was surprised by that family's lack of formality, so different from Libaninha's parents, always bowing and scraping with false courtesy.

I followed Aninhas down a hallway, heavily plastered with designs and flowers, according to the taste of the time, and with a long crimson runner. We saw first her parents' room, furnished with an enormous bed of carved walnut. Opposite there was a room where Aunt Generosa stayed when she came to Oporto. And next to it was Paulino's room, furnished with a plain single bed, a bookcase filled with books, mostly for school, a wardrobe, and a dresser with toys he had outgrown. Opposite Paulino's room there was a small office with a desk, chairs, a well worn armchair, two bookcases overflowing with books, and a piano. I stopped for a second to read some of the titles. There were works on theology, philosophy, history, geography, literature, and natural science, but most of them were medical.

"What do you like to read?" I asked, pointing to the bookcases.

"None of these. They're almost all from last century. My father inherited them from my grandfather. He was a doctor, but he liked to study everything, even religion. He was also a passionate collector of old books. Some of these are really valuable. At least that's what my father says."

"I didn't know books had any value beyond their content."

"Of course they do! Some books are extremely rare. For example," and she took down one, with a frayed spine, and opened it to the front page, "This is one of the first books printed in Portuguese."

"*Vita Christi*," I read, carefully articulating each syllable of the Latin title.

"*Christ's Life*," she translated.

"I see you know Latin, Aninhas," I said, impressed.

"Yes, a little."

"Now I know whom to ask when I find myself confused by some passage in Roman law."

"Always at your service."

Before we left the room, I pointed to the piano, over by the wall, and asked, "Do you play?"

"No."

I looked at her surprised. I had expected her to say yes, since she was, or at least at the time I thought she was, a spoiled girl from the bourgeoisie.

"My mother even sent me to piano lessons when I was little, but I gave up. I couldn't stand the teacher, a grumbling old woman who used to slap my wrists when I didn't hold them the way I was supposed to. Paulino's been learning and he can already play a few Mozart sonatas. But I don't think he'll ever become a great pianist. We aren't a musical family."

"May I?"

"You know how to play, Luís?"

"I haven't played in a long time. I learned at school in Braga. But I never got to the Mozart sonatas. I got stuck on Czerny's exercises and a few of Bach's inventions."

I opened the piano, sat down and tried out two scales up and down the keyboard. At first I made mistakes, but the second time I got every key right. A little more confident, I started to play some popular ditties I had memorized. They were not difficult. I played the melody with my right hand and some very basic accompaniment chords with my left. It did not sound too bad and Aninhas exclaimed, "Bravo, maestro! I wasn't aware of your musical talents."

"I promise to learn more serious pieces. But I'll only play for you."

"Traditional folk dances are good enough for me."

"Unfortunately I cannot recall *Für Elise*, much more appropriate for this listener."

Aninhas smiled and led me to the next room, which was her own. She took off her hat and put it on the bed, straightening her hair in the mirror over the dresser. Unlike her brother's room, hers was furnished with a double bed, less ornate than that of her parents, but even so, quite impressive, nicely carved and solid.

"Miss Aninhas, you sleep in the bed of a queen."

"A queen with no king."

The room was decorated with little feminine objets d'art, probably gifts from family and friends. I especially noticed a porcelain doll wearing a blue pleated dress, sitting on the bedside table. She also had a bookcase, and I glanced at the titles. They were mainly by French authors and collections of Portuguese poets then in fashion, such as António Nobre and Guerra Junqueiro.

Standing by the window, Aninhas opened the curtain and looked down on the street. I went over to stand next to

248

her. We could see part of the Douro river below us and a few buildings in Gaia, on the other bank.

"With a view like this, no one could ever be unhappy," I said.

"There are always the foggy, rainy days. That's when sometimes everything seems so melancholy, I feel like leaping into the river, like Hamlet's Ophelia."

I wondered to myself if she had suicidal tendencies. I looked at her face, her beautiful profile like a Greek goddess and it certainly did not seem to be the case.

"I read in the paper today the suicide rate in Portugal has increased a hundred per cent. If we add that to the deaths from the Spanish flu, tuberculosis, and malnutrition, pretty soon the country will be empty."

"Maybe that's what the politicians have in mind," she suggested. "Maybe they're trying to empty out the country to transform the whole place into a game preserve."

We laughed at her joke and I added, "What a topic of conversation for a time like this!"

"It's just as good as any other."

"Not if I were a real gentleman."

"And aren't you, Luís?"

"If I were a gentleman, I'd be telling you what a nice room you have, that the curtains are a cheerful color, that the bed looks very comfortable, that your knick-knacks and the way you've arranged them reflect the fine taste of their owner, that books show me what an intelligent, sensitive person you are, that the landscape we see from this window complements your big, moist, tender eyes."

Aninhas smiled mischievously and answered, "But, since you're not a gentleman, Luís, we'll just stick to suicide rates."

"It's safer."

"In what sense?"

"Otherwise, I'll end up embracing you, and kissing you, which is quite inappropriate, given that I'm in a serious young woman's bedroom, where I'm expected to behave with decency and respect."

Aninhas put her arms around my neck, gave me a quick kiss on the lips and said, "It's the first time I've ever kissed a man in my room."

"So, it turns out Aninhas likes numbers after all..."

"They're safer than people."

"Do you feel threatened?"

"Do you?"

"Not exactly threatened. Intimidated, maybe."

"Because of me?"

"No, I've never felt so safe with anyone."

I was about to tell her that, except for her, I trusted only the image on the four cent coin that had kept me out of danger during the war. She would not have understood the long explanation and that was neither the time, nor the place to try to go into it.

"We'd better go. What will your mother think about us taking so long?"

"It's not too hard to guess what she'll think. By now, she must be asking my brother to come upstairs to see what's going on."

"While we're waiting, do you mind if I return your favor?"

"Not at all."

I took her in my arms and kissed her tenderly. I felt her tremble and, when I was going to prolong the kiss, we heard the knock at the door. Aninhas broke away and went to open it. It was her brother with the bouquet I had brought her, asking where she wanted it. It was a good excuse to interrupt us. My future mother-in-law, if it had been her idea, was a very clever woman.

Aninhas took the flowers and sent him away, saying we would be right there. The boy left and she put the flowers in a vase on the dresser. She removed the silk roses and replaced them with the fresh flowers. The room, all in red, pink, green, white and cream, looked like springtime.

"They're beautiful, aren't they?" she said, setting the vase back on the dresser.

"You'd better put some water in the vase, or they'll wilt."

"But not the memory we'll have of them."

"Who knows? Memory is like the life of flowers."

She took the jar over towards the door and I followed her. We went back down the hall and she left me in the living room with Dona Leontina and Paulino, then went to the kitchen to fill the jar with water. While she was gone, I chatted with my future mother-in-law about the cost of living and the uncertain future of the country. When Aninhas came back, about a half an hour later, she joined us, now wearing a different dress and hat.

"Shall we go?" She asked.

I had completely forgotten that I had invited her to lunch.

Her mother made several suggestions, as if we were children. Be careful with the traffic, watch out for pickpockets, a real problem in Oporto, and above all, be careful near the river, especially near the containing wall. I promised I would have Aninhas back for the afternoon snack.

Although I was somewhat out of sorts due to having slept so poorly the previous night, the rest of the day was very pleasant. We had lunch at a restaurant Aninhas suggested. Before that, though, she wanted to show me Lello's Bookstore, where she usually bought her novels. I got her one that had just come out and seemed to interest her, *The Amputee,* by João Grave.[50] It was the story of a fellow who goes to Flanders and, when he returns, mutilated from an injury, it turns out his fiancée has replaced him with someone else. As far as I knew, João Grave was never in the trenches and heard from others everything he wrote about them. I confess I did not read the book, but Aninhas did and was singularly unimpressed. She used to say she was far more impressed by the things I told her.

251

I asked the salesman to wrap up the novel.

"It's the second present I've received today and so far I haven't given any," she commented.

"What better present could I have than your company?"

We were at the counter and I was waiting for the salesman to give me change. The man, who overheard the conversation, looked at us disapprovingly. Aninhas smiled, squeezing my hand. The fellow finally decided to give me my change and we left the bookstore holding hands, which the salesman undoubtedly thought was provocative. But we were not trying to provoke anyone that day. We were happy together and nothing else mattered.

After lunch, Aninhas took me to see a film, in a theater near the building of the newspaper *O Comércio do Porto*.[51] There were two matinee sessions. The first one we watched was with Harold Lloyd. I cannot recall the title, but I know it was about two swindlers who were fooled by a girl that worked as the assistant to a medium named Professor Galosh, or something like that. We had a great time watching it. Perhaps because it was Saturday, the theater was full and the carefree atmosphere was contagious. The piano player was mainly off key, but nobody seemed to care. Aninhas, at my side, laughed uncontrollably at the actors' antics. Every once in a while she looked at me, and if I was not laughing along with her, she poked me with her elbow.

The next film was a Charlie Chaplin. It had been much talked about for at least a year, but I had not yet had a chance to see it. It was called "Shoulder Arms," and it started out with the character in a close order drill session and the sergeant disciplining him for not keeping step with the rest of the platoon. Rato would like this film, I thought. We laughed a lot at the little fellow's military ineptitude, until he finally lay down in the tent and fell asleep. With that, I started feeling anxious because of the images of the trenches, the rain, mud, shooting and explosions. Aninhas, who in the meantime had stopped laughing, faced with visions of the trenches where her cousin had died, realized that I was not feeling well and asked if I wanted to leave. I told her I didn't.

So, we watched the rest of the film holding hands, in silent anguish, while everyone around us laughed hysterically every time Chaplin kicked a Boche in the seat of the pants. The film had a happy ending: the hero, thanks to his cleverness – or innocence – managed to capture the German generals and Kaiser William himself, and put an end to the war. In saving from the German clutches a beautiful damsel with whom he was hopelessly in love, he had saved the world from their tyranny. It was just too bad it turned out to be a dream, which was revealed in the last sequence of the film, when the little fellow wakes up in his tent.

We left the theater holding hands and, as we walked down to the river bank, back to Aninhas's house, we did not say anything for a long while. When we reached the river, she asked me, "Is that what the trenches were like?"

"Except for the water in the shelters, which was exaggerated in the film, yes, that's what it was like."

"So, you didn't have to swim in the shelters?"

"The shelters were uncomfortable, but not that much."

"And Luís, how many girls did you save?"

"Unfortunately, in all our trenches, no man's land, and the Boche trenches, there were no girls to be saved."

"And outside the trenches?"

We stopped in the middle of our stroll, Aninhas was gazing at me seriously. Was she about to have a fit of jealous rage? I took her in my arms, oblivious to any passers-by, and told her war was horrible and that there were no saviors, no saved, no winners and no losers. Then I added, "I love you, Ana Maria, and you are my savior. You're my little Chaplin soldier."

I saw her shed a tear and we remained there for a long time, without saying a word.

XXII

The three days Rato and I spent in Enguinegatte were a real warriors' rest after the first battle. Madame Gavroche, the aged Madame Léonor Pigeard, and the children gave us a particularly warm welcome. We were not just two ordinary soldiers dropping by. Having taken a liking to us, they felt the weeks we had been away were yet another loss. It was the first time they had seen men coming back from war safe and sound. Madame Gavroche's husband had gone missing in action, and her two brothers had been killed in the first months of the war, like all the other able-bodied men from the village. The English soldiers who had been there before the Portuguese had never come back, either killed or sent to other sectors. Thus we were the first soldiers they saw returning from their baptism by fire.

During the days we spent on the farm, Rato repaired the water pipes, the roof, and the cart. Even I pitched in, trying to help him, despite my limited ability for manual work. We also helped dig up potatoes and carry them to the barn. A good part of the harvest would be sold to our Quartermaster Service if the war lasted much longer. By then there was hardly anyone who did not think it would, considering the fiasco of the English offensive in Passchendaele, where, after one hundred thousand men had been killed, the front line had moved forward only half a dozen kilometers. At that point, the Great War, particularly on the Western front, had killed more people than all the wars fought in Europe over the last five hundred years.

The day we arrived in Enguinegatte Madame Gavroche made us take a bath. Rato managed with a basin of hot water, while I enjoyed the privilege of the bathtub. She left me alone. After I had got out of the tub, rubbed myself dry with a towel, and put on a somewhat clean uniform, she walked into the room to pick up the soiled clothes. She saw my uniform was not really clean and decided to lend me some of her husband's civilian clothes. I told her I was forced by regulations to be in uniform at all times, and if someone saw me in civvies, they might think I was a deserter.

"Nobody will see you inside the house. Who cares? I'll wash all of your uniforms tomorrow. Don't worry, nobody'll see you."

I had to take off the uniform in front of her and then put on some trousers, a shirt, and a vest she fetched from another room.

"Those trousers are a little big for you. My husband was heavier."

"Have you had any news from him?" I asked, as I buttoned up.

"No."

"I'm sorry. How long has it been?"

"I haven't heard anything about him for over fifteen months. I've been told it takes two or three months for captured soldiers to be able to contact their family through the Red Cross, which seems to be the only organization the Boche will let into their prisoner-of-war camps."

I wished I could say something comforting. But what can you tell a woman who has lost her husband?

"You know what really makes me sad, Monsieur Vasques? It's the fact that I can't wear mourning like I'm supposed to. It's very sad, to have someone missing in combat. There's no tomb where you can go to pray, or to lay some flowers on when you miss him. And then there's always a faint hope that he might come back some day, even when you know that's impossible. But let's not talk about painful things. You're our dear friends, here for a visit. You should see happy faces."

She picked up the soiled clothes and added, as she walked out, "Dinner will be served in ten minutes."

When I went downstairs I found Rato arguing with Madame Pigeard. He was trying to explain to the old lady that

255

he could not sit at the dining room table, that his place was in the kitchen, with the cats. The old lady kept on saying, *mais non, mais non,* as she pointed to a seat at the table.

"Stop making a fuss and sit down," I ordered him.

He sat by me, seemingly embarrassed. He grabbed the napkin next to his plate and tied it behind his neck like a bib. I nudged him with my elbow and pointed at my napkin, draped on my knees.

"French things," he grumbled, struggling to undo the tight knot.

To tell the truth, I was glad to have him sitting by me.

Even though they gave us much more than we could offer them, we had brought a bottle of wine, biscuits, and a few cans of fruit preserves, which were a novelty, and as such a big treat for the children.

At dessert, Madame Gavroche told us the village had quieted down after the Portuguese troops had departed. That was both good and bad. The presence of our troops had livened things up and was good for business, and the soldiers had helped with the farm work. But now there was also less prostitution and less trouble, Madame Pigeard added. The Portuguese were good boys, certainly better than the English. When the English got drunk, they smashed everything in sight and insulted everyone in their language. But you just couldn't ask soldiers, be they Portuguese or English, to behave like altar boys. After all, we were in war.

After dinner, François was allowed to play a record, and soon the lively voice of a fashionable male French singer was flowing out of the huge horn of the gramophone, which had not been played for many long months. Nannette grabbed François's hands and they started dancing. But they were too tired from digging up potatoes and, after some prancing around, they stopped and sat down. We were all tired and soon said good night to one another and went to bed. Rato had to sleep in the barn, as there was no room for him in the house. He did not seem to mind. That was the first night in nearly two months that we slept without fear of grenades or shells.

I lay down on the bed, by now like an old acquaintance, and, snug under the blanket, I enjoyed the comfort of the clean sheets, the soft mattress, and the smooth pillow. War was a distant roar, like the pounding drums during St. John's festivals along Avenida Central in Braga. From the window of my father's office, I used to make an effort to figure out where the din came from.

I closed my eyes, allowing my body to be overcome with languor. I imagined myself in my teens, in my room at the family estate. I started to touch and caress myself sensually, in a way I had not done since I was fifteen or sixteen. Then I heard a discreet tapping at the door. In a hushed voice, I asked who it was.

"Constance," was the barely audible reply.

I was confused whether I should get up or just tell her to come in. Against the rules of etiquette, I decided to tell her to come in. I simply could not get up in that state. What would she say if she saw that pointed thing sticking out under my long johns?

Madame Gavroche walked in, holding a candlestick, and closed the door behind her. I started to get up but she told me not to bother. Better that way, I thought.

"I'm sorry if I woke you up."

"Don't worry, I wasn't asleep. Is there something wrong?"

"I went to bed, but I couldn't fall asleep. And then I thought... I thought that maybe you wouldn't mind if I came over to chat a little."

"Oh, of course I don't mind. Please sit down, make your-self comfortable," I said, pointing to the edge of the bed.

"I don't have many opportunities to talk. The men have either died or disappeared. The only one left in Enguinegatte is the *maire*, and he's a troubled man. And talking to women

257

ends up being boring. The children can't understand it, and we should not frighten them with our concerns and our fears."

"We are friends, Madame."

"Monsieur Vasques, vous êtes très gentil."

Sitting on the side of the bed, she talked for about an hour. She talked about her husband, the war, her brothers killed defending their land, the weariness of the farm, her children's education, the uncertain future, the sadness of being a presumed widow, her longing for her husband, the price of potatoes, the horse the French army had requisitioned, again her husband and how she suffered greatly knowing she'd likely never see him again, and how she wished she'd been the best of wives while he was still at home, alive and in good health.

I was fighting sleep, making an effort to pay attention to her, when she started crying softly. The candle on the night table was nearly burned down and the wax was spattering. I leaned forward, pulled her toward me, and embraced her. Then I lifted the blanket and made room for her next to me. We fell asleep in each other's arms and nothing happened between us. When I woke up in the morning, I was alone. I got up, opened the shutters and realized it was mid-morning. There was an eerie silence in the house that made me wonder where everybody might be. I put on Monsieur Gavroche's clothes and went downstairs. The dining room table was set for breakfast, with a saucer and a cup, a wicker basket filled with sliced bread, and a jug of cold milk. There may also have been some butter, cheese or preserves, but I cannot recall for sure. In the kitchen I found a pot of hot coffee on the iron stove. I took it to the table, sat down, and helped myself.

"Maybe they've gone to the field to dig up potatoes," I thought.

After eating, I went to the kitchen door and called out to Rato. Since there was no answer, I risked advancing a few meters into the garden, until I could see the potato field. It was all silent and deserted. The family dog, which was about the

258

size of a lapdog and of the breed known among the Portuguese troops as pussy-licker, came close to my legs, wagging his tail and sniffing my trousers. Maybe he recognized his master's scent. I bent over, scratched his hairy nose, and asked him if he knew where everybody was hiding. The dog yawned widely, sniffed my trousers again, turned around, and went to lie down at the entrance of the farm like a relaxed canine sentry.

I went inside, just in case some passer-by might see me in mufti, sat at the dining room table, pushed aside the empty cup, and wrote a letter to my parents. I had a lot to tell them, but could not say much. I censored my soldiers' letters and, since I did not have a censor above me, I exercised self-censorship conscientiously. I filled about a page with banalities, saying I was well, that they need not worry, that the war would soon be over and that we would soon meet again. I finished off by asking them to send me an astronomy book with a map of the constellations. I intended to fill my long trench nights identifying the stars in the Milky Way.

Having finished the letter, I walked around the house. I found several photograph albums in the china cabinet and started leafing through them. Some must have been more than fifty years old, which I found astonishing. In nineteenth-century Portugal, only the rich and famous could afford the luxury of having themselves photographed. But in France, it looked like it was common for families to have photographs taken on special occasions such as christenings, first communions, weddings, and funerals. One of the albums was reserved for family funerals. When someone died, a photographer was called to make a portrait of the deceased before he or she was placed in the coffin. The body was washed, dressed, and, if necessary, made up. In the album the deceased were shown lying in bed with their hands crossed on their chest, or sitting in a chair as if they were still alive. At that time that seemed macabre to me. But when I think about it now, I see those photographs as the last reminder of a loved one who has left this world. Nonetheless, if asked if I would like to have a photograph of my parents in *rigor mortis,* I would answer in the negative. Every man is subject to the culture in which he was born and raised, and it is through that lens that he sees and judges other cultures. If the Germans had known that, or at least thought about it, maybe they would not consider other people inferior, and might not have tried to force their *Kultur* on them. They might even have used it to build a fairer and safer world.

I leafed through the entire album of the dead. The last seven pages were empty. They would never hold the photographs of Madame Gavroche's brothers and husband, consumed by the flames of war.

When I was about to pick up another album I heard the dog barking. I went to the window and saw the women and Rato approaching. Only then did it dawn on me that it was Sunday and they had gone to mass. Madame Gavroche apologized for not having woken me up. She had thought I needed to catch up with my sleep. Rato, an early riser, had offered to accompany them to church and so I had been left by myself.

The rest of the morning was rather busy. While the ladies made lunch and saw to household chores, Rato and I did some repair work. There was no field work on Sundays, since those people took the Lord's day very seriously. But it was tacitly accepted that certain small household jobs were allowed, such as repairs, gardening, laundering, and cleaning up.

After lunch Rato and I went back to doing repairs. Madame Gavroche washed our clothes and hung them to dry behind the house. The afternoon was sunny, with a light breeze, and by nightfall they were dry.

While we were mending the porch roof, a few meters away from Madame Gavroche, who was scrubbing our uniforms in a zinc washtub, Rato whispered to me, "Madame is quite happy today."

"It's because of our visit."

"Certainly not mine."

"What do you mean by that?"

"She won't stop looking at you, sir."

"Nonsense."

"When we went to mass, she asked me about you."

"What did you tell her?"

"What could I tell her, sir? I didn't understand her questions too well. You know I don't quite get their parleyvoo."

"How could you then tell she was asking about me?"

"Well, *Monsieur Vasques* ain't hard to figure out. And she repeated your name several times. Just to say something, I said to her: *Monsieur Vasques très bon homme!* The way she smiled, she must have understood. And now while she's washing, she keeps looking at you, sir."

"Maybe she's looking at you."

"No way, sir! She knows quite well I'm married with children. The way I see it, she's taken a fancy to you."

"Don't talk nonsense. She's a married woman, with her husband missing in action, and she's suffered a lot."

"As you say, sir, missing. Do you reckon she'd invite you to come here, and do all these nice things for you, if she didn't have a soft spot for you? I doubt it."

"We're good friends, that's all."

"If you say so, sir."

And that was the end of our talk.

After we dined on the leftovers from lunch, Madame Gavroche let the children play the gramophone again. They danced while the adults talked. Even though I wanted to, I did not mention the album of the family dead, because I was afraid they might be offended by my curiosity. We talked about the harvests and the high price of some products, particularly fabric for clothing. Nearly all cotton and other materials went to the uniform factories and it would not be too long before people started going around naked.

We must have talked until ten o'clock, when the children were sent to bed. Madame Pigeard followed them and Rato, not wanting to be the third wheel, retired to the barn, with the dog trotting after him. I stayed in the living room with Madame Gavroche, again talking about the war. As I have mentioned, she was in the habit of reading the newspaper every now and then. She told me about what was happening in the French lines, or at least about what censorship allowed the papers to print. I told her what little I knew about the way the war was going. I did not give her any information on our troops in particular. Although she was no Mata Hari, I could not talk about our troops' positions, morale, or material situation, without flouting military regulations, which forbade talking about those subjects with civilians, including friends, lovers, fiancées, or relatives. Such loose talk could bring out charges of espionage and treason.

"Monsieur Vasques, since you have been at the front, do you think the Allies will win this war?"

"That's what politicians and generals think. If you believe them, victory is at hand, in a matter of months. They say the German Army is running out of men and equipment. When the German people start starving, they won't resist much longer and will rise up."

"And do you believe that?"

I thought for a while. I recalled my trench experience, the contact with the enemy, invisible but always present and active, waiting for our slightest distraction to pounce. I said, "No, Madame Gavroche. In my opinion, the war will last. The English campaign in Passchendaele isn't having the expected effect. Even though the Germans have retreated for strategic reasons, they're still well entrenched and their defenses are impregnable."

I was about to add that, in contrast, our defenses were fragile and that, if the Germans attacked the Portuguese sector with their assault troops, we would be decimated. The open breach would allow the Germans to move in, outflank the English, and win the war even before the French Army, stationed further south, could react. But I kept quiet. That was an idea Captain Rebelo used to spin out to kill time, but it might alarm the French lady. Besides, it was confidential information about our troops' situation, which I must not disclose.

She told me about the revolution in Russia and the danger that the Russians might sign an armistice with Germany. The German divisions posted in the East would then move to France, outnumbering the Allied divisions. Since I did not know much about what was going on in Russia, I was very worried.

It was getting late and we had to get up at the crack of dawn. Rato and I were supposed to report to the Reserve Depot to take those soldiers to l'Epinette, and the ladies and the children would go back to digging up potatoes.

As I made a motion to stand up, she said, "I'd like to apologize for having bothered you last night. And to thank you for your patience in listening to me. You are a true *gentilhomme*, Monsieur Vasques."

"I'm not always a *gentilhomme*, Madame."

"And nobody could demand that you were," she said ambiguously. "There are times when a woman prefers less courtesy and more daring from a man."

As she said that she touched my arm. I told her I'd be honored to be more *oseur,* more daring, if she so desired. She smiled, let go of my arm after pressing it lightly, and suggested I'd better go to my room, as she'd be busy for another half hour or so. I went upstairs, took off her husband's clothes and hung them on the back of the chair. On a chest I found my uniform, washed, dried, and pressed, ready to be worn the next day. I lay down and, while I waited, felt apprehensive. Scruples, maybe. But if she did not feel them, or had momentarily set them aside, why should I not do likewise? After all, it was more than certain that her husband was dead. And if he was not, who would worry about such moral details in wartime?

Half an hour went by and she did not show up, and I began to think I had misunderstood her. Maybe I had misinterpreted her last words. I began to feel relieved, but that did not last. About ten minutes later I heard a light tap on the door. I said, "Come in." She walked in on tiptoe, this time without a candle. I made room for her in the bed and she lay down by me, facing me. The moon must have been on the wane, as some of its light seeped through the cracks in the shutters, letting us glimpse each other's contours.

She caressed my face and hair and then kissed me. I felt her tremble while she kissed me and I decided to act. I moved back a little and ran my fingers over her thin lips, her small nose, her light eyes, her forehead, her long, wavy hair, her ears, her neck. But she would not calm down. Quite to the contrary. She pulled down my long johns, sat on top of me, pulled up her nightgown and made me penetrate her. I felt my penis entering the humid flesh of her vagina. She sighed and was quiet for a few moments, feeling me inside her, her face turned to the ceiling and her eyes shut. Then she turned to me and started moving up and down, varying the rhythm, sighing, trembling, and groaning more or less discreetly so as not to wake up the household. When I was about to come I tried to pull out. She stopped moving up and down and whispered it was not necessary, it was safe. But if I wanted to do it in a different way, she would change her position. I agreed and she moved over. That brief interval made me feel good. I calmed down and managed to get rid of my long johns, caught around my legs. She stretched out next to me, took off her nightgown and, in the twilight I caught a glimpse of her naked body. Though over thirty, she was still a beautiful woman. She had strong, muscular thighs, and a delicate, soft-skinned belly. Her breasts were large and I lay my face down on her cleavage. She opened her legs and let me penetrate her. Lying on top of her, with her mouth brushing my ear, I heard, *"Mon chéri! Mon amour!"*

I could not tell whether she was referring to me or to the absent husband she felt in me. But I did not have the heart to ask her. Nor, at that point, did it matter.

XXIII

The vacation was coming to an end. A few days after I had returned from Coimbra, Rato appeared at the estate. He wanted to know if I had written Madame Constance Gavroche and if she had answered. I felt like a kid caught stealing oranges from the neighbor's backyard. Deciding that lying would be the safest policy, I said I'd written her and was waiting for an answer.

"As soon as you hear something, sir, could you send me a message?"

"And how are things at home?"

"Not good. There's hardly enough money for bread and Vicência won't get off my back. It's tough to get work these days."

"What about the grape harvest? It's just around the corner."

"You can't feed a family on grape harvests. The owners pay a pittance. Or else they expect a man to pick grapes for free. They give us some snacks and wine and think they're being real generous."

"But you'll be coming to our..."

"I can't say, sir. Like I said the other day, I've been doing day work over at Santa Madalena and the grape harvest there is set for the same day."

"It's up to you. You know that with us you can make the money you need to get your train ticket to France."

Rato looked at me suspiciously, trying to figure out if I was pulling his leg or if I was serious.

"I'm almost certain the letter from Madame Constance Gavroche will get here any day now and you'd better be ready for the trip," I added.

The grape harvest on our estate was coming up in about a week. After scratching his head a few times, he ended up saying he'd help out.

Rato went about his business and I sat down at the desk to write to Madame Gavroche. I had promised I would write when I got back to Portugal and, since I had not yet done so, I felt somewhat awkward writing several months later and asking a favor on top of it. I started the letter saying I had arrived safely and that I was gradually adapting to civilian life. I apologized for my delay in writing her, due to the many tasks that demanded my attention since my return, especially preparing for my upcoming university examinations. It was a white lie. In fact, most of the time I had been traveling with Rato, lazing around the beach or flirting with Aninhas. But I could not write that to a woman who was trying to pick up the pieces of her life and that of her family. Toward the end of the letter, I mentioned Rato and his difficult economic situation, asking her if it would be hard to find work for him on a farm in Enguinegatte or perhaps nearby. He would be very grateful if she could send some information. I ended the letter thanking her again for the warm welcome she had given us and for the laughter and tears we had shared. I did not mention anything else shared to avoid embarrassing her, in case she intended to show the letter to her mother or children.

I also owed a letter to Professor Oliveira Salazar regarding his invitation to become a member of the Portuguese Catholic Center, but first I needed to talk to my father about it. I did so at dinner that very day.

My father was reticent about both the invitation and the man who had extended it.

"How old is this Salazar fellow?"

"He must be around thirty,"

"That's the age when political ambition starts."

"I don't think Professor Salazar has political ambitions. At the most, I'd say, academic, like almost all the professors at Coimbra."

"If he didn't have political ambitions, he wouldn't have joined this so-called Catholic Center, which in fact is a political party, or if it's not, that's the idea. All you have to do is gather together a bunch of monarchists and the Catholics opposed to the current republican regime. It's not just a coincidence this Center supported the Northern Monarchy proclaimed in January this year in Oporto, and is sympathetic to Paiva Couceiro."

"And this means...?"

"What it means is, it seems dangerous to me, at least at this point, for you to join a party, a movement or whatever it is that opposes the government. It wouldn't surprise me one bit if this government, using the excuse of national security, were to start imprisoning and firing people left and right. It wouldn't be the first time. The republicans, as you very well know, are scared to death of the old forces, supported by most of the Portuguese and still active right under their nose. If someone is able to unite these forces, the current regime, brought to power against the will of the people by a dozen opportunistic bourgeois, will topple over like an old poplar."

"Sidónio Pais tried, and look what happened to him."

"Sidónio Pais was pretentious and vain, with little or no notion of politics and economics. I confess I voted for him. He was sure better than the riffraff that's ruined the country. He was a victim of his own naive view of the reality in Portugal. He could have survived if he'd surrounded himself with more competent people. Instead, he surrounded himself with military men, who didn't know any more than he did."

"People say if he hadn't been assassinated, he could've saved the country."

"Oh, Luís, there are no saviors. The only one who deserved to be called that was Christ. And look what they did to him. Sidónio Pais ended up with the only thing he could have: a bullet."

"And do you think, Father, that Professor Salazar might be the man to join these forces?"

"I don't know him. As far as that goes, you'd know more

than I do. But based on what you've been telling me, it doesn't seem like it. Still, you never know. With all the mediocrity in this country, anything is possible. Nobody ever put two cents on the Marquess of Pombal,[52] and nonetheless, he was in power for over twenty years. King João V thought he was an opportunist and never appointed him to any official position. It was only after King João's death, in King José I's reign, that Pombal managed, with great effort and thanks to influent supporters, to make his way into the government. But I don't believe Professor Salazar is like Pombal. I'd even say they're completely different types. But who knows?"

"So you think I shouldn't accept the invitation?"

"If I were in your place, I wouldn't."

"But why not?"

"I've already told you: it's dangerous, at least in the current state of affairs. You'd better wait to see how it's going to turn out. The regime won't last long and people are expecting an upheaval."

"More than what's already afflicted the country?"

"I'm no prophet. But you don't have to be. All you need to do is read the newspapers, pay attention to what's going on and to what people say."

"So what should I tell the Professor?"

"Don't tell him anything."

"I said I'd write. He'll think I was rude."

"Don't write. By now he's already forgotten you and is extending invitations to other people. Politicians have short memories."

"You know, Father, classes start in a few days and it's more than likely I'll run into him at Coimbra."

"Be friendly. Especially since he extended the invitation, it means he holds you in esteem. If he brings it up again, tell him you're thinking about it. At most he'll criticize your hesitation and try to make persuasive arguments to help you decide."

"And then what do I do?"

"Keep putting it off. Before you know it, you'll have reached the end of the academic year and graduated."

In December that year, about three months after that conversation with my father, Professor Oliveira Salazar, with a few of his colleagues from the Catholic Center, were dismissed from the university by the government for having supported the monarchist revolt in northern Portugal. I no longer needed to worry about the invitation. If I had accepted, Aninhas told me, I'd probably be some obscure cabinet minister in the current regime, I'd live in Lisbon with my family, wear a black suit every day and have people arrested for any trifling matter. *Libera nos domine!*

So that is why I did not write to Professor Oliveira Salazar. That late September I wrote Aninhas daily and went to visit her twice in Oporto. The second time, she took me to the tuberculosis sanatorium at Francelos beach, where Apúlia was interned. His coloring seemed better. He said he was sick of the sanatorium, the nurses, the doctors, and of eating the crappy food they fed him. He wanted to go home. He missed his family and his fishing boat.

I tried to make him see that if he went home before being completely cured, he'd end up dying. So he'd better let his family and fishing boat wait. He'd spent two years in Flanders and had put up with missing all of that, so now he would just have to wait a little more. Aninhas helped me convince him, arguing that the doctors would send him home as soon as they were sure he was cured. But in order for that to happen, he'd have to follow their instructions to the letter: the treatment, the rest, and the diet.

As we left the sanatorium, we talked to Dr. Juvenal Pereira, Aninhas's dandy friend. He told us the patient was showing some signs of improvement, but that it didn't mean much. The bacteria was still spreading in his lungs. The medication had managed to slow down the process to a certain extent, but it would take a miracle to save him. And since none of us believed in miracles, we all felt very apprehensive.

Dona Leontina had invited me to tea. As we sipped our tea and ate homemade cookies, I remembered to ask if Aninhas could come to our estate for the grape harvest, adding that Paulino could also come, if he wanted to, so she shouldn't consider my invitation inappropriate. Dona Leontina had a few reservations and, stalling, she said she needed to talk it over with her husband. Maybe she thought it unbecoming for a young single woman to go to the home of her sweetheart. I do not know what happened. Two days later I received a letter from Aninhas saying I could count on her and Paulino's company for the harvest and to meet them at the railway station in Braga.

On the day of the harvest, Rato also showed up to help. He brought along his daughter Evangelina and the two boys. My father, who had a terrible backache, had put me in charge. It was a tough day, yet very pleasant. First thing in the morning, I went to the station to meet Aninhas and her brother.

My parents received them graciously and, judging from both of their wide smiles, they liked Aninhas. My father, seated in an armchair because of his sore back, gave me a wink. My mother, when she caught me alone, told me Aninhas was a charming girl. And Aninhas thought they were both very nice. I was happy they had already got along so well. My parents had never cared for my relationship with Libaninha. She was a very picky girl and they considered her frivolous. That is why, when she called off the engagement, they showed no signs of disappointment. They did not like the idea of a daughter-in-law with a shrill voice, given to hysteria over the slightest hindrance, whether a broken nail or a loose thread in her hemline.

It was apparent Aninhas was a naturally nice girl, modest though tasteful in her appearance, discreet in her way of speaking, warm and intelligent. She could converse on any topic, proving herself to be just as well informed as anyone else. She was also clever, much more so than I, when it came to figuring out other people.

I left her with my parents and went out to the harvest.

By then the workers had already started. I went to the wine press, where they were stomping the grapes, and then to the trellises surrounding the estate. I took Paulino with me. The temporary workers, about twenty men, were climbing ladders to pick the grapes, which they placed in small baskets. Then they handed down the baskets to older women and children, who emptied them into much larger wicker baskets. When these were full, the younger women and girls carried them, on top of their head, to the ox cart, which then took them to the wine press. It was hard work for everyone, but the atmosphere was cheerful. The men, on top of the ladders, were telling jokes and calling down flirtatious comments to the girls, who answered them right back.

Paulino wanted to pick grapes, so I got him a small ladder. To make sure he did not get hurt, I asked Rato to keep an eye on him. Once again, Rato was his guardian angel. It would have been disastrous if the boy had fallen off the ladder and broken an arm or leg.

There was a lunchtime break and the temporary workers sat on a rock or wall and ate from their lunch pails. The invited guests were given a meal. Unfortunately, it was logistically im- possible to feed all those people. Although I had promised to pay them, I considered Rato and his children my guests and they sat at an improvised table near the wine cellar, where they were served along with the estate caretakers and a few men my father usually invited as a courtesy. Paulino and I went to the house to have lunch along with my parents and Aninhas.

Paulino ate without much appetite – he had eaten too many grapes. During the meal he kept talking enthusiastically about what he had done, seen, and heard while hanging from the ladder cutting down bunches of borraçal grapes.[53] He said Rato had talked about the war, the trenches, the bombs, the grenade fragments, the rats, and the Boche.

"Living in the trenches must have been neat. I wish I'd been there. But now the war's over..."

"Don't worry. There'll probably be another one someday," my father said with a touch of irony.

"Really?"

Although the topic was not funny, we all ended up smiling at the innocence of my future brother-in-law.

"Rato told me there were soldiers in the trenches that had rifles equipped with a telescopic sight who spent all their time on the look-out for the enemy. When they saw someone, bang! And he was done for. The enemy was killed without ever knowing where the shot came from. I'd sure like to have a rifle like that."

"And what for?" I asked.

"From the window of my room back in Oporto, it'd be real fun to shoot at sparrows, gulls, and cats climbing on rooftops."

"Oh Paulino," Aninhas interrupted him, "whatever will our hosts think of you? Will you please do me a favor and be quiet and eat your lunch."

"I'm not hungry."

"Why aren't you hungry? The food is excellent. If you don't eat, you're going to offend these kind people who were nice enough to invite us."

"I ate too many grapes and now I don't feel like having anything else."

"All the more for us," said my father, sticking his fork into a chicken thigh from the tray.

When lunch was done, Aninhas called me aside to ask if she could go to the harvest. I asked her if my parents were getting on her nerves.

"No, no. They've been so kind. But I didn't come here to spend the day with them. I came to spend the day with you."

By then we were treating each other very informally, ever since the day we had visited Apúlia at the sanatorium. She insisted, "I want you to take me to the harvest."

"You cannot follow me around the fields, Aninhas. You'd

get your clothes and shoes all dirty. You'll be more comfortable here at the house. You must realize I cannot keep you company. I have to tell the men what to do, keep them motivated. We're running a little late and it's impossible to pick grapes at night."

"I don't want to follow you around the fields. What would people say? 'There goes the little spoiled brat, tagging along after the boss's son!' I want to help with the harvest."

"Help with the harvest?"

"Didn't you just say you're running behind schedule?"

"Well, yes, but I don't think this is your kind of work."

"And why not?"

"Now, Aninhas, it's hard work. I don't think you'd be able to carry a basket on your head."

"From the window I saw girls younger and more slender than I am carrying baskets."

"But they're country girls. They're used to carrying heavy loads."

"And why shouldn't I get used to it?"

"Because you don't need to."

"And why shouldn't I pick grapes?"

"Because you'd have to climb a ladder. It's impossible."

"Why is that impossible?"

"First, because you wouldn't be able to stay up there very long. And second, it's inappropriate."

"Inappropriate?"

"Women don't climb ladders."

"But why not?"

"Well, because they wear skirts. Now, you don't want the men to be looking up at your legs, do you?"

"That's a good argument for keeping women in their place. But one day, it will be irrelevant."

"I don't see how."

"When women start wearing slacks."

"When pigs fly, maybe."

"You may be mistaken."

And I was mistaken after all. A few years later, it was not unusual to see women wearing slacks, especially in Oporto and Lisbon, which led the clergy to campaign against modern fashion, inspired by the Devil.

One thing was certain, at that moment there was no argument to convince me to let Aninhas get on a ladder and pick grapes.

She sulked a little, and to settle the dispute, I asked if she wanted to come along and pick up grapes off the ground. That was the only way to keep her busy and near me without attracting attention and with little risk. But she'd have to change her clothes. She could not go out in the fields with her long beige dress, her flowered hat and her little high-heeled patent leather shoes. I asked Maria, the maid, to lend her a blouse, skirt, apron, scarf for her hair, and some clogs. And when she was all ready, she should come meet me at the wine press. I'd go over there in a while to see how things were coming along, after I'd checked out the harvesting.

I was watching Old Felício work on the crusher, cleaning out the pieces clogged with pomace, when I saw walking into the wine cellar the prettiest farm girl who had ever showed her face in that region. Old Felício stopped working to look at her.

"Luís!" Aninhas called out.

"Luís?!" Old Felício exclaimed indignantly. "Listen here, lassie: you watch your tongue. You're speaking to the boss. Show a little respect, d'you hear? Or didn't your mother teach you nothing?"

"Leave it be, Felício. Don't get worked up on my account. She's new here," I explained.

"It don't matter if she's new or not. Good manners's good manners, specially with the boss. Who's ever heard of such a thing...?!"

Aninhas could not control herself and broke into laughter. Old Felício hit the ceiling.

"But lassie, are you losing your mind or what? Ain't you got no work to do? Get going, you little fool. There's lots of baskets to be carried."

"Come now, Felício, you'll end up frightening the girl. Just carry on with what you were doing and I'll deal with her."

"You deal with her, Master Luís, you deal with her... If it was up to me she'd be out of here with her tail between her legs and stinging ears."

Aninhas followed me out of the wine cellar with her clogs hammering the tiles. She could not stop laughing and I ended up laughing along with her.

"That man," she said between her hiccups "that man thought I was a farm girl, come to work the harvest."

"Well, aren't you? Just a little while ago you were offering your services."

I took Aninhas to the field and put her with a group of two old women and four children who were following the grape pickers along one of the trellises. She crouched and started getting her little white delicate hands dirty with the fallen grapes. The old women looked at her and thought, perhaps, that she should be using her little body to carry baskets. I decided to let them know she couldn't bear their weight and she was doing the best she could.

"If you say so, sir," said one of the old women.

It was a sunny afternoon, which helped us make up for the time we had lost that morning. Some clouds accumulating in the south promised rain for the following few days. It had certainly been a good idea to set the harvest for that date.

I walked all over the estate encouraging the men, pointing out an overlooked grapevine, helping one girl or another place the basket on her head, coordinating the comings and goings of the ox cart, supervising the wine press. I passed Aninhas several times and we exchanged glances and smiles. She got involved in the conversations with the older women and the harvest workers. One young worker, she told me later, allowed himself to get caught in her spell – which was no surprise, since Aninhas was easily the most attractive farm girl working that harvest. He flirted with her and she, in the strongest Oporto accent she could muster, put him off.

"You're not from here," the boy apparently said.

And he insisted she tell him where she was from, who her parents were, and how she had ended up at the Quinta de São Francisco.

Aninhas, who did not want to say she was the owner's son's sweetheart because it would have made the workers very uncomfortable, came up with the idea of saying she was Old Felício's niece, working as a house maid.

"Oh, you're a kitchen maid!" the young man exclaimed from the top of his ladder, somewhat disappointed.

"Do you have something against kitchen maids?" she asked.

"Not me. But everyone knows who they are and what they do in the house."

"And what do they do?"

"You should know, I'm not a kitchen maid," he said laughing.

One of the older women told Aninhas what the common folk thought about kitchen maids.

"They're a lot of lazy girls who live the high life in rich people's houses. They got a soft bed and lots of good food. And, since they ain't got to slave away in the field like us, they's always warm and fresh."

"But, see here, Alfredina, they work a lot," Aninhas answered, basing herself on the maids she had known. "A housemaid spends the whole day working and goes to bed exhausted, completely spent."

"But it ain't nothing like working in the fields," Alfredina countered. "Not to mention the bosses' little gifts...."

"What little gifts? So the masters give them gifts?"

276

"Don't you know, girl? Little gifts like a skirt, a blouse, a handkerchief, new clogs, things the master usually gives them in exchange for little favors."

"Little favors? What little favors?"

"It's easy to see you're new at all this. But you can be sure I ain't going to explain. You'll surely find out on your own one of these days. Now get me that bunch of grapes we left behind."

And that was how the conversation on kitchen maids came to an end. The farm boy, disappointed, did not bother Aninhas again. Few men would ever want a kitchen maid for a sweetheart, no matter how pretty she was.

We managed to harvest everything just before dark. The workers put the ladders back in the shed and I said goodbye to each one of them, thanking them for their efforts and paying them the agreed-upon wages. In contrast to legend, no one complained. I asked Rato to stay for supper along with his children. I wanted him to help Old Felício stir the new wine in the press.

Back at the house I found Aninhas and Paulino in the living room. They were exhausted. Aninhas had a backache from having spent the entire afternoon bent over, and the boy's legs hurt from climbing up and down the ladder. My mother was really upset to find them in that state and blamed me. I shouldn't have allowed our guests to help with the grape harvest as if they were common day workers. Since they were in no condition to make the trip back to Oporto, she thought it better they stay overnight at the estate. Aninhas, sitting in an armchair, still wearing the maid's clothes, did not have the energy to protest.

So their parents would not worry, someone needed to telephone them. The problem was that at that time we had no telephone at home and the closest one was at Quinta de Santa Madalena, that is, Libaninha's parents' estate. We thought about sending the message via one of Rato's sons, but Libaninha's parents might have been offended. And so, while Aninhas and

Paulino took a hot bath and got ready for supper, I mounted Ruddy and rode to Quinta de Santa Madalena, wondering how I would be received by Libaninha's parents. Would they have the nerve to refuse me entry and to deny me the use of the telephone?

Benvinda, the maid, met me at the door and announced my arrival to Senhora Dona Libânia, my very dignified, very proud, very dry ex-fiancée. Right there in the living room, I explained confusedly that something unexpected had happened during the grape harvest and that I needed to make an urgent phone call. I'd be very grateful if she would let me use their telephone.

"But of course," she said stiffly.

She accompanied me to the hall where the telephone was installed and left me alone.

Aninhas's mother answered and I explained it would be better if her children spent the night at our house. It was already late and they were really tired. Dona Leontina, to my surprise, offered no resistance. She confessed she'd been afraid that might happen. After all, grape harvesting was not for everyone. She would meet her children the following day at the railway station. After listening to a few words of advice, that she knew she need not remind me that under no circumstances was I to forget my gentlemanly behavior, she hung up.

I returned to the living room where Senhora Dona Libânia was waiting for me. She asked me, in a slightly worried tone, what had happened, if everything was all right with my parents. I said they were fine, and asked after hers. She told me they were in Caldelas, taking the waters. They would be back in two days for the grape harvest. It had been set for that day, but they had been obliged to postpone. The grape pickers had suddenly become unavailable. Apparently there was another harvest they couldn't miss going to that same day.

She said that with a touch of irony I pretended not to notice.

278

"And how is your husband?"

"He's in Lisbon. He works in the Ministry of the Colonies."

A politician, I thought.

After a few seconds of silence during which she studied me from head to toe, she continued, "Mr. Luís Vasques, you seem to have lost weight."

"And Senhora Libânia's slightly..."

I hesitated, I was going to say 'fatter,' but it would have been rude.

"...graceful." I ended up saying.

"You're just being polite."

"Why are you here at the estate? Don't you like Lisbon?" I asked. "In the capital, you'd be closer to your husband, of course."

"I hate Lisbon. And my husband also hates for me to be there."

Those two statements could have led to a long conversation. But I could not stay, because they were probably already holding supper for me. I thanked her for having allowed me to use the telephone and took my leave. Dona Libânia insisted on accompanying me to the gate. As I was preparing to mount my horse, she said, "Luís, you know..."

She rubbed her hands together, with their long, manicured nails, and hesitated over what she wanted to say, or how to say it.

"I wanted you to know that it was not my idea to break off our engagement."

"What's done is done, Senhora Dona Libânia."

"Don't you believe me?"

"It no longer matters. You are a married lady now, Ma'am. Whether or not I believe it doesn't change anything."

"I don't want you to think poorly of me, Luís, that I broke off the engagement because I didn't care for you. That..."

"Goodbye, Libânia."

"Stop by again, when you can. I'd like very much to talk with you, to clarify what happened. Promise?"

I shook the reigns and my horse trotted off along the dark road to the village.

After supper, I went with my father to the wine cellar to see the press. He leaned on my arm to go down the steps. We found Old Felício and Rato, duly supped, stirring the must with rakes.

"We have here one fine wine press, I'll say," my father said. "What have we got, eighteen casks?"

"Maybe nineteen, sir," Old Felício corrected him.

"Somehow I reckon it's nineteen casks and half a dozen demijohns," Rato suggested with a mischievous smile.

"You shut up, you wretch!" ordered Old Felício, who did not like jokes. Then, turning to my father, he added, "Sir, we'd better pray."

"Very well, let's pray."

We all took off our hats and my father recited several short prayers accompanied by Hail Marys and Lord's Prayers said in chorus by all present. It was a superstition my father respected and that was harmless to maintain. In fact, it would have been a serious mistake, with Old Felício present, to not carry out the ritual. The wine might go bad.

We put our hats back on and Old Felício got a jug of old wine, filled a bowl and gave it to his boss. My father threw some into the press and drank a gulp. He handed it to me, I drank, then passed it to Old Felício, who did the same and, after hesitating briefly, handed it to Rato, who finished it off. The ritual was carried out in silence and with strict respect for the rules and hierarchy.

While my father talked to Old Felício, I asked Rato to come back the following day. I wanted to keep him near the press. He asked me if I'd had news from France yet. I promised I'd let him know as soon as I heard anything.

280

Back at the house, my mother told me our guests had retired.

"They were all worn out," she explained. "Aninhas even wanted to wait for you, but I made her go to bed. The two of you will have plenty of time to talk tomorrow."

Then she went back to harping on me for having allowed them to help with the grape harvest.

"They're from the city and they're not used to this kind of work. Whatever will their parents say when they find out we made them work like common day laborers?"

There was no use trying to explain that the whole idea had been theirs. As far as I was concerned they would have stayed home looking out the window.

As I walked by the guest rooms – there were two – I stopped outside the doors. I wondered which one might be hers. I could have knocked and put my doubts to rest. Instead, I walked on to my own room. A basin of hot water and a bar of soap were waiting for me. I washed my hands and feet and went to bed.

XXIV

I got back to Madame Gavroche's at lunch time after spending the morning at the depot, checking out the marching orders for the twenty-four replacements I was supposed to take back to l'Epinette, where they would join our battalion. Having verified and signed the forms a sergeant put in front of me, I went out to meet the men. There were twenty privates, three sergeants, and a second lieutenant named Moreira, originally from Chaves, who would replace our comrade who had lost his hand in a recent attack. He seemed a decent fellow, apprehensive about what awaited him. Those men had just arrived and were being sent to the front with hardly enough training. I felt sorry for them.

We would not get many more replacements. By the end of 1917, the dead, the wounded, and the sick would no longer be replaced, for lack of reserves. It was the beginning of the crisis for the Portuguese Expeditionary Corps.

I left the greenhorn second lieutenant in charge of the men and gave him instructions to have them ready to move out after lunch. He was billeted on a farm near the depot and invited me to lunch. I thanked him, but did not accept.

Back at the Gavroche farm, I found Rato, Madame Gavroche, and the children in the field, digging up potatoes. Thanks to Rato's help, they had made good progress. Madame Leonor Pigeard had not finished preparing lunch and I started helping to fill the burlap bags. Madame Gavroche came over with a pail full of potatoes and asked me to hold one of the bags open. While we were at it, she said in a low tone, "I'm very happy, Monsieur Vasques. But my happiness is a bit troubled because I know you'll be leaving for the front again. Promise me you'll be back."

"I will, Madame," I said, even though I knew the value of such a promise, tied as I was to the hazards of the war.

She looked at her children and Rato, bending over the ditches where they were digging up potatoes. They were too far away to overhear us. She asked me not to think of her as an easy woman who would go to bed with anyone. She was aware that French women had that reputation, but she wasn't like that. She'd never gone to bed with any man other than her husband. She'd done it with me because, deep inside, she felt sure she was already a widow. So she hadn't violated any moral code. Besides, she liked me. I was a handsome, sensitive man, and very respectful. If I'd been an Englishman, she'd never have allowed herself to be so intimate as she'd been with me. I said the English were not all brutes. After all, they were known to be gentlemen.

"A gentleman is not a *gentilhomme*," she replied. "Being a *gentilhomme* is more than greeting politely, holding a door open for a lady, or standing up like a soldier. Being a *gentilhomme* means being refined, kind, and unassuming." She paused, and added, "A gentleman is like a grandfather clock; a *gentilhomme* is more like a curtain, softly fluttering in the breeze."

François came over with a pail and we stopped talking. About half an hour later, Madame Pigeard yelled from the porch that lunch was served.

When I had bought the bottles of bagaço for Captain Rebelo at the depot, I had also got one of port. I opened it after lunch and poured a glass for everybody, including the children. They enjoyed the wine, sweet and aromatic. Madame Pigeard proposed a toast *à votre santé*, meaning mine and Rato's, and we responded with another toast, *à la santé* of the *mesdames et des enfants*.

We got ready to leave. We had to be at the depot before the two o'clock parade. Madame Gavroche loaded us with homemade delicacies and insisted on seeing us off at the gate. The dog, having woken up from his after-lunch nap on the porch, came trotting along. She thanked us for helping to dig up the potatoes and for fixing things around the house, and renewed her invitation for us to visit the farm whenever we had a chance and felt like it. I shrugged on my knapsack and stretched out my hand.

"*Au revoir, madame.*"

"*Au revoir, Luís,*" she said, shaking my hand.

Rato also shook hands with her and we left. At the first bend of the road I turned back. She was still by the gate with the dog at her feet. She raised her hand and waved a final goodbye. Rato noticed it and said, "She's a good lady, this Madame. If I had my way, I'd stay here forever."

"The only ones who stay here forever, Rato, are those who get killed. There's a cemetery full of Portuguese soldiers near Neuve-Chapelle."

"I meant at the farm, sir."

"And what's there about the farm that makes you wish to stay here forever?"

"The land, sir. Have you seen how many potatoes came out of each ditch? It's like a gift from God. And also the people. They've all been very nice. And Madame Constance..."

I began to wonder what Rato might mean by that. Did he suspect there had been something between the two of us? If he did, that conversation did not go any further. He was discreet enough not to raise the subject, and since I did not confide in him, the matter was dropped.

When we got to the depot, Second Lieutenant Moreira had the men formed up and ready to go. We double-checked the numbers on the list against the number each soldier had sown on his collar, and left.

I am now racking my brain trying to recall the details of our trip back to l'Epinette. Most likely, other than the march, which was a soldier's main activity in Flanders, and the trivial incidents related to it, such as blisters, fatigue, and having to chew out stragglers, nothing memorable happened. Or maybe I was so absent-minded that I did not pay attention. I was walking to war happy and contented, unlike the wretches under my command, who were apprehensive and scared by the booming of the guns, increasingly louder. But they had not spent two days in paradise and did not know that, after that, death ceased to be important. I was ready to die, should fate so determine.

We arrived at the cantonment at l'Epinette, turned the men over at Battalion Headquarters, and went back to our billets. Rato rejoined the platoon, lodged in a barn, and I went to Madame Eveline Piñata's, where Nigeria and I shared our little room.

At the end of September, our battalion marched to Penin-Mariage. It was the end of our month-long rest, a privilege we would never again enjoy. We were going to relieve the 8th Battalion in the support line of the Penin-Mariage sector. During the week we spent there we had a night attack with mortar shells and gas grenades. At the same time, the first line, defended by the 8th Battalion, was being raided. The gas alarm bell went off and we had to put on our masks. Since we had not worn them for a while, the gas caused a few casualties before we could adjust them. A dozen soldiers had to be evacuated to the hospital with sores in their eyes, mouth, and throat. Nobody died, but after the war those who had inhaled mustard gas started having respiratory problems and emotional troubles. When a man was seen in public singing, talking loudly, or babbling nonsense, people would say, "That one's been gassed!" Even if he had not. In Portugal in the 1920's, "being gassed" was synonymous with being crazy.

From late September to the end of the year, our battalion alternated a week in the support line at the Penin-Mariage sector and a week in the first line at the Ferme du Bois sector. Three damp, freezing months. Trench routine was regularly disrupted by raids and bombardments. Someone who has never been there might think it was a daily hell of shooting and explosions, but actually that was not the case. Shots and explosions were exceptional. Our routine included standing guard, waiting, parading, and periods of quiet, during which we picked lice and flees, and above all tried to stay warm.

When we were in the first line, we were raided twice, both times in November. Once the Boche penetrated our trenches – a sentry must have been asleep or simply not paying attention. We fought back as best we could. The raid left a balance of one dead and thirteen wounded, either shot or bayoneted. When I heard the alarm shouts I was sitting on an ammunition box in the dugout, scraping the bottom of one of Madame Gavroche's preserve jars. Nogueira was sitting next to me on one of the cots and cleaning out a can of corned beef. Captain Rebelo was lying on the other cot in a drunken stupor. By then he had already polished off the bottles of bagaço I had brought him and was drinking rum and whiskey, which were easier to obtain in our sector. Nogueira and I jumped up, startled, barely missing the ceiling, and ran out at once to see what was going on. The Captain did not even budge.

Nogueira and I split a few meters from the shelter and ran toward the area guarded by our respective platoons. We could hear shots and screams. As I passed by several men manning the fire steps and guarding the parapet, I told them to stay in their posts and keep their ears and eyes peeled, because the enemy might attack from any direction.

I got to a periscope, told Corporal Fontes to fire a Very light, and tried to see if there was anything moving in no man's land. Nothing was moving in front of our position.

"Do you think the Boche have got in, sir?" asked Tibães, who was on one of the fire steps.

"They sure may have," I said. "If anyone comes up from inside the trench, not knowing the password and talking funny, just let them have it, for they're certain to be the Boche."

I reiterated my recommendations and walked on in the direction of the shooting and screaming. Only then did I realize I had forgotten to bring my rifle. I drew my pistol and aimed ahead as I walked. A few meters ahead, I ran into Rato on a fire step, aiming at no man's land. Private Semelhe was next to him. Each position was always guarded by two men. I told Rato to come along with me and ordered Semelhe to stay sharp.

I could still hear shooting and screaming and thought the Boche had attacked the company on our right. The man at the last sentry post guarded by my platoon confirmed it. The Boche had taken advantage of the moonlight to attack our lines. Otherwise it would have been impossible for them to find their way in no man's land, jump over the parapet and fire at our soldiers.

When we reached the attack area, the Boche were gone. You could hear our heavy machine guns combing no man's land, but by then the Boche had either reached their own lines or were hiding in some shell-crater, waiting for our machine gunners to run out of ammunition or enthusiasm. I considered sending some men after them, but I lacked the authority to do so. Such an order had to be given by the Major or by one of the company commanders, which at that point was impossible. The Major was out of reach somewhere in the rear, Captain Rebelo was nursing his drunkenness, and the Captain of the company under attack was somewhere else. I joined those taking care of the wounded and helped apply a few compresses. I recall a dead soldier, stretched out at the bottom of the trench. His face was covered with mud and his tunic was soaked with the blood that had oozed out of his chest. The bullet must have hit a lung and it took him a few minutes to die. His sentry post partner was telling a sergeant he had tried to be brave and resist after being told to surrender, and they had shot him through the chest.

The wounded were moaning and their comrades tried to calm them down. The noise they were making was a hazard and I asked them to be quiet, since the Boche could easily pinpoint us and start firing a mortar. But it was too late. All of a sudden we heard a mortar round screech by and burst a few meters over the parapet, sending dirt and bits of barbed wire on top of everyone in the area. A wire fragment sliced through a stretcher-bearer's face. I immediately ordered to have the wounded removed by any means possible – on stretchers, dragged, or stumbling – and to evacuate the area.

I went back to the shelter, urging the men to stay alert, even though I did not think there would be another attack that night. Unlike us, who trusted luck and supernatural forces more than military tactics, the Germans only ventured a raid after considering all the risks and deciding which objectives had some probability of being reached. Thanks to that, ninety per cent of their raids caused damages. By contrast, our raids had a success margin of less than five per cent. The heroic Portuguese navigators who had conquered the oceans had long faded into history.

I found Nogueira, Coutinho, and Captain Rebelo in the shelter. Comparing notes, we figured the subsector defended by our company had escaped unscathed. The report we would send the Major the next day would be the usual one. The company on our right, however, would have to describe the attack and account for the dead soldier, the thirteen wounded, and a few who had been taken prisoner.

"At this hour the Boche must be interrogating them," Nogueira said.

"They're out of luck," Coutinho said. "I doubt they have anyone who can speak Portuguese. And even if they do, the Minho accent is so thick they won't be able to figure out what the prisoners are saying. If they say anything."

"They're from Minho, and so they can talk a blue streak."

"Maybe we do," I said, "but that doesn't mean we can't clam up when necessary. And even if one of my men were interrogated and talked, he'd babble so many lies and so much nonsense that they'd think he was crazy, or if they believed him, they'd think there were a million of us here instead of just fifty thousand."

The next day we were visited by General Gomes da Costa. It was the first time a general had ever descended to the first line. He was accompanied by the Major commanding our battalion and a few paper-pushers. The sun was shining, but that did not prevent our illustrious visitors from getting their boots splattered with mud. They chatted with the soldiers, handed out cigarettes, and promised we'd be back home soon. Private Tibães stood at attention and requested permission to speak. When it was granted, he asked the General when they would have a home leave. The General twisted his mustache, looked up at the sky as if doing some mental calculations, and answered, "Maybe at Christmas."

A month later, by mid-October, the President of Portugal, Bernardino Machado, paid a visit to the Portuguese Expeditionary Corps, but he stayed at General Headquarters, way back at the rear. Before the sumptuous lunch in his honor, he decorated forty-five soldiers with the War Cross. None of them was from my platoon. As the top brass saw it, no brave deed had been done by the soldiers under my orders. Two weeks after the President's visit, the figures of Portuguese dead in Flanders were released: 258 killed in combat and 94 from disease or accidents. In about six months in the front line, that averaged two dead per day.

The second attack against our sector took place three days before my birthday, which I spent in the field hospital because I was wounded.

In the evening of November 22nd the first line was the target of intense shelling. Our Captain, drunk again, was sleeping in the dugout, seemingly undisturbed by the explosions that rocked everything around him. The other two junior officers and I made the necessary decisions. Since we could not phone Battalion Headquarters, as the cables had been damaged by the first mortar rounds, each of us went to the area held by his platoon and, using what cover was available, encouraged the men to resist.

As chance would have it, the next attack took place in the subsector defended by our company. Shortly after the guns went silent, the sentries sounded the alarm and started firing into no man's land. Despite that, the Boche managed to cut the barbed wire and jump over the parapet. Rushing in the direction of the alarm shouts, I ran into Rato, who said the Boche had got into the trench. Realizing I had left my rifle in the dugout again, I raced ahead of him along the duckboard, quite damaged in places by the bombardment, and suddenly we ran into two Boche soldiers.

"*Halt!*" one of them yelled.

Reacting almost instinctively, I punched the one closer to me, branding his face with my family signet ring. The other German reacted by plunging his bayonet into my left arm. I leaned back on the parados, holding my wounded arm, and while he prepared to stab me again, Rato fired. While he reloaded his rifle, the two Boche ran away. Rato fired two or three more rounds into the dark trench, but by then they must have already jumped over the parapet into no man's land. I told him to stop firing, to prevent him from hitting one of our own.

We could hear shooting and yelling on our left as Rato helped me back to the shelter. The cut on my arm was long and I lost a lot of blood. The Captain had woken up and, although still under the effects of alcohol, sent a runner for medics and stretcher bearers for the wounded. Nogueira and Coutinho joined us and we reported on the situation: besides my wound, eight soldiers had been hit by grenade fragments and bullets, and Sergeant Rosado had been rifle-butted in the head. Fortunately, nobody had been killed. The Boche had withdrawn after the raid, leaving no casualties behind.

The Captain, who hated having his sleep interrupted, was furious.

"Can't these fuckers leave us alone? We're trying to take it easy, like sportsmen, and the sons-of-bitches just can't leave us in peace! I swear they're going to find out what we're made of, and that's a promise!"

I sat down on an ammunition box and the Captain, who had received some first aid training at the Military Academy, decided to treat my wound. I felt like saying I could hold out until the medics arrived, but he insisted. There was no point in arguing with a drunk. He made me take off my tunic and ripped my shirtsleeve up to my shoulder. The bayonet cut went from the elbow to the wrist and would have been worse if it had not been for the clothing. He cleaned off the blood with a rag soaked in whiskey and applied a compress. To minimize the pain he made me drink what was left in the bottle.

The medics and stretcher-bearers arrived, and after administering to the seriously wounded, they carried those who could not walk to the first aid post. The others and I walked. As we crossed the communication trenches, I recall hearing our heavy machine guns combing no man's land. I wondered if the Boche Rato had shot had reached his lines alive, or if he was bleeding to death in the mud of Afonso Costa Avenue. But the Germans never left their dead or wounded behind.

To prevent infection, rather than letting me go back to the trench, the doctor who sewed up my wound sent me to the Brigade Field Hospital, where I spent a week convalescing. I had hoped to be sent back home, but as it turned out my wound was not that serious. To be repatriated, I would need to lose a lot more blood, or maybe an arm or a leg. But although my wound was not very serious, I was left with a scar that my family makes me show our visitors.

I owed Rato my life. Had he not intervened, I would have been impaled by that Boche's bayonet. We commented how odd it seemed that the Boche had managed to escape after having been shot at point-blank. Rato blamed the poor visibility, but I suspect he did not kill that soldier because he did not want to. The time would come when Rato would have to choose between killing or being killed, but that was still a few months ahead.

During the time I could not use my arm, I did not answer any letters. My father wrote me with news about our estate and the country. In Lisbon, due to the scarcity of staples, bakeries and groceries had been looted. He commented that whenever things got that bad in Lisbon, the government would fall.

But this time the government did not fall, it was deposed. In early December there was a military uprising headed by Colonel Sidónio Paz, who had been Ambassador to Berlin, putting an end to the corrupt Afonso Costa administration. When it became known, there were smiles on the faces of the soldiers and some officers, myself included. Rato told me there was a rumor that Sidónio Pais would soon order the withdrawal of our troops from Flanders. Even though I knew he was a germanophile on good terms with the German Government, I did not believe he would do that. It would be dishonorable in view of our commitments to our allies. Besides, at that point a withdrawal would be impractical. Some said that, in view of Sidónio Pais's sympathies for the Boche, we might receive orders to do an about-face and start firing at the English. That would have been a supreme irony of war.

To go back to my father's letter. He also mentioned some apparitions supposedly sighted in Fátima since May. The last one had occurred on October 13, attracting thousands of people and a handful of journalists to the area. It seemed that, except for the shepherd children, nobody had managed to see the Virgin, which was somewhat odd, to put it mildly. There was, however, a strange phenomenon witnessed by many people.

The news of the apparitions spread fast throughout the country, and the people, always keen on miracles and prodigies, flocked to the region. As I found out later, Old Felício had visited that place with some fellow members of his Brotherhood of Our Lady of Good Fortune. He told me there were so many people that only a few managed to see the three children at the place where the Virgin supposedly had appeared to them. It had rained heavily all morning, soaking people's clothes and churning the ground into a muddy field. Around one in the afternoon the rain ceased, the clouds opened up like theater curtains, and something like a dark silver disk spun off the sun, spinning around like a fireworks wheel. It moved, stopped, moved again, and fluttered over the crowd like a dead leaf. When it got very close, it became transparent and he saw three faces inside it. Then it zigzagged upwards and entered a golden cloud. When the wind blew the cloud away, the disk had vanished and the sun was back in its usual place. Everyone said the sun had moved, but that is not what Old Felício had seen. The sun had remained up behind the clouds, and he saw something else. Some people said the three faces were the Holy Family – Saint Joseph, the Virgin, and the Infant Jesus. But Old Felício was not sure about that. Why couldn't they be the persons of the Holy Trinity? Or the three Wise Men? Or three demons? It was known, he said, that one could not trust the Devil, and the so-called miracle of the sun could well be one of his tricks for fooling innocent Christians.

What was really extraordinary was that after the phenomenon people suddenly found their clothes had dried, and some of the sick, who had come on stretchers or wheelchairs, started saying they had been cured. I suggested this was further evidence it was not the Devil's work, but God's, but Old Felício still did not agree, and never set foot in Fátima again. Every year around May 13, when he saw his neighbors and relatives leave for Fátima on pilgrimage, he started grumbling heresies. I asked him several times about what he had seen and his story was always the same. One might suppose our caretaker was a free-thinker, but that was not the case. Old Felício was a devout Christian who fulfilled his obligations to the Church. He belonged to the Brotherhood of Our Lady of the Good Fortune, and several times at Easter he was appointed Steward of the Cross. But let nobody mention Fátima to him. When his Brotherhood, following the priest's suggestion, decided to place an image of the Virgin of Fátima at the church, he was the only one who voted against it.

According to what my father wrote in his letter, the phenomenon of October 13, 1917 was publicized in the papers, particularly *O Século*,[54] which was republican and anti-clerical, and therefore a reliable source of information that something extraordinary had indeed taken place, whether it was the work of God or the Devil, or Nature's whim, or something we have not yet been able to figure out.

Supposedly the Virgin told the shepherd children the war would end on that very same day, but this prophecy was not fulfilled, since the war only ended a year later. Could the Lady have got the dates mixed up? Or, as Old Felício thought, was it another of the Devil's tricks meant to fool us? The Fátima apparitions, as my father commented, were not something unheard of. All over the country there were dozens of known cases of shepherds, young and old, who swore they had seen the Virgin while herding their goats in the fields. Nearly every mountain village boasted a sanctuary consecrated to the Virgin at the top of a nearby hill or knoll. He also mentioned the case of a little shepherd from a hamlet near Ponte da Barca,[55] who said the Virgin had appeared to him one or two days before May 13 of that year.

What was unusual about Fátima was the hullabaloo in the newspapers, its political and religious exploitation by the Church and the opposition to the republican regime, and the resulting eagerness with which the ignorant masses flocked there as if it could solve all of life's problems. For the opposition to the regime, the Fátima apparitions could hardly have been handier.

On May 13, 1924, Aninhas, impressed by those stories, asked me to take her to Fátima. She practiced Catholicism casually but had many doubts about her faith. Unlike thousands of pilgrims, we were not keeping any promise, but simply visiting. Or at least that was what I thought. Aninhas never told me what her real intentions were. It was my first trip to Fátima since I had driven there with Rato, and I was surprised to see the construction work underway and the village growing in the middle of the wilderness. The Catholic Church certainly knew how to take advantage of the shepherd children's stories. After the open air mass, Aninhas went to the chapel to pray and give alms. Most of the people had scattered outside the sanctuary, looking for a place to sit down and eat their picnic lunch. It was a pleasant experience for the faithful who would rather not be crowded and wished to have some silence and peace for their devotions. I waited for Aninhas outside the chapel, watching the construction work. Suddenly I noticed some people around me looking up and pointing at the sky. It was raining white flowers. I stretched out my hand but did not manage to catch any. The petals vanished as soon as they came a little over our heads. As far as I was concerned, what was falling could just as well have been snow flakes. However, there were no clouds, without which there is no snow. Maybe a passing airplane had dropped the flowers. But there was no sign of any airplane. When the flowers stopped falling, I turned my eyes to the chapel, looking for Aninhas among the pilgrims. That was when a sudden impulse led me to the chapel, as if an inner voice were telling me to go and kneel before the Virgin's image.

Aninhas was quite surprised when she saw me kneeling down beside her. At that point, due to lack of practice, I did not remember the usual prayers I had learned at catechism as a child. Nevertheless, to my surprise, I found myself reciting Hail Marys and Hail Holy Queens without any hesitation or error. Until then I had been rather skeptical about apparitions, and I am still convinced that place is conducive to telluric phenomena, as some researchers call them. It is quite likely that my sudden inner voice had something to do with that. What makes me have some reservations is my positivistic streak, as Aninhas calls it. There is also the fact that the Church, or some of its representatives, have manipulated the story of what happened, silencing the only one of the shepherd children still alive today[56] and stifling any alternative versions.

A letter from Madame Gavroche cheered me up a little. It was affectionate without being sugary. She wrote she thought about me every day and prayed that nothing bad happened to me. She asked me to write her. I need not write much, a *carte-lettre* would suffice for her to know I was well and had not forgotten her. When my arm healed and I could hold a pen, I wrote her, without mentioning my wound. If we ever met again, she would see the scar and it would not matter much, but if I mentioned it then she might have worried.

I spent my birthday at the hospital, which consisted of a few wood and tin huts on stilts, where the cold crept in through the cracks. Since it was forbidden to leave the perimeter without a medical pass, I killed time reading in bed, or walking around and talking to the other patients. I had the advantage of being able to walk, but most of my companions were bed-ridden, or at best they could only hop around on crutches. There were about thirty beds, whose occupants had quite a variety of problems. Most had been mutilated, shot, gassed, or, like me, bayoneted. A few suffered from tuberculosis and were waiting to be transferred to a sanatorium, and a few were asthenic. I asked an orderly what kind of illness that was, since it had no apparent symptoms, and he told me it was an illness typical of pusillanimous soldiers. I asked him what he meant by that.

"I dunno, sir. Maybe you'd better ask the Doc. He's the one that says asthenic soldiers are pusillanimous. It's gotta be some medical word."

Unlike the orderly, I knew pusillanimous was not a medical term, but rather a word of Latin origin that meant cowardly. The orderly tried to explain, "Fellows with that disease, sir, they spend all their time shaking. They ain't got no strength, can't stand up, nor hold a rifle."

"And what kind of treatment do they get?"

"None, sir. They just stay moaning and shaking day and night, and saying they gonna die. The first ones what came, the doctors said they was just malingering and sent them back to the trenches. But since the English doctors told us about asthenia, we been keeping them here. There just ain't nothing you can do for them."

More than the men who had lost their arms, or who had gunshot wounds in their chest or their belly, or had shot up faces and bandaged eyes, groaning and coughing, more than the smell of rot, gangrene, dried blood, pus, vomit, piss, and shit, more than all that, it was the asthenic patients with their mental infirmity that impressed me most. I was ashamed of being there. My wound was no more than a scratch in comparison to what my comrades had to withstand.

In the morning of the first day I spent at the hospital, they found out four men in nearby beds had died during the night. Within a few minutes the nurses removed the bodies, frozen stiff. In a little while, the beds were taken by new patients.

Love, I thought, created men. War, pain and death.

XXV

The morning after the grape harvest, I heard a knock at my door. I told whoever it was to come in, thinking it was my mother. It turned out to be Aninhas.

"Good morning. Did I wake you?" she whispered, closing the door behind her.

She was still in her nightgown and was wearing a robe my mother had lent her. Slightly thrown off by the unexpected visit, I sat up and started fixing the sheets, totally disheveled as a result of my tossing and turning during my nightmares.

"What happened here?" she asked, taking in the mess. "Some sort of nocturnal battle?"

"I had a restless night."

"I hope it wasn't on my account," she ventured, with a dash of irony.

"Oh no! Of course not. Although, truth be told, trying to sleep, knowing that the damsel of my heart is sleeping right next door can be very disturbing."

She laughed and I asked, "And you? Did you sleep well?"

"Like an angel. I woke up with the rooster crowing. It's been ages since that's happened."

"And how's your back?"

"I still feel it a little, but nothing to worry about."

She sat down on the edge of the bed, modestly wrapping the robe around her legs, and added, "I wanted to apologize for not having waited for you last night. Paulino and I were so tired, your mother made us go to bed."

"I'm the one who should be apologizing, first for getting the two of you involved in that mess at the harvest and later, for having left you after supper."

"Oh Luís, I want you to know that even though we got tired we're so happy we came. Paulino had a marvelous time and, from the looks of it, he's made a friend."

"A friend? Who?"

"One of Rato's daughters. What's her name again? I think it's Angelina."

"Evangelina. Rato has two daughters, one's twelve, Evangelina, and the other one's two, named Fátima."

"It's the older one, of course. He came to tell me he'd met a girl, a very pretty, nice girl. If he weren't only twelve years old, I'd say he's got a crush."

"Children!"

"But I also wanted to tell you how happy I am that I've come, in spite of the hard work picking up grapes. It was a pleasure to meet your parents, they're so charming, and to see the house where you were born and to be able to come into your room. So, this is where you sleep!"

"The room's too big for me, and a little too cold. I'm going to convince my mother to have it remodeled, to make it more modern, more comfortable."

"And what for?"

"Maybe someday I'll be sharing it with someone..."

Aninhas gave me her hand and I held it and kissed it.

It was time to get up and she left so we could get dressed. We met again at breakfast. My parents said goodbye to the siblings ceremoniously and I drove them to Braga to catch the train. Before getting into the automobile, Aninhas let me embrace her and, with her mouth touching my ear, she murmured, "I love you, Luís."

A few days after the grape harvest, I received a long letter from Madame Gavroche, in her right slanted handwriting, without any smudges but with slight variations in the color of the ink, suggesting it had been written in more than one sitting. Part of it must have been written at night, by candlelight, because in some places the handwriting slipped off the lines. That was where she confessed she'd missed me a lot since my return to Portugal. She was not criticizing me: *C'est la vie*! she wrote. When a war is over, soldiers should go back to their countries, back to their families. The soldiers in her family hadn't come back home. Her two brothers and her husband were but three among the millions of unfortunate people that the war had devoured. Very few men from Enguinegatte had returned. And the few who had were either mutilated, or had bad lungs, or had simply lost their minds. That's why there were so few hands to farm the land, or to work in factories or construction. Rato would be welcome and she would be very happy to give him a job on the farm. Now that the Portuguese soldiers had left, the French were selling products to the Germans at good prices and she was in real need of some help. The Germans had apparently exhausted their food supplies and French potatoes, meat, and grains were staving off their hunger. Life has many twists and turns, she commented. She ended the letter wishing me much success in my studies and in love. She would never forget me, and she knew that I too would never forget her, in spite of the distance and the changes life puts us through. In a *post scriptum*, she added she would be very happy to find out someday I had met *une fille gentille* who would give me the satisfaction and joy she herself had felt in my company.

On the very same day that I received the letter, I sent Delmiro to tell Rato I had news for him. He arrived within a half an hour, breathless from running.

"I was out in the backyard watering some collards," he explained, interrupting himself to catch his breath, "when Delmiro got there telling me you've got news for me, sir...."

"Madame Gavroche wrote. But have a seat. Do you want a glass of water?"

"Don't go to any trouble, sir. But what did she say?"

"She'll give you some work on the farm."

Rato was very pleased with the news and asked when he could leave.

"The sooner the better. She wants you there as soon as you can go. So take care of the paperwork, get yourself packed, and tell your family goodbye."

"I ain't got a lot to pack, sir. I'll just go with the clothes on my back, not much more."

"Well, it's true you don't need to worry about that. Madame Gavroche still has the clothes that belonged to her brothers and husband. I'm sure she won't mind giving you some. Unless she burned them or gave them away in the meantime. Just in case, you'd better take two shirts, a pair of pants, and some underwear."

A few days later, while I drove him to the railway station at Braga, I asked him what Vicência thought about him going. He said she was very happy about it. She was sick and tired of having him around with no real work, just watching the collards grow, hardly helping at all to support the children. The work at Quinta de Santa Madalena had been short-lived, and with the end of the grape and corn harvests, the day workers had been let go.

"Ever since I came back from the war, sir, things just ain't been good."

"I know, the country's going through tough times."

"I don't give a damn about the country! I'm talking about me and Vicência. It's between us two that things is bad."

Since I was watching out for potholes, I did not answer, and he continued, "Vicência says I'm different, she says I ain't the same man she married. Do you think it's possible we've changed so much, sir?"

"When a man goes through what we went through, he just can't stay the same. And it's the people that know us best who really notice the difference. Poor Vicência must have been confused when you got home. She looks at you, recognizes your face and mustache, but the fellow inside is a stranger. It's as if you were someone else."

"You've got it, sir. You explain what a man with no learning tries to say, but can't. To my mind, what little I get, that's just what happened. At first, I was real sore. She wouldn't even sleep with me."

"So where did you sleep?"

"First in the boys' bed, then in her bed, to be more comfortable like. But what I mean to say by sleep ain't really sleep, if you get my meaning, sir. I guess you do, sir, since you've got so much schooling."

"So, she refused to…"

"That's right, she refused. Always coming up with something, feeling under the weather, women's aches and pains, and I don't even know what all else, just to get out of doing her duty. Just last night I got up close to her, tried to sweet talk her, but she just turned her back on me. Told me to go find some French woman to take care of my needs."

"Well, it's possible that once you're gone, she'll miss it."

"Maybe so, sir, but then it just ain't nothing I can do 'bout it."

We arrived at the station and I bought him his ticket and accompanied him to the train. Before he got on the car, he thanked me for everything I'd done for him and wished me happiness.

"Don't let Miss Aninhas get away, sir. She's a jewel of a girl. If you want my advice, you marry her. It'll be a happy day for me, sir, when I get that letter, telling me you've married her."

"Give my regards to Madame Gavroche, to her mother and the children, too."

"I'll do that."

"And come back alive, would you? Sometimes civilian life is more dangerous than life in the Army."

"I'll make sure I do."

The whistle started blowing and he held out his hand, but I stepped forward and embraced him.

Nearly nineteen years would pass before we were to meet again.

In 1919, almost forty thousand Portuguese left the country in search of a better standard of living. Close to one third were war veterans who went back to Flanders to replace the men killed in the war. The friendships resulting from contact with the local population during war, as well as familiarity with the land, contributed to their decision to return to that devastated region, in spite of what they had suffered.

A few days after Rato had left for France, I went back to Coimbra. I took the *Minerva* to be able to carry everything I needed: books, law readers, and clothes. I would not have been able to take everything if I had gone by train. Besides, with my automobile in Coimbra, it would be easier and faster for me to get to Oporto to visit Aninhas. My mother did not favor the plan because she thought it was dangerous for me to be out on the Portuguese roads, which at that time were either macadam or dirt. She thought the train would be safer. Since I insisted, she convinced my father to withhold the gasoline money, but her plan was to no avail. My savings from Flanders were more than enough to pay for the gasoline. And not only that, I argued, if they hadn't wanted me to drive the automobile, why had they given it to me? To stay in the garage, building up rust? If I had my automobile in Coimbra, I wouldn't be out carousing with other students. Since they didn't have any place to go in their free time, they spent it ruining their livers with the terrible wine served in filthy taverns, disturbing the other inhabitants of the city with their night antics and violence, pursuing single females, and harassing married women or widows, especially the young and pretty. But my mother did not budge. The money my father handed me in an envelope in front of her was to be used strictly to pay for my food and lodging until Christmas. I'd have to pay for my own revels.

As we said goodbye and embraced, my father whispered me to have a look underneath the seat of the automobile. Once I had the motor started, I reached down and found another envelope. I put it in my coat pocket and only opened it once I got to my room in Coimbra. It contained three one hundred escudo bills, the most valuable banknote in circulation at that time. It was only the following year, if I remember correctly, that they began issuing one thousand escudo banknotes. It was enough money to buy gas until the end of the world.

The first time I drove to Oporto to visit Aninhas, I had a conversation with Dr. Gouveia. Dona Leontina had invited me for lunch on a Sunday and, before we sat at table, Aninhas's father took me to his office, invited me to sit down, lit a cigar without offering me one, and went straight to the point.

"Mr. Vasques, I'd like you to tell me what your true intentions are regarding my daughter. I'm well aware she's a feisty one and frankly, if I were you, I'd think twice before making any decisions. I don't mean to be negative about my own daughter. I am very fond of her. But I don't want my future son-in-law to complain later that he's been fooled. I want everything out in the open. She's an honest girl, the daughter of honest people. It's her manner that leaves a little to be desired. She's far too modern and obsessed with the idea that women are entitled to independence, freedom and equality and a lot of other nonsense. As if we were all the same and the world were different than it is. She thinks women weren't meant to spend all their time cooking or embroidering. I can't imagine who put those ideas into her head. I swear it wasn't me. Nor her mother, for that matter. Must be her friends. And reading. She reads all these magazines they're publishing nowadays, with no censorship, and foreign books filled with hogwash. That's why I'm telling you to think it over carefully before you say anything to me. If you choose Ana Maria, you won't have a woman like all the others. But if that doesn't bother you, all the better, for both of you."

"I like your daughter just the way she is, Dr. Gouveia. Whether I'm going to marry her, I don't know. It's not only up to me."

"What do you mean?"

"I haven't asked Ana Maria yet if she really wants me as her husband."

"And why wouldn't she? Don't tell me she's been flirting with you just to pass the time!"

"You're speaking in jest, aren't you, sir?"

"Yes, I am, but with women, you never know. They're just too modern these days for my taste. Don't misunderstand me, son. I trust my daughter to the fullest. If you marry her, you can be sure you're getting a trustworthy girl. We're a God fearing family of very high morals. I tolerate no monkey business in this household."

I felt like laughing, but I managed to remain circumspect by staring at my shoes. Talking about a daughter as if she were a piece of steak you're about to buy at the corner butcher's, recommended for its integrity, struck me as outlandish. But in those days, that was still the way parents negotiated their daughters' future.

The conversation did not take long. Especially since Paulino came to call us to lunch. I reiterated my noble intentions regarding Aninhas and asked permission to call on her. The request was a tad late, given how things had already progressed, but better late than never, and I certainly did not want to disrupt the carefully negotiated protocol for dating, engagements, and weddings so alive and well at the time.

Our romance followed the expected trajectory. I would get into my automobile on Sunday morning, when Dona Maria das Dores left for mass with her children, and head for Oporto. I would have lunch at the Gouveias's or, not to wear out my welcome, I would invite Aninhas out to a restaurant. Then, if there was a film we wanted to see, we would go to a matinee. Around that time we saw *The Vagabond*, one of Charlie Chaplin's comedies, which we enjoyed enormously. Chaplin had the role of the Tramp, making a living by playing the violin. One day, just by chance, he goes to a gypsy camp where he recognizes a beautiful blond girl, the daughter of very important people. She had been kidnapped by wicked gypsies. She falls under the influence of his beautiful playing, which leads to a series of unexpected events where there is no dearth of kicks, missed punches, escapes, chases, dunkings, and split heads. The Tramp manages to escape spectacularly with the girl in a gypsy wagon. When it looks like the two of them are about to start living happily ever after, an artist paints a portrait of the girl, and the painting, upon exhibition, eventually leads the girl's parents to her. Aninhas and I laughed delightedly. I believe it was the first time I laughed my heart out in a long, long while.

After the movie, we would take long walks by the river, sit on a bench in the gardens and talk. If it was raining, we would go to a café. In the late afternoon, I would take her home and drive back to Coimbra. Dona Leontina almost always offered me a light meal before I left, which I would try in vain to refuse. I had practically become a member of the family. After I had eaten the codfish fritters and sweets, accompanied by tea, barley, or a glass of white wine, Aninhas would accompany me to the door and we would say our goodbyes, first squeezing each other's hands, followed by a kiss on the very same, and then, if no one was watching us, a kiss on the cheek.

In mid-November, one afternoon when saying goodbye, I drew her towards me. Just for an instant, she resisted, but I persisted, my arms around her waist. She ended up in my arms and I was able to kiss her mouth. The following day, she wrote me a ravishing love letter. I answered her in kind, perhaps a little less ravishingly, since I my amorous vocabulary is poorer, though not less sincere.

That kiss and the letters that followed increased our intimacy, and from then on, when we met, we tried to be alone to kiss, sigh, and tell each other how much we were in love. We were like two mischievous children.

One afternoon, in the darkness of the movie theater, in a sudden impulse that I immediately regretted, I put my hand on her thigh. Aninhas trembled feeling my hand on her dress and, very delicately, removed it. On another occasion, before getting in my automobile to go back to Coimbra, I just barely touched one of her breasts while we kissed. She caught my hand without interrupting the kiss. A week later, late one rainy Sunday afternoon, since we could not go for a walk, we took a drive to Foz do Douro[57] where we watched the rain, the river, and the ocean while we talked. At one point I pulled her close to me and kissed her. It was a long, ardent kiss, so much so that our lips ached. During the kiss, she allowed me to touch her breasts and her thighs through her dress. But when I tried to reach my hand beneath her dress, she asked me for God's sake not to, and closed her legs like a mussel when touched and disentangled herself. I recoiled like a spoiled child upon being denied a lollipop. Aninhas reacted.

"I'm sorry Luís. I didn't mean to make you mad. But you know how I was brought up, to think you should only do things like this after marriage. I ... you know I like you a lot. I'd do anything to make you happy. It makes me sad to see you looking so glum. When you're like this, it's as if you were absent, far away in the trenches, in the war. Please, say something. I don't want you to be angry at me. Come here, let me hold you."

"I can't, Aninhas, at least not right now. If you hold me, I'll end up trying the same craziness all over again, and you don't want that."

"No, Luís. I do want to, I have the same desire... But you know we can't."

"And why not? We like each other, you know me, and I know you. One day we'll be husband and wife. Why put it off? Why should we be tantalizing each other with this unnatural, ridiculous abstinence?"

"We girls have been taught some things are only permitted after marriage. It's not that I agree. But I understand. It comes from our need to protect ourselves. And we're so fragile! Men can get away with whatever they want and they never get hurt. For us, just a hint of rumor or gossip and we've lost everything. You know Celeste, my girlfriend and classmate, she's been in

307

a terrible state because her fiancé left her. Their romance was like any other. But he started to want more. She kept telling him no. But he persisted. One day he told her that if she didn't do what he wanted, he'd leave her. Celeste gave in and he had his way once, twice, three times. When he was tired of her, he dropped her. As an excuse, he said he couldn't marry a girl who was so easy. And that's the reason, my darling, why women try to avoid these situations. To protect ourselves."

"And you think I'm capable of such a thing, of what that scoundrel did?"

"Of course not, I know you. You're a decent man."

"But you can never be too sure..."

And that was how I found myself romancing Aninhas on Sundays and going to bed with Dona Maria das Dores, my landlady, during the week.

As I have already mentioned, I do not sleep well, especially if I have to sleep alone. It takes me a long time to fall asleep, I toss and turn and have nightmares and cold sweats. It so happened that my bed was made of iron and squeaked when I moved around. My landlady's room was right next to mine and, without my realizing it, the squeaking bothered her. Out of politeness, she put up with it and never said anything. One day at breakfast, however, just before Christmas vacation, she asked me if I had a hard time sleeping in that bed. She said she'd be willing to change the mattress or even the bed itself. I told her the problem wasn't exactly the bed, but the fact that, since the war, and even during the war, I'd sleep very poorly. The danger to which I'd been exposed meant I'd had to be constantly vigilant. A soldier never sleeps. I dozed, but always with one eye closed, the other open, and my ears perked up. The pressure was such that my body and mind started getting used to a state of wakefulness.

The following night, she knocked at my door and asked if I wanted to change beds. Hers was made of wood and didn't creak. I got up drowsily, wakened from one of my trench nightmares where rats, mud, the stench of filth, and the thunder of howitzers were a constant, and followed her to her room in my long johns. I lay down and she left, closing the door behind her. But I must have continued tossing and turning, since she decided to keep me company. I woke up in the morning with her clinging to me. I have no recollection of anything happening that night, but on the following nights, that changed.

Although she was in her thirties, Dona Maria das Dores had a lovely, sweet face, long black hair, and a neck that would lead any man astray. Otherwise, she was somewhat full figured, probably because she spent so much time at home, a certain path to plumpness. When she was twenty, she must have been extremely attractive. The late sergeant had very good taste and, when his military duties permitted, he likely took advantage of his good fortune.

So there I was, once more consoling a widow, as she did me. Consolation was shared equitably. She administered tenderness and other caresses on my deprived body and I responded with my company, which she so desperately needed since the loss of her husband. And thus we lived happily in her house, exchanging physical and verbal favors. She knew I had a girlfriend whom I met on Sundays. Although she said she didn't mind, I knew she was jealous. The issue was dealt with in bed, in her room, the one that did not creak. Aninhas had my platonic love, the widow had all of me. Not for very long, she knew only too well, because I would finish my studies and be on my way. I never led her on. Every once in a while, spent from our activities under the bed sheets, she would whisper how much she was going to miss me when I was gone.

She managed to overcome her husband's death. Not that she had forgotten him: she still respected his memory and used to tell me what a fine man he was. He was slightly awkward in bed, due to his limited instruction and his life in the barracks, but he was fond of their children, very considerate, and a good provider. When she received the letter from the War Ministry, offering condolences for his death in the battle of April 9, it was as if she herself had received a bullet in the chest, where it remained, burning. She said my kind words and caresses had finally dislodged the bullet. Instead, she now had something wonderful that she couldn't describe. She would kiss me deeply, probably like she had never kissed the poor sergeant.

Actually, it was Dona Maria das Dores who was a great lover. At first, she was slightly uneasy, perhaps for lack of practice or because her husband had not been much of a teacher. Later on, however, she became extremely interesting. Portuguese women are just as good as all the other women. They just need to get over their moral prejudices based on atavistic religious fears. When I explained to her that there are a lot of ways to prevent pregnancy without compromising pleasure, she looked at me in wide-eyed shock. She confessed that she had often refused to make love to her husband for fear of getting pregnant. She discovered it would have been so easy to please him without any risk, and for her to enjoy herself without fear as well. I think that is why she was so enthusiastic in her lovemaking and our voluptuous games were so frequent.

That last year in Coimbra, Dona Maria das Dores was very fine company in every sense. She was an excellent cook, her house sparkled in cleanliness and, in spite of her limited means, she was finely groomed. Since she did not read, her conversation was limited to the goings on in the neighborhood and to her children. When I was not in the mood to study my law readers, I would sit and listen to her talk about the little dramas that took place on our street.

That relationship was never detrimental to my relationship with Aninhas. On the contrary, I stopped pressuring her sexually and she gained confidence. At first she thought it was strange I had backed off and she even asked me if I was entertaining myself with some tart in Coimbra during the week. I laughed, gave her a kiss, and she never brought it up again.

That year in Coimbra ended poorly, although I felt well,

or at least, not too bad. A new Spanish flu epidemic swept the country in December, killing nearly three thousand people. Aninhas, who did volunteer work at the infirmary of the hospital in Oporto where her father worked, fell ill. Throughout the month of January, her family and I were extremely anxious.

XXVI

I woke up freezing. Aninhas had risen earlier to give the kitchen help instructions for our Christmas Eve supper, leaving me in bed without my source of warmth. I got up and opened the shutters. Sunshine entered the room and I felt some comfort, if not physical, at least psychological. The ground, trees, and sheds were frosted all over the estate. Even so, there is no comparison between this cold and what I had to put up with in Flanders twenty-one years ago. At this time of the year there, temperatures used to get down to fifteen degrees centigrade below zero. The unfortunate Portuguese soldiers, unaccustomed to such weather, practically froze. The double rum rations and sheepskin jackets issued to every man did not help. Ice and dampness got into our flesh and bones, our hands were swollen with frostbite, and our lips were so chafed that it hurt to put anything in our mouth. A few tried to cheat the cold by smoking, but with chaffed lips even that was painful. We spent about six months stomping our feet, our teeth chattering. When they saw us in sheepskin jackets, the Boche started shouting "baaa-baaa-baaa," as if we were sheep. Actually, if we were not sheep in the flesh, in spirit we certainly were like lambs on our way to the slaughterhouse. We were about to sacrifice our blood at the altar of war erected in 1914 by the politicians and the powerful.

I have promised Pedro that we will go out to collect the moss for the manger scene we will set up in the living room. He must still be asleep. During vacations he can afford to stay in bed till mid-morning, a privilege he does not enjoy at the Seminary. I am writing this in my study. The fireplace is not lit and lighting it is too complicated. While I wait for Pedro to get up and come fetch me to go for moss, I recall Christmas twenty-one years ago in the mud of Flanders.

Our battalion was in the support line at Sanechal Farme,

three kilometers behind the Ferme du Bois Sector II. We had spent a week at the front. While guarding Ferme du Bois, we used to spend a week resting in Penin-Mariage. But this time, as a Christmas gift, we were ordered to Sanechal Farme, a somewhat less damp place, though neither less cold nor less dangerous than any other. It was a common saying that one got killed more easily in the support line than in the front line. Never having checked the statistics, I do not know if that is true or not. But one did hear about soldiers getting killed by a mortar shell while eating lunch or hanging their laundry to dry.

It was our first Christmas away from home. In spite of the letters and packages we received from our families, there was a generalized malaise that was difficult to fight. A few days earlier we had received news that the High Command would issue codfish, potatoes, oil, rice pudding, and port wine to every battalion. But the quartermasters soon ran into a problem: How could the codfish soak overnight? The water containers froze during the night and the men would have to eat the codfish still salty, which was unpalatable. But on Christmas Eve the problem disappeared, because we had the usual menu, except for an extra ration of corned beef. The codfish, certainly dispatched from Lisbon, had either gone down with the ship, or been delivered to the top brass.

The Portuguese soldier is brave, daring, and resilient. But without support from his family and friends, and above all without decent food, he becomes fragile and insecure. On that day I heard several privates and officers complain, and apparently only the sergeants, who were professionals, remained indifferent or hid their feelings well. When I asked Sergeant Rosado why he didn't complain like the others, he told me he was used to spending Christmas away from home and pulling barracks duty year in, year out. However, he wouldn't pretend not to be annoyed at spending Christmas in the middle of a war in a foreign land, and without codfish to boot. But anyway, who was he to question anything? He was a sergeant who was there to obey orders, that's all. If I gave him an order that he could carry out, he'd do it without batting an eye. That's what he got paid for.

I gave him my orders, even though on that day I did not feel like ordering anyone around. There was a Christmas Eve supper for the officers, probably featuring codfish, at the mess dugout, the dining room of the battalion's makeshift command post, but I did not attend. I stayed with my platoon, under a half-wrecked shed, around a small fire fed with pieces of wood taken off doors and windows. We were not supposed to let the fire get too bright, we did not want to become the target of a series of mortar rounds that could blow up everything around us. A little after half past nine, we were supposed to move on to the first line. On that night we had orders to do repairs in that sector, especially the parapets, the communication trenches and a few posts that had crumbled or been destroyed during the day. The men hoped the Boche would pause for Christmas Eve supper, but I was not counting on it.

Rato offered to fix me a separate supper, but I did not accept. Christmas meant sharing, and at least once in that war, I wanted to share everything with my soldiers: the sorrow of being away from home, the cold, the corned beef, the hard crackers, the rancid fruit preserves. While we ate, Sergeant Rosado, sitting on a wooden box next to me, fat dribbling down his chin, shining oddly by the fire, asked, "Sir, don't you think it's a good omen that we ain't hearing no shots right now?"

We listened but actually could not hear a single shot. Even the thundering of the big guns in the distance had died down.

"Maybe the generals've decided to declare a truce for Christmas Eve," suggested Corporal Fontes.

"Sure thing," Rosado quipped. "I can even see Foch and Douglas-Haig sending a *carte-lettre* – with our dear Tamagnini's signature in the lower right corner – wishing Hindenburg and Ludendorff a merry Christmas, and suggesting a truce for Christmas Eve supper!"

That was funny, but nobody laughed. We were so cold that not even Charlie Chaplin's jokes could have shaken us out of our torpor.

But our illusion did not last. Around seven o'clock we started hearing the whish-whishing of shells and grenades. It was our own artillery ruining poor Fritz's Christmas supper. Ahead of us, in no man's land, the first bursts could be heard.

"Sons of bitches!" Corporal Fontes growled. "They just had to screw up Christmas for everybody."

"They're not the ones who's stuck in the trenches," Rato said.

They were those fellows at Brigade, or Division, or Head-quarters, whoever had given the order to open fire.

After supper, our Chaplain, Father Cruz, paid us a visit. After greeting me, he whispered that my absence from the supper at the mess-dugout had not sat well with the other officers. I told him I had nothing personal against my fellow officers. I simply wished to spend Christmas with my men.

"As you know very well, Padre, it's a way to lift their morale. If every officer did that, the men would be in higher spirits."

"I won't discuss strategy," he said. "But I understand you. Several of the boys came to me crying today, and I didn't know how to console them. I've been to the field hospital, where things are a lot worse than here. Young men without legs, without arms, without a face, others poisoned by gas, coughing, moaning, shouting. It was terrible to feel so helpless before so much suffering. I said mass and those who could, attended, and then I ran away from that place, like a coward."

"I also understand what you're saying, Padre. God must not really like war, having abandoned us all here."

"Don't get God mixed up in this. He's not responsible for men's mistakes."

"I'd rather not discuss theology with you, Padre. You know enough to run circles around me. But what little I know

315

leads me to think that, if man is capable of such barbaric acts, and if God created man, then God bears the ultimate responsibility."

"You can't really make your parents responsible for your errors, can you?" said the Chaplain, well trained in argument.

"Well said, Padre, well said," I finally replied, defeated but not really convinced.

I asked Sergeant Rosado to gather the men and Father Cruz prayed the rosary with them, spoke briefly about the birth of the Child God, and added a few words about the meaning of Christmas. Although it was not midnight yet, for the sake of convenience he had them all kiss a small Infant Jesus image he had brought along. At the end, he greeted each man personally and wished them all a merry Christmas.

"I've got to go," he said, taking his leave. "I have to say midnight mass in a shed near the command post. It's a shame your platoon cannot attend."

"Our duty calls us, Padre."

"Merry Christmas to you."

He left and we prepared to march toward the first line trenches, carrying shovels, picks, and rolls of barbed wire. The men seemed more cheerful. A few started humming "The Child is Asleep" and I had to tell them to be quiet, so we would not become an easy target for the Boche mortars in response to our fire.

As we crossed the first communication trench, the overhead whistling started again.

"Here comes Fritz's answer!" someone said behind me.

But it was not the Boche artillery yet. It was still our own.

I take up this narrative again after a few hours' interruption. Pedro came to the study to let me know he was ready for us to go collecting moss for the manger scene, and we took off, each holding one side of a wicker basket. On the patio we ran into Afonso, busy on the Minerva. When he comes home on vacation he likes to pass the time cleaning, tuning up, and lubricating the old jalopy.

"Where're you headed?" he asked.

"We're going to collect moss," Pedro said. "Don't you want to come along? You could help carry the basket."

"Why? Don't tell me you can't do it. Don't the priests feed you at the Seminary?"

"I eat better than you."

"You don't look it. You're as skinny as a dog that hasn't been fed for months."

"You're the skinny one. Either you don't eat in Coimbra to save money for drinking, or you get your food straight from the privy."

"I'll show you who's eating from the privy!" Afonso exclaimed, half-offended, half-amused.

"What? You're threatening to beat me? Don't you know you can be excommunicated for hitting a churchman?"

"Some churchman you are!"

"Cut it out, you two!" I exclaimed. "Let's go, Pedro. Leave your brother alone, he's got work to do. If he manages to make that car run, we can ride it to midnight Mass. I'm sure you don't want to miss it."

"Sure," Afonso added in a mocking tone while he tightened a nut with the wrench. "If you miss midnight Mass, the Devil will certainly save a warm place for you in Hell."

"You know which warm place you should stick that wrench."

"Some priest you're going to be!" Afonso said, laughing at his brother's rudeness.

We left Afonso with the old car and his wrench, and took the dirt path leading to the woods. As we walked along, taking care not to slip on the ice, I asked Pedro about his studies. He is fourteen years old and has been at the Seminary for two years, by his own choice. I would rather he were attending high school,

317

studying Natural Science in preparation for medical school. But that is not his choice. Can one make a sensible choice at his age? No matter how much I think about it, I cannot see myself with a priest for a son. Pedro is too independent to accept the Church's hierarchy and the required obedience. But people change, and maybe with training and discipline the priests will manage to shape him in their own image. Let's hope not.

In the woods, under the oaks, we found some moss, but so frozen that it would fall apart when touched. Pedro said, disappointedly, "That's no good. If we come back in the middle of the afternoon, maybe it'll have defrosted by then."

"That's possible. But just in case it doesn't, we'd better collect moss off the walls."

"It isn't nearly as pretty," he protested.

"Maybe not. But still, it's moss. And it isn't frozen."

And to prove my point, I went up to the stone wall that separated the woods from the road and pulled out a piece of moss easily. Pedro shrugged, resigned, and started helping me, and in a short while the basket was full. As we worked, he asked, "When you were in the war, did you also make a manger scene?"

"We were right inside the manger."

"How come?"

"Do you know what a manger is?

"Sure, it's a kind of trough where they put fodder for the animals to eat."

"There you are."

And I did not say anything further.

After we had collected the moss, my son suggested we cut down two small pine trees. I had my reservations. He argued that since there were too many trees, cutting two of them would benefit the others. That simple argument sounded to me like a metaphor of war: the deaths of some men benefit the community. I thought my son had a knack for politics. Maybe he would end up a deputy, or perhaps a minister. At that point, however, I would not have bet a cent on his religious vocation.

When we got back home, Aninhas was waiting for us. She announced that a hot bath was ready. Pedro excused himself, saying he had already taken a bath at the Seminary last week.

"At the Seminary?" she said. "And since when can you take a proper bath at the Seminary? Kindly get into the tub right away, young man. Your underwear stinks. And please make sure you soak really well."

"Come on, Mom, it's cold!"

"I want you washed and scrubbed for Christmas. Remember your cousins'll be here tonight and it would be embarrassing if you were stinking when you greeted them."

"Or with those dirty ears," I added.

"You're treating me like I'm a boy."

"Nonsense! Of course you're still a boy. And a lot more childish than your sister, who's already taken a bath and is in the kitchen, helping Guiomar with the French toast and the Christmas pudding."

Inês is twelve years old and already a young woman. About a month ago Aninhas proudly whispered to me that our daughter had had her first period.

Pedro, who likes bathing as much as a cat does, tried to postpone his sacrifice, "What about the manger scene? Wouldn't it make more sense to put it together first and then take a bath?"

I came to the help of our future priest, "Well, Pedro's right. After all, he'll get all dirty setting up the platform and spreading out the moss."

Aninhas finally agreed, warning he wouldn't have dinner if he didn't get into the tub and scrub off those crusts. Not even a dispensation from the Archbishop would exempt him from that penance!

The manger scene was set up in a corner of the dining room, Pedro took his bath, I took mine, and now, after lunch, I am back at my desk to finish my narrative of Christmas in the trenches.

I had received several letters wishing me happy holidays, but I cannot very well recall whom they were from. I used to keep all the mail in a bundle in my knapsack. But like most Portuguese soldiers who were in the front line during the attack on April 9, 1918, I lost my knapsack and everything in it. I recall a *carte-lettre* with a snow landscape, from Madame Constance Gavroche, wishing me a merry Christmas, but I did not reply. There was also a letter from my father and one from Libaninha.

Libaninha's letter surprised me, because our relations were severed on account of her having broken off our engagement. It was just a short, bland note wishing me a happy holiday, but I did not bother to reply. I was still in pain.

Libaninha wrote me again at Christmas two years later. This letter was related to my visit to Quinta de Santa Madalena on grape harvest day to telephone Aninhas's parents. I wonder if I kept it. More likely, I burned it in the fireplace. It was too compromising.

Let me recount what happened.

When I came home from Coimbra for Christmas my mother handed me a letter. I did not recognize the sender's name. It was a man's name and I opened the envelope indifferently, thinking it might be from some former Army comrade I no longer remembered. It was a short note signed with the letter "L," which I recognized from its shape. Clearly, Libaninha would rather not be identified. She wished me a happy holiday, adding she would like to talk to me. On December 22 she would be waiting for me at the *Café Brasileira* in Braga, between three and four in the afternoon. She would be very happy if I came. Now I wonder whether it was really the 22nd. It might just as well have been the 21st or the 23rd. Why have I then written the 22nd, if I do not have the original letter here to confirm the exact date? Narrative strategies of verisimilitude, a literary scholar might say. But I am not writing a novel. I am not a writer, nor do I intend to be one. I do not even feel any sympathy for writers, those vain good-for-nothings who think they are better than others, when in fact they are just some poor devils seeking fame and public recognition, which always come too late.

Let us go back to Libaninha's letter and my reaction to it.

I decided to go and meet her. I can't remember exactly why. It was sheer madness. What did I expect? An apology? A new opportunity? A brief affair with my former fiancée? A mischievous little revenge? I do not know. The fact is that, on the day she had suggested, I stopped by the *Café Brasileira*. It was very cold and there were no other customers on the terrace. Libaninha was sitting at one of the tables, facing toward me. She saw me and got up before I approached her. She walked past me without turning and went out. She walked along the street and I followed her. She stopped to look at the manger scene in the window of a store that sold saints' images. I stood by her and she asked, without looking, where I had left my car.

"Next to São João do Souto's," I said.

"I'll be there in five minutes."

I went to the car, leaving her admiring the oversized infant Jesus surrounded by the Virgin, Joseph, a dwarfish cow, and an ass. When she arrived, I asked her if she would like me to take her to some place in particular.

"To Falperra, maybe."[58]

I realized she wanted to be alone with me in a discreet place. It might be problematic if we were seen together.

We drove off to Falperra, remaining in silence while in town, I paying attention to the road, she wrapped up in her own thoughts. She was wearing a dark winter dress and a dark hat with a veil covering her face, as was fashionable among society widows at their husbands' funeral. As we approached our destination, I asked, "Are you in mourning for someone?"

"Not that I know of."

"I mean, since you're wearing black, Dona Libânia..."

321

"Please, Luís, don't call me that."

There was another period of silence, and as the road began to climb, through pine and oak trees, she took off her hat. She wore her hair short, as was beginning to be fashionable, and it made her look different, maybe more attractive.

"And your husband?" I asked.

"He came from Lisbon yesterday for the Christmas holiday. He brought me to Braga. He had to take his car to the garage – some problem with the brakes, it seems. We're supposed to meet at six at the *Café Brasileira*."

"So we have about two hours to talk."

"Yes, we do."

"And what do you want from me, Dona Libânia?"

"Please, I beg you not to call me that."

"I'm just trying to be polite."

"Just call me Libânia."

"You're a married lady now."

"Oh well, as you wish."

I parked the car under some oak trees next to the seminary, we got out and started walking in the deserted park, toward a small church. She began by asking me to forgive her for everything she had done to me. Even though she felt guilty, she wanted me to understand that her parents had forced her to end our engagement. When they found out I was leaving for the war they were very apprehensive, and their first concern was to protect her interests. They had made her write that letter breaking up with me. They thought I would be killed in the war or come back wounded or crippled, and it was best for her to forget me and find herself another fiancé.

"I loved you, Luís. I loved you so much that I cried for days on end after the letter was sent. It broke my heart to know that you were in the war, far from me, and that I'd contributed to your suffering."

I was silent while she talked, and went on walking next to her, looking at the leafless oak trees and the frost piled on the grass we were trampling. When we got to the church we stopped. She turned to me, tears streaming down her face. I found a handkerchief in my pocket and gave it to her. She took it casually, but did not dry her tears.

"Do you forgive me, Luís?" she asked, looking at me like a shipwrecked person staring at a buoy in the middle of the sea.

I did not have the heart to say I forgave her. I had suffered too much to be able to forgive her at that moment, regardless of whether she was guilty or not. I could not forgive her weakness before her parents, her nice girl's submission. I could not forgive her the days and months of despondency and bereavement after having received her letter. But she went on looking at me, her big eyes, transparent like water, and her fleshy, half-open lips, waiting for an answer.

I embraced her, touching my lips on hers. They tasted salty.

When we got back into the car, she asked me to park in a more discrete place. I drove up the road and stopped among some oak trees by Santa Marta's baroque church. She pulled up her dress and asked me to take her. I did not hesitate and it was with great fury, the car shaking like an unhinged cart, that we rediscovered each other's taste and fulfilled our desire. She screamed madly, and as I prepared to pull out, feeling I was about to climax, she begged me to stay inside her, called me *my love, my darling*, while I came, fully and warmly.

We drove back to town in silence. I left her not far from the café, and before getting out, she asked me when we could see each other again. I reminded her it wouldn't be appropriate since she was now a married woman. Sooner or later we'd be seen together, her husband would find out, and we'd only cause more suffering to each other and to our families.

A stain remained on the fabric of the car seat, the mark of two fluids that would never get mixed again.

The following Christmas when, already married, I went

to the family estate for Christmas, my mother's report of what had taken place in the village included the news that Libaninha had given birth to a daughter and had named her Marta.

Let me get back to Christmas in the trenches, which is what I meant to write about this evening. But memory has its whims and flies away like a grenade fragment.

Our night in the first line was relatively quiet. The Boche received our Christmas gifts but did not bother to reciprocate. My platoon carried out the assigned repair jobs without being disturbed, except by the cold, which made it difficult to breathe and cramped our joints. When we were about to install barbed wire at the top of the parapet overlooking no man's land, Rato called me.

"Listen, sir. Sounds like the Boche are singing."

I climbed on a fire step and listened. From beyond the snow-covered no man's land came some strands of a familiar melody. The German soldiers were singing "Silent Night."

XXVII

Rato came over today to wish me a happy New Year. Under his arm he carried a rooster, its legs bound.

"For your New Year's Eve supper, sir."

It was an impressive rooster. Guiomar would need help to cut off its head.

"You shouldn't have bothered. We've got plenty of hens."

"But not a rooster like this one," he said proudly.

"That's for sure. Not like this one. It looks like an elephant."

He laughed merrily.

To prevent a fight with the rooster we kept in our coop, which like all roosters, is jealous and would likely lose his crest if they fought, we put Rato's bird in the barn. Once he had removed the band from its legs, it started crowing and strutting around. Then I took Rato to the cellar, filled up a demijohn with white wine and took down one of the hams hanging from the ceiling. He would not accept them, protesting he had not brought me the rooster to receive anything in exchange. I insisted that if he did not take my gift, I would never again accept anything from him. He knew I did not mean it, but played along and accepted.

"It's for your New Year's Eve supper."

"There ain't no New Year's Eve supper in a poor man's home, sir."

"Nonsense. You're not going to tell me you don't have some codfish soaking and a fat hen ready to be plucked, nor that your wife and daughter aren't going to fix a tray of French toast for desert."

"How did you guess, sir? But that's a poor man's fare. I don't reckon the rich eat codfish and French toast on New Year's Eve."

"Who told you that?"

He grinned, and our talk then turned to other matters, and we agreed that in January, by the new moon, he would come to help trim the vines. We parted with a strong handshake, wishing each other a prosperous new year, with plenty of health and happiness. Nevertheless, I felt apprehensive as I watched him walking toward the gate, coughing hoarsely and bending under the weight of the demijohn in one hand and the ham, resting on his shoulder like a shovel.

Then I told Aninhas about the rooster and came back to my study.

I have not written a line for nearly a week. The cold has not helped much, and my fingers are numb. Besides, with my three children at home, I spend a lot of time with them, especially the two young men. Inês, the youngest, naturally seeks her mother's company.

Yesterday I went to a business lunch that dragged on until late in the afternoon. For a few years now, Dr. Mateus, one of the region's best-known lawyers, has insisted on inviting his colleagues to a stew at year's end. It is a way of minimizing any misunderstandings that may have arisen during the year, to plan strategies, cut deals, and above all, to eat well.

This time he also invited a judge, which I did not like. Too much inbreeding. I heard the other colleagues say it was a smart move, to make sure of having the judge on his side. But in my opinion a judge should not be leaning towards either side of the scale, but rather stay in the middle. I came back home feeling indisposed, either because of the food, which was basically pork, or the conversation. We talked about Hitler, Franco, and Salazar, all champions of the West against the demon of Communism. My learned colleagues unreservedly support the crusade against this evil of our century. I actually agree with some of Communism's ideals, but I have no sympathy for its mentors' rampant struggle for power, particularly as they try to impose the dictatorship of the proletariat upon the world. One of the worst consequences of that struggle is Bolshevism, a monster nourished by a band of opportunistic criminals who, pretending to act on behalf of freedom, have turned Russia into a huge slave ship. But the champions of the West do not convince me either. Still, it seems to me the fight against Communism is a pretext for something bigger and far more frightening. Just look at what has happened in Spain, where Franco and his supporters persecute as a communist anyone fighting for freedom and democracy.

I was rather worried by a brief speech the judge made after the dishes had been cleared away, while we waited for the French toast with honey. He said our government should imitate General Franco's crusade against Communism, to prevent Portugal from becoming a satellite of Moscow.

"But it's already being imitated!" one of the lawyers said. "Every time a Spanish red crosses the border trying to escape, he gets handed over to the Nationalist forces."

"Yes, that's true. But what about our Portuguese communists?" the judge asked.

We all looked at him as if he had touched a key point in a complex judicial case.

"Gentlemen: It's only through the conscientious vigilance of every citizen that it'll be possible to fight Communism in our country."

The judge was defending informants as an effective means to destroy the enemies of the Fatherland. I considered saying that in Spain thousands of innocent people were murdered every day by Franco's supporters, not because they were communists – that was a feeble excuse – but because they defended freedom. However, the conversation had shifted to praise Salazar, and I opted for stuffing a piece of French toast in my mouth.

The judge commented smugly that, ever since Professor Oliveira Salazar had accepted to be Prime Minister, Portugal had all the means to become an orderly, pious, and hard-working country. I thought of asking him if freedom, democracy, and progress were also on the Prime Minister's agenda. But I did not want to be a wet blanket. Besides, when among snitches and boot-lickers, it is wiser to keep quiet. So, without much remorse, I ate another piece of French toast.

I find politics increasingly disgusting, probably because there is no room for real debate. Gone are the days when everything was discussed. Discussion is no longer possible, and praise for the current state of the country is all that can be said in public.

Let us go back to the trenches.

Two days after Christmas 1917, our battalion went back to the first line. The only difference between the first line and the support line was that in the first line we were constantly on alert watching no man's land, and in the support line we filled time with training sessions and repair work. The cold, the poor food, the atrocious lodging conditions, fatigue, and danger were the same.

On December 30, three months after arriving in the front line, our battalion left the trenches and marched to the Paradis cantonment, four kilometers from Lestrem, where it would stay until early February as a divisional reserve. The name of that village was promising. Maybe it had been a real paradise before the war, but by the end of 1917 it was just a hodgepodge of tents, wood-and-tin huts, vehicles, beasts of burden, heavy guns, ammunition boxes, firing stands, and thousands of men working hard to turn the area into a muddy, stinking hell.

The month our battalion spent in Paradis was supposed to be a rest from the hardships of war and a cure for wounds of the body and the mind. But it did not quite work out like that. Since the rigor of winter precluded military exercises, the soldiers were kept busy working in the so-called line of the villages. New trenches were dug, existing ones repaired or deepened, shelters built, and kilometers of barbed wire laid. As we found out later, all that would be for naught.

At Epiphany, early in our stay in Paradis, our battalion

got orders to form up in full kit. Colonel Barbosa, the new Minho Brigade Commander, reviewed the troops, who paraded before him to the sound of a military band. At the end there was a fraternization party. The codfish that had been promised for Christmas finally arrived and each soldier was issued a portion. Wine and quince jam were also issued. The soldiers got together in groups and sang songs celebrating the Wise Men, accompanied by banging cans and helmets with their bayonets, which cost them an oral reprimand from their company commanders.

The officers were offered a banquet presided by Colonel Barbosa. The military band played popular tunes and after dessert there were a few inebriated patriotic speeches. Some officers even recited their poems, mostly doggerel written in the trenches. It was quite apparent that the Expeditionary Corps was not destined to produce a new Camões to praise the glorious deeds of the Portuguese in Flanders. Anyway, there was nothing to praise, since neither side performed any heroic feats. Maybe the only heroes were the carrier pigeons used during the bombardments, when telephones stopped working and communication trenches became impassable.

At night we went to our billet in a semi-wrecked farm house inhabited by an elderly couple. It was a big house, and we managed to spread out comfortably in the rooms. Dozens of battalions – French, English, Scottish, Canadian, and Portuguese – had been through it before us. Paradis was one of those highway hubs where battalions were sent to rest after a spell in the front line. In all of Flanders, it must have been the place with most *estaminet*s per square kilometer. A few were just wood-and-tin huts fitted with a board set up on bricks by way of a counter. Where there are men, there is thirst. If it is hot, they drink to cool off; if it is cold, they drink to get warm – not to mention other reasons, more personal than weather-related. The inhabitants of Paradis figured that out fast, dropped their plows and went into the beer, wine, and liquor business.

Paradis was also a love nest for men returning from the mud and filth of the trenches. A number of *estaminets* offered complementary facilities and, for half a franc, soldiers could relieve themselves, thanks to prostitutes who worked the railway from Calais to Metz. According to rumor, a few of them boasted having done the other side as well. It was said they were used as spies, either by the Allies or by the Boche. How they managed to cross no man's land was a mystery, at least to us junior officers. One story was that they used to go across at night, by airplane or submarine, thus infiltrating the enemy. The airplane would land in a clearing, drop the prostitutes, and take off. The submarine would come near the coast, unload its cargo, and dive again.

I thought those stories were all nonsense, but a few officers took them seriously. In Paradis they even hunted down a few prostitutes who, unable to explain how they had got there, were accused of being spies, which I thought was absurd. Even though the Mata Hari case was well known, those poor women were only trying to make a living. What precious information could they possibly get from soldiers who knew nothing about positions, armament, strategy, or troop movements? And only in five minutes, which was about the time they allowed a client for half a franc. Rato, who used their services, said the time was so short you could only concentrate on what you were doing, with no chance of chatting. I asked if there was really no talking and he conceded there was, but just like this:

She: *Vite! Vite!*

He: *Oui, oui, madame!*

She: *C'est bon! Ah, c'est bon!*

He: Oh yeah, oh yeah, I'm coming!

And he explained they shouted *c'est bon!* to pretend they were enjoying it and so to encourage the soldiers to hurry up. Those French women were no fools. By the time we were in Paradis things had quieted down, but according to rumor the French had executed several prostitutes on espionage charges.

Insofar as I know, the English never did that. So much for the so-called French chivalry toward women.

In that kind of environment, the number of victims of venereal diseases would eventually surpass the number of war casualties. Some statistics include soldiers who died from syphilis or other venereal diseases among those killed in combat, those mutilated in bombardments, gassed, or wounded in accidents, suicides, those executed by a firing squad, and those who died from tuberculosis.

When we got to Paradis I wrote my parents and Madame Gavroche to give them my new address. Madame Gavroche wrote back almost at once, inviting me to spend a few more days in Enguinegatte.

Since there was not much to do, I requested a five-day leave for Rato and me. Captain Rebelo did not mind letting me go as long as I could convince one of the other junior officers to take charge of my platoon during my absence. Nogueira wanted to go to Paris on leave in spring to see the Eiffel Tower and Notre Dame, where it was said one could find the most beautiful women in the world. I agreed to take over his platoon at that point, if he replaced me during the five days I wanted to spend in Enguinegatte. I filled out an application for both of us and it was forwarded to the Major, whose approval was needed.

The leave was authorized for me alone. I could not take Rato because, since it was not a service trip, I was not entitled to an orderly. That was a general norm, intended to prevent off-duty officers from using their orderlies as servants. Orderlies could be servants, but only in the barracks; elsewhere, officers had to fend for themselves. I understood the norm, which prevented abuse, but in my case, I considered Rato a friend more than a servant. I felt safer when he was around and it was good for him to have some time away from the war madness. I mentioned that to Captain Rebelo, who passed the message on to the Major, who sent back word that besides the fact that leaves for other ranks were cancelled by superior orders,

Portugal was no longer a monarchy, and so the time of lackeys was gone. I was offended and went to talk to the Major, taking Rato along. The Major received us in his command post on the second floor over a grocery store. He was in a bad mood and busy with a pile of paperwork on his desk. I asked him if that was actually his response to my application. He looked at me with scorn and said nothing. I explained that Rato, although my orderly, was not my servant, let alone my lackey, but really a friend. And if I had requested a leave for him it was out of my esteem for him.

"You are aware of the regulations, aren't you?" he finally said.

"Yes, sir."

"Well, then, just follow them. Dismissed!"

And he plunged his head back into paperwork. Rato and I saluted and, as we left, we heard the Major's sarcastic voice, "Your protest will be duly noted."

When I mentioned this conversation to the Captain he suggested that, instead of a five-day leave, I might reapply for just a weekend. That way Rato would be able to accompany me, as he was entitled to spend the weekend wherever he wished. In that case the application did not even need to go to the Major.

Thus bypassing the red tape and the regulations, I was able to leave for Enguinegate with Rato. He said he did not mind spending two days and then return to Paradis without me. Why should I not enjoy a five-day leave? I replied in the negative: we'd leave together and return together.

We left for Enguinegatte on Army transportation and then took the train. At that point I felt rather down. There was a general malaise, but the soldiers were in worse shape. An officer who had an influential relative or some friend in the government or at the War Ministry, usually managed to go to Portugal on leave. And those who did usually managed to stretch their leave indefinitely, thanks to a courtesy medical certificate. To make things worse, Sidónio Pais's government stopped providing fresh troops, so casualties due to death, illness, prison, or desertion were no longer replaced. We were left to our own devices, and to Fate.

Thus I thought it would be good for us to spend those days among friends. But I was mistaken. Despite all the attention received, we did not end up feeling any better, and, through my own sheer stupidity – or rather, drunkenness – I made a fool of myself and offended Madame Gavroche.

When we arrived in Enguinegatte on Friday evening, Rato slipped and mentioned my wound. I had then to roll up the sleeves of my tunic and shirt to show my scar. Rather concerned, Madame Constance Gavroche, wishing to take a close look, held my arm and examined it from several angles. The two children crowded in, trying to catch a glimpse.

"Did it hurt a lot?" François asked.

I tried to explain that the real pain was not from the wound, but from having been wounded by a Boche. For a warrior, it is humiliating to be wounded by the enemy.

"How come?"

"Because that means that either he is better and stronger than you, or you just didn't pay enough attention and couldn't defend yourself as you should have."

"How many Boche did you kill?"

"As far as I know, none."

I was about to add, "and I hope I'll never kill any," but I held my tongue. That might sound offensive to those people who had already had three of their loved ones killed by the Boche. I am sure that if I had said I had killed half a dozen, they would have considered me a hero. But, as I said before, in that war the true heroes were the pigeons.

By the end of the war, when I read that "Private Millions"[59] was decorated by the Portuguese government for having saved the honor of the Portuguese Expeditionary Corps by machine gunning dozens of Germans on April 9, 1918, I was indignant. How can a man be considered a hero for sending to hell three dozen wretches who simply had the bad luck of crossing the sights of his machine gun? What kind of hero is that, who acts more like a murderer than like a medic? However, from a military viewpoint, since we were there to kill, a high number of enemy casualties should be cause for praise. Furthermore, if we did not kill, we would get killed. But that was not how I saw our mission in Flanders. We had not been sent there to kill, but to defend an invaded land and prevent the invader from advancing further. As to "Private Millions," some will say that by having wiped out the Boche who walked in front of his weapon, he prevented them from killing our own troops, and thus saved their lives. The logic of this argument is skewed. To kill some to spare others is morally justifiable in war. If Rato had not shot the Boche who bayoneted me in the arm, I would likely have been killed by his next thrust. Rato killed an enemy to save my skin. Therefore, my reasoning won't hold water. When it is a matter of saving one's life or a comrade's, any argument against war and violence turns out to be rubbish.

I was really dejected when I got to the Gavroche farm. Madame Gavroche paid special attention to me and came to my room on the first night. She embraced me and ran her hands and mouth all over my body, but somehow I would not respond. It was as if war had rendered me insensitive.

"*Mon chéri!*" she whispered. "What's the matter with you?"

She rested her head against mine and caressed the scar on my arm. But I just could not react to her warm, fragrant, and gentle presence. I felt like crying like a boy with a skinned knee after roughhousing. But she was an experienced woman and set to work to arouse my desire, even though I was dirty, since there had been no time for a bath, and I ended up doing what was required of me to quench her pent-up desire.

The next morning I found Rato at the barn, fixing a rotten step in a ladder.

"It's a good thing we ain't come here for four days, sir."

"Why do you say that?"

"Ain't nothing to be done here. No farming, on account of the cold."

"We've come here to rest, remember?"

"I get enough rest from a good night's sleep, sir. Even so, I've been tossing and turning. My body's so used to hard work and marching that it feels funny if I try to relax."

After lunch with the Gavroche family, we went out for a walk. The fields were covered with ice and we could not walk long on account of the cold wind. As Rato used to say, we were more protected in the trenches.

We walked into the *Gentillet*, the *estaminet* where young Gisèle, the Rapunzel-like girl, used to work, and started drinking. Even though it was Saturday, there were few clients around. I remember there were some sergeants playing cards. Since I did not know anyone, we stood at the counter, near a brazier, and drank brandy and beer.

"The war turns us into beasts of burden, sir. It makes us into stubborn beasts, and we just go wherever our master cracks his whip."

After my third beer I went out to piss and when I got back I saw a patrol of the National Republican Guard, which served as Military Police, checking the papers of all Portuguese soldiers. Rato did not have his papers on him and the corporal in command was taking down his identification number.

"May I know what's going on here?" I asked.

"None of your business," the corporal said, gruffly. "You just wait your turn."

"What manners are those? Stand at attention!" I ordered.

The man looked at me, saw my insignia, and said, "Sorry, I didn't see you."

"That's no way of talking to an officer."

"I talk like that to captains and majors, and I sure talk

like that to a second lieutenant," the corporal said cheekily.

I pulled out a piece of paper and pencil and demanded to see his papers.

"Are you kidding me? I'm the one who asks for papers here. So please identify yourself before I get angry and tell you to come along to the station."

To avoid a confrontation I was not keen on having, I showed him my papers, and while he tried to read them, I told him the private in question belonged to my platoon and was with me. He had left his papers at the farm where we were billeted. If the corporal would like to come along with us, the private would show him his papers.

"We got better things to do. This here private's got eight hours to show his identification and his pass at our station in Enguinegatte. If he don't, a report will go to your Brigade's Provost's Office, and he'll have to fend for himself."

I said that if that happened, I would file a report on him for acting disrespectfully to a superior officer. He laughed like a jackass and left with the other two guards. They probably went to bother the clients at the *estaminet* next door.

I thought it was abusive for a National Republican Guard noncom to have the right to question, report on, and arrest anyone. And even though he was entitled by regulations to question a superior officer, he was required to address him respectfully and call him "sir." Those were important details of military etiquette, and ignoring them might entail punishment. But the National Republican Guard, one of the pillars of the republican regime, could not care less about military regulations. I found out about other similar cases which, despite protests and written reports, did not lead to anything. In Flanders as in Portugal, the National Republican Guard enjoyed rather special privileges.

On Sunday, Rato went to the National Republican Guard station, showed his papers, and everything was straightened out, but for the remainder of Saturday afternoon, we stayed at the *estaminet*, talking and drinking. I was not much used to drinking and ended up drunk. Rato, who either had more resistance to alcohol or drank less, helped me to walk back to the Gavroche farm. I cannot remember anything from that day. I woke up on Sunday, alone in my bed and with a splitting headache. The house was quiet, and I assumed everyone had gone to mass.

After lunch, which was a lot less lively than at other times, we took our leave and got ready to go back to Paradis. I felt I must apologize to Madame Gavroche for having got drunk. She said she understood, and suggested I had better be careful with drinking. It was a shame to see a man acting silly and talking nonsense. I almost told her the British Army, and probably the French Army as well, gave soldiers rum before launching an attack. It seemed that alcohol made them braver and more courageous. But I thought the purpose of that healthy procedure was to use alcohol as a narcotic to make them less aware of the risk of getting killed. It was a way of saving on morphine.

XXVIII

At first they thought Aninhas had caught the influenza, commonly known as Spanish flu, at the hospital where she did volunteer work. The initial symptoms were the same: high fever, congested breathing, weakness, and pain all over her body. At that time, at least in Portugal, there were no methods for determining exactly what kind of virus or bacteria was responsible for an infection. Even so, the doctors concluded that she did not have the influenza but rather pneumonia. To prevent it from getting worse, or turning into some infection that might prove fatal, they sent her home. Her father, Dr. Gouveia, would watch her closely and keep up an appropriate treatment. She managed to overcome the infection, but remained very weak.

I spent many hours by her bedside, both at the hospital and at home. I did not do it out of compassion, but for my love for her and the children I believed we would have. She was the woman of my life.

When I got back to Coimbra, after having seen her in her sick bed, ill and breathing with difficulty, I decided to find another place to live. Out of respect for my future bride and for myself, I felt I could not go on living at Dona Maria das Dores's. A man who cannot control his passions and vices, and lets himself get involved with any skirt that comes his way, is not an honorable man.

When I told Dona Maria das Dores I was moving out, she hit the ceiling and called me ungrateful and opportunistic. I did not argue the point because she was right. I only told her that was the way I felt and I did not wish to continue taking advantage of her hospitality, nor to compromise her honor. Thinking I was making fun of her, she screamed a slew of barracks curses she had probably learned from her late husband.

I packed my things, loaded them onto my automobile, and drove around looking for another room. I felt bad about it. I was afraid of losing Aninhas and felt guilty for having deceived her. But I also felt bad for having taken advantage of an emotionally deprived widow and now having rid myself of her as if she were worthless. Only it was I, and not she, who was worthless.

I do not consider myself different from other men. I have made mistakes and trespassed in matters of decency and morality. Other men, or at least many of them, manage to live without scruples and pass themselves off as models of respectability. They feel clean and renewed if they help carry the image of Our Lord of the Steps on Palm Sunday, or the Cross at Easter, or if they hold one of the poles of the canopy in a Holy Week procession. They are happy and sleep in peace. Unfortunately, I am not like that. Every time I make a mistake or do something wrong, it gets added to a list that casts a dark shadow on my days. Maybe I used to read too many morbid and pessimistic authors when I was young. Or maybe my naturally melancholy personality has been exacerbated by the war, which has ruined so many bodies and minds.

On one of my visits to Aninhas, when she was well on her way to full recovery, I noticed she received me rather coldly. I asked her what was the matter and whether she was not happy to see me. She pointed to the night table, where I saw an envelope.

"Maybe you could explain why I've received that."

"May I open it?"

"It's open."

I picked up the envelope and pulled out a sheet of paper.

"May I read it?"

"Yes," she answered curtly.

It was a letter telling about my relationship with Dona Maria das Dores, my former landlady. It was neither graphic nor naughty, as such letters tend to be. It started with a polite greeting and suggested Aninhas should find out, in case she did not yet know, who the man she was dealing with really was. In Coimbra it was widely known that I was living maritally with a widow. If Aninhas cared about her honor, she should think about it carefully and act accordingly. There was no signature, but it ended more or less with these words, "someone who likes you and wishes you well."

I folded the letter, put it back in the envelope, and studied the postmark. It was dated from Coimbra four days earlier. I wondered if Dona Maria das Dores had been bold enough to write such a letter.

"Can you explain to me why I've received that letter?" Aninhas asked, looking very stern. I remembered the advice lawyers give every client: whether innocent or guilty, always deny everything, even against the evidence. After hesitating a few seconds, I answered, "No. I can't explain it."

"How is it possible that I received an anonymous letter postmarked from Coimbra, telling me you're betraying me with another woman, and you can't tell me anything about it?"

"What can I tell you? That there's someone trying to do me harm?"

"And who could that person be?"

"I've no idea. Maybe some jealous fellow student. Or some neighbor who holds something against Dona Maria das Dores. As you know, she's a widowed lady and there are people who don't like the fact that she's got an unmarried tenant."

Aninhas stared at me in silence and I held her stare, trying to keep a neutral attitude. She probably suspected I was hiding something.

"Whoever wrote that letter knew my full name and address. How can that be? I don't know anyone in Coimbra."

"The mailman delivers your letters to an elderly lady in the building, and she then distributes them among the various residents. Considering how nosy neighbors can be, I wouldn't be surprised if someone found out your name and address."

Obviously that was not the case, and Dona Maria das

340

Dores's finger was certainly in all that. She was the one who handed me the letters, and I'm sure she read them on the sly, since I left them in the bookcase in my room, together with the course readers and books.

"Well, maybe it would be better if you'd leave Dona Maria das Dores's house and find a room elsewhere, so that won't happen again."

I nodded in agreement, and to avoid further suspicions, I did not mention I had already moved five days earlier.

"It would be a good idea," Aninhas added, "if your new landlady were old, toothless, and illiterate."

"As for being illiterate, that's not easy. Coimbra is a town of scholars."

"You don't mean the landladies attend the university!"

"They don't need to. Being in contact with the students is enough to educate them. Besides, to know more than the students, all they have to do is to keep their ears open."

"If the students don't study, what do they do? What do you do during the week in Coimbra? Tell me."

I was relieved with the change in subject.

"There are several kinds of students, and it would take too long to describe them all. Basically, it depends on which school they attend. I can tell you about those in Law School, who are the ones I know best. Anyway, the typical Coimbra student goes to Law School. He dresses in black, wears a cape, grows a mustache, combs his hair back, keeping it in place with pomade or oil, sleeps by day and goes to the fado by night."

"Does he also sing the fado?"

"What I mean by fado is not the song. It's the wild life, drinking, whoring."

"Whoring?!"

Aninhas seemed shocked by the term and I begged her a thousand pardons for having used it.

"Such a virtuous young woman as you shouldn't have her ears defiled by such coarse words."

"I should smash that vase on your head!" she said, pointing at the vase with silken flowers on the night table.

I took her hand and kissed it. She smiled and said, "You're a fool, that's what you are. And I'm even more foolish for liking you. Here I am, bedridden, while this scoundrel enjoys the wild life, drinking, and doing shameful things in Coimbra."

"In Coimbra there are also some who study, go to classes, and memorize the course readers."

"You surely aren't among those. Maybe some bookworm who goes to the Catholic Center meetings and will be a minister some day. By the way, you've never told me what you did about that invitation from your professor – what's his name?"

"Oliveira Salazar."

"Yes, that one. Has he mentioned that subject again?"

"I never saw him again. He was fired from the university in December. They say it was because he supported the Northern Monarchy. What this government has been doing is deplorable, and it portends no good. It's disgraceful to fire someone because his ideas are different from the government's. But we couldn't expect anything different from the republicans. Liberty, equality, and fraternity are only for those who think just like them."

"Well, at least you didn't get involved. You didn't get a bad reputation with the professor, nor with the republicans, who could have marked you."

"I'm already marked. They know perfectly well I don't agree with their ideas."

Our conversation was interrupted by a knock at the door. It was Aninhas's mother, bringing a tray with a snack for the poor sick girl. Aninhas adjusted her pillows and took the tray. Dona Leontina sat on the bed.

"I need to ask a favor of you, Mr. Luís Vasques."

"At your service, ma'am."

"Clorinda, our maid, is going to marry a police corporal, and since he's been transferred to Elvas, she's going to leave us. We're very sorry, and so is she. She's a very good maid, she's been with us since she was twelve, and is almost a member of the family. But that's the way life is – we can't do a thing about it. And what's worse is that it's getting more and more difficult to find a maid that's honest, discreet, obedient, and hard-working. There are lots of girls who'd like a job, especially nowadays, when there's so much poverty. But you just can't trust someone you don't know, especially here in Oporto. Some of my lady friends have been complaining about maids from certain disreputable districts. They're ill-mannered, lazy, and steal everything they can get their hands on. In the long run they have to be let go. So, as you can see, we have a problem."

"Well, if I could, I'd come work here myself," I suggested. "But you certainly wouldn't want a servant who can't even fry an egg."

Dona Leontina burst out laughing at such nonsense and went on, "The favor I'm asking isn't that difficult. It's really very simple. What I need is for you to ask your good mother if she knows some reliable young girl in your area, who might want to come and work in Oporto."

"I'll be glad to ask my mother," I said.

"The younger the better, because that way she'll have fewer bad habits. And she doesn't need to know much about housework, either. We'll teach her everything."

We talked a little longer about maids and I said goodbye, wishing Aninhas a quick recovery, and telling her not to worry about the letter. Her mother asked what letter we were talking about, and Aninhas told her it was a love letter.

"A love letter?" her mother asked, warily.

"Luís has received an anonymous love letter," Aninhas lied.

"There's nothing unusual about that," Dona Leontina said. "Your father, even after we married, received several. Some women have no sense of shame, that's all there is to it. And it's even worse when the letters cease to be anonymous. That's when Mr. Luís Vasques ought to be careful, or he'll get hopelessly entangled."

343

I smiled at Aninhas, thankful for her pious lie – I should have been more discreet – and left. Dona Leontina saw me to the door, I said goodbye effusively, and left for Braga.

That night I found a letter from Madame Constance Gavroche waiting for me. She mentioned the arrival of Monsieur Joaquim Domingues and how glad everyone at her home was to see him again. Too bad he'd come alone. At that time in the year there was not much work at the farm and he was keeping himself busy fixing things around the house and in the barn. Other neighbors, having noticed how handy he was, started hiring him at good wages. Although he missed his family and his Portuguese friends, he was getting along fine. He complained about the cold, but he said that it was easier to put up with when you have dry clothes and your feet are not in the mud of the trenches. She also said they were planning a spring visit to Neuve-Chapelle and Fauquissart. Monsieur Joaquim Domingues insisted on visiting the abandoned trenches again. He also asked for news from his wife and children.

The following day, Saturday, I mounted Ruddy and rode to Rato's house, where I found Vicência hanging the laundry.

"Good morning!"

"Good morning, Master Luís. What are you doing around here? Out for a ride?" she asked, about to hang a rag on the clothesline.

"I'm bringing you news from Joaquim."

"And what's he got to say?" She sounded uninterested.

"He says he arrived well in France, found work, and is missing his family."

"Oh, is he now. He been gone more than three months and this is the first time he sends news."

"So, he hasn't written you?" I asked, surprised.

"If he did, I ain't received nothing. He must've forgotten the address."

"Not even at Christmas?"

"Not a word."

"Well, he can't write, and surely it must be difficult to find someone in France who can write letters in Portuguese for him," I said, trying to find excuses for him.

"But haven't you just said, Master Luís, that you got news from him?"

"Well, not exactly from him. The news came from a French lady who gave him work." And I showed her the envelope, adding, "The letter is written in French."

"Ain't nobody here knows French. Anyways, it couldn't have been too hard to stick some franc notes into an envelope and ask that lady who gave him work to write our address and post it. When he was in the Army, the War Ministry, or whatever it was called, used to send a little money to support his children. But now there ain't nothing coming to us. And we been going through hard times."

"Oh!" I exclaimed. "Of course, he did send money with the letter. Forgive me, Dona Vicência, if I didn't mention that earlier."

I opened my wallet and pulled out two five and one twenty escudo bills. It was all the paper money I had on me. She wiped her hands on her patched apron, took the bills, and commented, "These ain't francs. They look like Portuguese money."

"Yes, they are escudos. Since it's difficult to change francs here in the village, I took the liberty to change them for you. I hope you don't mind, Dona Vicência."

She looked at me suspiciously. Did she realize that money had not been sent by her husband? Then, remembering Aninhas's mother's request, I asked if she knew of some young girl who might work in a home in Oporto.

"Why, my Evangelina," she said, tucking the bills in the pocket of her apron. "She's about to turn twelve and I ain't yet found a home that would hire her. I'm sure you know, Master Luís, how hard things is these days. Your dear father was good enough to hire my Delmiro, but that was a miracle. The middle

345

one, Fernando, he goes to work with me, when there's any. The young 'uns, they have a hard time finding work these days. If they can, they go to Lisbon, or to Brazil. The others stay here, and get by as best they can."

"Well, Dona Vicência, if you don't mind sending your daughter to Oporto, there's a chance for her to go into service."

"And this home, is it a good one?"

"It's my future fiancée's home. Their maid is getting married, and my fiancée's mother needs to hire a girl to replace her. The job is your daughter's, if she wants it."

"Of course she wants it! Why wouldn't she?"

"Wouldn't it be better to ask her? She might have a different opinion."

"What opinion could she have? But if you say so, Master Luís..." She turned into the house and yelled, "Lina! Come here!"

A young female voice asked what she wanted.

"Come here, girl, I got something to ask you."

A young girl appeared at the door, carrying a child. She was tall for her age, wore her hair in a long braid and her brown eyes, large and expressive, reminded me of Rato's. Unlike her father, she was rather fair skinned. She probably spent a lot of time indoors, taking care of her younger sister, Fátima, born while we were in Flanders. Her breasts were beginning to show under her blouse. If she stayed in the village, in two or three years the young men would start sniffing at her door. It would be a good thing for her to leave that hole. Maybe in Oporto she would also meet a police sergeant and marry him, I thought.

"What do you want, Ma?"

"Come, girl, ain't you going to greet Master Luís?"

"Good morning, Master Luís," she said, somewhat embarrassed.

"Good morning, Evangelina," I said.

"What was you doing?" her mother asked.

346

"I was wiping Fátima's ass. She crapped again."

"Watch your language, girl. Ain't I learned you that ain't no way of talking?"

"What did I say, Ma?"

"You said what you done said. We'll talk later. Let me have your sister. Master Luís wants to ask you something."

Evangelina handed the child over to her mother and looked at me open-mouthed, as if it were something extraordinary for someone like me to want to talk to her.

"Have you been to school, Evangelina?" I asked, to get her to talk.

"No, sir."

"And can you read?"

"No."

"And why not?"

The girl stared down at the ground in silence.

"Life is hard, Master Luís," her mother said finally. "She been helping me a lot in taking care of this little one. Also in the house work."

"Tell me, Evangelina , how would you like to work in the home of a good family in Oporto?"

She hesitated, looked at her mother, who nodded in agreement.

"Yes, I would."

"That's it, then. Next week I'll talk to Dona Leontina Gouveia. If she agrees, you'll come along with me to Oporto. All right?"

Her mother answered, "Yes, Master Luís, anything you say."

I said goodbye to them and rode Ruddy out of the village.

The following weekend I came home again and on Sunday afternoon I drove Evangelina to Aninhas's home in Oporto. Probably with the money I had given her, Vicência had bought a new skirt and blouse for her daughter. Everyone found her

347

attractive when she walked into the Gouveia's home, in spite of her noisy clogs and sing-song Minho accent. During the trip she listened attentively and asked a few questions while I gave her some pointers on how to please her masters. I summed it all up in a few rules: she should obey orders, even if they sounded silly; listen quietly and never talk back; pay attention and learn the household chores fast; do them well, or as best she could; never say or show she missed home; never cry, and only laugh when others laughed; and never eat anything unless they told her she could.

"Not even leftovers?"

"Not even leftovers. If there are any, wait until they tell you can eat them."

"And if they don't?"

"Don't eat them."

"But they can go bad, and my ma says that's a sin."

"You can always let your mistress know there's something that may go bad if it isn't eaten. She'll tell you what to do."

"Very well."

"If you have any free time, ask Aninhas to teach you to read."

"To read? What for?"

"It's a good thing to be able to read."

"Why? Delmiro can read and he's still an idiot."

"But you're a smart girl, and if you learn how to read, you'll be able to get a much better job, at a lady's shop. I'll ask Aninhas to teach you."

"Aninhas is your fiancée, ain't she, sir?"

"More or less."

"More or less?"

"We aren't engaged yet. We're just sweethearts."

"And when are you going to be engaged?"

"That's something I've been forgetting to ask myself."

"She's very pretty."

"Yes, she is. How do you know?"

"I seen her at the grape harvest."

"Oh, yes. You were there too."

"I went with my pa and Delmiro. I was filling the baskets. I also got to know Paulino."

"Aninhas's brother?"

"Yes, him. He's very silly, Paulinho is. He kept pulling my braid all the time."

"Well, mind you, he liked you."

"Really? He didn't seem to."

"When boys like a girl, they like to pull her braid."

We stopped talking and I spent the rest of the trip thinking about my relationship with Aninhas. I decided to formalize our engagement. Aninhas was out of danger and her father had promised to let her get out of bed and lead a normal life if she regained a few kilos. That would be a good time to ask for her hand in marriage. However, I did not have a chance to do it, because we were not alone for even a second. Her parents, her brother, and Aunt Generosa were at home, and Aninhas was spending her time sitting in the living room with her legs wrapped in a blanket, looking rather fragile.

Having dropped off Evangelina, I drove on to Coimbra. I did not know it then, but I had just started something I would regret bitterly. I did it, however, in the best of intentions, thinking I was helping a needy family and doing my future mother-in-law a favor. But the gods, or whoever guides human destinies – assuming anyone does – simply pulled the rug from under my feet.

XXIX

It is February and the shrubs at the entrance of the estate are dotted with little red flowers. Ever since I was a child, the blooming of those shrubs has meant to me the end of winter and the onset of spring. Those shrubs – I cannot recall what they are called, even though my father told me many times – are unremarkable the rest of the year. Nobody ever notices them. In October they shed their small leaves and in winter they look like a bundle of bare dry sticks. As the temperature begins to rise in February, they burst into a festival of red. I once asked my father if he had planted them. He said he had not. As far as he could remember, they had always been there, next to the gate. Maybe, he suggested, they were planted when the house was built in the 18th century, by some ancestor from the days of King João V.

When I was an adolescent I tried to look up that ancestor, and, like the hero in *A Ilustre Casa de Ramires*,[60] I penned an historical narrative, which is probably still buried in some notebook from my high school days.

But I do not intend to write about my ancestor. Rather, I am writing about a younger version of myself who was in the trenches in Flanders more than twenty years ago.

In February there were not yet any signs of spring. The fields were frozen, the trees dormant, the ditches iced up, and the trenches filled with trampled mud.

Early in the month, our rest in Paradis came to an end and our battalion departed, first to Laventie, and then on to the front subsector of Fauquissart I. Two days earlier, a few officers had reconnoitered that sector, which was totally unfamiliar to us. On the day we marched, Laventie was bombed. It is possible that the Boche, by means of balloons or an airplane, had detected the movement of our troops and decided to wipe out a few of us. But neither my platoon nor our company had any casualties. There would be time for that.

While we remained at the front, the battalion command post was set up in the Red House, to become a resistance bastion on April 9, which was just around the corner. Later it was commented that in February the Boche had already decided to attack the front defended by the Portuguese, which they thought – correctly, as it turned out – was the most weakly defended sector. The Portuguese soldiers were unmotivated – the war meant nothing to us –, poorly equipped, and in dismal physical and sanitary conditions. Therefore, it was not surprising that the Germans would unleash all their military power against us. They bombarded us almost daily, trying to wear us out as much as possible prior to charging us with assault troops.

During our twenty days at the front, the first and second lines in our subsector were intensely bombarded twice. Both the parapet and the parados in our trench were destroyed by mortar shells and heavy machine gun fire, making it far more difficult for us to maintain lookout posts. We were also raided by three good-sized patrols, but fortunately we were alert and managed to repel them back to their trenches.

The day we left for Laventie to resume a reserve role, we were heavily shelled and had several dead and wounded. Throughout our stay in that village rumors of intense activity in the enemy lines portended no good.

In early March we relieved another battalion in the first line. The Boche started shelling the Champigny subsector on our right. We were warned by telephone – on that day the wires were not hit – that one of our companies was being attacked by assault troops. The situation was very serious and Captain Rebelo wanted to go to help that company. The Major forbade it with a direct order, telling us to hold on to our positions, just in case the Boche attacked our subsector. Consequently, they managed to penetrate the trenches next door and capture some boxes of corned beef – a delicacy they apparently lacked – and a few prisoners, likely caught asleep or with their pants down.

A few days later, while we were back on reserve at Laventie, we were summoned to help defend the front at Fauquissart I, which was under attack.

In early March we found ourselves once again in the first line. We suffered another bombardment and a night raid. The next day, several airplanes flew over our lines but did not drop any gifts. They were reconnoitering, taking photos of our positions to help their artillery pinpoint targets with more precision. We tried to bring them down with machine gun fire but they were too quick. Private Frossos, one of our company's best shots, leaned back on the parados of the trench, aimed his Lee-Enfield, and managed to hit the rudder of one of the airplanes. But the .303 caliber cartridge was too small to do much damage, and the airplane went on flying around as if on a pleasure cruise.

The shelling went on nonstop until the end of the month. In our unit, however, besides a few scratches from grenade fragments and a couple of men who inadvertently shot themselves in the foot while in the latrines, there were no casualties.

Suddenly, in early April, everything went silent. Nights became serene and nearly completely quiet. Sporadically you could see a Very flare, or hear a shot or the drone of an airplane. Someone reported hearing sounds of automobiles or even a train beyond the enemy lines. I heard nothing.

"Might it be the Boche heading home, sir?" Rato asked me once as he handed me a plate of bean stew at dinner.

"I don't think so. They're still there, waiting."

"Waiting for what, sir?"

"Waiting for us to attack them, which isn't likely, since we don't have the means and they know it, or for an order to attack us."

"And so?"

"I'd bet on the second hypothesis."

"Well, we'll be waiting for them. Until now, not a single one has gone through."

I did not want to alarm Rato. Telling him what I really

thought and feared might have a catastrophic effect on morale – his own and the soldiers he talked to. I only said, "I want you to promise me that, if this starts getting hot, you'll do everything to get out of here alive. In this war, there aren't any heroes. At best, there are only survivors."

"There you go again, sir! How can this get hot if it's already cooled down? We ain't heard a single mortar in days. The way I see it, the Boche have given up on the war and they're still there just to stop us from chasing them."

"What makes you think that?"

"That's what everyone's saying, sir. There's a rumor we'll be going home in a month."

"May the angels say amen."

"On October 13, in Fátima, the Virgin said the war was going to end soon."

"The Virgin didn't say the war was going to end soon. From what I read in the papers, she said it was going to end the next day, that is, on October 14. That was six months ago."

"Oh, that shepherd girl, Lúcia, she must have misheard it, sir. You know how children are. You tell them one thing and they get another. Anyway, I've promised the Virgin a candle as heavy as me if I manage to get out of this pigsty alive. And I'm sure I'll be able to keep my promise."

"How's that? Has the Virgin appeared to you too?"

"You shouldn't joke about them serious things, sir. How could the Virgin appear to a poor sinner like me? She only appears to holy people, like children, who don't know nothing about sin. Or to the nuns at the convent."

"But didn't Jesus say he'd rather be with sinners than with sanctimonious men, always pounding their chests and acting like whitewashed tombs?"

"Sure, but he also said, 'Let the little children come to me.' In Fátima the Virgin didn't appear to people like us, she appeared to three children."

"Assuming she did."

"Do you doubt it, sir?"

"There are lots of people who've been there and doubt it. I haven't been there and haven't seen anything; how could I believe it?"

"Begging your pardon, sir, you sound like you ain't got much faith."

"And you sound like you have too much of it."

"I have every reason for that, sir."

"Maybe you don't know that it's easier to believe than to doubt. Doubting requires a lot of thinking."

"Well, sir, you sure know more about them things than me. But even so, I do believe the Virgin appeared in Fátima, whether you believe it or not, sir."

"I'll think about it."

In Fauquissart I often thought of Madame Gavroche. I cannot tell if I felt any passion for her, but it was certainly a blend of affection and desire. With every step I took in the trench I found myself dreaming about her scent after washing, her white, warm skin, her soft lips, her gentle voice, her blond hair touching my face, her long hands turned rough by the hard work she was forced to do. Our letters did not mention love. Or at least they did not include the typical epistolary flourishes with which lovers used to make up for the impossibility of exchanging something more substantial. All the same, when I finished writing a letter I kissed it, and I am sure she did likewise. Those were invisible kisses which only we, who wrote and read those letters, were able to perceive.

At that point, Libaninha was just a faint memory. The fact that I did not reply to her at Christmas probably made her give up writing to me again. Our courtship had been rather conventional. Of all the well-born marriageable young women in the neighborhood, she was the most convenient. At that time our parents were in favor of our courtship. The wedding, planned by them, would take place after I graduated from Law School, and I would then go to live at Quinta de Santa

Madalena, together with my dear in-laws. I was too young, too naive, and could not imagine what awaited me.

The Fontoura e Azevedo family, of old, though plebeian tradition in the land, had come from Brazil shortly after the republic was proclaimed in Portugal in 1910. Libaninha was born in São Paulo. Mr. Arnaldo Fontoura e Azevedo had left for Brazil as a child, fleeing hunger and poverty in his village and his family of fifteen siblings. He had been taken in by an uncle who was in the meat business in Brazil. The boy grew up, got smart, and went into business for himself, becoming the main competitor of his uncle, who certainly cursed him forever. In a few years he owned half a dozen butcher's shops and a slaughterhouse. When his uncle died from intestinal problems, Senhor Arnaldo bought off the heirs, two work-shy mulattoes who proceeded to fritter away the money on whores and drink. Senhor Arnaldo, then in his thirties, thought he needed an heir and married Dona Eleutéria de Brito, a brunette with Brazilian parents in whose veins flowed a good mix of Europe, Africa, and America. She was beautiful – the portraits I saw at Quinta de Santa Madalena showed it – and he did not hesitate to choose her as the mother of his heirs. The bride's parents had a lot of money, which helped increase the estate.

At forty five, Senhor Arnaldo was tired of the meat business and, having learned the King had been deposed, thought a new era was about to dawn on Portugal and decided to come back. He came alone at first, to reconnoiter. He went back to his village, saw his mother, the few siblings who were still around, and started looking at property for sale. Santa Madalena had been abandoned for years, and the owners, who could care less about it and lived in Lisbon, sold it to him for a song. He hired a contractor to fix up the house, had one of his brothers keep an eye on the job, and went back to Brazil. Once there, he sold his butcher's shops and the slaughterhouse and came back to Portugal with his wife and daughter.

Libaninha was fifteen years old when I first saw her at

the village church where I used to attend Sunday mass with my mother. She was an exotic beauty to the eyes of a dolt like me, who had seen nothing or nearly nothing of the world. Her black hair was naturally wavy, her skin was naturally tanned – both certainly inherited from her mother – and she had dark eyes and fleshy lips. She did not walk like the other girls; rather, she sort of danced, with her head high, always smiling. But it was mostly her way of talking, her tropical Portuguese, full of open vowels, sweet and colorful, that most attracted me at the time.

She went to a young women's school in Braga. My school, also in Braga, traditionally threw a party before the Easter holidays, inviting all the others, particularly those for young women. It was the only time in the year when young men and young women could get together. I was probably seventeen years old, and she sixteen, and it was during one of those parties that we first talked. I played the role of a lawyer in a short play. She recognized me and came to congratulate me after the play. We became friends. During the vacation she would invite me to spend afternoons at Santa Madalena, to play the piano for her and her mother, to read, or just to chat. Since her parents considered me a good catch, they approved of it, and when I finished my first year in Law School we became officially engaged. I was then twenty, and she nineteen.

As soon as we became engaged, our courtship became more conventional. When I called on her on weekends or during school vacations, we sat in the living room, talking about inanities, while her mother did some embroidering and kept an eye on us. If her mother was not available, she sent one of the maids. On hot afternoons we were sometimes allowed to go to the porch and sit on an iron bench in the shade of a camellia tree. Vigilance was then more discreet. Dona Eleutéria showed up at the window every now and then and, if we were too close together, she just coughed and Libaninha jumped like a cricket to the other end of the bench. When we least expected it, a maid walked by carrying a basketful of laundry or a bunch of collard greens for dinner. In the meantime we exchanged kisses, at first quickly and discreetly, and later wet and deep. We were never caught, or at least that was what we believed. Now I wonder whether her mother, or a duly instructed maid, had not simply ignored those saliva exchanges as means of reinforcing our future union.

One Sunday afternoon in June, while we were sitting on the bench under the camellia tree, one of the maids brought us a basket of cherries. We ate them up and Libaninha felt like having more.

"Shall we go and pick them?" she suggested.

"If you wish..."

She grabbed the empty basket, called to her mother, struggling with her embroidery in the cool of the living room, to let her know we were going for cherries, and led me along a dirt path into the interior of the estate. Her mother did not have time to react. In a little while we were among some reeds next to a reservoir used for watering the crops, sufficiently hidden from inquisitive eyes. She dropped the basket, embraced me and we kissed each other avidly. Suddenly I felt her hands inside my pants. Feeling my hardened penis, she cried out excitedly, "The little rascal wants to have some fun."

I was getting excited but could not do anything about it. Brazenly, she said, "Take off your pants."

"Take them off? What for?"

"Why, to make love, of course. Or don't you want to?"

"Sure I do. But it'd be better if you took off your dress."

"Why me?"

"You don't want to get it all dirty and wrinkled. What would your mother say?"

She took off her dress and hung it on a reed. It was a pink dress. She kept on her hat of the same color, her black patent leather shoes, her corset and her bloomers. It would be too complicated to take off all that, and anyway I had no idea how to handle all those buttons and strings. She knelt down, lowered her bloomers a little, and I was bowled over at the black, abundant hair that covered her sex, like oak trees in a valley between two hills. I was surprised she did not feel any shame about showing it to me. On the contrary, she seemed proud of it, and, wiggling her bottom, she even asked me, "Do you like it?"

"Yup, a lot," I think I replied, stammering with emotion.

"Well then, what are you waiting for?"

I unbuttoned my fly, felt for her opening hesitantly, as if in the dark, and bending my knees slighted, penetrated her. She was quite humid and I had no difficulty doing it. I wondered if she was still a virgin, for she did not bleed and that was the first time I was with her. At the time I was prejudiced enough to think about that. But it did not occur to me right away. Rather, I concentrated on the task at hand. With her left hand she held on to a reed that shook as I thrusted, and with her right she rubbed herself underneath. We moaned and grunted, softly, so no one would hear us. I finally came inside her and as I was about to pull out she asked me to stay. I kept on, without the initial enthusiasm, with my penis almost limp, but as she wiggled and moaned, I felt aroused again, I felt her quiver several times, and in a short while I came again. Finally I pulled out, wiped my penis with a handkerchief, and buttoned up. Libaninha stood up, a bit dizzy and blushing, pulled up her bloomers, adjusted her corset, brushed the grass off her knees, hung herself on me, and asked, "Did you enjoy it?"

I took a deep breath and said I did.

"We'll do it again. Often."

And we did. What is amazing is that I never saw her worry about getting pregnant. We did not take any precautions. She did not get pregnant out of sheer luck. At our next meeting I asked her if everything was all right. She said I need not worry, and as I seemed in doubt, she explained that there was no danger, as long as we made love one week before she had her period.

"I read about it in a medical book."

"In a medical book?"

"Yes. There was one, in French, in the school library. The nuns wouldn't let us read it. But one day, when the nun in charge of the library wasn't paying attention, I read the section on reproduction. Everything was explained very clearly."

Much later, a doctor told me that was not absolutely safe, and confirmed it was out of sheer luck that I had not become a father.

In the meantime we were informed that the 2nd Division, to which we belonged, would soon be relieved by an English division. Only one of our battalions would be kept in the trenches. On April 7th the soldiers from that battalion mutinied, claiming it was unfair to keep them at the front while all of their comrades took a rest.

Despite intense shelling on April 6th and 7th, aimed particularly at the second line and the command posts, we were in high spirits. We thought the war was just about over for us and we would go home. On April 8th we found out we would be relieved the next day. Having been informed about the situation of the Portuguese forces, the Commander-in-Chief, Marshal Sir Douglas Haig, had ordered their immediate withdrawal and relief by an English division.

April 8th was a holiday in the sectors defended by the 2nd Portuguese Division, which at that point were, from left to right, or from top to bottom, depending on how you looked at it, Fauquissart, Champigny, Neuve-Chapelle, and Ferme du Bois. That area, which covered eleven kilometers, was defended on paper by twenty-five thousand men, but in reality by fewer than five thousand. The missing men were either dead, or sick, or stuck in some warehouse or office in the rear. The English knew about that, hence the withdrawal order. The question was the extent to which the Boche were aware of our weakness.

"We're going home, sir!" Rato exclaimed enthusiastically as he served my lunch outside our shelter.

"That's the way it looks, Rato," I said.

"Do you still doubt it, sir?"

"You know what makes me worry?"

"What, sir?"

"This silence."

"Oh, please, sir. There you go again with the same story!"

"Haven't you realized that today we haven't heard a single shot from the other side?"

"No, I hadn't noticed it. And I guess the others haven't either."

"You men haven't been paying attention, thinking about going back home."

"But what does it matter if the Boche have decided to be quiet today, sir? Just yesterday they sent a few shells and grenades our way. I even heard that the landlady of the Red House started having her furniture removed. She was afraid the shell fragments might ruin the varnish. I bet our Major ain't got a chair to sit in."

"He can always use a corned beef box."

That afternoon I censored more than thirty letters. Enthusiastic about the announcement of our withdrawal, the soldiers hastened to send the good news home.

In my two rounds I found the men, even those on sentry duty, busy dictating or writing letters. That would be their last letter from the trenches. I myself sat down at the entrance of our shelter, under a patch of blue sky, and wrote my parents and Madame Gavroche. Among other things, it was forbidden to mention troop positions or movements in our letters. Consequently, it was also forbidden to mention our withdrawal. But since that would be our last relief and we would be far from the trenches when the letters were mailed, I figured there was no danger and did not black out any references to our forthcoming relief. In my letter to my parents, I enthusiastically explained we would leave the front line, adding I would be home in a month. But when I started writing to Madame Gavroche, I felt some doubts and toned it down somewhat.

I felt almost certain that the Germans would soon launch a massive attack. Otherwise, there was no explanation for the movements we perceived on the other side of no man's land, the constant reconnoitering flights over our lines, and the shelling of the preceding weeks. Maybe we would not take the brunt of the assault. But it might begin while we were on our way to the rear and then we would be forced to come back and repel the attack. On several occasions, a battalion on reserve or resting had been called back to the trenches in an emergency. Even if none of that happened and we managed to reach our embarkation points, I thought I should warn Madame Gavroche about the danger she and her family ran in Enguinegatte. I advised her to move further down south, to a place where she had relatives or friends.

None of those letters, however, would ever reach their destination.

A little before evening stand-to, Captain Rebelo summoned the company officers to the shelter for a final briefing on our relief by the English the next day. The tobacco smoke exhaled by everyone, except me, made breathing impossible inside the dugout.

"Let's hope they won't be late," concluded the Captain.

"The English have a reputation of being punctual," Coutinho said, flicking ashes on the dirt floor.

"We'll see if they're like that when the going gets tough," the Captain replied.

"Sir, do you think..." Nogueira began.

"I think nothing. And even if I did, I wouldn't say it."

We were rather crestfallen, sitting on empty ammunition boxes and looking at each other, and when we heard the Captain's answer, we looked down at the floor.

"What's the matter? Aren't you happy? What the hell, we're leaving the trenches! Come on, let's see a smile on those mugs!"

He threw away his cigarette butt, grabbed a bottle of brandy, took a swig and passed it on to Nogueira, adding, "Come on, let's drink! A toast to this trench, which has kept us alive until now."

"Some have died, sir," Nogueira added, holding the bottle, hesitating between taking a swig and passing it on.

"It was their fault, for being stupid. They should have taken shelter. The trench protects you, but it doesn't make miracles."

"It may be a man's bad luck to be in the wrong place, or a shell fragment coming from where you least expect, or a leaking gas mask, or just Fate, which no amount of precaution can prevent."

"Yes, yes, Nogueira. You're quite right. And since you are right, drink to Fate, which has kept us alive to this day."

Nogueira drank and passed the bottle on. After the toast, the Captain dismissed us and went on sipping what was left in the bottle.

Except for a reconnoitering visit by enemy airplanes by the end of the afternoon, nothing else happened on April 8th that might be mentioned in the report every officer had to fill out. Silence and quiet were not relevant. Reports privileged events, not their absence.

The night started somewhat agitatedly, not because of the Boche, who remained quiet, but because of an order from Minho Brigade Headquarters, directing some platoons to reinforce the 8th and 20th Battalions, which at that point did not have enough men to defend the first and second lines. My platoon stayed behind to defend the support line. Captain Rebelo, Nogueira, and Coutinho left for the front with the rest of the company.

A little after four in the morning, the Boche seemed to wake up from their lethargy and started the biggest shelling we had suffered until then. They began methodically by the rear lines, shelling the command posts, the supply depots, the ammunition depots, and the telephone lines. A few soldiers burst out laughing, happy to imagine what the pen pushers were suffering. But the laughter soon died out when they realized the range was being shortened back as far as the support line, and then further back to the second and first lines, forcing them to take cover as best they could.

Around eight in the morning, couriers started bringing news that the Boche had broken into the English sector on our left. That was the beginning of Operation Georgette, conceived, planned, and executed by General Ludendorf, aimed at breaking through the Western front and putting an end to the war once and for all. We took the first attack, which would be known as the battle of La Lys. Our battalion lost sixty per cent of its strength. General Hacking, commanding the 11th Army Corps, ordered the 2nd Portuguese Division to hold the line of villages and the support line to the last man. That order confirmed the rumor that we were no more than cannon fodder.

The battle of La Lys inflicted on the Portuguese Army the worst debacle in its history since the battle of Alcácer Quibir.[61] This time, however, there was no Dom Sebastião to disappear. Or maybe those who vanished, and whose families are still waiting for them on misty mornings, are, each one of them, Dom Sebastião.

XXX

Aninhas set the date of our engagement ceremony after speaking to her parents and gaining their approval. It was to be a family event, during which I would formally ask for her hand in marriage. It took place on a Sunday afternoon at the Gouveias's home and my parents were also present. There were rings exchanged, speeches, port with crackers, rissoles, and cod cakes. The wedding date was set for the last week in July, whether or not I had graduated from Law School. In the worst-case scenario, in September I would retake any exam I still needed to pass. The head of a family needed to have the means, present and future, to support his loved ones.

During our first year of marriage we would live in Oporto, in my in-laws'. At first my parents objected. I would be too far away from them and they were afraid they would end up seeing their son only sporadically. I promised I would visit them every week. I would work as a legal intern with Mr. Trancoso, a lawyer friend of Dr. Gouveia's, and, after my internship, we would move to Braga. There would be plenty of work for a young lawyer, and since my father still kept his office, even though he no longer practiced, the many people he had served over the years would become my clients. There was no lack of inheritance disputes, scuffles and brawls at fairs, fights and deaths resulting from conflicts over water rights in the summer, arson, rapes, church burglaries and vandalism, thefts of chicken and fruit, quarreling neighbors, tavern knifings and contempt cases.

Dona Maria das Dores showed no more signs of life, either because she realized the anonymous letter had come to nothing or, more likely, because she had found herself another renter to make her forget our escapade. If that were the case, all the better for me, certainly for her too, and for Aninhas, who by that time had recovered her coloring. In March she had taken up her volunteer work at the hospital, much against her parents wishes, who wanted to keep her as far away as possible from anyone that might infect her again. On weekends, I would go to Oporto. In order for us to meet on Saturdays and Sundays, I often stayed at a pension I knew near the railway station. Out of politeness, her parents invited me to stay in their guest room. I refused, because it would have been very awkward for them to justify to others, and to themselves, that their daughter's fiancé was sleeping under their roof. It would not do at all for a young man to sleep at his fiancée's home. What would their neighbors think? What would their friends say? After all, they lived in Oporto, not in Lisbon.

One Sunday afternoon, Aninhas wanted to take me to a football match. It was a very pleasant day and I wanted to take her to the beach. But apparently it was an important match between the Oporto team and I cannot recall which visiting team. I had already watched a few matches in Braga and Coimbra and had even played a little at school. But in 1920 what little enthusiasm I might once have had for that sport had entirely vanished, and it was at great sacrifice that I watched that match, sitting next to Aninhas at the stadium.

I may be accused of elitism, of having aristocratic airs, given my lack of interest in football. There might be some logic to that if the sport only held the interest of the plain folk. But I have been seeing more and more people in important positions becoming fanatics over this particular sport, turning into dedicated fans of this or that football club, and transforming that passion into their raison d'être. There is a judge in the Braga district court, whose name I decline to mention, who allegedly passes down sentences on Monday according to whether or not his team has won or lost on Sunday. If it is true, and I suspect it is, because I have had clients condemned by him with insufficient evidence, that judge is a real idiot.

I do not like football, just as some people do not like to listen to piano music. In school, I was on the football team sometimes as left back, sometimes as goalkeeper. Those positions were usually played by clods. At first I was green with envy watching skillful players. It seemed amazing to me how, with their two legs, shoulders, chest and head, they could do so much with the ball. And I was afraid of the ball. If a hard and fast one came towards me, I avoided it, which earned me a mass of insults from my teammates. In the highly unlikely circumstance that I did receive a pass, I would quickly lose the ball either because I could not dribble the ball to pass it to a teammate, or because I made a stray kick, giving the ball to an adversary who would then score a goal. As defense, I was a disaster, since I rarely intercepted. I was even worse as goalkeeper, for when a hard kick came at me, I either turned my back or covered my face with my hands.

I was better at chess. But since there was no one who played at my level, except my father, I never rose above the level of a mediocre player.

In the match I watched with Aninhas, young men in blue and white striped shirts ran around kicking other young men in red and white striped shirts. What I saw in that match was a representation of war, with enemies facing each other on either side of the field, and no man's land in between. Aninhas cheered excitedly, elbowing me, wildly applauding things that would leave any reasonable person cold. When the blue team made its first goal, she hugged me and gave me a big kiss, which earned catcalls from the locals sitting near us. One of them asked us if we would not prefer to go play ball elsewhere. We were distracting him. I stood up, to make him eat his words, but Aninhas stopped me.

"You should have let me punish that fellow," I murmured.

"This isn't the Army. Here, if you get involved with one of these ruffians, you'll end up in the hospital, and that's if you're really lucky."

"And if I'm not?"

"You'll end up in the cemetery. And no matter how you look at it, neither choice is pleasant, especially on a beautiful afternoon like this and when our team is winning."

When the match was over, the Oporto fans left the stadium singing their victory. Aninhas was very happy, and I enjoyed seeing her like that. She had recovered from her illness and had renewed enthusiasm for life.

As we left, we ran into Dr. Gouveia and Paulino, who had also come to the match and were ecstatic with the victory. They turned down my offer of a ride, saying they were going to celebrate with friends. We drove away and, since it was still early, we decided to have tea at the Majestic. To change the subject – for Aninhas could not stop talking about the match and kept enthusiastically describing the spectacular plays – I asked her about Evangelina, Rato's daughter who was working as a maid in their house.

"She's a very clever girl, very quick. She catches on fast. And she already knows how to do a lot. My mother's taught her how to cook, wash, and clean. In a month or two, the other maid, Clorinda, can leave to get married."

"I promised her you would teach her how to read when you have time."

"I have the time. But she doesn't. By the end of the day, she's exhausted, poor girl, and she asks permission to go lie down."

"Where does she sleep?"

"In the attic, with Clorinda. It's a little cold in winter, but we don't have anywhere else in the house where they can stay."

"So the girl spends the entire day working?"

"Maids work all day long. That's what they're for and that's why they're paid, isn't that right? Or are the maids at your house different?"

"No, no, they're not. I just feel sorry for the girl."

"That's life, Luís."

367

"I know, but we could make things better."

"Just giving her work already improves her quality of life. What kind of life did she have in the village with her mother and brothers? Just barely getting by. She's far better off with us. Of that you can be sure. In our house the servants are almost like members of the family. When Clorinda gets married, she'll have a dowry from my parents and she'll be able to visit us whenever she's so inclined. Out of the maids that I recall working in our home, and there weren't many, I think, three since I was born, all of them come to visit us whenever they can."

"I believe it."

"Of course, not everyone treats their servants so well. There are a lot of very arrogant masters, people who believe their maids are no better than slaves."

"People with neither scruples nor principles."

"And no background. The nouveaux riches are the worst. Before working for us, Clorinda worked for a family living in a mansion, who'd made their fortune in Brazil. Her master was a Portuguese man who had gotten rich exploiting rubber in the Amazon and he tried to rape her several times. His Brazilian wife treated her like a slave girl. Clorinda got fed up with the abuse and disrespect, and she quit."

It was starting to get late and I had to go back to Coimbra. While I waited for the check, I said to Aninhas, "Promise me you'll try to teach Evangelina how to read. Even if you have to do it on the weekends."

"On the weekends, I'm with you. During the week, I'm working at the hospital and, when I get home Evangelina is making dinner or taking care of the thousand and one tasks that always need to get done in a household. By the end of the evening, she's so tired she has to go to bed to be able to get through the next day's work. But I could have Paulino tutor her every once in a while."

"Paulino?"

"Yes, my brother can easily teach her to read and even

to write. He has almost every afternoon free and gets bored at home. I'll ask my mother to release her from her duties for an hour or two. While he's doing his homework, he can get her started on learning to read."

"That seems like a good idea to me. Tell Paulino I'll get him a very special surprise if he manages to teach Evangelina the alphabet by... Let me think..."

"No deadlines. I'll only mention the surprise if he's reticent. Sometimes youngsters need motivation."

But there was no need to motivate Paulino. He took on the task immediately. He liked the company. It was Dona Leontina who was hesitant. She didn't want her son distracted from his homework, nor the little maid to waste her time learning to read. What for, she asked, if to cook, clean house, and wash clothes reading was entirely useless?

Instead of answering the question, Aninhas said I had made the request and she had promised me.

"Well, if this is your fiancé's request, and he's insisting," Dona Leontina backed down, "then we mustn't displease him. After all, two hours a day won't make that much difference. And, since the girl's smart, she'll learn to read quickly. Besides, at Fátima, the Virgin Mary told Lúcia she had to learn to read. And if she said that to a ten-year-old girl, a common girl, then it must be important."

"After all, Mother, knowledge doesn't take up any space."

"But it can take someone's place."

"Whose?"

"If everyone knew how to read, dear, the world would be filled with unrest and wars. Everyone would be clamoring for their rights. And as you well know, not everyone can have the same rights."

"As for the wars, they happen because very important people want to push others, less important people, around. They want to impose their will by force. As for the rights, you're

369

very mistaken, dear Mother. We're all born the same way and eventually, we die the same way too."

"You've been reading too much, dear. Too much reading is bad for your eyesight and creates illusions."

"And you don't live in the twentieth century, Mother, you're still in the past."

"Are you calling me old?"

"Oh Mother, dear! I'm just saying you're reactionary."

"And is that bad?"

Aninhas kissed her and went to take care of other things. She could not explain what a reactionary was or else she would have offended her mother.

After this conversation, Evangelina started reading lessons with Paulino. Within a month, she could read anything given to her from the worn out primary school reader they were using, and Paulino decided to introduce her to the mysterious world of numbers. He was surprised to discover she managed to do the four basic arithmetic operations in her mind, even before learning her numbers.

Five years later, he was eighteen and she was seventeen, and they fell madly in love with each other without anyone realizing what had happened. By then, Aninhas and I were married and living at Quinta de São Francisco. Evangelina had grown into a beautiful young woman. I do not know the details of their romance. But it is not difficult to deduce what might have happened. They probably exchanged amorous words, promises and secret caresses, unaware of the possible consequences. What is certain is that she got pregnant, and when she started showing, Dona Leontina wanted her to identify the cad. Evangelina refused to tell her. My mother-in-law threatened her. Either she confessed or else she would have to leave the house. She preferred to go home to her mother, in spite of the shame she would have to endure back in the village.

Paulino was distraught with the absence of his loved one and wrote her passionate letters behind his mother's back. Back then, dialogue between parents and children was extremely limited. Dona Leontina and Dr. Gouveia noticed how sad and drawn he looked, but it never occurred to them to ask him what was going on. They imagined it was some innocent problems in his love life. The idea that he was the cad never crossed their minds.

Around that time, Vicência visited us at the estate and brought along a small bundle of letters from Paulino to Evangelina. Aninhas chose one at random. It was a love letter in which the boy told his loved one not to worry. He would work out a way to help her and the child when it was born. He was planning to go to Brazil, where he had an uncle. When he had made his fortune, he would return and they would be married and live happily ever after.

Aninhas told their parents immediately and they, beside themselves, forbade Paulino from seeing the maid or writing her. As for the pregnancy, they refused to assume any responsibility whatsoever. It could have been the milkman, some coachman or a street sweeper, how in the world were they to know? Any butcher boy she'd fooled around with could have done it.

I was really disappointed in my in-laws, and from then on my relationship with them was distant. Up to a point, I understood it was hard for them to allow their son to assume paternity and marry a maid. Maids did not marry the sons of their employers. It was the rule and, although it may seem ridiculous, no one ever questioned it, except perhaps novelists, those creators of fantasy worlds. My disappointment had more to do with their categorical refusal to accept the more than evident fact that their son had been responsible for Rato's daughter's situation. In talking it over with Aninhas, Dona Leontina apparently said that above all, Paulino had to be protected. Aninhas asked, "And who is going to protect the girl? She's the one with child, not Paulino." Dona Leontina then asked if Aninhas had any suggestions.

Aninhas was aware that marriage, at least right then, was out of the question. They were too young and too immature for such a big step. In addition, Paulino would be going to the university that year and had no way of supporting a family. The only solution was for them to provide the future mother with financial support, discreetly, but effectively. My mother-in-law argued that, by doing that, they would be acknowledging Paulino's paternity and that could lead to pressures and demands from the girl. There was no convincing her that Evangelina was not a little hussy that had taken advantage of the trust of those who had taken her in. Whether or not Paulino had anything to do with it, the point was that she was guilty of lack of self-control, allowing herself to be seduced like a cat in heat. Slips like that come at a high price.

Aninhas was angry at her mother and told her she planned to do everything within her reach to help Evangelina. As for me, I was feeling guilty for having placed her in their home, and I supported my wife. We did everything possible, without drawing attention to the situation. Aninhas trusted neither the midwife, nor the hygienic conditions of her work. As a nurse, she would naturally be more capable of assisting at the birth, and so she had asked Evangelina to call her when labor set in. That, however, did not happen.

The child was born with the help of her maternal grandmother, who was very experienced, and the local midwife, an old woman who had assisted in the birth of most of the living, as well as the dead, of that village. Father Ruas used to say that there were even more of the latter than of the former. I don't know the statistics as well as he does. After all, his daily life is composed of registers of the parish baptisms and obituaries.

As I was saying, the child was born and they named her Isabel. Aninhas wanted us to be her godparents but, after much thought and following advice from my mother, who in such situations usually had very sound ideas, we did not proceed with the plan. Had we done so, we would have set ourselves against Aninhas's parents' wishes and, since the relationship was already tense, there was no point in making the situation worse.

Shortly after the delivery, Paulino decided to call on us behind his parents' back. We were somewhat surprised to see him, and when he insisted on visiting Evangelina and the child, we tried to make him see it was a foolish idea. He would more than likely be turned away by her mother and siblings, who viewed him as a young man that led innocent women astray.

"But the child is my daughter!" he argued.

"Just how can you be so sure?" Aninhas asked, putting him to the test.

"I heard it from Lina."

"What do you mean, 'you heard it'?"

"She wrote me saying the baby girl was born and the two of them were doing well."

"But don't you know she can't be writing you? Mom intercepts her letters before you ever get them?"

"I wrote her saying she should write to me at a friend's house."

"You really are a fool! And what if your friend reads the letters? What is he ever to think?"

"He knows what's going on."

"And what does he have to say about it?"

"That it's not the first time, nor the last, that a fellow falls in love with a maid and..."

"Ruins his life and hers. Did your friend also mention that?"

"No, he didn't. He said I should carry on, that love's more important than anything else."

"Has this friend of yours been reading romantic novels, by any chance? Life is not a novel, dear brother."

I got him in my car and, in spite of his protests, took him to the railway station, which I only left after the train had departed for Oporto.

I thought of writing Madame Gavroche and asking her to tell Rato that he had become a grandfather. I had not had news from her, nor from Rato, for over five years. Perhaps I was to blame, for I had not written them either. My marriage and my professional life occupied both my mind and my spirits. I stuck to the old adage that no news is good news.

I had a few doubts when I started the letter. What if Vicência had already told him he was a grandfather? My writing to tell him about what had happened to his daughter, and my own involvement in the situation, would not be at all tactful. One thing was certain, he was not going to be pleased to discover that the young man he had once saved from drowning in the ocean at Póvoa had made one of his daughters pregnant. He might have, with reason, blamed me for what had happened. So that is why I set my pen down and turned my attention to Afonso, already four years old, and leaning against my desk asking for a sheet of paper to draw on.

Let us take leave of Evangelina nursing little Isabel, happy mother, happy baby, the former having forgotten the past suffering and the latter, oblivious of that to come. Let us turn to Afonso, my eldest.

One Saturday in early May 1920, about three months prior to our marriage, I took Aninhas to Póvoa de Varzim. We went to visit Apúlia, who had returned home and was in the process of making a full recovery. We left a few gifts, mainly used clothing and foodstuffs. We went to have lunch with Aninhas's aunt, Dona Generosa, and we took the opportunity to invite her to the wedding. In the afternoon we went for a drive along the coast. The ocean was rough. Even so, Aninhas wanted to get her feet wet. I stopped the car near the Vila do Conde fortress, we took off our shoes and, holding hands, walked down the beach towards the waves. I felt the ice-cold water reach my ankles and instinctively withdrew. Aninhas squealed and grasped me, then I got hit by a second, stronger wave, which sprayed my rolled up slacks and soaked the hemline of her dress. We both laughed and, taking her in my arms, indifferent to the waves lapping at our feet, I kissed her. She took my hands and pulled me into a race along the shore. I tripped and fell, bringing her down with me. We lay there on the sand, she on top of me, and we kissed again. A wave surprised us, covering us like a sheet, soaking our clothes. I was afraid the cold water could be harmful to her, since another cold or pneumonia could be fatal. I helped her up.

"Now what?" I asked her. "We can't leave here like this. If we start driving all wet, you'll certainly get sick."

"We'll dry off first."

"How?"

"In the sun."

"In the sun? But we've got to get out of these clothes."

"So, we will."

"Right here on the beach? The fishermen or people along the coast might see us."

"We'll go up to the rocks. No one will see us there and we'll be protected from the wind."

She took me by the hand and led me to the nearest rocks. I could see we were indeed sheltered from everything there, except perhaps an unsuspecting wanderer or a curious seagull. And it was there among the rocks, surrounded by limpets, mussels, and sand crabs watching us suspiciously that we took off our clothes, set them out to dry, and lay down on the bare rocks. The sun was hot and we were soon dry. We wore only our underclothes and most probably, the seagulls up above confused us with some of their relatives. We dozed off and when I woke up, Aninhas was curled up against me, one arm over my chest, and a leg over mine. Her eyes were closed and her lips were parted in a subtle smile. I caressed her head and she woke up. She smiled at me.

"I love you, Ana."

Perhaps because of our surroundings, or maybe because she had forgotten what she had told me a few months earlier about pre-marital relations, or simply because we were engaged with our wedding date set, Aninhas decided to give up her virginity. And because of that, slowly and passionately, with the roar of the ocean in the background, in the company of crustaceans and mollusks, and scraping my knees, I became a father.

XXXI

There is a military saying that when you run away from a battle that you cannot win, you stay alive in order to fight again. Strategists favor the term withdrawal, possibly because running away has connotations of fear and cowardice. But as we say in Minho, cemeteries are full of heroes and brave men. The approximately two thousand Portuguese soldiers killed during the German offensive of April 9, 1918 were unanimously acclaimed as heroes. Nobody can take that title away from them, nor question their bravery in dying for the Fatherland in the field of honor, as the military like to call that quagmire where people kill and get killed. Those approximately two thousand Portuguese soldiers are rotting in cemeteries in Flanders.

According to the strategy manuals, my men did not run away. They obeyed my orders to withdraw to a more advantageous defensive position in order to carry out a more effective counter-attack.

At this point it is fitting to tell what happened to me at the battle of La Lys. Many have written about that battle, with scenes full of details, emotion, heroism, much blood and a lot of shooting. With few exceptions, those battle chroniclers write about something they did not witness because they were comfortably installed in an office in the rear. I will tell only what I saw, what I lived through, and the decisions I made as a platoon commander.

As I have already said, the 2nd Portuguese Division, which included the Minho Brigade to which my battalion belonged, was supposed to be relieved on April 9 by an English unit. We were finally going to get out of that war, or at least we were going to stay away from it for a while.

The day before was one of the quietest we spent in the trenches. The silence and stillness on the Boche side led many soldiers to think the enemy had withdrawn. After dark, I did

376

my first round of the posts manned by soldiers from my platoon, which was in the support line, and then I sat on an empty ammunition box by the shelter entrance, and looked at the stars. The sky was clear and I started identifying the different constellations. When I was a boy, my father used to take me on walks around our estate, on February and March evenings, which were ideal for star-gazing. As we sat on a wall, he would point out the various constellations. Facing north, we saw the constellation of Cassiopeia on our left, looking like a poorly drawn M. Then there was Camelopardalis, a little above Polaris, the North Star, which could hardly be seen. And on the right was Ursa Major, or the Great Bear. Facing south, we could see other constellations: Leo in the middle, Cancer on the left and, lower and to the right, Orion.

Once I told him that Ursa Major did not look anything like a bear.

"It looks more like a cart without wheels," I added.

"The rear of the cart," he explained, lines up with the North Star, in Ursa Minor, or the Little Bear constellation. The North Star is very important. It used to make it possible for sailors to find their way at sea, in the old days before navigation instruments were invented.

"And why is it so important?"

"Because it points north. If a sailor got lost, all he needed to do was to find the position of that star in relation to the other constellations. That way he knew where he was and could find the right direction. If you ever find yourself lost in some unknown land, without a compass or any point of reference, the North Star will be your only hope of finding your way."

"If only sailors had chosen a star that shone more brightly, it would be easier to see it."

"Stars don't shine."

"But I can see them shining. Or twinkling, which amounts to the same thing."

"That's because of our planet's atmosphere. The light

from the stars enters the atmosphere and is deflected by the air in movement. It's an optical illusion."

"Old Felício says the stars are the souls of the dead. And so many people have died, that's why there are so many stars that we can't count them."

"Some men can believe whatever nonsense they wish. But you're an intelligent young man and shouldn't believe that. Besides, the stars we can see with the naked eye have almost all been counted, and they're not as many as it seems."

"Even so, it looks like there are a lot of them."

"There are many more that we can't see. The ones we can see from here are just a tiny part of the Milky Way."

Since the universe was so big, I asked, could there be more worlds? He told me about other planets of the solar system and the notion that there were intelligent beings on Mars or even on Venus. But he did not believe that. He thought even if other inhabited worlds existed, they would be in stars so far away that it did not make much sense for us to think about them.

Sitting on the ammunition box by the shelter, I recalled my chats with my father about astronomy. I thought we were too insignificant before the vastness of the universe. On a cosmic scale, that war did not matter any more than two electrons clashing inside an atom.

My train of thought was interrupted by Rato, bringing up the usual rum ration. I did not feel like it.

"More for me, then," he said, drinking from the tin mug.

I told him to sit next to me.

"This is the last night we'll spend in this trench, sir. Once we're gone, we'll never believe we were ever here."

"Some day you'll miss this."

"Now that you mention it, sir... A lot of the men are going back to a life that's a lot worse than this. Back home there's just work and tiredness, cold, heat, hunger and poverty. Here, at least, nobody goes hungry. A lot of cold, not much heat, but work ain't never been too hard. The shitty thing about this is, we're so far from family and scared of being done in by a bomb or a bullet. Myself, I thank God I'm alive and in one piece. And tomorrow, goodbye trenches!"

"Better not count your chickens before they hatch."

"There you go again with your persismism, or however you call it, sir. What the heck, it's just a matter of hours! When it starts getting light, the Limeys'll come to relieve us. I've already packed up our kits. I'm taking some keepsakes home."

"What kind of keepsakes?"

"Oh, just a few small things. A couple of grenade fragments, rifle cartridge cases, an ashtray made out of a grenade, an insignia from the helmet of a Boche who must've croaked around here."

"And why are you dragging all that junk with you?"

"Like I said, they're keepsakes, or soovenirs, like the French say. Back home there's bound to be someone interested in them. And if nobody don't want them, I'll make them an offering to the Virgin."

"Father Ruas may think scrap metal isn't an offering fit for the Virgin."

"Well, sir, if the Padre don't like the idea, I'm sure Bigarrilha'll be glad to have it for his tavern. He can put it all on the shelf with the brandy bottles, or stack it on top of the barrels, next to the portrait of the Republic with her tits hanging out. Lots of folks'll like to see this stuff. Something to chat about of a Sunday afternoon."

"So Bigarrilha has a portrait of the Republic with her tits showing?"

"He sure does. Ain't you ever seen it, sir? She sure is a knockout, the Republic. No wonder she's turned the country upside down. It was her tits what drove everyone crazy, beginning with the politicians. And by the way, sir, I've also stuck a few things in your knapsack. I know you don't care about them things, sir, all you care about is your four cent coin.

I don't blame you. Every man's got his good luck charms. Mine's a medal of the Sacred Heart of Jesus."

"Madame Léonor Pigeard gave me a little medal of Jeanne d'Arc. I always have it on me."

I searched in my tunic pocket and showed it to him.

"I didn't know you believed in them things, sir."

"I'm not telling you if I do or don't."

"No need to. I figure holy medals are easiest to carry and give the most protection to folks wearing them. I know fellows who carry miniature Bibles in a pocket, or a bone of Saint Blaise in a scapular hanging from their neck, or a hair lock from their missus or their youngest child, or the Pope's photograph, or a crucifix blessed in Rome, or a vial of holy water from Lourdes, or a rabbit paw, or I don't know what else. There's even some what carry a coin..."

"You're pulling my leg and I am listening to you!"

I got up, turned around and went to lie down. Captain Rabelo and the other two junior officers were in the first line, supporting the thinned-out companies. I had the dugout all to myself.

I asked Rato to wake me up at five for stand-to.

"If you see anything out of the ordinary before then, come over at once, on the double. In the meantime, check your rifle and mine, and get us a full complement of ammunition."

"Are you planning on going hunting, sir?"

"I don't want to be caught unprepared on our last night in this trench."

"A man warned is worth two. Since there's two of us, we're four. But don't you worry, sir. You'll wake up with the birds singing, you'll see."

"May God hear you."

I stretched on the cot and covered myself with a greasy blanket full of rat holes. But the silence would not let me fall asleep. I missed the lullaby of gunfire in the distance, the machine gun clatter at half-hour intervals. Too tired to walk around the trench, I just lay on the cot. I found the four cent coin in my tunic pocket and rolled it through my fingers, caressing the young woman's breast, which I could not see in the darkness of the shelter. I imagined Libaninha's face while I caressed the breast of the woman on the coin, but that was someone else. The young woman on the four cent coin was the one I had seen in passing at the Campanhá station, as the train was leaving for Lisbon. I had to get out of that war alive and tell her...

I must have dozed off, for I woke up with Rato shaking me.

"Sir, they've started shelling us again."

"Shelling?" I asked, half-awake.

"That's right. Can't you hear it?"

In fact, a bombardment was going on. That was probably what had made me fall asleep.

"What time is it?"

"Past four-thirty. The shelling started about fifteen minutes ago."

I got up and went out after Rato. The shells were whizzing overhead and landing further behind, in the line of villages and probably on the 2nd Division Headquarters area.

"Those are going straight to the pen pushers," Rato said.

"Let's hope the Boche won't shorten their range."

"It would be a real pain in the butt to spend our last few hours in the trenches under a shell shower."

But soon the bombardment spread a storm of fire and molten iron over the entire sector. We had to run back to the shelter for cover. The telephones stopped working around five o'clock– they never worked when we needed them most – and I lost contact with Battalion Headquarters and with the companies on either side of us. I called Sergeant Rosado and ordered him to keep all the soldiers from our platoon in the available dugouts, and to make them put on their gas masks at the first sign of gas. He protested, saying that the sentry posts would be left unattended.

"We're in the support line, Rosado," I said. "The Boche won't attack a line that's under fire from their own artillery. As soon as the shelling stops, the men can go back to their posts."

"Yes, sir."

He saluted and left. I let four more privates into the shelter and they settled down as best they could. Rato was already in there, and Tibães, Apúlia, Semelhe and Frossos joined him. Rato found a bottle of bagaço left by the Captain under a box and asked me if he could wet his lips. I said he could and told him to pass the bottle around.

"Ain't the Boche overdoing, sir?" Tibães asked at a certain point. "This has been going on for half an hour. At this rate, the English won't come to relieve us today."

At that moment a shell fell at the shelter entrance, whistling like a snake.

"Gas!" one of the soldiers shouted.

We pulled the masks out of the bag we carried around our neck and put them on. While I put mine on, I ordered Apúlia and Frossos to grab the shell and throw it as far as possible. Even so, some gas seeped into the shelter and we had to get out and distance ourselves. At that moment the range was shorter, pinpointing the first line.

It was getting light, and with all that smoke, gas, dust, and fog, we could not see what was going on in front of us. When we stopped hearing the shells bursting, I tried the telephones again, but they were still out of order. I decided to send two runners, one to the company on our left and another to the company in front of us, to see if they could find out something. Tibães and Semelhe left and came back in a little while. Semelhe could not get through because the communication trenches had been destroyed. Tibães brought some worrisome news. The company on our left had managed to send a runner to Battalion Headquarters in Laventie, and he came back saying the Boche had broken into Fleurbaix, the English sector to the left of the Portuguese sectors. I recall looking at my watch: it was eight in the morning.

In the meantime, we began to hear intense small arms fire ahead of us. Since fog and smoke prevented us from seeing anything, we held on to our positions. Captain Rebelo's orders, given to me the day before, were to defend that subsector. The developing situation had rendered those orders obsolete, but since I had no others, I did my best to obey. I put Sergeant Rosado in command of half of our platoon and kept the other half with me. Our armament consisted of our individual Lee-Enfield rifles and two Lewis light machine guns. The Vickers heavy machine guns, which had more firepower, had been moved to the front by independent squads outside my command.

We leaned on the parapet, aiming our rifles, and waited. Next to me, Rato exclaimed, "The Boche had to ruin our party on the last day!"

"It's our farewell party," Tibães said.

"If this goes on, I doubt the Limeys will relieve us today," said Apúlia.

"What bugs me most is that I ain't had a bite to eat," said Semelhe, hungry as usual. "It's a pain to start the day on an empty belly."

"If you get out of here alive, count your blessings," Apúlia said. "You'll have the rest of your life to eat."

Around ten o'clock, a corporal and three privates from the 8th Battalion straggled into our support line. Two of the privates were lightly wounded. I asked the corporal if they were coming from the front, and he said there was no front line left, or if there was, we were in it. The enemy artillery had destroyed the parapets, the shelters, and the communication trenches of the first and second lines. When the big guns stopped firing, the assault troops attacked. The few men of the 8th that had not been buried just could not put up an effective resistance.

Those who had not been taken prisoner were retreating. There was nothing left to defend. I realized we had better retreat also, because the Boche were about to fall on us. There were too many of them and we would be squashed like snails if we didn't get out of there.

I ordered the corporal and the other three privates to stay with my men to defend our position. He hesitated, I frowned at him, and he ended up obeying. It was not worth it, at least at that point, to argue with an officer supported by ten armed men he could rely on. The newcomers leaned onto the parapet and waited, while our medic bandaged the wounded.

In the meantime, we started hearing shots and grenade blasts toward the rear. It was a bad sign that could mean the Boche had managed to surround us. I called Sergeant Rosado, posted some fifty meters away, and asked what he thought. He had more experience in war, having done several tours of duty in Africa. He thought the shots were coming from Rue Tilleloy, some twenty meters from our trench. Since it was unlikely our troops would be shooting at one another, it was more probable the enemy had flanked our positions and reached the road.

"Any suggestions?" I asked.

"We have two options: either we resist here or we withdraw to a safer place."

"Come now, Sergeant, any private could say that. What do you think our chances are if we stay here?"

"None. And in that case, we'll be either killed if we resist, or forced to surrender."

"So you think we should withdraw?"

"As a soldier, I can't say that, sir. You've ordered me to resist, and that's my job. But as a family man, I got to tell you, we'd better withdraw. Ain't no point in us staying here. We'd be no more than a thorn the Boche could brush off just like that."

"All right, Sergeant. Thanks for your sincerity. Here are my orders: when the Boche get within our range, we'll let them have it with everything we've got. When the men are down to their last clip, we'll try to withdraw to the right, since we can't move back. You'll go first with your men. If the Boche have made it to Rue Tilleloy, they're likely to have reached Laventie and the Red House. In that case, if you see things are bad in that area, move on to Lestrem, where Division Headquarters is."

"Very good, sir."

"And please don't try to be a hero. When all this is over, I want you to report to me with all the men safe and sound."

"You can count on it, sir."

"Good luck, Sergeant."

"May Our Lady of Fatima protect you, sir."

He saluted and left. Yes, at that point I surely could have used some help from the Lady of Fátima, whoever she might be.

When we spotted the first Boche among the smoke and fog that was beginning to lift, I gave the order of fire. Ten minutes later we were down to our last rounds. Our ammunition supply services certainly left a lot to be desired. Since the nearest ammunition depot was on the other side of Rue Tilleloy, it was out of the question to send someone to pick up two cartridge boxes. The Boche set up a Maxim machine gun and started spraying the parapet. We had to duck and could not return their fire. Some of our men got scratched by spent bullets. I sent Frossos to tell Sergeant Rosado to withdraw at once. I remained in the trench, or what was left of it, with the ten men from my platoon and the four from the 8th Infantry.

When I saw the last men disappear around the trench bend, I put Corporal Fontes in command and told him to withdraw with the remaining men. I would stay behind with Rato and Tibães to cover their withdrawal.

"But sir, we can't leave you here with no protection!"

I had to yell at him, "Do as I tell you, damn it! Scram!"

Crouching like a mouse, the corporal moved away with the men trailing in single file after him.

I waited with my two soldiers, hunkering down at the bottom of the trench and holding our rifles high.

"What are we doing here, sir?" Tibães asked, impatiently.

The firing overhead kept on. The Boche were getting closer and started throwing rifle grenades, against which there was no protection.

"They know we're here," Rato said.

"Be still and keep quiet," I whispered. "If they don't hear anything they may think there's nobody alive here."

We stayed there until the Boche, moving in from the left and front, ran into us. Rato moved to point his rifle but I ordered him to lower it. We threw down our rifles, raised our arms, and I shouted, "*Portugais camarades, bonnes!*"

We were surrounded by more than thirty Germans with their Mausers pointed at our heads. One who seemed to be their officer ordered two soldiers to search us and collect our weapons. Then he said in German-accented French, "*Portugais prisonniers!*"

Pointing in the direction of our first line, toward no man's land, he added, "*Allez, allez!*"

They turned around and left by the right, leaving us unguarded.

"What did he say, sir?" Tibães asked.

"He said we're prisoners and ordered us to go toward their lines."

"And we're going to?"

I thought for a moment. I did not like the idea of spending time in a German prisoner-of-war camp.

"We'll try to escape," I said finally.

"Which way do we go, sir?" Rato asked.

"We'd better go down to the first line and then turn left. If we turn right, we'll run into the Boche and they'll send us back – if they don't shoot us for disobeying orders. Since we know the Boche have got into the Fleurbaix sector, we'll have to walk some four or five kilometers to the left until we find some English unit that's still resisting."

"And when we get out of here and into an area we don't know, how do we know if we're going left or right, sir?" Tibáes asked. "The trenches must've turned into a real bog and we for sure won't find our way inside them. Most likely, we'll end up running into the Boche again."

"Don't worry about that. We'll find our way by the sun by day, and by the stars at night."

"We're done for!"

"If Apúlia were here, he'd tell you that's how fishermen find their way at sea."

"A good thing he ain't," Tibáes said.

We took off our helmets and, with our hands crossed over our heads, we started walking through the bombed-out trenches. Waves of Boche went past us and looked at us with curiosity. We saw a few stealing boots and food from our dead comrades. The fog was lifting and we could see the destruction in our sector clearly.

"We have to avoid getting into no man's land," I said, as we walked on cautiously to avoid tripping.

We walked in circles, keeping our hands clasped over our heads, moving slowly to the left, and crossed Rue Pincantin. German battalions were walking on the road toward our line of villages. A German officer stopped us. He probably thought we were either up to something or really lost. He pointed toward no man's land and shouted something in German. We obeyed, at least for a while.

"This way we'll end up in their lines, sir," Rato warned.

As we got near what had been our front line parapet, we ran into two dead Boche in a demolished machine gun post. It dawned on me that we might get out of that quandary by disguising ourselves as German soldiers. I ordered Tibáes and Rato to take off the dead men's tunics, trousers, and boots. One of the tunics had blood spots in the back where the bullet had gone out, but the other was clean. They put on the dead men's clothes and helmets, which looked like chamber pots. The boots were too big for Rato.

"These boots fit me like a pair of boats!" he complained.

"It would be worse if they were too small," I said.

Two unloaded Mauser rifles laying near the bodies were added to our disguise. The idea was for Tibães and Rato to pass off as the escort of a prisoner officer. Maybe that way we would not be noticed. I told them that, if we were stopped and interrogated, they should just answer, *Ja, ja.* As the prisoner officer, I would try to explain things in French. Since we were unshaven, I feared the Boche might be suspicious, and so I told Tibães and Rato to rub mud on their stubby faces.

Thirsty, hungry, and tired, we managed to get into the Gleurbaix sector, defended by the 40th English Division. That was where the Boche had entered, surrounding the Portuguese troops. Everywhere we saw dead English soldiers. Every now and then a group of Boche waved at us, fooled by my comrades' helmets. I told Tibães and Rato to wave back.

It must have been about three in the afternoon, the temperature had risen, and our thirst was getting to be unbearable.

We heard a moan coming from a damaged shelter where several English bodies lay. Rato went to inspect and found a British sergeant still alive. He had been hit in the head by a shell fragment and had passed out. When the Boche walked by they probably thought he was dead. The Sergeant thought Tibães and Rato were Boche and raised his hands. I approached and said in broken English, "Portuguese. Friends."

He did not seem to understand how those two could be Portuguese, dressed like Germans as they were. I made them take off their helmets, and said, "You see? Disguise. Mask."

The Sergeant, his forehead covered with dried blood, laughed in relief.

"You, Portuguese! Friends!" he exclaimed.

I helped him to stand up and lean on me as we moved on. We walked past a few Boche soldiers, who ignored us. The English Sergeant was a big help, for he knew the sector well and guided us through the ruins of the communication trenches.

We stopped by another group of English bodies and checked if anyone was still alive. They were all dead. Rato found two canteens with water and we sat down to drink and rest a while. The Sergeant found a pistol the Boche had overlooked and hid it inside his tunic. I tried to explain to him that our goal was to reach the English lines, to get as far as Estaires and then move on to Lestrem, where our headquarters was located. I had to repeat it several times, once in French. Then I drew a sketch on a piece of paper and he finally got it. He doubted we would manage it. At that time, the Germans would have reached Lestrem. If that was the case, I thought, the entire Portuguese 2nd Division would be lost.

Changing directions constantly and lying low among the demolished trenches, we managed to approach the English lines that had not yet fallen to the Boche. There was only one problem: to reach the lines, we had to walk through the Boche, and that would not be easy.

We moved forward cautiously, since both sides were firing at each other. Suddenly we were challenged by two German sentries, who asked Tibães and Rato something. They replied as I had instructed them, *Ja, ja.* They repeated *ja, ja* several times, and the sentries became suspicious and pointed their rifles at us. The English Sergeant – I never found out his name – took the pistol out of his tunic on the sly and fired point-blank. The two Germans went down. One of them was still alive and Tibães finished him off with the bayonet fixed to his Mauser. We collected their weapons and ammunition and divided them up among ourselves. I took off my pants and tunic, and put on those from one of the German soldiers, and also his helmet. It was the first and last time I tried on that kind of military clothing. I decided to keep my own boots. I suggested to the Sergeant that he should do likewise but he refused. He would never put on an enemy uniform. If he had to die, he would die wearing the glorious uniform of the army of His Majesty, the King of England. I did not feel like arguing about military pride and we moved on.

I told Tibães and Rato to fire if any Boche challenged us again.

"No talking to the Germans. Only fire," said the Sergeant. "And then run!"

We arrived behind a trench defended by six Boche, who were firing a heavy machine gun toward the English line. They had their back to us and either did not see us coming, or thought we were on their side. If only we had a grenade, I thought, we could finish them all at once. As it was, we would have to shoot them, and although we had trained with the Mauser rifle in Portugal, it was harder to handle than the Lee-Enfield. The Sergeant aimed at the two Boche on the left, I aimed at one on the right and left the others for Tibães and Rato. I was a lousy shot and had to rely on their marksmanship. If we missed one of the targets, they might sound the alarm and we would be in trouble. The Sergeant fired first and a Boche fell. Tibães and Rato fired next, and two more fell. I fired but did not see anyone fall. The Sergeant reloaded, fired again, the other two did likewise, and I did not have to shoot again. The whole operation took less than half a minute.

"Run!" the Sergeant shouted.

We sprinted toward the English line, dropping the helmets and taking off the tunics as we ran, to make sure the English marksmen would not mistake us for Germans. We heard some shots and sprawled on the ground.

"English! English!" the Sergeant shouted. "Don't shoot!"

The bullets stopped cracking overhead and we saw some English helmets peering over a parapet some twenty paces away.

By then the Boche behind us, possibly alerted by the shooting and shouting, started firing. We crawled as far as a small shell-crater and took cover as best we could from the shooting that was now going on between the two sides. I was worn out and fell asleep, rocked by the shooting. I woke up with Rato shaking me. Night had fallen and it was a good time to get out. The problem was to figure out in which direction to go. If we made a mistake, we might end up in the German lines again.

I looked up at the starry sky, spotted Ursa Major, followed the line that began at the pointer stars Merak and Dubhe, and located the North Star. The English trench was due north, some fifteen paces from where we were.

"Follow me," I ordered.

As we approached the barbed wire we heard a voice, "Halt! Who goes there?"

"We're English!" whispered the Sergeant. "Don't shoot!"

"Jump over! Quick!"

We went over the parapet and found ourselves in a trench, surrounded by English soldiers.

XXXII

The wedding of our maid Guiomar and Delmiro, Rato's eldest son, took place yesterday. I let them hold the banquet in the large covered shed where farming tools and hay are stored, and I also provided a fat pig and two barrels of wine, one red and one white. The young couple and their families took care of the rest. Although traditionally the task of organizing the wedding is the bride's parents' responsibility, Vicência and Rato took over and had their hands full for the last few days. Guiomar's parents are a poor elderly couple totally lacking in ability or patience to organize anything. For them to even come to the wedding – and at Guiomar's request – I had to fetch them and drive them back. I would never refuse that maid of ours anything, as she never refused anything I asked her.

As promised, I made them tenants in charge of one of my best estates, vacant since Old Felício's death a few months ago. When they left the church after receiving their blessings, I wished them much happiness and wealth, in riches as well as in progeny.

Rato was very pleased. It was the second son he had married off. He must have sipped too much white wine, and by the end of the afternoon he was so merry he started dancing with the bride to the tune of the accordion played by Bigarrilla, the tavern owner.

Evangelina, who currently lives in Matosinhos, came to the wedding with her husband. This husband is not my brother-in-law Paulino. That relationship ended after Isabel was born.

(I had better backtrack a little. These memoirs have so many parentheses that I am beginning to think anyone who ever reads them will need a lot of imagination to fill in the many gaps and inconsistencies I am leaving behind.)

Vicência and Evangelina came to visit us at the estate about a year and a half after the baby was born. We invited them to sit in the living room. Aninhas and my mother were charmed by little Isabel and covered her with caresses. Aninhas gave Evangelina a lot of advice on how to take care of the child and took her to one of the bedrooms to give her a few of little Afonso's old clothes. My mother went along with them while Vicência and I went on talking. I asked her about Rato and whether he had sent news and was well.

"He can't write, Master Luís."

"What about money? Has he sent you any?"

"If he has, it ain't got here. He took off for France and now he don't want to have nothing to do with his wife and children. I reckon he's got some French hussy and, begging your pardon, is shoving all his earnings up her butt."

"I'll find out about it, Dona Vicência. I haven't heard from him in about six years. But since I haven't written any letters, I can't really expect to receive any."

"And who might you write to, Master Luís?"

"To Madame Constance Gavroche. She's a lady friend of mine, who found work for your husband."

"This is the first time I hear about that madam. And if you want to know, Master Luís, I'm beginning to be suspicious. Who's she?"

"She is a widow who owns a farm in Flanders. Her husband died in the war."

"Ah! A widow! You don't need to tell me nothing more, Master Luís! I get the picture."

"Now, Dona Vicência, Madame Constance Gavroche is a serious person. I don't think Joaquim... Besides, she's too old to get involved with your husband or with anyone else."

I had to use my legal savvy to try to convince the judge, in this case Vicência, of something I knew not to be completely true.

"But didn't you just say, Master Luís, that madam's husband died in the war? Or was the French so short of people they had to draft old men?"

Again I had to resort to legal reasoning, "Her husband did die in the war, but he wasn't a soldier. As they told me, he was working in the field when a grenade fell at his feet and killed both him and his horse."

"May he rest in peace!" she said, crossing herself.

"Well, Dona Vicência, I suppose Joaquim may be having health problems, or maybe some difficulty at work, and that's why he won't send you news, nor money – he may be incapacitated, or perhaps feeling embarrassed. I'll find out what's going on and will let you know."

"I'll be much obliged, Master Luís. Anyways, it wasn't Joaquim I wanted to talk to you about, it was Evangelina."

"Of course, go ahead."

"My daughter, she needs to find work to support her child. But she can't go back to the Gouveias', not after what happened. Might you know of someone in need of a maid, Master Luís, that you could put in a word? That would be a huge favor. Life's getting harder by the day, I work my hands to the bone to feed the children, and now there's two more mouths to feed."

"Well, Dona Vicência, as you know, we don't need any more help here at home. We can't fire our maid to hire Evangelina. I mean, we could do it, but it wouldn't be a good idea, for many reasons."

"My daughter, she don't want to take nobody's job away. Besides, she don't want to stay around here. She's fed up with people gossiping. You know how it is, unmarried mothers don't get no respect. If my Joaquim was here, he'd do something about it. The scoundrel that done it would have to marry her, even if he had to be dragged to church. But since I ain't got a man..."

I let her blow off steam. It would not do to defend my brother-in-law, and to tell the truth, he did not deserve being defended.

In the meantime, my mother, Aninhas, and Evangelina came back to the living room with the child and a bag of clothes.

Having been told about our conversation, Aninhas suggested there might be some household in Matosinhos where Evangelina could be hired as a maid. She would write her friend Celeste about it. At worst, maybe Evangelina would be able to get a job in one of the fish factories, but in that case she would need to find a place to live, which would entail expenses.

"And wouldn't you know of a household in Oporto, Miss Aninhas?"

"In Oporto? I thought you didn't want to go back there."

"I wouldn't mind it. I already know the city..."

"This daughter of mine, she just won't learn," Vicência said. "Everyone knows what happens when you play with fire..."

She was referring to Paulino, who continued living in Oporto with my in-laws. He would likely try to contact his loved one, and that would cause a lot more problems.

About two weeks later, Aninhas sent for Evangelina and let her know a family in Matosinhos needed a maid. The only problem was that she would not be able to bring her child along. After some hesitation, Evangelina made up her mind to accept. Her mother and Fátima, her younger sister, would take care of little Isabel, at least as long as she could not be with her mother.

At that time Paulino was studying medicine and, although he often asked Aninhas about Evangelina and her daughter, his passion for her seemed to have cooled off. His main diversion, besides being a fan of the Oporto Football Club, was a hussy who sold nuts near the stadium on match days.

Evangelina adjusted well to her new job in Matosinhos and even secured permission to visit her daughter twice a month. She would get on the train on Saturday evening and get back on Sunday.

In the meantime, however, little Isabel fell ill with meningitis. Hygiene conditions in those days were deplorable, medical care was even worse, and infant mortality levels were among the highest in Europe. She did not recover and died when she was three years old. Nobody was really very sad, and I would not be surprised if some even felt relieved – my in-laws, for instance, and probably Vicência as well. She had one less mouth to feed and the fruit of her daughter's slip no longer shamed the family. Aninhas's brother, pining for the nut seller, probably just shrugged. The child was buried in the village cemetery.

Evangelina went back to work, served in several homes in Matosinhos and avoided contact with men. She used to say, "fool me once, shame on you; fool me twice, shame on me." A few years later she met a fellow from the Oporto area, younger than she was. By then she would have been about twenty seven years old, but still pretty and lively. The young man worked on the docks and would not miss a chance to flirt with her when she went out on errands. I am not aware of the details, nor do they matter, but the point is that they were married about three years ago. We were not invited to the wedding. Aninhas was annoyed at such inconsideration, but I did not blame the young couple. Evangelina wished to bury her past, and our presence at the wedding would have been a reminder. Without telling Aninhas, I bought a bolt of white fabric for her linens and handed it to Vivência personally.

Aninhas's own trousseau was on her mind in the spring of 1920, after we had become officially engaged and had known each other biblically among the rocks that afternoon on the beach, with the breaking of waves keeping the rhythm of our movements. At that time Evangelina was twelve years old and was learning to be a maid at the Gouveias'. Paulino was teaching her to read, and when no one was looking, he would tug her blonde braid.

I was invited to spend St. John's Eve in Oporto. Despite the war, the Spanish flu, hunger, misery and political instability, people went out on the streets to celebrate as though they lived in a paradise. I took Aninhas to have dinner at a food stand, where we ate grilled sardines with corn bread and drank jug wine. My fiancée was very happy and dragged me to dance near a stand where a band was playing waltzes. The place was packed, and because we started bumping into other couples, we gave up and went out for a walk. As was traditional in those days, every now and then passers-by would rub a leek stalk on our noses, so we bought a leek stalk and started doing likewise. Besides the smell of garlic I remember the scent of the flowers from the large tilia tree in the garden. I looked at Aninhas, took her hand, and told her I loved her. She touched her mouth on my ear and whispered, "You deserve more than a kiss, but I can't give it to you here, with all these people gawking at us."

"We can fix that," I said.

"How? Only if you're a magician who can make them vanish so we'll be left alone."

"Do you trust me?"

"I don't know. Sometimes you're very naughty."

"If you don't trust me, I can't show you my magic."

"Well, let's see what you can pull out of your hat."

We walked toward the boarding house where I used to stay, and where I had reserved a room for that night. The place was practically deserted, as the guests were out celebrating St. John's Eve. I asked for the key at the desk and led Aninhas to my room. Before the iron bed, I said, "Here we are, magically alone."

She looked around, considering the shabbiness of the room, and said, "At least you could have a more tasteful magical wand..."

"It's the magician's fault, not the wand's. But for next time I promise you a room worthy of a princess, with a four-post bed with a tester and curtains embroidered in gold, Persian rugs and a Chinese porcelain chamber pot."

"You're crazy! As long as I have you, why should I want a Chinese porcelain chamber pot? As for the rest, it's fine as is."

She embraced me and we kissed, standing on the worn-out burlap rug.

We got married at the end of July at a church in the Lapa district in Oporto. I had taken my last Law School exam a couple of days earlier. Since I did not yet know the result, my concern about whether I had finished the course cast a shadow on the good humor a groom must display at his wedding.

To spare us the discomfort of traveling from Braga on the day of our wedding, at my parents' suggestion I reserved two rooms at the Grand Hotel. The wedding was set for eleven o'clock and we arrived at church in my car ten minutes early. My father looked like a minister from a kingless kingdom, and I, his aide. While we waited at the altar for the bride and her retinue, my father told me that it was not the first time our family's Goth blood would be mixed with plebeian blood through holy matrimony. In 1754, when King José I reigned and the Marquess of Pombal was his prime minister, my father's great-great-grandfather, Dom Gonçalo Vasques, had married a very beautiful and well-dowried lady, the daughter of a shopkeeper in Oporto. That lady, named Sara Ester Pereira, had made Dom Gonçalo very happy, increasing the estate and the income of Quinta de São Francisco, and giving him many children. Were I equally lucky, the family's name and coat of arms would exist for another hundred years.

I considered telling him that we now lived in a republic where no one cared about those things, but I did not wish to disturb my now elderly father. It was my wedding day, and all I wanted was to leave church holding my bride's hand, both wearing our wedding bands, and head off for Cascais, where we would enjoy a week-long honeymoon.

I invited some former Army comrades to the wedding. Captain Rabelo and Second Lieutenant Nogueira came, and two soldiers from my platoon, Apúlia and Tibães, showed up with their wives. The others neither came nor sent a reply. I had no reason to feel bad about that. Why on earth should anyone go to the wedding of a fellow who had spent two years giving him a hard time with orders, reprimands, and punishments?

At church, with my father and mother by my side, I found myself missing Rato. After all, he was the cause of my being there. If he had not saved Aninhas's brother at the Póvoa beach, I might not have met the girl of the four cent coin. While I waited for my bride I took the coin out of my pocket and rolled it through my fingers. Until then it had been my charm, my companion in moments of sadness, anguish and loneliness, but after I married Aninhas, my relationship with that coin ceased to be meaningful, and so I dropped it into the collection purse during mass.

The bride arrived with her parents and guests. There was neither singing nor nuptial marches. At the time that was a luxury reserved for the sons of ministers, and I was the son of a man who merely looked like a minister. The priest, a distant relative of the bride's father, spoke very slowly, and the ceremony lasted too long, with flowery phrases in Latin, rites, blessings, and an abundant sprinkling of amen's. Fortunately it was cool inside the church and we did not suffer from the heat. While the priest blathered away, Aninhas, kneeling next to me, summed up the morning's activities. With the excitement of the wedding, she had slept poorly and felt queasy. When she got up, the house was sheer bedlam, with everyone trying to use the bathroom at the same time, guests arriving and expecting to be received, her father hunting for a white tie, her brother asking for shoe polish, and her mother running to and fro, trying to take care of everyone and herself. Poor Evangelina had to open the door for guests as soon as the door bell rang, while making a valiant effort to carry out four orders at the same time. The bride's veil got torn at one end and had to be darned very carefully so the mending would not show except under very close inspection. Transportation was late and as she climbed into the carriage, one of the horses started urinating, splashing people nearby. She was lucky because she had already got in, but her father and Paulino got badly splashed, which was not at all pleasant, considering the heat.

"I told my father," she said, "that he should have hired an automobile. It would have been cleaner, faster, and more comfortable. But he thinks it's smart to come to church in a horse-drawn carriage..."

"Well, if it gets hotter, when we leave church some will be smelling like a horse," I said.

"Too bad," she smiled.

"I love you, Ana Maria," I whispered.

"I love you too, Luís."

"Do you want to marry me?"

"Yes, I do."

I smiled and squeezed her left hand, as the right was busy holding her bouquet. From behind us came a *pssst!* from either my mother or the bride's.

About an hour after the beginning of the ceremony, the priest gave us his final blessings and administered the seventh sacrament. When he uttered, *Ite missa est,* there was a general sigh of relief. However, we still had to go to the sacristy to sign the registry book and leave a donation for the church. As we walked out there were shouts of *long live the newlyweds!* and we were pelted with rice and candy. I ducked instinctively, and Captain Rebelo, one of the first to throw a handful of rice, said laughingly that I need not be afraid, since we were no longer in the trenches.

Apúlia, standing next to Captain Rebelo, seemed in good health. Having once seen him close to dying, I was very happy to see him there, all spruced up in a suit. He extended his hand to congratulate me, but I broke the protocol and gave him a big hug. Aninhas, standing next to me, did likewise. He was the only male guest to be embraced by the bride.

After spending our wedding night at the Grand Hotel, we left for Cascais in the Minerva. Going to Cascais was one of my father's good ideas, since he knew the area well. During the time he used to live in Lisbon he would go to Cascais for sea bathing and other activities he would not tell me about.

He suggested I take Aninhas to Sintra, Queluz, Belém and, of course, Lisbon, although in the latter city there was not much to see, other than corrupted politicians and cheap whores.

In Cascais I called up a classmate and found out that I had passed the last exam. To celebrate, I decided to take Aninhas to a fado tavern in Alfama. At first she was not keen on the idea for she had a dim view of such places attended by riff-raff. I explained there were some decent restaurants where respectable people could go. The fado singers were no longer necessarily prostitutes, nor were the accompanying guitarists necessarily pimps. She did not know what a pimp was, and I had to explain, "They are procurers."

"And what's a procurer?"

"He's a man who exploits a woman sexually."

"And how does he exploit her?"

"He finds her clients and keeps a percentage of her fee, when not the whole sum."

She had heard about such practice, although she did not know the name by which those types were known. But in spite of my arguments, she told me she would rather go to the opera to see the *Traviata*. I commented that the women involved were all prostitutes, from the last chorus singer to the soprano playing the role of Violetta Valéry, herself a prostitute in the story.

And so we went to a fado tavern. Driving along the road from Cascais to Lisbon, we parked on Praça do Comércio, not far from the place where King Carlos I and Prince Luís Filipe had been shot to death. We easily found the restaurant my father had recommended, called Martinho da Arcada, on the right hand side of Arco da Rua Augusta. At the table next to ours there was a man in his thirties, nearly bald and with a thick mustache, scribbling on a piece of paper. I thought he was doing figures, but Aninhas said those were verses, and to make sure we decided to ask him. He turned out to be an engineer named Álvaro de Campos and said those were life's accounts. So we were both right.

As I paid the bill I asked the waiter if he knew of a fado tavern not too far from the restaurant. He did not, but the verse writer who looked like an accountant asked permission to suggest an establishment in Alfama. Following his directions, we arrived at a tavern where we were impressed by the quiet and by the seriousness of the customers, sitting at tables and eating rice and beans with codfish fritters while listening to fado songs. Since we had already had dinner, we only drank a glass of port. I cannot recall the name of the singer, a young woman in her twenties with a masculine countenance, her hair as black as her dress. But her voice was charming and soon Aninhas pulled out her handkerchief and discreetly wiped a tear.

We left the fado tavern feeling rather moved and walked hand in hand towards our car. As we walked down a narrow street we were accosted by two tough-looking types, one of whom said to me, very courteously, "Would you please hand over your wallet, sir, if you'd be so kind."

Frightened, Aninhas held on to me, and without losing my composure, I said, "I can't give you my wallet, since I don't have it on me."

"But surely, sir, you must have some change you could kindly give these two luckless wretches."

"Oh yes, that I do."

I searched my jacket and pants pockets, making a point of turning them inside out to show I only had a few coins and a crumpled five escudo bill, which I passed on to the fellow who had spoken. He counted the money, sniffing at such meager pickings, and pointed to the watch chain hanging from my vest pocket, "Your watch too, sir, if you'd be so kind."

I gave him my watch but he did not seem satisfied, and pointed to my old ring with the coat of arms and the wedding band. Then Aninhas said that was too much, and if they didn't go away with what they'd got, she'd start screaming. To my surprise, the fellows apologized for the inconvenience, bowed, and disappeared in a side street.

"I think we should file a complaint at the police station."

"It isn't worth it. After all, they only took some loose change I had."

"And your watch."

"It wasn't worth much."

"I'll give you a new one for your birthday. But it'll be a wristwatch. I don't like chain watches, they're too old-fashioned."

"Whatever you say, my love."

And right there, in an alley in Alfama, after having been robbed and with our ears still charmed by the guitar strumming and the fado singer's voice, we kissed each other for a long time.

XXXIII

The children are home for the Easter holidays. Yesterday afternoon a violent storm broke out and Inês curled up on my lap, frightened by all that lightning and thunder. While the windows turned white with flashes of light and the house shook with the rumbling, she asked me if that was what war was like. I told her yes, it was pretty much like that. But in a storm, if we were sheltered at home, nothing bad could happen to us. In war, on the contrary, bombs burst through roofs and walls, and no place was safe and nobody was free from danger.

"And weren't you afraid, Dad?"

"I certainly was. We were all very much afraid. Even those who wanted to pass off as valiant and brave. Fear was with us all the time, and in the end we got used to it. It was like having a toothache."

The storm moved eastward and Inês, more relaxed, climbed down from my lap and went looking for her mother. I stepped outside to check the damage. The wind and rain had shattered branches, blown off leaves, stripped blossoms off the fruit trees, and flattened the barley in the fields. It looked as if a Boche division had been trampling all over the place, only there were no corpses.

I came back to the house, sat at my desk and wrote the above lines about the storm. I am now trying to recall what happened to the remains of our 2nd Division after the German offensive in Flanders on April 9, 1918.

Rato, Tibáes and I spent the night in the relative safety of the lines defended by the English. The Major who had given us shelter put us together with some Portuguese soldiers from other units who had managed to get to the English trenches, and the next morning he fed us combat rations and sent us off to Aire, with me, as the ranking officer, in command. The English Sergeant we had saved, and who had saved us in the end, was not able to tell us goodbye, as he had been sent to a field hospital to have his head wound treated. But the Major thanked us on his behalf and promised to cite us in the order of the day, which he would then forward to our battalion Headquarters. We never received a citation, but that did not bother us, because we had not performed any heroic deed. We were just trying to get out of no man's land alive. We ran into the English Sergeant by chance, and he was the one who deserved a citation. It was because of his intervention that we had managed to get into the English trench before the Boche killed us.

"And what good is a citation?" Tibáes said, "if not for wiping your ass when you run out of newspaper."

The rear was in total chaos, with thousands of soldiers, wagons, and carts moving in all directions. Everybody looked discouraged. Almost everyone felt the war was lost and the Boche would soon move in and wipe us all out.

We were exhausted when we got to Aire, where a pompous ass from the Portuguese General Headquarters ordered us to join the survivors of the Minho Brigade. We found Captain Rebelo with what was left of our battalion and our Company. I saw his face light up with joy when I approached him. He embraced me and nearly cried.

He told me Second Lieutenant Nogueira had also escaped and was in the field hospital with a wounded leg. Second Lieutenant Coutinho was missing. I asked him how many of us were left and he told me our battalion had lost about sixty percent of its strength. Counting the dead, wounded, and prisoners, the Minho Brigade had suffered three thousand casualties. We had no more than twelve hundred men left.

I made a brief report of what had happened to me and the men in my platoon, and he summed up what had happened to him and the others from our company who were in the first line when the Germans attacked. A little before the Boche shortened their range, he ordered the platoons to withdraw to the second line and take cover as best they could. When it became impossible to keep that position, and seeing the assault troops advancing, he decided to order a withdrawal to the support line, and so on to the rear.

"We lost more than half of the men in our company in these war games. But we might all have been killed if we'd followed General Hacking's orders, or whoever the hell gave them, to die in the second line. Our death would've been pointless, because the Boche would've got through just the same. And so here we are, reorganizing the defense."

"And your orders for me, sir?"

"You'll collect what's left of our three platoons and find out who's alive and who's missing. I'm going to find out what those pen pushers at Headquarters intend to do with us. Ask Sergeant Rosado to help you."

"So he managed to escape?"

"Thanks to you, who told him to get going with the rest of your platoon."

"I ordered him to withdraw..."

"And that's what'll go on my report, which you're going to write."

We went our separate ways and I went after Sergeant Rosado and the men from my platoon. I found them sitting in the shade of a wall, scraping out some ration cans. I ordered them to fall in so I could assess our losses. There were twelve men, among them Rato, Tibães, Apúlia, Frossos, and Corporal Fontes. I asked if they knew about anyone else. Three were in the field hospital and two had died defending the Red House, but they did not know about the others. Semelhe, Cabanelas, Padim, and Tenões were missing. I asked Sergeant Rosado to take down the names of the missing in action. I still hoped they might show up.

We repeated the procedure with the other two platoons. In the meantime, Captain Rebelo came by and gave us our marching orders. We were bound for Crecques, where we would spend the night, and the next day we would leave for

Ledingham. We reached the Hubersent cantonment on the third day. The troops involved in combat were withdrawing and were replaced by fresh troops, who counter-attacked and stopped the German offensive. The war was not lost after all. The Boche stopped advancing and had to set up a defensive line. But we only found this out later. During our three days on the road, we were totally in the dark about what was happening at the combat front. As we marched along the Flanders roads we instinctively looked back, afraid that the Boche might be coming after us. We ran into some English troops on their way to the front and asked them questions, but they knew little or nothing about what was going on.

At the Hubersent cantonment we were able to rest for a few days. The two Braga battalions, or what was left of them, were merged into one. Since we had lost our personal baggage and many had lost their weapons, armament and uniforms were reissued. I got a complete uniform and helmet, two gas masks, a pistol and a brand-new Lee-Enfield rifle, which clearly had never been fired in that war.

We remained cantoned in Hubersent for the rest of April and most of May. To keep the men busy, we followed a regular schedule: arms drill, physical education, marches, bayonet fencing, and theoretical instruction.

In the meantime, we started getting news about what had become of more than six thousand of our comrades. About two thousand had died and the others were in prisoner-of-war camps in Belgium and Germany. It was said that there were far fewer dead than originally thought. The High Command probably considered those figures a trifle – and, for the English and the French, they certainly were. In some battles of the Great War up to thirty thousand were killed on a single day.

During a rest period I asked Sergeant Rosado what had happened after he had obeyed my order to leave our trench. He told me he had managed to reach the Red House, where the defense was being reorganized.

"I was questioned by a cavalry lieutenant, and he ordered me and my men to take combat positions in a ditch. I told him, with all due respect, I didn't think that made sense. The Boche were about to arrive and if we didn't withdraw to a safer place, we'd be totally crushed. The guy, in them riding boots and spurs, asked if I hadn't got his order. I said, 'I got it very well, sir.' And he said, 'Then get on with it. That's what you're here for.' And so I did. In less than half an hour, the Boche reached the street and started firing on us. Our Major, he'd organized the resistance around the Red House with the help of that lieutenant, and he was making the rounds, waving his pistol to keep the men going. He was completely out of his mind and wouldn't listen to nobody. You know, sir, he was more stubborn than a mule. And he had to stick to that spot instead of withdrawing, and so several men got killed. Maybe he wanted to play the hero and save Portugal's honor by trying to keep the Boche from advancing. Or maybe he just went crazy and couldn't think straight no more. In my opinion, that resistance he insisted on putting up, it was totally reckless. And the pity is that now they're saying he's a hero 'cause he faced off the Boche. In my opinion, that was sheer stupidity."

"Mind how you talk about our Major!" I warned him.

Although I had my reasons not to like the Major, I could not let a subordinate talk that way about him.

"Sorry, sir. I was just blowing off steam. Sir, you know I always do my best for our unit and I've always obeyed orders, even when they've been against my conscience or common sense. But then don't nobody ask me to keep quiet. The time of the Monarchy is past, and if something is wrong, we've got a right to speak up."

I did not wish to discuss politics and just asked him what had happened next.

"The Boche kept coming by the hundreds. The Major, with that lieutenant and a few cooks and orderlies, kept losing ground and took shelter in a bombed-out building some fifty meters behind the Red House. More than half of the eighty or so men that was there got mowed down by the heavy machine guns the Boche had set up along the road. I was still in the ditch with the men from our platoon. We had water up to our knees. A couple of them had been hit. If we stayed in that ditch we'd all be killed. All the Boche had to do was to throw a couple of stick grenades at us. So I ordered them to withdraw. Frossos said he'd cover us, and while we walked down the ditch going west he started firing and shot down four Boche as they moved in."

"Four? Isn't that a bit too many, Sergeant?"

"I saw two fall down, sir. The other two, he told us about them later, 'cause we'd gone round a bend in the ditch and couldn't see what was going on. But you know, sir, that Frossos, he's one of our best marksmen, and nobody ever caught him telling no lies. If it hadn't been for him, I reckon the Boche would've caught us."

"We should put him up for a medal," I said, ironically.

"Well, he surely deserves it."

"And what happened then, Sergeant?"

"Well, we got to a barrier behind Laventie that was being held by an English cyclist company and a few of our gunners who'd lost their guns. We were pretty safe there. Frossos managed to leave the Boche behind and joined us later."

"And what about the Major?"

"Last time I seen him, he was still alive. Hit at least twice, bleeding on his head and one hand. Even so, he kept on shooting at the Boche and yelling at the soldiers to hold their ground. I saw a poor devil climb a tree to shoot at the Boche. He got hit and then climbed down, bleeding in the chest, and the Major, instead of telling him to take cover, he made him climb back up on a roof and go on with his target practice. He must've bled to death on that roof."

I thanked the Sergeant for the information and made up my mind not to include any of it in the report I was supposed to write about the events of April 9. Military reports should not mention petty human trifles.

Even though our battalion needed all the surviving officers to control the men, who were getting increasingly restless and unruly, I managed to convince Captain Rebelo to grant me a two-day leave during the weekend to call on Madame Gavroche in Enguinegatte. I found her very frightened and worrying that the Germans might advance as far as her village. During my previous visit, I had suggested she should leave the farm for a safer place, but she decided to stay. That was her home, where she kept animals she could not abandon, and her fields, which needed to be tilled if she wanted to have a harvest that year.

I tried to calm her down, telling her the Allies had been able to hold back the Germans. Although we had lost some ground, the front line had been re-established and stabilized. She wanted to know what had happened. She had read in the papers about the Boche offensive in La Lys and the routing of the Portuguese Army, which had not been able to hold out. Some people were criticizing the Portuguese, saying they were incompetent, poorly trained, and should not have gone to war. I told her that was true. The politicians had blundered in sending us to Flanders. But she should not think it was the soldiers' fault. They were just as good and brave as any others. It was only that they didn't have the physical training and equipment required to hold back such a gigantic onslaught. At the battle of La Lys there was one exhausted Portuguese soldier for every nine Germans, rested and well-armed. We never stood a chance.

She wanted to know how I had managed to escape and I gave her a general idea of my misadventures on April 9. She said I was a hero and should get a medal for having saved myself and my men. If the Portuguese government wouldn't give me a medal, I'd get one from the French government. She herself would talk to the *maire* about it. I told her the best reward I could possibly get was to be in her company. She smiled and told me to go and take a bath, for I smelled like a *cochon*.

410

At night she came to my room. I was somewhat apathetic and she did her best to cheer me up with kisses and whispers. She got me inside her several times, sighing and trembling, but I, covered with sweat and panting from the exertions of love, remained like a rock, a column, with an erection but lifeless. We spent the night in naked embraces. I caressed her face, her hair, and the small of her smooth, warm back, and she caressed the hair on my chest, whispering French words I did not understand.

Although we continued to exchange letters, we never saw each other again.

In mid-May the Minho Brigade moved to the area of the 2nd Division in Ambleteuse. As no transportation was available, we had to go on foot, carrying all our equipment for forty kilometers, in a semi-forced march under a scorching sun.

Although surrounded by water, we had little to drink during the march. Since it was too hot and the equipment was so heavy, the men soon emptied their canteens and had only one chance to refill them from a fountain of drinkable water. The water in the ditches and wells was not fit to drink and it was preferable to go thirsty than to risk contracting dysentery. Since the new uniforms would not fit in the knapsacks, we rolled them up in the two heavy blankets each man carried, with unsightly results. Bending under the weight of their packs, the Portuguese soldiers looked like a band of beggars.

We were cantoned in Ambleteuse for more than a month. There were no billets in civilian homes, so we stayed in canvas tents that were useless when it rained, and where we roasted when it was hot. In early June, the Brigade underwent a medical inspection. Out of the twelve hundred men on active duty, a hundred seventy were diagnosed with lung infections, more than a hundred eighty with heart problems, and a hundred thirty with several other incapacitating diseases. All the sick moved on to the port of Cherbourg and were repatriated. They would die at home.

I now belonged to a battalion thrown together with the remnants of the two battalions from Braga, plus a few stray officers and noncoms. We had a second lieutenant from São Miguel, in the Azores, whose thick accent the soldiers did not understand. There was also a sergeant from Miranda do Douro who spoke Mirandese and neither understood, nor was understood by anyone.[62] A few days before June 24, Saint John's day, my new battalion left for the Herbelles area. Working under orders from the English, we were kept busy building trenches to the rear of Blendecques. It was hard work but the men considered it a real vacation. Danger was remote and we were convinced the war was over for us.

About a month later our battalion left for the Nieppe Forest. We remained there as a tactical reserve until mid-October and were once again kept busy building trenches and repairing railways. We were near Merville, a town abandoned by the Boche after the Allied counterattack. By then we had been downgraded from soldiers to diggers, and were treated like the Chinese, the Indians, and the Africans. The French and the English no longer considered us their equals – assuming they ever did.

At about that time a bugler from another battalion incited his comrades to rebellion. They demanded better conditions and leaves to visit their families in Portugal, like the officers. When the soldiers in our battalion would not adhere, the rebels came to our camp armed and threatened to kill our soldiers if they did not turn over their weapons and ammunition.

On top of the soldiers' rebellion, widespread along the whole Western front, there was bad news from Portugal. Sidónio Pais, elected President in late April, proclaimed martial law in October, in the wake of a failed revolutionary attempt in Coimbra and Évora. At about the same time, an outbreak of Spanish flu killed thousands of people. My father wrote me about the death of several relatives and acquaintances. The carnage was even worse among the poor on account of bad nutrition and awful hygiene conditions. Since people lived in crowded quarters, it only took one person to get sick for the whole family to be contaminated. Nonetheless, the flu was strong enough to wreak havoc among the rich. Only the strong or the naturally immune managed to survive.

Inflamed by the bugler, the rebellion precluded our battalion from participating in the offensive that would decide the outcome of the war. The rebellious battalion was disbanded and the men were dispersed among other battalions unrelated to the Minho Brigade. The generals figured that dividing the troops would eradicate insubordination. Fortunately they did not think of having a few soldiers shot, as the French did.

During the five days the rebellion lasted, company officers continually received orders to put an end to all that by hook or by crook. Rebellion was dishonorable to the Portuguese Expeditionary Corps and to Portugal's glorious name. Captain Rebelo passed the order on to me and commented, "What's dishonorable is for those sons of bitches in Lisbon to send us to war without enough men or equipment to do what they ordered us to do. The soldiers aren't to blame, poor devils. The ones to blame are those clods sitting pretty in their offices, wearing shiny boots and sipping tea while they give orders by telephone."

I summoned my platoon and tried to convince those who were still undecided not to join the rebellion. I talked frankly to them. It wouldn't do any good. The Portuguese government wouldn't send them back home any earlier. More likely, they'd be sent back to the front to get killed. And if they didn't get killed, when they got back to Portugal they'd be court-martialed for treason and spend a long time in a military prison.

Speaking partly for the others, Tibães told me about the dissatisfaction that was eating him. They thought there was no reason to be there. If only they were in the trenches, they could fill their time killing a few Boche or running away from them. The others laughed. Nobody would likely trade a place in the rear for one in the trenches.

"This's a waste of time, sir," Corporal Fontes said. "We're even putting on weight. Looks like the big brass only want us for digging holes. Let them hire more Chinks and darkies to do that. We Portuguese ain't never been nobody's slaves."

"I ain't no darky," Tibães said, rather offended.

"Maybe the English got a different opinion," Rato said.

I told them to be quiet and ended the talk by warning that I would personally shoot anyone who joined the rebellion. I heard some muffled laughter but could not pinpoint where it came from. They knew what a poor shot I was. Or maybe they figured I would never have the heart to do it.

Our battalion was disbanded and I found myself commanding a new platoon. Only Rato remained with me, because he was my orderly and I pleaded with my superior officers. My new platoon was a patchwork. There were four reckless, petulant types from Beira, who talked with a lisp; six slow-witted brutes from Trás-os-Montes; three long-winded bums from Alentejo; a fellow from Algarves who spoke in sing-song, the most selfish type I ever met; three Lisbon ruffians who seized every chance to clean the others at cards and ended up being cleaned out by Rato when he figured out their tricks; two foul-mouthed braggarts from Oporto; and half a dozen types from all over Minho, respectful and sheepish. My second-in-command was the sergeant from Miranda do Douro I mentioned earlier. Since nobody could understand him and he could not understand anybody, we all lived in peace. I spent my last day of the war with this platoon, guarding a trench in the English sector.

Except for some occasional encounters, for the rest of the war I did not see the soldiers from the platoon with which I had left Braga. I once ran into Tibães and Apúlia on the way out of an *estaminet*. Tibães, though somewhat discouraged about the delay in being sent back home – the war had been over for more than two months – was in good shape. Apúlia, very thin, was coughing, possibly a symptom of the tuberculosis that was eating away at him.

414

On November 11th, 1918, the fog lifted and the rumble of the heavy guns ceased. The machine guns and snipers' rifles on either side of no man's land, which used to seek easy targets, were silent. Rato climbed onto the parapet and, without bothering to use a periscope, took a peek at the enemy lines.

"The war is over, sir. We're going back home."

"Alive," I said.

"We'd never go back dead. The poor devils who fell here are in the cemetery."

"You're right. We'd never get out of here dead. But then it wouldn't have mattered."

"You speak for yourself, sir. If a shell fragment sent me to the other side, I'd be turning over in my grave if they didn't bury me in my town's cemetery, so the wife and the children could come once a year to lay down some flowers, light a candle, and say the Lord's Prayer."

Rato had a coughing fit, cleared his throat noisily, and spit out on the barbed wire. A thick, yellowish glob got caught on the wire and dripped slowly to the ground. I looked at no man's land. It was green. The autumn showers and the limited traffic in that sector had stimulated the seeds carried over by the wind. If it were not for the shell holes and the bundles of barbed wire, one might think we were looking at a meadow where the cows would come and graze the good grass.

"I wonder if the Boche are still there," Rato said, pointing at the trench facing us.

"Most likely."

"I wouldn't be surprised if the snipers was looking at us, hiding like cowards."

"Because of the cease-fire, they aren't supposed to shoot. Otherwise, by now we'd be in the bottom of the trench with a hole in our chest."

"You know something, sir? Since I first got here, my big dream's been to cross no man's land and bum a cigarette off the Boche."

415

"That's an odd dream. Your comrades would rather go over and wipe them all out."

"I don't hate them, sir. They ain't done nothing to me personally. Besides, I can't hate someone I don't know."

"Maybe you're forgetting they're the reason we're here. If they had stayed in Germany minding their own business quietly at home, we wouldn't have spent a year and a half being shot at in the mud."

"Do you think, sir, that if I dare go to no man's land, they'll shoot at me?"

"That's a good question. Just think what you'd do if you saw a Boche coming over toward us now."

"Well, I sure feel like a Boche cigarette. Just to find out what it smells like."

"Boche cigarettes must be a lot worse than ours. The prisoners have told us that since they can't get tobacco on account of the sea blockade, they roll up their cigarettes with leaves of corn and other plants. Giving them a cigarette was like giving them two minutes in Heaven."

"I know fellows who can smoke a cigarette a lot faster than that."

"With a bit of luck, we'll all be sick in the lungs when we get out of here. If dampness and mustard gas doesn't do it, tobacco will."

"I've always heard tobacco clears out a man."

"Don't you believe that. Doctors say smoking is a poison."

"Which don't mean they smoke any less than we do. I know you quit smoking, sir. But you got to respect other people's vices."

I yelled down the trench, "Stand to! One of our own's going out into no man's land."

The men climbed onto the fire steps and rested their rifles on the parapet with their fingers on the trigger.

"Thank you, sir. I'll make sure to ask for two cigarettes,

and I'll offer you one. If you don't care to smoke it, you can have it as a keepsake."

He took a white handkerchief out of his pocket, tied it to the end of a stick, raised it above his head, jumped over the barbed wire in front of our trench, and started advancing on the grass. Every ten meters he stopped, listened for some noise from the other side, and shouted, "*Je, camarade bonne!*"

At the parapet, we watched him through our rifle sights. It was pointless, because if the Boche decided to open fire on Rato, we would be of no help to him. I was beginning to blame my own folly in letting him go.

We watched him approach the enemy parapet and jump over. We waited for more than ten minutes. I was about to send two men for him when I saw him reappear. He waved at us and walked back without stopping, as if he were taking a country walk. He no longer carried his makeshift flag. When he got back I asked him, "Well, then?"

"Nobody there, sir. Them trenches's empty. The Boche are gone."

The men next to me heard that and passed the word. Then we heard shouts of joy.

"Are you sure?" I insisted.

"I climbed down into their trench, shouted them things in French, walked all around at will, got into two shelters, and the only thing I seen was the rats. The Boche must've withdrawn to their second line."

One of the fellows from Beira, standing next to me, lisped, "Shir, if we attacked now they'd shtart running non-shtop back to Shermany."

"Listen, Peneda," I said, "the war's over."

"Even sho, Shir."

"Besides, the Germans are too careful to withdraw without having their rear well covered. I suspect this withdrawal has been planned for a long time."

I turned to Rato and asked, "What about those cigarettes?"

"Nothing. They took everything. They didn't even leave their sausage cases, or whatever it was they ate. The trenches are clean. Their rats are walking skeletons. As for cigarettes, I didn't find a single butt."

"Too bad."

"That's an odd trench, sir."

"Why?"

"Because it don't reek of piss like ours."

"Maybe they don't pissh!" Peneda said.

"Their piss got to be different from ours. It don't smell," said one of the privates from Alentejo, who tended to mull over deep subjects.

"How come, different? Pissh ish pissh!" Peneda protested.

"They just don't piss anywhere, you pigs," the Alentejo man explained. "Besides, their pissing holes have to be spick-and-span."

I had to interrupt their discussion and dismiss them. We climbed down the parapet and went to celebrate with a bottle of port I had been saving for that occasion.

The war was finished, but that did not mean our travails were over. Military discipline was maintained and we went on with our arms drills, gymnastics, and weapons maintenance. Instead of building trenches, we demolished and filled with dirt the trenches on both sides of no man's land. It was said that the land along no man's land and the adjacent trenches, if planted, would suffice to feed all of France for a year, and there would still be enough food left over to feed the Germans for a month. Maybe that was why the former owners hastened to go back to the ruined villages and started reclaiming their burned-out, disemboweled lands. A few must have died of sorrow when they saw their devastated farms without a single standing tree, fields pock-marked with shell holes, and houses destroyed.

Rato told me a few days ago that when he visited Fau-quissart with Madame Gavroche, he did not see any signs of war. The houses, including the church, have been rebuilt, the trenches dismantled, and no man's land graded and turned into plowing fields, just as it used to be before the war. Bewildered, he asked an old man who was passing by on a bicycle where the trenches were.

"Here," the man said, pointing to the middle of the road. "You're standing on them, Monsieur."

Rato knelt down on the step of the newly rebuilt Crucifix at Neuve-Chapelle and prayed for his dead comrades, giving thanks for the grace of having been spared. Then he visited the cemetery where the two thousand Portuguese who gave their life for the Fatherland, whatever that might be, are buried. The graves were marked by wooden crosses identified by a number. If those wooden crosses were not replaced by others made of stone or cement, they would soon rot away. He was indignant at how the cemetery was neglected. The graves were covered with weeds and brambles were growing on the walls. The English, French, and German cemeteries, and even an Indian cemetery, were well-cared for, showing those countries' respect for those who had died for them.

The Portuguese cemetery in Flanders spoke loudly of the scorn and disregard the government heaped upon the men it sent to war for the purpose of aggrandizing the glorious name of Portugal.

XXXIV

Today is Easter. We all woke up very early and went to the seven o'clock mass. Afonso drove the old Minerva and took Pedro with him. I followed in the Ford with Aninhas, Inês, and my mother. After mass some firework rockets went off. As I was walking out of the church, I instinctively lowered my head. Aninhas held my hand, as if telling me not to be afraid: those were just fireworks. My brain, still used to the sounds of war, cannot yet distinguish the blast of a mortar shell from a firework rocket.

Having left Pedro with the Easter procession making the rounds of the parish, we came back home. Father Ruas has again put him in charge of the bag of alms for Saint Peter. Our home will be one of the last to be visited.

I am sitting at my desk. I have nearly the whole day to finish this memoir. The window is open and I can hear the procession bell ringing throughout the fields and paths of the village. It announces the resurrection of Christ, who paradoxically is taken to all the houses on a cross to be kissed. To me this is just another holiday on the calendar. I do not know whether Christ resurrected or not, nor do I care. To me, the only true Christ is that of the trenches, with maimed feet and arms, without the cross, tied to the trunk of a poplar torn up by mortar shells. There is a sonnet by José Régio[63] about the cross of a vanquished god, while off in the distance angry crowds clamor amidst smoke and dust. It is a perfect description of my Christ.

I look out the window. The sparrows are chirping in the camellia trees in front of the house. The morning is cool, but the sun is getting warm and the flowers are aromatic. There are no roses in the garden yet. The wood sorrel shrubs look like a bride's dress. I am always astonished when I watch this renovation of nature, this clockwork machinery built by a beauty-loving god as cruel as Nero, poet and butcher.

Rato came to the house yesterday afternoon. He brought me a big, fat rabbit he raised especially for me. I left the animal in the kitchen and we went for a walk around the estate. I asked him how he and Vicência were getting along. Not too bad, he said. She calmed down after she made him see the healer.

"The healer?" I asked, surprised.

He told me that Vicência, seeing him so despondent, decided to follow the advice of the women in their neighborhood and take him to a healer who lived in the village of Cambedo. He didn't want to go. He said his illness couldn't be cured with prayers and blessings. But his wife and children insisted so much that he finally gave in. They borrowed two mules and rode to Cambedo on a Saturday before daybreak. They had to ask for directions to the healer's house. Some helpful people pointed the way, while others either wouldn't reply, pretending not to see them, or scolded them, saying that calling on the healer was a sin that would doom them to hell. From the top of a ladder, an old man, pruning a poplar, even insulted them. Rato wanted to get off the mule and teach him a lesson, but Vicência told him to leave the old man alone with his stubbornness, and they went on their way.

Some charitable soul pointed out an estate gate, they dismounted, tied the reins to an iron ring outside, and walked in. The gate opened directly onto a shed where agricultural tools, firewood, and sacks of potatoes were stored. There were already a few people waiting, sitting wherever they found a place. Rato and Vicência greeted them, but only one woman grudgingly returned their greeting. She was sitting next to another woman who seemed pregnant. They also saw a middle-aged couple with a young woman who must have been their daughter. The healer had not yet begun to meet with people. They sat on some oak stumps and waited. Finally the man, who had a big white mane, came from a nearby house. He greeted those who were waiting and went into a small partition next to the shed, which Rato guessed had been a cow pen. As business started picking up over the last few years, they had moved the cows somewhere else, so the healer would have a place to see his possessed clients.

Their turn came and the old man asked them to enter. He was sitting in a chair and asked the patient to sit down in front of him. Vicência sat in a corner and summarized her husband's ills, telling the healer about the war, the years spent in France, and his despondency since his return. The healer listened to her prattle without paying too much attention and, when she finally stopped talking, he mumbled a prayer, laying his right hand on Rato's left shoulder. Then he was silent for a while, eyes closed, as though asleep. Rato cleared his throat, the old man opened his eyes and repeated the prayer. At last, he raised his eyes to the cobweb-lined ceiling and started shaking. Turning to the table at his side, he dipped a pen into the inkstand and started scribbling on a foolscap folio. Vicência dragged her chair closer. She wanted to see what the old man was doing.

"Here," he said, "is the trench."

And he drew a somewhat wavy line lengthwise across the page.

"And here is the barracks."

And he drew a small rectangle.

"And over here, this is the path to a farm."

And he drew a path.

"The farm house faces the path."

He dipped the tip of the pen and drew a small square.

"And this is where the problem is," he exclaimed, pointing at the small square.

"And what's the problem, Senhor Antonino?" Vicência asked.

"The problem is a hex they've put on your man."

"And who did it?" she asked.

"That's not for me to say."

"Was it a woman?"

"It must be."

"And what should we do?"

422

"First he has to be fumigated. Then, at home, he must drink the tea I'm going to give him."

"And what do I want that tea for?" Rato asked, suspiciously.

"To cleanse your inside," the healer answered.

Having determined the prescription, the old man got up and prepared the fumigation. He poured wine into a bowl, grabbed an iron that had been heating in a small fireplace, and dipped it into the wine, releasing a cloud of wine-smelling smoke that filled the air. Rato was urged to bring his face close to the bowl and inhale the smoke. When he could stand it no longer, he tried to move away, but the old man forced him to breathe that mixture for a few more seconds, while he muttered some prayers against the evil eye.

Having undergone the cure and received the healer's advice, Rato paid for the consultation and returned home with Vicência. At supper, instead of boiled potatoes and collard greens, he drank the tea she put in front of him. He spent the night in the privy, in the throes of diarrhea. That was the cleansing prescribed by the healer.

When he had finished his narrative, I asked him if there was any reason for Vicência to think he had had some love affair while in France.

"Sir, a man ain't a stick of wood," he said, immediately trying to justify himself.

"No, but he likes to stick it in... Tell me, what happened?"

"There's things a man shouldn't tell. A man's lived them, they're over, and there ain't no more to be said."

"If that were true, Vicência would have no reason to take you to the healer. Those years you were away, sending neither news nor money to support your children, aren't something that can be forgotten. She's a good woman and took you in when you came back without a penny in your pocket. Another woman would have slammed the door in your face. She had plenty of reason to do that."

"I ain't saying she didn't. On the train, while I was crossing France and Spain, I thought about that a lot. How would Vicência greet me, after I'd left her with the children to bring up?"

"Your decision to leave this place wasn't wrong. What was wrong was staying there, doing whatever you were doing, and forgetting you had a wife and children who needed support. You acted like a sparrow that leaves his mate and nest."

"Sir, maybe you don't really know what you're talking about."

"If I don't, then tell me what happened. Maybe that way I can understand it and forgive you, although it isn't really for me to do so. You haven't offended me, but your family. And if they've already forgiven you, then there isn't really anything more to be said about it."

We were walking along a path next to a rye field. A blackbird, startled by our presence, took off from the middle of the rye. On its beak it carried what looked like a locust.

Rato stopped, his hands stuck in his pockets, and watched the blackbird's flight. Then he looked down at the ground and said, "I had an affair with Constance."

"With Madame Constance Gavroche?" I asked, stopping next to him.

"There was no other."

I folded my arms, looked at him and waited for him to say something else. But he kept quiet. He started walking again and, a few meters ahead, made a comment about the vine buds, which were a little late for the season. Our conversation drifted to agriculture, the tasks to be done in spring, his son Delmiro, who was now my caretaker, and Rato's plans to dig wells for several farmers in the neighborhood. People were beginning to realize wells were more reliable than springs. They could be dug in practically any kind of land and were a solution for a number of irrigation problems. Rato believed an increase in the number of wells would lead to better harvests and also to a decrease in the number of lawsuits over water rights in summer.

I pointed out that would ruin my law practice. Lawyers also needed to make a living.

He could not understand why nobody had ever thought of digging wells to provide water for the households and irrigate the fields. There were so few wells because it used to be so difficult to dig them. But now, with the use of concrete rings and pulleys, a well could be dug in a month, whereas earlier it would have taken a year or longer. He also believed pumps were a great invention, thanks to which now everyone wanted to have a well. In the past, wells were not very practical because it was difficult to draw water. Buckets were of little use for irrigating corn fields. With a gasoline pump, however, you could irrigate a field in next to no time. In France, he said, wells were used a lot, and every farmer had a gasoline pump for drawing water. Those who had hand pumps eventually replaced them with mechanical ones. An armament factory, once the war was over, started making irrigation pumps instead of heavy machine guns. They cost less than machine guns and were more useful.

"Come along," I said. "Let's tap a barrel of white wine and see how it is. It's from the same vintage as the barrel we opened for your son Delmiro's wedding. I want to open it today, so there won't be any surprises tomorrow, when the Easter procession comes by. If it's good, you'll take a demijohn."

"Vicência'll enjoy wetting her lips."

"And you won't?"

"Oh, I'd rather drink red. It's more manly."

"Well, then, you'll take two demijohns."

"It's up to you, sir."

We went down to the cellar and he helped me tap the barrel. I handed him a bowl, he opened the tap and gave it back to me full.

"There you are, sir. Boss tastes first."

I smelled the wine. It had a faint aroma of Muscat grapes. I sipped it, swirled it in my mouth, swallowed a little, and it seemed all right to me.

"Now you taste it."

I handed him the bowl and he sipped it.

"It's fine. With this wine, we'll make the women sing. If that offer's still good, let's see the demijohn."

I found an empty demijohn, he put it under the tap and, using a tin funnel, filled it. Then we moved on to a barrel of red wine, and he filled another.

Meanwhile, Inês brought a tray with two large slices of sponge cake.

"Mother sends you these," she said, placing the tray on the wine press wall.

"Thank you, Inês."

She went away and I invited Rato to help himself.

He had a coughing fit while eating and unclogged his throat with the bowl of white. Two bowls later, when only crumbs were left on the tray, he started telling me what he had not been able to, half an hour earlier, by the rye field.

In autumn 1919, he arrived in France and was taken in by Madame Constance Gavroche. At first he slept in the barn with the horse and the chickens. He helped in the work on the farm and worked for wages if a neighbor needed an extra hand. He had a hard time in winter, when it was extremely cold.

"In the war, when we slept in the barns, we leaned against each other in the straw to keep warm on cold nights. But I was there alone and just couldn't get them hens to come and warm my feet."

He caught a cold, which grew worse and turned into a flu – he never found out if it was the Spanish flu – and nearly died. Seeing him so ill, Madame Constance Gavroche put him up in an empty room in the house, and, with the help of hot soup, syrups, and much care from her and from Madame Pigeard, he managed to pull through. When he was able to get up and was getting ready to move back to the barn, she told him he could go on sleeping in the room. She did not want to see him get sick again because of the cold.

426

Madame Léonor Pigeard passed away in early spring. Madame Gavroche was extremely upset, not only because she cared very much for her mother, but also because she had been so helpful in household chores and fieldwork.

I asked Rato if there had been any news about what happened to Madame Gavroche's husband.

"By the time I arrived, she'd given up hope."

At that point, war prisoners had already returned from Germany. Some Enguinegatte men had come back but none had seen Monsieur Gavroche. Neither the Red Cross, nor the veterans' associations, nor the War Ministry knew anything about him. He'd been listed as missing in action and it was most likely he'd died in battle and ended up buried in a trench or in a common grave.

"After the old lady's burial, Constance came at night to the room where I slept and got into the bed with me. Until she died last year, we always slept together."

"Did her children know about it?"

"Eventually they did. François took it poorly and never forgave his mother. Nannette couldn't care less. That little one, she was very friendly to me."

"And how did she die?"

"Who? The mother or the daughter?"

"I meant the daughter. But since you mention her mother..."

"The old lady died from old age, I guess. She had a heart problem and went off like a candle. Constance died from a bad thing."

"A bad thing? Can't you be more specific? A bad thing can be many things."

"A bad thing in her stomach. At least that's what the doctor told me when I took her to the hospital and she stayed there a spell."

We kept silent for more than a minute. Rato looked glumly at the empty tray and the bowl. I broke the silence, "But

427

tell me something. In all those years you spent there, didn't you save anything?"

"Everything I got was in Constance's hands. When I needed money to buy a drink or cigarettes, I asked her. She died and I was left with nothing. The money was all in the bank under her name. Nannette married a Frenchman who went to work for the government in Algeria. They couldn't come to the funeral. François, the same day his mother was buried, kicked me out of the house, threatening me with the police. I told him I'd only leave when I got back the money I'd asked his mother to deposit in the bank."

"So the money wasn't under your name?"

"No, it was under Constance's name. The young man said I wasn't entitled to no money. That his mother had done enough for me, keeping me all them years. I came close to punching him. But I figured it'd only make things worse. I was just a foreigner and had no way to claim my rights. I was an ass, that's what I was. I picked up my belongings, which wasn't many, and came back."

I pondered what he had just told me, and thought there might be a legal way for Rato to claim part of that money, or, at worst, a compensation for having worked on the farm for almost twenty years.

"Maybe it isn't all lost," I said. "One could find witnesses to prove you worked on the farm for no salary all those years, and the heirs would be forced to compensate you. There's still time to claim that. If you wish, I'll take care of the lawsuit for you."

"It ain't worth it, sir. If you pardon the expression, one shouldn't stir up shit."

"Were the years you spent with Madame Gavroche that bad?"

"Bad? No, they wasn't bad at all. We got along well. We grew a lot on that farm, and there was good profit. I worked digging wells and ditches when people asked me. Constance was very kind to me. We had a good time together."

428

"And what did she say about your family?"

"She didn't like when I talked about the wife and children. She was very jealous. That's why I couldn't send no letters and no money. Sometimes I told her I felt bad about it, but she said if I didn't like it, nobody was holding me. But I didn't want to come back to this miserable life."

"You enjoyed being with her, that's what happened."

"That must've been."

"She never asked you to marry her?"

"No, never."

"What about children? How did you manage not to become a father?"

"We was very careful about that."

"How did you go about it?"

"There was lots of ways. One was not to grab her on them days when she said it was dangerous. It looks like there's days when women can get knocked up more easily than on other days. Just like bitches and sows. If a hog mounts a sow when she's not in heat, no matter how much he humps her, there won't be no new litter."

"But just think that it's on those days that women like it best."

"I know. As she wouldn't let me stick it in, for fear of getting knocked up, she asked me to rub her and other things I won't talk about. She did the same thing to me. French women, in those things, are way ahead of the Portuguese."

"It's for us to initiate them. Once they get used to it, they won't settle for less."

"Well, you probably have your reasons for saying that, sir. Ladies of quality, they always know more than our women folk. The wife, she don't even dream of what a man and a woman can do in bed. For her, sex means opening her legs in the dark and letting me stick it in. That's another reason why I stayed in France."

He took the bowl I had refilled with white wine and drank half of it.

"Not bad, this wine. It goes down nice."

"Didn't you say you preferred red?"

"Since we're drinking white... But do you know, sir, what bothers me most? It's not having sent Vicência any money as I earned it. It would've helped support the children, and since Vicência's very thrifty, we'd have a nest egg to buy a piece of land with a little house. The way it is, we go on living in the shack, and paying rent to boot. If I'd done that, all my work would've come to something instead of just fattening up Constance's son's belly. I was an ass. I was afraid. Afraid Constance might send me away. Afraid to lose her, to have to come back here and not be able to put up with missing her. "

"Did you like her that much?"

"She was a very attractive woman, sir. You tell me where we can find that kind of woman over here. I mean, not meaning to be disrespectful of Dona Aninhas, who's got her qualities, that's sure. Constance was older than me and looked like she was my daughter. In the war, when you was billeted in her home, and later, when we visited her, she only had eyes for you. I don't know if there was ever anything between you, and it don't matter now. Those invitations to spend a few days on the farm, I always suspected they wasn't just out of friendship. Anyways, you know, sir, she was very attentive, like only a Frenchwoman can be. Later on, when I lived with her, I found out about her bad temper. When she got mad, she sure hit the ceiling. If we was here in Portugal, I'd just slapped her round a little and she'd calm down. But in France you can't do that. Besides, I was in her house. I listened and kept my mouth shut."

"And she never mentioned me?"

"She never brought up the subject. Sometimes I mentioned the war, my comrades and you, sir. She'd say Monsieur Luís was a *gentilhomme* and she had very pleasant memories of you. She just wished you was happy in Portugal with your wife and children."

"And how did you two communicate?"

"At first it was hard for me make them sounds. I could understand most everything the French said, but speaking was harder. But I got used to it and in a while I managed to parleyvoo as much as I wished. I tried teaching Constance to speak Portuguese, but she said our language was *très difficile*. I guess she just didn't care about it. I soon figured out the French were too full of themselves and thought they was bigger, smarter, finer, and more civilized than anybody else. I even think that's why the Boche invaded them, to cut them down to size. And what they done to the Boche after the war, piling up demands on them and starving them to death, that wasn't right neither. And now the Boche are strong again, I wouldn't be surprised if one of these days they marched back into France. And we'll have to go defend them like we done before. I mean, we, the Portuguese. For me, the war's over. And for you too, sir. But there's our sons. May our Lady of Fátima protect them from such a fate."

"We don't learn from our mistakes," I said.

"What good's come of us going to war if the Boche start a new one? Vicência never understood what we was doing in Flanders. She once asked me and I said, we was standing guard. Standing guard over what, she asked. And I said, standing guard over the trenches. But she couldn't figure out what there was in them trenches that was so important to stand guard over, and I had to tell her that, really, besides us, there wasn't nothing. She didn't get it. Why the heck did we have to guard a place where there wasn't nothing important to guard? I tried to explain that the trenches was like a melon field that you've got to guard so the thieves won't steal them, with the difference that the melons was us. Even so, she couldn't figure it out. She said I'd spent two years in the war keeping watch over she didn't know what, while she needed me in the house. 'You've turned out to be a big rascal, you and all of them as started a war that didn't bring us nothing but unhappiness,' she said. And she warned me, if I wanted to have peace in the house, I must never mention them

431

trenches again. If I wanted to talk about them, I should come and see you, sir. And so here we are."

We left the cellar and wished each other a happy Easter. I stood there, a little clouded by the white wine, watching him go through the gate and stagger away, a demijohn in each hand.

There is nothing surprising about his affair with Madame Gavroche. Rato's arrival in Enguinegatte must have been a godsend to her. It did not matter to her that he had a wife and children to be brought up. When it comes to such things women can be rather selfish. As to Rato's savings, there are legal ways to try to recover them. I will check out the French legislation on that subject.

I can hear the procession bell coming closer. The procession must be some ten minutes from here, maybe less. Even though the coat of arms is still covered with black cloth on account of my father's death three years ago, I have asked Inês to scatter lily flowers and leaves all the way from the gate to the stairway.

I look back into the past once more and see a trail covered with cut flowers – a pathway for time and its whims. The soldiers I commanded and who remain in Flanders, pierced through by a bullet or a grenade fragment. Madame Constance Gavroche, a true war godmother, and her mother, the affable Madame Léonor Pigeard. The little Isabel, a victim of caste prejudice. My father, the image of monarchic, liberal Portugal. Myself, in days gone by. Aninhas, my beloved girl on the four cent coin. My future grandchildren and all who will follow, flowers cut and trampled by time. The young man with the bell is approaching the gate. I have to go now.

EPILOGUE

A young man came here a few days ago and asked to talk to me. My health has been rather shaky and I did not feel at all like seeing him, so I asked my daughter to tell him I was ill. But he insisted, arguing that, if I was that sick, all the more reason for him to talk to me. He explained to Inês that he was a student in Letters at the University of Oporto and one of my former caretaker Delmiro's grandsons. Inês came back to the study where I was taking my after-lunch nap in an armchair and passed that information on to me.

"Well, let the young man in," I told her.

He was a good-looking man who reminded me of someone. He said, "Good afternoon, sir," and stood before me, without daring to offer his hand.

"You'll forgive this intrusion, Dr. Luís Vasques," he said, "but I really needed to talk to you."

I explained to him that if he meant to ask me for a favor, he was wasting his time. It would be better to talk to my daughter, the lady of the house. She was the boss. I was just billeted here.

"You're just what, sir?"

"Billeted. That's a term used in the Great War when military men were officially lodged and fed in private homes. Instead of sending me to an asylum, which is where I should be, my daughter does me the charity of keeping me here and putting up with me."

"I'm not here to ask for any favors, I mean, actually I am, but it isn't anything that you cannot do, sir."

"What is it then?"

"My grandfather Delmiro, who used to be your caretaker..."

"And how is he?" I asked, not really interested.

"He died from pneumonia last winter. He talked a lot

about you. He used to say he owed you almost everything he had."

"Let me tell you something, young man, your grandfather was an ingrate. I brought him up, sent him to school, let him marry one of my maids, Guiomar, put him in charge of one of my best estates, and one day he told me he'd got a job in Braga as a street-sweeper and left with his whole family. I never saw him again."

"Even so, he always said you were like a father to him, sir. He chose to become a street sweeper because working in the country was way too hard. He wanted to give his children a different future."

"And did he?"

"Yes, sir. His children got good jobs. My father is a civil servant in the Finance Ministry and..."

"Well, then," I cut him off, "he belongs to the biggest band of thieves we have."

The young man seemed somewhat offended, and I, to make things more comfortable, asked him, "And how's your grandmother?"

"My grandmother Guiomar?"

"Yes. She used to be a maid in this house, I don't know if you knew that. She was a good cook. I always liked her."

"She's fine. When I told her I was coming here, she asked me to give you her greetings."

"Tell her I've received them, and give her my greetings. Your grandmother was a good young woman. Really good."

And at this point some shreds of memories from a week, more than forty years ago, when Guiomar had kept me company, came to my mind.

"My uncles are all fine," the young man went on. "They emigrated to France and are still there."

"I see," I said, coming back to reality. "They followed in your grandfather's footsteps."

"Excuse me, sir, but my grandfather Delmiro never went to France."

"I'm not talking about your grandfather Delmiro, but rather about your great-grandfather, Joaquim Domingues, better known as Rato, who was your father's and your uncles' grandfather."

"Oh yes, of course. Well, sir, that's who I'd like to talk to you about."

"Well, then? What do you have to say?"

"My grandfather Delmiro told me that you and his father had been in the war. You see, I'm studying Letters in Oporto, and my professor of Portuguese Culture has suggested I write a paper on the First Republic. I've been reading a few things and, since I knew my great-grandfather went to war in France, I thought of writing a paper on our participation in the war. I wanted to find out more about my great-grandfather, so I asked my uncles and aunts about him, but couldn't find out much. Then my grandmother mentioned you'd been his colleague..."

"Colleagues my arse, young man. I never was your great-grandfather's colleague. He was a soldier in the platoon I commanded. For reasons that would be too long to explain, I appointed him my orderly. But go on, what do you want to know about him?"

"I'd like to know everything," the young man said.

"You can never know everything. As a student in Letters, you ought to know that. What we know or can tell are small bits, portions of the past, transformed by time and memory, which is always imperfect and unreliable."

"Yes, I know that. It was a manner of speaking."

"Your great-grandfather was a man dissatisfied with what Fate had given him, which was unusual in those days. Most people, especially those who were guileless and ignorant, were contented with what God or life's circumstances gave them. They worried about having something to eat, a place to sleep, being healthy, procreating and not going to hell. Your great-grandfather sought other paths, but either because he didn't make the right choices, or because he wasn't able to take the good things they might hold, he ended up returning to his old path and never managed to overcome his dissatisfaction."

"Do you remember when he died, sir?"

"Rato died in the fifties. I remember a conversation we had a few months before his death, about Humberto Delgado's candidacy for the presidency of Portugal."[64]

"That was in 1958. Admiral Américo Tomás won the election."

"Exactly. There's nothing like having a Portuguese Culture specialist handy. Your great-grandfather and I supported Humberto Delgado's candidacy and voted for him. Oddly enough, when the votes were counted, there wasn't a single vote for Humberto Delgado in our district."

"That's further proof there was fraud at the polls."

"We were talking about your great-grandfather. He had lung trouble and died from it. He'd caught trench fever. The mayor wanted to ask the Braga Regiment to send a platoon to render him the military honors he was entitled to as a war veteran. But Rato had told me that, when he died, he wanted to have no honor guard and no rifle volleys. He wanted to be buried in peace. In the end, we promised each other that, if one of us died, the other would prevent them from sending an honor guard. Since he was the first to go, I had to see to it. He was buried on a sunny, cold, quiet day."

I looked at the lit fireplace, over which hung the old Boche insignia with the eagle and the motto, "*Mit Gott für Koenig und Vaterland.*"

"A little later," I went on, "Vicência, your great-grandmother, died. Then a strange story made its rounds. They said that, when the news of the La Lys disaster reached the village, your great-grandmother vowed that, if her husband managed to survive, she would donate a dress to the church's Infant Jesus. But she ended up forgetting her promise. When she died, her wake was held in her house. The next morning, in the room

436

where her coffin was kept, the family found a wash line with clothes hanging on the walls around the coffin. They called the priest, who said that was certainly a joke in poor taste. But soon the news spread out throughout the village and many people decided it was a miracle. One of the daughters of the deceased, I can't remember which one, recalled the promise her mother had made, and which she often alluded to, and went to talk to the priest again. To calm things down, the priest ended up accepting the fact as a divine omen. Since Vicência hadn't kept her promise, God had chosen that way to remind the family. As long as the promise remained unfulfilled, the soul of the deceased would not enjoy eternal rest. After the burial, the family hired a seamstress to make a dress for the Infant Jesus. There's a detail about that dress: the two top buttons in back were from your great-grandfather's military uniform. I don't know if the dress still exists, but you can easily find out at the church."

"Dad," my daughter said from the door of the study, "don't overdo it. Remember your heart condition. If this young man wants to, he can come back tomorrow to continue your conversation. Now you must rest."

"But we've barely started..." I protested.

The young man took his leave, somewhat flustered, promising to come back the next day, in the late afternoon, so as not to disrupt my nap. After all, he was on vacation and could come over when it was most convenient for me. He went away, but I could not rest.

I am ninety three years old and my legs weigh down on me. It took me a great effort to climb the stairs leading to the attic, where I had put away a trunk in which my war memories are kept. I lifted the top and went through the contents: remnants of a junior officer's uniform, a second lieutenant's insignia, a gas mask, a few letters I wrote my parents, with Coimbra and Flanders addresses. At the bottom of the trunk I discovered a waterproof portfolio. Inside it I found a sheaf of foolscap paper written in my small longhand from fifty years ago. On the first page I read, "I am staying home with the maid while Aninhas and my mother are spending a few days in Póvoa de Varzim with Aunt Generosa, who is sick and needs some help." That page was written on November 11th, 1938. These are the memoirs from the first quarter of my life, with references to people who took part in it, including Rato, the great-grandfather of the young man who called on me, causing me to rummage through my past.

I returned my faded, moth-eaten uniform to the trunk – I must have forgotten about the letters – dropped the top, and walked out of the attic. Then I sat down, looked for three blank foolscap sheets in the portfolio, and scribbled this. Tomorrow I will give it all to that young man. Maybe he will find in these pages what he is looking for, or maybe he will find what he is not looking for, which is what life – the dust and ashes into which all is turned – has reserved for him. My daughter is coming with the glass of water and the pill that will keep me alive for another day.

EDITOR'S NOTE

I am Joaquim Domingues's great-grandson, and I am writing this note in the study that used to be Dr. Luís Vasques's. I bought this house and part of Quinta de São Francisco from his heirs five years ago. I had it remodeled and moved in with my family about two years ago.

I have kept the pages written by Dr. Luís Vasques for almost twenty years. He handed them to me personally and I used them to write a Portuguese Culture paper for the university. Unfortunately, it did not get a very good grade. The professor was sympathetic to the republicans who favored Portugal's intervention in the war, and did not like the fact that I wrote such a negative description of Portugal's role in the conflict. After April 25th,[65] certain politically involved intellectuals tried to whitewash the crimes committed by republican politicians up to 1926, when Marshal Gomes da Costa put an end to the party and imposed the dictatorship, which would commit even more crimes than the preceding regime. But politics is not what I intend to write about in this note.

Dr. Luís Vasques died a few months after our meeting. Dona Inês, his daughter, told me at the funeral that he passed away in his sleep from a cardiac arrest. A peaceful death, it seems.

Dona Inês, who by now has also passed away, was a widowed lady who inherited the estate, where she lived with a maid and half a dozen cats. Her children lived in Lisbon and rarely visited the estate. When she wanted to see them, she had to travel to the capital. At her father's funeral, I asked about her two brothers. She told me that Afonso, the elder, had fled to France in 1946 or 1947, she could not remember which year. He had been involved with the communists, the political police suspected him, and started to watch him. Dr. Vasques, afraid of losing his son – at that time Salazar used to send the reds to Tarrafal[66] – made him leave the country. He married a French woman and found a job as a professor in an Engineering department at the Sorbonne in Paris. His brother, Pedro, was ordained, but in the sixties, after the Vatican Council II, he left the Church and married a nun he had met during some national prayer meetings in Fátima. He had four children and taught history at a secondary school. The two brothers are a good example of some of the splits in Portuguese society in the twentieth century.

I hesitated for some time about publishing these pages. First, because I thought I did not have the right, since their author had not expressly authorized me. Second, because these pages include comments that might somehow displease the descendants of persons referred to. I myself was not very happy, at least during the first reading, about the passage in which the author mentions his relationship with my grandmother Guiomar, and I even thought of omitting it. But then I decided the case no longer mattered, since the persons involved are dead. Deep inside, it did not displease me to learn that Dr. Luís Vasques, that rascal, had shared my grandmother's bed. The two families were carnally united.

It took me about two years to transcribe the manuscript on the computer, due to the fact that dampness had caused the ink to fade considerably in some chapters, and to my difficulty in interpreting the handwriting and spelling. Dr. Luís Vasques ignored the 1911 orthographic reform and wrote like a nineteenth century author.

Braga, April 9, 2008

Notes

These notes are intended to assist readers unfamiliar with Portugal, its language, geography, and history, in making sense of some terms and names of persons and places, as well as historical and cultural references.

[1] **Póvoa de Varzim:** A coastal resort town in northern Portugal. **Coimbra:** The University of Coimbra was founded in 1290 in the city of the same name. **Braga:** The oldest Portuguese town, going back to Roman times, located in the Minho region of northern Portugal. **Famalicão:** A town near Braga.

[2] **Dona:** A courtesy title used before a woman's first name, e.g. *Dona Ana.* A more deferential form of address would be *Senhora Dona Ana.* **Aninhas** is a familiar diminutive of Ana. (See Note 50).

[3] **Boche:** Disparaging World War I French slang for Germans, particularly soldiers. *Mit Gott für Koenig und Vaterland*: "With God for the King and the Fatherland." **Raul Brandão** (1867-1930): A Portuguese Army officer, journalist, and author. *Húmus* (1917), a monologue-novel, is considered his finest work.

[4] **Escudo:** Portugal's old currency, replaced by the euro in 2002.

[5] **Esmoriz:** A town in the Minho region.

[6] **The New State (Pg. Estado Novo):** The dictatorial regime inaugurated by António Oliveira Salazar in 1933, which lasted until 1974.

[7] **Fado:** Portugal's best known popular music genre. **Fátima:** A town in central Portugal, where a sanctuary celebrates the supposed apparition of the Virgin to three shepherd children on May 13, 1917.

[8] **Ministry of the Sacred Union (Pg. Ministério da União Sagrada):** a government organized in response to Portugal's declaration of war on Germany. It lasted from March 16, 1916, to April 25, 1917. **Afonso Augusto da Costa (1871-1937):** A lawyer, law professor, and republican politician who was Minister of Finance and Prime Minister. He died in exile in Paris.

[9] **Quinta:** A rural estate, operated as a farm and usually including a large residential house.

[10] **Alfama:** The oldest district of Lisbon, known for its restaurants and fado taverns.

[11] *A Monarquia* **("The Monarchy"):** A conservative newspaper, banned by the government after the attempt to reinstate the monarchy in Oporto in January 1919 (see Note 41). **Integralism:** A traditionalist, monarchist, and Catholic party founded in Coimbra in 1914.

[12] **Manuel de Oliveira Gomes da Costa (1863-1929):** An Army General, author of *O Corpo de exército português na batalha do Lys* ("The Portuguese Army Corps in the Battle of the Lys"), 1922.

[13] **João Pinheiro Chagas (1863-1925):** A journalist, politician, and Prime Minister of Portugal from September to November 1911.

[14] **Sidónio Pais (1872-1918):** An Army officer, Ambassador to Berlin (1912-1916), who led a coup d'état (December 1917), and was President of Portugal from April to November 1918, when he was assassinated.

[15] **Tancos:** A village in Northern Portugal and the site of several military installations, used as a training ground for troops in World War I.

[16] *The Lusiads* **(Pg. *Os Lusíadas*):** An epic poem by poet Luís de Camões (1524-1580), celebrating the great Portuguese navigators.

[17] **Bom Jesus do Monte ("Good Jesus of the Mount"):** A sanctuary and pilgrimage site near Braga. It has a baroque stairway with 581 steps that stretches 116 meters (381 feet).

[18] **Ricardo Reis:** One of the heteronyms used by poet Fernando Pessoa (1888-1935).

[19] **Joaquim Mouzinho de Albuquerque (1855-1902):** An Army officer and onetime Governor of Mozambique.

[20] **Matosinhos:** A town near Oporto.

[21] **Apúlia, Esposende:** Coastal villages in northern Portugal.
[22] The Inquisition started in Portugal from the middle of the 16th century and was formally abolished in 1821.

[23] **Chaves:** A town in northern Portugal, near the border with Spain, known for the quality of its hams.

[24] **Doutor ("Doctor"):** In this case, not a medical title but a courtesy title given to university graduates, particularly in Law.

[25] **Figueira da Foz:** A resort town near Coimbra by the mouth of the Mondego River.

[26] **Joanina Library:** Named after King João V, it is a baroque building dating from the 18th century.

[27] **Beja:** A town in Alentejo, in SE Portugal.

[28] **Leiria:** A town located some 70 km (ca. 44 mi) to the south of Coimbra.

[29] **Cova da Iria:** The name of a tract of land where, according to tradition, the Virgin appeared to three shepherd children in 1917, and which soon became a site of pilgrimage.

[30] **Santarém:** A town in central Portugal.

[31] **Monastery of Santa Maria da Vitória ("Saint Mary of the Victory"):** Located in the village of Batalha ("Battle") and also known as the Monastery of Batalha, it was built to celebrate Portugal's victory in the battle of Aljubarrota (August 14, 1385).

[32] According to tradition, poet Luís de Camões (1524-1580), shipwrecked in India, supposedly saved himself and the manuscript of his poem, *Os Lusíadas* ("The Lusiads"), published in 1580.

[33] **Poilu ("hairy/ hairy one"):** Familiar slang for French soldiers in World War I.

[34] **Neuve-Chapelle:** A village in the Pas-de-Calais region, where several battles took place.

[35] **Republican National Guard (Pg. Guarda Nacional Republicana):** Portugal's paramilitary police force.

[36] **Northern Monarchy (Pg. Monarquia do Norte):** In January 1919 an armed movement in Oporto tried to reinstate the monarchy. Presided by former Army officer Henrique Mitchell de Paiva Couceiro (1861-1944), the so-called Northern Monarchy was quickly suppressed by the republican government.

[37] **Sapateiros ("cobblers"):** Critics of the republican system called it the *República dos Sapateiros* ("Cobblers' Republic") because it was strongly supported by the working classes.

[38] **Ginja, ginjinha:** A typical Lisbon liqueur, made from an infusion of **ginja** berries (sour cherries) in wine-based brandy (*aguardente*). **Intendente** is a downtown Lisbon district then known for its lively street life. *Puta(s)* is a slang term for whore(s).

[39] Vasques is quoting from the *opéra comique, Le jour et la nuit* (1881) by Charles Lecocq (1832-1918): *Les portugais sont toujours gais / Qu'il fasse beau, qu'il fasse lais, / Au mois de décembre ou de mai, Les portugais sont toujours gais!* ("The Portuguese are always happy / In fair weather or bad / In December or May / The Portuguese are always happy!")

[40] **Pas compris:** "Not understood;" from Fr. *je n'ai pas compris* "I did not understand."

[41] **Vinho verde ("young/unripe wine"):** a wine with Protected Designation of Origin, made in a region between the Minho and Douro rivers in NW Portugal.

[42] **Bagaço:** Eau-de-vie or brandy made by distilling pomace, that is the remnants of grapes crushed in wine-making.

[43] You shitty Boche! Go home! Your mothers are a bunch of whores! Victory is ours! After we win this war we'll go to Germany! Seriously! We'll go there to screw your mothers and your fiancées!

[44] **Senhor:** A courtesy title used before a man's first or last name. Its feminine form is *Senhora* (see Note 5).

[45] *Primum vivere, deinde philosophare*: A Latin proverb meaning "Live first, then philosophize."

[46] **Rabelo boats:** Square-rigged, flat-bottomed vessels once used to ferry wine barrels to warehouses in **Vila Nova de Gaia**, on the south bank of the Douro River, opposite Oporto, and currently used for tourism activities.

[47] Portugal became an independent nation by seceding from the Kingdom of León and Castile in 1139.

[48] After 24-years-old King Sebastião disappeared in 1578 in a battle against the Arabs in the region of Ksar el Kebir (Pg. Alcácer Quibir) in today's NW Morocco, an Arthurian-like cult, *Sebastianism,* centered on the myth of his return to restore Portugal's grandeur.

[49] **Decauville:** A train running on light narrow-gauge tracks assembled with steel sleepers, for transporting personnel, equipment and supplies along the front, named after its inventor, railway pioneer Paul Decauville.

[50] **João Grave (1872-1934):** A Portuguese journalist and writer.

[51] *O Comércio do Porto* **("The Oporto Commerce"):** The second-oldest newspaper in Portugal, published from 1854 to 2005.

[52] **Marquess of Pombal:** Sebastião José de Carvalho e Melo was a diplomat and Prime Minister of King José I between 1750 and 1777. A representative of the Enlightenment, he introduced many reforms, some controversial.

[53] **Borraçal:** A red grape variety, one of many grown in Minho and used to make *vinho verde* (see note 47).

[54] *O Século* **("The Century"):** A Lisbon daily published between 1880 and 1977.

[55] **Ponte da Barca:** A small village in the Minho region on the Portuguese-Spanish border.

[56] Lúcia, the eldest of the three shepherd children, was born in 1907 and died in 2005. Her other siblings were Francisco (1908-1919) and Jacinta (1910-1920).

[57] **Foz do Douro:** A small town at the mouth of the Douro River.

[58] **Falperra:** A mountain range NE of Braga, where there is a baroque chapel, dedicated to St. Martha.

[59] **Private Millions (Pg. Soldado Milhões):** A pun on the name of Private Aníbal Augusto Milhais, who at the battle of La Lys kept shooting at advancing German soldiers with his Lewis machine gun. According to tradition, a superior officer told him, "Your name is Milhais, but you're worth millions (*milhões*)!"

[60] *A Ilustre Casa de Ramires* **("The Illustrious House of Ramires"):** a novel by Eça de Queiroz in which a young country

gentleman, Gonçalo Ramires, writes a story-within-the-story about a medieval ancestor.

[61] **Alcácer Quibir:** See Note 48.

[62] The accents of the varieties of Portuguese spoken on the Azores Islands, and particularly that of the island of São Miguel (known as *Miquelense*), can differ considerably from the accents heard in Continental Portugal. Mirandese (*Mirandês*), spoken in Miranda do Douro, a small town on the border with Spain, is sufficiently different from Portuguese to have been officially recognized as a separate language in 1999.

[63] **José Régio:** pen name of Portuguese poet and polymath José Maria dos Reis Pereira (1901- 1969).

[64] **Humberto Delgado (1906-1965):** An Air Force general who opposed the Salazar regime, went into asylum in Brazil, and was murdered by the Portuguese political police (known as PIDE) near the Spanish border in 1965.

[65] **April 25th, 1974:** Date of the Carnation Revolution, through which the military put an end to the "New State" dictatorial regime installed in 1933 by António de Oliveira Salazar (†1970).

[66] **Tarrafal:** A camp for political prisoners in Cape Verde, formerly a colony of Portugal.